"*Lives of the Saints* is simple, moving, and compelling."   —*The Spectator*

"A beautifully paced and measured first novel . . . an extraordinary story—brooding and ironic, suffused with yearning, tender and lucid and gritty . . . perfect pitch and brilliant descriptive powers."

—*New York Times Book Review*

"Nino Ricci's complex and skillfully fashioned tale of life in an Italian Apennine village offers pleasure too seldom present in contemporary fiction: full and involving characterizations, an exhilarating combination of tightly knit plot and episodic looseness, and a rich sense of lives lived truly communally, in conflict and in balance with one another . . . exudes a dazzling breadth and richness."   —*USA Today*

"A book to celebrate—a wise, poignant, and poised novel."

—*Wall Street Journal*

"A fine, artful piece of work . . . a powerful tale."   —*Washington Post*

"This seems to me to be literature at its best, a sense of life lived, a sense of life felt, not without dreams, not without poetry, but without fakery."

—*Toronto Star*

"In a forgotten village lost to time and the world, Nino Ricci unfolds a tragedy of nearly mythic proportions."

—*Le Monde*

Praise for in a glass house

"Splendidly, even forcefully written, this is a novel which nags at the soul."

—*Glasgow Herald*

"Compelling in its artistry . . . [Ricci is] an extraordinarily subtle writer."

—*The Guardian*

"Ricci has written a profound essay on the human soul." —*Sunday Telegraph*

"Full of sensitive, insightful writing . . . a strongly voiced and engaging book . . . Ricci's observations about family dynamics . . . are frequently elegant."

—*Boston Sunday Globe*

"Lyrical."   —*Los Angeles Times*

"A superbly sad story . . . Nino Ricci's triumph."   —*Washington Post*

"*In A Glass House* is a haunting, lyrical, intelligent coming-of-age novel . . . the acuity of its observations, the eloquence of its prose, and the hard-earned wisdom of its final pages make it a genuine achievement."

—*New York Times Book Review*

Praise for where she has gone

"A superb stylist whose unpretentious prose carries an emotional charge that gathers so slowly and surely that we're surprised to find ourselves so moved by his characters' stoically borne crises."
—*Kirkus Reviews*

"Ricci's poetic prose and fluid plot create a tense and beautiful story whose sad ironies achieve resolution in a haunting conclusion."

—*Publishers Weekly*

"Ricci has spun out a delicate and soulful novel."
—*TIME*

"Outstanding . . . the work of a writer arrived at startling maturity . . . The novel's language and rhythms are quietly extraordinary, both loose-limbed and intense, moving with fluid grace between the sharp here and now of Toronto or rural Italy and the brooding landscape of Victor's mind . . . vibrant with life."
—*Times Literary Supplement*

"Ricci manipulates our expectations with an adept, steady hand."

—*Time Out London*

"Absorbing and moving."
—*Sunday Times*

"The smooth surface of Ricci's prose belies the novel's richness as it builds surely and lucidly toward a poignant, bittersweet conclusion: Ricci's exploration of the rupture between old world and new is masterful."

—*The Observer*

Praise for testament

"In the beauty of its language, its rich detail of place and character, its humanity and grace and sense of wonder, Nino Ricci's *Testament* both transcends and revalidates the so-called historical novel. Religion aside, history aside, this is a lovely work of fiction."
—TIM O'BRIEN, author of *July, July*

"A hypnotic, deeply lyrical presentation of four gospels . . . A writer of impeccable craft . . . recreating, in his incantatory prose, the very aroma and the wild, sorcery-filled world through which Jesus walked."

—PICO IYER, *Los Angeles Times Book Review*

"Nino Ricci pulls off a genuine tour-de-force. *Testament*'s last fifty pages are grisly, wrenching, and utterly absorbing—Yeshua's all-too-human suffering and death have a real and terrible power, unrelieved by lightning flashes of divinity or miraculous interventions."   —*Washington Post*

"*Testament* is a remarkable retelling of the Jesus story, doing what great art always does—making what is familiar suddenly fresh, daring, challenging. You will never think of the characters of the gospel accounts in the same way again, which is the good news of this stunning novel."
                                   —REVEREND STEPHEN KENDRICK, senior minister,
                                                  First and Second Church, Boston

"The sum of these various reminiscences makes a highly readable narrative . . . There is, moreover, an element of suspense that is sustained throughout the novel despite—or even because of—the universally known outcome of Jesus's career."   —*Toronto Star*

"Ricci has given us a contemporary Jesus. Like a palimpsest, with each fresh image superimposed on earlier images, Ricci's Jesus testifies to the inexhaustible power of story, reminding us that enduring myths are not windows through which we view objective truths, but mirrors framing our own evanescent mortality and morality plays."   —*Globe and Mail*

"*Testament*, a refracted biography of Jesus, becomes too an examination of storytelling itself, for what is Jesus of Nazareth if not a teller of stories? . . . From the good book Ricci has fashioned a great story."   —*Quill & Quire*

"Covers new, daunting, and unexpected territory . . . Much of this retelling accumulates a mysterious power of its own, even as it roils the reader."
                                                                —*Commonweal*

"A uniquely down-to-earth treatment of the life of Christ that plunges the reader into the sounds, smells, and emotions of his Jewish world."
                                                               —*Utne Reader*

"Ricci transcends the stale confines of 'the historical Jesus' debate and invites us into that imaginative region where Jesus finds a living context."
                          —DR. BRUCE CHILTON, director, Institute for Advanced Theology,
                          Bard College, and author of *Rabbi Jesus: An Intimate Biography*

"This is a remarkable work—immensely savvy about the nature of human longing, compassionate about human failure, and illuminating about the trajectory of the hero. It's beautifully written, an endeavor both humble and risky."   —BARRY LOPEZ, author of *Arctic Dreams*

the origin of species

the origin of species

a novel

Nino Ricci

other press · new york

Other Press edition 2010

Production Editor: Yvonne E. Cárdenas

This book was originally designed by Kelly Hill.
Design revisions for this edition by Simon M. Sullivan.

Epigraph on page 1 from *Illuminations*, translated by
Harry Zohn (New York: Harcourt, Brace & World, 1968).
Epigraph on page 121 translated by Samuel Butler.
Epigraph on page 331 translated by Gayatri Chakravorty Spivak
(Baltimore: John Hopkins University Press, 1976).

10 9 8 7 6 5 4 3 2 1

LIBRARY OF CONGRESS CATALOGING-IN-PUBLICATION DATA

Ricci, Nino.
The origin of species / Nino Ricci.
p. cm.
"First published by Anchor Canada in Canada in 2008."
ISBN 978-1-59051-349-1 (paperback original) –
ISBN 978-1-59051-371-2 (ebook)
1. Graduate students–Fiction. 2. Self-realization–Fiction.
3. Montréal (Québec)–History–20th century–Fiction.
4. Psychological fiction. I. Title.
PR9199.3.R512O75 2010
813'.54–dc22
2009041070

In memory of Esther

. . . as with the individual, so with the species, the hour of
life has run its course, and is spent.

CHARLES DARWIN
The Voyage of the Beagle

one

There has never been a document of culture which was
not at one and the same time a document of barbarism.

WALTER BENJAMIN
"Theses on the Philosophy of History," VII

The girl standing in the foyer when Alex went down to get his mail, trembling slightly on her cane, was Esther. Not a girl, really: a woman. Everyone in the building knew her. Or everyone, it seemed, except Alex, who, in the few months since he'd moved here, had never quite managed to be the one to open a door for her, or put her key in her mailbox, or start a conversation with her in the oppressive intimacy of the building's elevators.

She was looking out through the plate glass of the entrance doors to the street, where sunlight now glinted off the morning's earlier sprinkling of rain.

"I wouldn't go out there if you don't have to," Alex said, then regretted at once his admonitory tone.

From the confusion that came over her, plain as if a shadow had crossed her, it was clear she hadn't understood.

"The rain," he said.

"Oh!" She looked up through her thickish glasses at the now cloudless sky and her whole face seemed to twist with the strain of trying to follow his meaning.

"Chernobyl," he said, making a botch of it. "The fallout. They say you shouldn't go out if it's rained."

"Oh-h-h!" She drew the word out as if in understanding. "Really? They say that? Oh!"

"They're saying the clouds might pick the radiation up over Russia, then dump it somewhere else. At least, I think that's what they're saying."

It suddenly occurred to Alex, though the story had been practically the only thing in the news since the Swedes had broken it a few days before, that she didn't have any idea what he was talking about.

"You know, I heard about that," she said, and Alex was relieved. "About Chernobyl. Isn't it awful?"

They stood there an instant while Alex half-turned, not wanting to put his back to her, and awkwardly retrieved his mail, which was just junk, it looked like. But in that instant's lull it seemed he'd lost whatever conversational thread there'd been between them.

Esther was still standing at the doors, neither going out nor coming in.

"You wouldn't happen to have a cigarette, would you?" she said finally, looking right at him. "I mean, if you could spare one."

That was how the day had got started. Alex did indeed have cigarettes, but up in his apartment, and although he'd considered lying—he didn't like the idea of giving a cigarette to someone who was clearly Not Well—it finally ended up, despite his protestations that he simply fetch one for her, that Esther followed him to his place to get one herself. There weren't any more awkward silences from then on: in the elevator Esther launched at once into a disarming rush of revealing personal anecdote, so that by the time they got out at Alex's floor he was dizzy with excess information.

"What about you? I don't even know your name."

"Alex. It's Alex." Then he added, stupidly, "Alex Fratarcangeli."

"Oh! Really? Frater—oh! That's interesting."

"Don't worry," he said quickly. "I can't even pronounce it myself."

Alex's apartment was on the seventeenth floor, which had been the chief selling point when he'd rented the place, some feeling still surging in him—hope? vertigo?—each time he opened his door to the expanse of cityscape and sky through his living room windows. He'd left the radio on, tuned to the CBC: there was an interview coming up with the prime minister that Alex was perversely anxious to catch, largely because he despised the prime minister, from the very depth of his being, despised every false word that dropped from his big-chinned false mouth. He could hear the interview coming on as he unlocked the door, Peter Gzowski's honeyed coo and then the mellow low of the prime minister, false, false, although Peter, and this was the side of him that Alex couldn't stomach, simply carried on in his fawning amiability as if the man was actually to be taken seriously.

Esther was still talking. So far, Alex had learned that she was a student, as he was, at Concordia, though he hadn't been able to gather in exactly what; that she'd grown up in Côte St. Luc, a possibly Jewish neighborhood somewhere on the outskirts of the city, though he couldn't have said exactly where; that she lived in the building because it had a pool in it, though he couldn't quite reconcile this detail with her condition, which seemed to involve some issues of motor control. The fact was he was finding it hard to attend to her, not only because he was a bit overwhelmed by her barrage of talk and because he couldn't quite help trying to catch the interview going on in the background, but because of a host of other matters clamoring for attention at the back of his brain: his appointment with Dr. Klein, for which he somehow already seemed destined to be late; his class at the Refugee Centre, for which he'd hardly prepared; his final lesson at Berlitz with Félix, his cash cow, and the concomitant prospect of a depressingly low-income summer; his theory exam the following day, for which he'd hardly studied. Then there was the phone call home he had to make, the post-exam party he had to host, the grant forms he had to fill out, and in the middle and not-so-far distance the questions he did not even dare to give a shape to at the moment, though they were the pit above which everything else seemed precariously suspended.

In the background, the prime minister, having dodged the subject of Libya, was going on about Chernobyl, trying to cast himself as the calm leader in troubled times. Please, Peter, please, Alex thought, ask him a tough question. Though in truth, Alex revered Peter: he credited him with his own discovery of Canada, which had happened, ironically, in the couple of years since Alex had left Canada proper for the foreign country of Quebec. And he revered him despite his occasional fawning, his boyish stutter, his too frequent feel-good pieces on apple baking or native spiritualism or peewee hockey; and also despite, or maybe because of, the comments you sometimes read, usually buried by timid editors in the last paragraphs of lengthy profiles, that the instant the mike was turned off—though Alex could understand this perfectly: the mike was who he was, what he gave everything to—he turned into an unmitigated bastard.

Esther, who by now had settled herself on his couch, was explaining to him the notion of something she called "an exacerbation." With a start, Alex realized she had been telling him about her illness. It began to sink in that she'd actually named it and he'd let that crucial bit of information get by him. Somehow, she'd managed to slip the thing in as if it were just a casual aside: *Oh, by the way, I have blah-blah.*

"So what about you, Alex? What do *you* do?"

"I'm at Concordia, too," he said, realizing, guiltily, that he ought to have brought this up earlier. "I mean, I study there."

"Really? You don't say! What a coincidence!"

In fact, it wasn't much of a coincidence at all: probably half the people in the building were students at Concordia, whose hub, the infamously ugly Hall Building, stood just kitty-corner to them.

When Alex tried to explain his program his description struck him as even more convoluted and opaque than Esther's had been of her own. He'd initially been admitted to the university under Interdisciplinary Studies, in a mix of literary theory and evolutionary biology, of all things. But then the university had decided it couldn't handle such a broad crossing of disciplines and he'd ended up in the English Department.

"I guess I'm trying to find the way to bring the arts and sciences together," he said. "You know, a sort of Grand Unified Theory."

"Oh—you mean—art and science—"

The shadow had crossed her again.

"That's just a fancy way of saying I don't really know what I'm doing."

Alex had long ago handed over the cigarette Esther had come for, but she had placed it carefully in the little pink handbag in padded silk that she carried over her shoulder, struggling a bit with the clasp, though he hadn't known whether to offer help. To have with her cappuccino, she'd said, which was where she'd been heading when Alex had run into her.

"Do you really think it's dangerous to go out?"

"I dunno, the rain's probably all evaporated by now. Anyway, I doubt we're any safer inside."

She had risen and stood leaning on her cane at his door. Alex didn't like to admit to his relief at finally seeing her go—they hadn't been together more than twenty minutes, yet he felt exhausted.

In the background, the prime minister's interview was winding to a close.

Well, Peter, I know Canadians just love what you're doing here.

"Say," Esther said, "you know what? I have an idea. I could buy you a cappuccino, in exchange for the cigarette. I mean, if you're not busy."

Alex's heart sank. It seemed unfair somehow to brandish his excuses at her, exactly because he had such good ones. It was that face, the transparency of it, the bit of desperation he saw in it now. She'd met a man, it seemed to say—even if it was as poor a specimen as Alex—and wanted him to like her.

"That would be great," he said, "I'd love that," feeling himself draw a little closer to the pit.

The entire mood between them shifted with Alex's acceptance, Esther's bright, false, coming-on personality replaced with a kind of childlike triumphalism. In the elevator, she hooked an arm in his and batted her eyes at him with exaggerated coquettishness.

"I guess you'll just have to help a po' little sick girl like me," she said, then added "Ha, ha, ha," to make clear she was joking. Alex had instinctively tensed when she'd taken hold of him as though expecting some jolt, some clammy frisson of diseased flesh, but in fact her grip was warm and firm. She had taken possession of him, it seemed to say, and would do what was needed to hold on to her claim.

Outside, they found the rain had indeed misted off into the ether, though whether the air hummed with evil ions in its wake, Alex couldn't have said. In Sweden, radiation had reached a hundred times the normal level, and people were taking pills to protect their thyroids. No one knew if that was the worst of it—on the news reports so far, there hadn't been a single image from the site. Instead, they kept replaying the clip from Soviet TV where a matronly anchorwoman, posed against a background of washed-out blue, had given the first official announcement of the thing, in four bland, unhelpful sentences.

Everything about the day, however, belied Alex's sense of threat: the sun was out, the air was crystalline, and winter was gone, gone. There'd been ice on the ground only two weeks before, right into mid-April, the bane of Montreal living. But then a warm wind had come up and thawed the city overnight. The trees in the little church park at St. James the Apostle already had the intimation of leaves, a flock of something, starlings or sparrows or finches, chattering in their limbs.

Then there was Esther, for whom Chernobyl seemed little more than a conversation point. It was indeed true that everyone knew Esther: there was hardly a person they'd passed on the way out who hadn't greeted her, and then once they were on the street all the shopkeepers called out to her as well, from the little depanneur on the ground floor of their building, from the hairdresser's next door, from the little sandwich shop at the corner of St. Catherine. Almost to a one they winked at her for the good fortune of having a man on her arm. If Esther saw any condescension in this she didn't show it, refusing nothing, no attention or offering.

"Oh, that's Ilie," she said, "he's the one who usually gives me my cigarettes," and "That's Claire, she gives me free haircuts."

To his surprise, Alex actually found himself liking the attention they were getting. The world seemed different with Esther by his side: he'd hardly even noticed the sandwich shop on the corner before, or, for that matter, the church park. He also had never been to the Crescent Street strip, where Esther was leading him. It was only a couple of blocks over from their building, but had always seemed hopelessly tawdry and touristy next to his former haunts on the Plateau. Today, though, in the spring sun, radiation or no, he couldn't understand why he'd avoided the place—it looked so sprightly and European and gay, with its little cafés all with their tables out front and their fancy railings and stylishly dressed servers.

The place Esther brought him to, however, was one of the cheesier ones, a glitzy bar called Chez Sud done up in an overwrought tropical motif like some Club Med resort, their cappuccinos actually coming out with little colored umbrellas on them. Normally, Alex would never have ordered a cappuccino; it somehow irked his ethnic sensibilities, this passion everyone suddenly had for them. But he had to admit he liked the taste.

"I love this place," Esther said. "I come here all the time." And indeed it was clear from how everyone greeted her that she was well known here, though the waitress gave Alex a conspiratorial smile behind Esther's back as if to sympathize with his having got saddled with her.

Alex pulled his chair a bit closer to Esther's.

"It's just great," he said.

Alex had planned to quickly down his coffee and then beg off back home to his work. But he wasn't quite as anxious to be going as he ought to have been: the sun was shining and he was out here in the world, with Esther.

"It's very interesting what you were telling me," Esther said. "About the arts and sciences. That's very interesting."

"Oh, well. Maybe not so interesting."

But then despite himself he found himself drawn out by Esther's probing. As it happened, he was at a crisis point in his work. The university had accepted him, from what he could tell, largely on the basis of a lone, fluky publication, a sort of spoof of contemporary literary criticism that had somehow garnered much more attention than it deserved; from it, the assumption had apparently been drawn that he actually knew what he was doing. Yet the further he had tried to get into his work, the more unwieldy it had become. His original notion, of finding a way to link evolutionary theory to theories of narrative, had foundered, largely because of his almost total lack of grounding in the sciences; and so he'd been thrown back onto drab, overworked territory like social Darwinism. Instead of trying to impress Esther with the wonders of his doctoral mind, then—what would be the point of that?—he discovered himself actually opening up to her about his fears, two years into a Ph.D. without even the beginnings of a cogent dissertation topic.

Esther listened to all of this with the kind of rapt, open-mouthed attention one often dreamt about but never got. True, she didn't seem quite to follow everything he was saying, but then Alex was so relieved simply to give voice to something that had been gnawing at him for so long, and that he hadn't been able to bring up with anyone else—not his advisor, not Dr. Klein, not even Liz—that Esther didn't have to do much more than sit there without yawning for Alex to feel a tremendous gratitude to her.

It was only when he'd finished that he saw how self-indulgent he was being: he was merely taking advantage of Esther's innocence and need as an opportunity for easy sympathy. Liz would never have let him get away with this sort of thing; she would have seen through him at once, how all his whining and vacillation were just part of an enduring immaturity and lack of focus.

"So are you saying you want to give it up?" Esther said.

Alex was taken aback. Where had she got that from? He realized, belatedly, that he had, after all, been trying to impress her. See what a stoic I am, he'd been saying, to soldier on against such impossible odds. Yet as soon as she'd spoken the question he felt a kind of release.

"Maybe I'm saying that. I'm not sure."

It would be so simple if he just fell back to what was normal, wrote a modest, unoriginal dissertation, finished it up in a year or two. Surely that was acceptable, didn't even require him to resort, as he easily could, to extenuating circumstance.

But Esther, with sudden force, said, "You can't give it up! Listen to the way you talk about it, how excited you get—I can't believe you would even think of giving it up."

This wasn't the response he'd expected: a real one. He himself, in Esther's situation, dealing with a new person he wanted to like him, would probably have been too self-conscious to do anything other than guess what it was the other person might want to hear, and say that.

"Isn't it important to you?" Esther said. "Just listen to yourself!"

"Well, yes, but, who knows, maybe it's just some crazy idea—"

"It doesn't sound crazy to me," Esther said. "It makes a lot of sense. It sounds important, except other people haven't been smart enough to see that yet."

Alex felt himself blushing. Who was this girl—woman—saying things like this to a stranger? What force had sent her suddenly hurtling across his path?

"It's the same with MS," she said. "People are always saying you have to accept this or that, you have to give in. But I'm never going to give in. I'm going to fight."

MS, that was it: multiple sclerosis. He repeated the name over and over in his head now to lodge it firmly there, though he still had no idea what it was, what was multiple about it, or sclerotic, if she was basically a well person with a few chronic but stable symptoms or if she was dying before his eyes.

"What is MS, exactly?"

"Oh," she said, rising to the subject. "Actually, it's very interesting."

Now it was Alex's turn to be mystified, as Esther launched into a discussion of nerve cells and myelin sheaths, pronouncing certain words like shibboleths, though to Alex they all quickly receded into the miasma of biological terms that had been consigned to a remote corner of his brain after Grade 12 biology and had never emerged again, for all the reading he'd done since in the natural sciences.

"It's kind of like AIDS," she said, which shocked him, because she made the connection so casually, as if proud to be associated with the disease of the moment. "It's"—and she stressed the word—"an *autoimmune* disease."

"Oh. I see." But what he saw was a vision of his friend Michael's ex-partner Mario, whom he'd seen about a month before he'd died, when he'd been slack-faced with dementia and wasted to skin and bone.

They had finished their *cappuccini*. There was an awkward moment, when Alex should have taken the opportunity to excuse himself or suggest he lead her home.

"Are you going back?" he said finally, but no, she had an errand at Ogilvy's.

He saw her eyes go to her cane.

"I could come with you," he said, before he could stop himself.

And he was quick to insist that he pay the bill, a privilege Esther was happy to concede to him.

Although Alex had passed by Ogilvy's any number of times and had stopped like everyone else to gawk at its elaborate Christmas windows, he had never actually been inside the place. He had thus avoided any taint of association with the reviled Anglo Establishment—most of which, at any rate, had been chased from the city by now—that the store seemed to represent. The truth was, however, that he was secretly drawn to the place: it had the air of Manhattan to it, of the 1950s, of Rock Hudson and Doris Day. Inside, it did not disappoint, with the look of some large yet intimate manor hall, marble-floored and crystal-chandeliered and humming with the background murmur of wealth.

Even here, Esther was known, several of the saleswomen smiling at her as she came through, though more than one rather tightly, Alex thought. Esther, oblivious, pushed on past the makeup tables and perfume counters that lined the ground floor to the old brass-doored elevators, where an actual attendant, a pale young woman in a dark uniform and cap reminiscent of the Salvation Army, escorted them upward. They got out, somehow predictably, at Lingerie. Esther, moving free from Alex now and managing quite well on her cane, headed at once past the rows of designer teddies and negligees toward the sale racks at the back.

Through this whole time, she had never really stopped talking.

"I don't think of myself as someone with a *disease*, do you know what I mean? You know, 'Oh, no, I have MS!' A lot of MS-ers are like that, that's why I don't like hanging around with them. Do you think that's bad? That I don't like other MS-ers?"

Esther's battle of the moment, Alex gathered, was against the loss of any more mobility. She had reluctantly consented to the cane after her last exacerbation, but was determined to go no further.

"'You have to accept it,' everyone's always saying to me. But I think if you just accept it, of course it's going to happen to you. I went to this meeting of MS-ers once and it made me sick, how everyone was just saying accept this and accept that. I'll never accept it. I'll never stop walking. I love walking. I'd die if I couldn't walk."

Esther was sorting unabashedly through bins of brassieres and discounted underwear while Alex stood discreetly to one side. Then, out of nowhere, Alex heard the strains of bagpipes. They must be coming through the speaker system, he thought, but no, lo and behold, an instant later a flesh-and-blood bagpiper emerged from a back aisle in full regalia and began wending his way through Lingerie, to the bafflingly less-than-astonished smiles and glances of the pretty much exclusively female clientele. Esther, for her part, barely looked up from her bin.

"What's going on?"

"It's just the bagpipes!" Esther said, shouting to be heard above them. "They do it every day at noon."

The panic rose in Alex: so it was already noon. Of all the things he might be doing at that moment it seemed inexplicable that he was standing here biding his time in Lingerie while a bagpipe played and Esther rifled through the underwear bin. The piper was coming right at him now, holding his eye with the steely stare of a Scottish raider, an onslaught of tartan and noise that seemed set to obliterate him like some poor, oppressed habitant. Then at the last instant he turned, veering off from the low-end racks toward the Chantelle bras.

Alex became aware that Esther was at his elbow, trying to get his attention.

"Alex," she whispered, "I have to use the bathroom."

"Oh. Sure. Oh."

There was an edge in her voice. Alex wasn't exactly sure what his role was here: he felt suddenly parental, as if he were on an outing with one of his nieces or nephews.

"It's on the next floor up," Esther said, the edge sharper. "We have to take the elevator."

But when they got to the elevators, one of them, to judge from the indicator, had just passed on its way up, while the other, with the Salvation Army girl at the controls, was apparently being held for the piper, who was at that moment making his way toward them.

"It's an emergency!" Alex said to the girl, but she couldn't hear him above the noise of the pipes. And then the piper was there, moving relentlessly forward, and they had to stand clear.

"Should we take the stairs?" Alex said.

"I don't know. Sure—I mean, okay."

The stairs were wide and old and unevenly worn; it was clear at once that it would not be an easy proposition for Esther to get up them. Alex could see more fully now the extent of her frailty; what she'd been able to mask until then with the occasional shuffle or lunge was exposed in the difficulty she had aiming her foot toward each step. But it was too late to turn back—she had already gone silent and grim with the effort of holding back whatever it was that wanted to come out of her.

It seemed an eternity before they reached the upper landing. Alex had had to resort to practically carrying her, surprised at how solid and heavy she was.

Coming out of the stairwell they ran into one of the salesclerks, an older, salon-haired woman who seemed to take their air of crisis as a sign of infraction.

"Can I help you?" she said, with a false, saleswoman's smile.

"We just need the washroom," Alex said quickly.

Esther, ignoring the clerk, had lurched on headlong without him.

"It's over here!" she said.

Esther was panting now, saying "Oh, oh, oh," with each breath. At the washroom door, the salesclerk's eyes still burning into him, Alex said, "Can you manage all right?" and Esther said, "Yes," before plunging ahead. She was hardly inside, though, before Alex heard her give out a long groan and her panting gave way to sobs.

"Esther! Are you okay?"

Without daring to look back at the clerk Alex pushed through the door. He found Esther collapsed in a heap on the tile floor, the seat of her jeans wet and a small puddle spreading around her.

"Oh, Alex," she said, her face torn with grief.

Alex helped her up. He led her, still sobbing, into one of the stalls and sat her on the bowl there.

He put a hand awkwardly on one of her shoulders.

"It's okay," he said, "it's okay."

The saleswoman was peering in through the doorway, her eyes going at once to the puddle on the floor.

"Is there something I can help with?" she said, in a tone that suggested she hoped not.

Alex wasn't certain what to do next.

"I could use a plastic bag," he said.

He handed Esther her cane from the floor as if to console her with it.

"Just wait for me here. I'll be right back."

He sprinted down the stairs back to Lingerie and made his way to the discount bin. After some quick sorting he picked out a medium panty, opting for the most workmanlike pair he could lay his hands on.

The saleswoman was waiting for him at the washroom door with the plastic bag. He handed her the tag from the panties.

"I'll pay for them on the way out," he said, and she pursed her lips as if to keep herself from suggesting otherwise.

Esther was still on the bowl.

"Can you get these on on your own?" Alex said.

"Yes, I think so."

"You can put the other ones in here," he said, handing her the bag.

He heard her jostling and grunting as she struggled with her clothes behind the stall door.

"Do you want me to help?"

"It's okay. I'm okay."

When she came out, finally, her cane in one hand and the plastic bag in the other, she seemed so chastened and forlorn next to the girl who'd locked an arm in his not an hour before that Alex could hardly bear to look at her.

He took the bag from her.

"I guess we should get going," he said.

"My pants are all wet." Her voice was cracking again.

"It's okay, we'll get a cab. I'll walk behind you. No one will see."

"Oh, Alex," she said, but half laughing now.

"At least you got a new pair of underwear. Ha ha."

"Ha ha," she said.

The saleslady was waiting nervously beyond the door. She was likely just some poor ex-housewife from Verdun, exiled here with all the clearance stuff on the store's shabby top floor.

He gave her a five-dollar bill for the underwear.

"I'll get your change, sir."

"It's all right."

They were able to get a cab right in front of the store, though it was still a good ten minutes of traffic and one-way streets before they were back at their building. The fare was four seventy-five; because the driver was francophone Alex felt compelled to add a couple of quarters onto the five he'd already pulled out in order to bump up the tip. Alex didn't like himself for it, but he couldn't help doing the math on what this little excursion had cost him, some fourteen dollars in all, money he could ill afford.

He escorted Esther up to her apartment on the eleventh. It seemed the two of them had crammed into a couple of hours several months' or years' worth of drama and intimacy and strain. How could they go back from that to mere politeness, to what in fact would have been the appropriate level of distance for two people who didn't really know each other?

At her door, he blurted out, "I'm having a party tomorrow night. If you'd like to come."

Esther's face lit up like a sunrise.

"A party? Well, yes, I'd love to!"

There, he had done it, had added another complication to things, just in case he hadn't enough of them.

He saw by Esther's watch—he didn't wear his own, a stupid affectation that caused him no end of trouble—that it was nearly one. Shit. Whenever he was late for a session, Dr. Klein always saw it as hopelessly significant, a habit that irritated Alex deeply, implying as it did that the only thing of importance in Alex's life was his relationship with Dr. Klein.

"I guess I'll see you tomorrow then," Alex said. "Eight o'clock?"

"It's a date."

Alex had the sinking feeling again. He thought of María, from his language class, and the big play he'd been hoping to make for her the following night.

"It's a date," he said, already backing up toward the elevators.

It was a thirteen-minute walk, all uphill, from Alex's apartment building to Dr. Klein's office. Up Mackay Street to Sherbrooke; past the Unitarian church and Le Linton apartments; past Chelsea Place on Simpson, with its beautiful courtyard and Georgian-style townhouses; past Percy Walters Park, which someone had rechristened, in graffiti, *Parc Merde de Chien*, and which sported, for some reason, a bust of Simón Bolívar. From the park you could just see the back of Pierre Trudeau's house, perched on the slope that rose up to Pine Avenue looking unrevealing and fortress-like, with its art deco austerity. The rumor was that you could see the Great Man himself heading off on foot every morning along Pine toward the law firm where he'd taken up a sinecure after quitting his job as the nation's leader. Alex often took a detour from the route up McGregor in the hopes of catching a glimpse of him, making his way up to Pine by the steps at the eastern end of the park, which came out not twenty feet from Trudeau's front door. But so far the only outcome of his skulking was that he had probably become a person of interest to the Cuban consulate across the street, which had boosted its usual phalanx of security cameras in the wake of a recent firebombing.

Dr. Klein worked from an outbuilding of Montreal General that served as some sort of rehab. It stood at the head of another steep set of stairs that came up from Pine—and the symbolism of all this climbing was not lost on Alex—and passed along the high-fenced schoolyard of the Académie Michèle-Provost, whose children's sounds and construction-paper-decorated windows always filled Alex with a not-so-obscure sense of shame. The rehab building sat four-square and gloomy amidst a clump of spindly pines at the top of the steps. To the west, above the treetops, you could make out the upper stories of the General; to the north, up the slopes, the red rooflines of the Shriners children's hospital and then the undifferentiated woods of Mount Royal Park.

Alex had never quite been able to determine what went on at the rehab except that everyone there seemed much crazier than he was, with either the vacant stare of the overdrugged or the weird, screwed-up intensity of the perpetually embattled. He had ended up there by fluke: after his breakup with Liz he had gone into the university's counseling center when his usual low-grade depression had taken a turn for the worse, and the center, being unequipped, it turned out, for any kind of long-term treatment, had sent him on to the health clinic for a referral. That was where he had met Dr. Klein, who worked shifts there as a medical doctor.

"Actually, I'm just setting up a practice," he'd said, clearing his throat. "I might be able to fit you in."

The look of him then had hardly inspired confidence. Everything about him was boyish and gawky, his mop of hair, his adolescent thinness, the way his doctor's smock hung on him like a disguise. Even the way he'd put the thing had sounded suspect, as if he was shilling for clients. But Alex had been feeling pretty black at the time. He had moved into the place on Mackay by then but didn't always trust himself to go out on his balcony.

The counseling center had warned him it might be months before he found a placement.

"When can you see me?"

Dr. Klein made a show of looking through his agenda.

"I could put you in tomorrow."

Alex hadn't even known Klein was a Freudian until he'd gone in the next day and seen the couch.

"The way we'll work is you'll lie on the couch and say whatever comes to you."

That had been pretty well the full extent of their discussion of methods. Indeed, in the three months that Alex had been coming in, five days a week, fifty minutes a day, the word *Freud,* or, for that matter, *psychoanalysis,* had not so much as crossed Dr. Klein's lips. Alex, though, who was not unfamiliar with Freud, recognized even these omissions as hallmarks of the Freudian system: the important thing was to keep the analysis free of all contaminating influences. Once, to test the waters, Alex had pointedly asked about Dr. Klein's education, and the doctor had put him off at once.

"I don't think it would be useful to the therapy to talk about that."

In fact Alex couldn't believe his good luck at first. Freud was about as close as anyone came to being a hero for Alex: back in first-year under-grad he had read the *Introductory Lectures* and had never looked back. He credited Freud with releasing him, finally and irreversibly, from the last shackles of the Catholic Church; he credited Freud with teaching him whatever little he understood about the mythopoeic mind. It had long been his dream to do an analysis, something he'd assumed would forever be beyond his financial means. But here in socialist Quebec, wonder of wonders, the treatment was fully and generously funded by the taxpayer.

The thirteen-minute walk to the clinic meant that Alex arrived, as he saw from the hall clock, some twelve minutes late for his appointment. He was happy to be spared waiting in what passed for the building's reception room, a squalid foyer with a torn vinyl couch and a few ratty chairs where there was not so much as a reception desk or even a sign to show what sort of facility one had entered. Alex hurried past the vaguely familiar presences shuffling through the halls—inmates? outpatients? cleaning staff?—to Dr. Klein's office, or at least the office he was to be found in, for there was no indication, such as a nameplate on the door, that it was actually his.

As always, when Alex was late, the door was slightly ajar. Alex gave a knock but then pushed through without waiting for a response. There at his desk sat Dr. Klein in all his sartorial splendor, perma-press-trousered and gabardine-jacketed, not poring over some new psychoan-alytic text or the notes from some other client, not even furrow-browed in concentration, but cross-legged and blank-eyed as if he had simply been waiting for Alex without a significant thought in his head. It came to Alex in a rush how contemptible he found this man—for his novice's exacti-tude and adherence to the rules, for his ill-fitting sports coats and anachronistically long sideburns, for his insipid commentary and insights. For the fact that he was such a boy finally, awkward and set to his task and blind to the plodding unimaginativeness of his methods. Alex would have liked to have been in the hands of someone he might comfortably turn himself over to, not this wet-behind-his-biggish-ears apprentice who was at most only a year or two older than himself.

Dr. Klein nodded to him as he came in, said nothing about his being late, expressed nothing in his body language that might give Alex a window into his character and hence interfere with the necessary process of transference—another word, of course, that had never crossed the doctor's lips.

At once, Alex removed his shoes and lay down on the couch. In all the weeks he had been coming here Alex figured he had not held Dr. Klein in his gaze for more than an accumulated total of five or six minutes: a few seconds when he came in, a few when he left, maybe one or two stolen ones while he removed or replaced his shoes. It felt increasingly ludicrous, this sort of relationship. Far from keeping Alex from any hint of Dr. Klein's real nature, it only seemed to heighten his sense of it.

Alex was on the couch.

"I met a woman in my building today who has multiple sclerosis," he said, in an attempt to follow the rules, just speak what was uppermost in his mind. But the more he talked about it, the more the whole encounter with Esther seemed tainted. There was no way he was going to mention the incident at Ogilvy's, though he could still feel the warmth in his hands of the bag with Esther's urine-soaked underwear.

"She seems quite an amazing woman," he ended lamely, thus flattenning out all the nuance of their meeting.

Dr. Klein had yet to say a word. Alex lapsed into one of the silences that were becoming more and more frequent of late, biding his time doing an inventory of whatever of the room's spartan furnishings he could make out from where he lay: the vaguely African etching above the couch, with its abstracted sea and animal images, in particular a largish fish that Alex figured must be somehow significant; the unframed poster on the wall opposite of the 1976 Olympics; the bookshelf near the window that held a few bound annuals from the Canadian Medical Association, a featureless tome that Alex supposed was a guide to antipsychotic pharmaceuticals, and a copy of *Time* that looked like it had been picked up in passing from the reception area. Yet all this evidence was ultimately inconclusive, given the uncertainty of the doctor's permanence here.

"Maybe you're talking about your new friend," Dr. Klein said finally, and Alex cringed at the phrase *new friend*, "because you don't want to pick up where we left off, talking about Liz. And maybe that's why you were fifteen minutes late."

Twelve minutes, asshole, Alex thought, though he also thought, You're damn right I don't want to talk about Liz, a topic he was thoroughly tired of but was one of the few Dr. Klein seemed to think worthy of his attention. This was a constant tussle between the two of them, what Dr. Klein deemed significant and what he deemed evasion, what he thought was the point of something, and what he thought was beside it. Once, Alex had spent almost an entire session talking about the shoe rack that had stood in the furnace room of his childhood home, a crudely fashioned thing that his father had cobbled together out of old wood scraps: in Alex's mind it had seemed suddenly like Proust's madeleine, the nexus of every important question that had ever pressed on him, because it had been so makeshift and dusty and insignificant and yet an integral part of his life for many years, and because now that his father had sold the farm it had probably passed away forever from the world, though his first Sunday shoes had sat there, and the shoes he'd got in Italy when he was thirteen, and then his father's mud-caked work boots, his mother's bloated loafers-turned-farm-shoes, the cracked hobnailed boots that his grandfather had brought over with him on the boat, a whole history of work and rites of passage and loss.

But Dr. Klein, when Alex had finished, had said, "Maybe you're still blaming your father for the fact that you were poor."

Wrong, wrong, wrong, Alex had thought. Why did everything have to go back to some childish sense of grievance? Surely it had to be possible to look beyond your little Oedipal struggles to the occasional bigger question—about the way things were in the world, for instance, and what they might mean. Take that shoe rack: what had become of it? And why did it hold such a numinous place in Alex's consciousness, as if the weight of existence rested on it?

"I don't know why it's more important to talk about Liz than about this person I've met who might be dying," he said now, surprised at how pleasant it felt to put on this show of indignation.

"Is she really dying?" Dr. Klein said.

Too late, Alex remembered he was speaking to someone actually trained as a medical doctor.

"Well, she does have MS."

Dr. Klein relented.

"I can see how that would affect you," he said, with what seemed almost like real sympathy, which of course had the result of making Alex feel obliged to speak about Liz again.

The truth of the matter, which Alex was only sporadically successful at hiding from himself, was that Dr. Klein was pretty much on target where Liz was concerned: the reason Alex didn't want to talk about her was that he still couldn't bring himself to face up to the weirdness the relationship had taken on its final awful months. Of course, Alex had more or less admitted from the outset that it was the breakup with Liz that had driven him here, though that had been a whopping evasion in its own right.

"The thing about Liz," he said, trying this on, "was that everything about her was a lie. She wanted to be this bohemian, this radical feminist, but underneath that she was just a conservative. Then she hated me because I pretended to believe in this other version of her."

"What makes you say that?"

"I just know it, that's all."

There was a silence while Dr. Klein gave Alex time to ponder the irrationality of his reply. Then, because the silence had to be filled, Alex said, "I saw it all at the end. How she just wanted someone to dominate her. But then she would have hated me for that too."

"Maybe," Dr. Klein said, "you're inventing a situation that couldn't possibly have worked so you can feel justified for having ended it. The same issue has come up, I think, when you've talked about your dissertation."

When had he talked about his dissertation? Clearly, that had been a mistake. There seemed something oddly puritan in the doctor's take on things, as if to go on with something was somehow always more psychically sound than to end it. In this case he was wide of the mark: breaking up had been the only thing in their relationship that he and Liz had been right about.

From the clock above the door, which he could just make out if he twisted his head, Alex saw that they were already at the halfway mark. A familiar panic went through him. What was he doing, forever fighting this man whom he'd come to for help? Why did he continue to avoid the most important things? He had yet to say a word, for instance, about

Desmond and the Galápagos; he had yet to say a word about his son. These were matters of far greater import than Liz or his dissertation and yet he hadn't gone anywhere near them, as if, for all his imagined self-knowing, he was as classically repressed as any of Freud's Viennese hysterics. Of course, it might also be the case that he was just an idiot, a bourgeois with too much time on his hands, bilking the already over-burdened health care system to the tune of forty-three dollars per fifty-minute session. If he continued to see the doctor at all it was only for this, that since he'd started his analysis he felt unaccountably better.

"I don't see what my dissertation has to do with it," he said, thus inviting exactly the mind-numbingly obvious reply Dr. Klein gave him.

"Sometimes there are patterns to what we do. That's what we're looking for."

He wondered if Dr. Klein didn't feel it too, that same sense of hollow-ness when he spoke as if they were merely following a script. More and more Alex saw their relationship less in Freudian terms than in purely animal ones: they were both of them sniffing the air, circling each other, making feints; all the rest, all the talk that passed between them, was just so much barking and clucking. It might really be as simple as that, call it transference or whatever, that the shaky respite Alex felt since he'd started here was due entirely to his making an enemy of the doctor, to his focusing on him all his simmering animal rage. Alex would have liked to talk to someone about that rage, which was pretty much a constant in his life, attaching itself to whatever was handy—Ronald Reagan, Liz, the rude servers at the Van Houtte's—and making him feel incessantly mean-spirited and exhausted and low, even when its targets were perfectly rea-sonable ones. And he would have liked to talk about the endless stream of vindication fantasies that ran through his head—I will finish my dis-sertation; it will be published to great acclaim; I will get tenure; I will win awards; a school of thought will be founded in my name—that was the other side of this rage, the gargantuan need for some sort of revenge against the world. Revenge for what? he had to ask. Against whom? The kids who had picked on him in high school? Did it really come down to this, that his main motivation in life was this simple need to get revenge for all his petty humiliations?

Somehow it was not Dr. Klein, however, with whom he wanted to discuss these things. That would have been too awkward, really, too demeaning. From there, it would have been only a short step to making incontrovertible what for most of his life he had striven to hide from the world, namely the dark den of banality and self-absorption that his mind truly was. There were the self-improvement fantasies that kept his revenge ones company—I will be more generous; I will quit smoking; I will learn Spanish; I will call home more often; I will stop plotting stupid revenge fantasies; I will become a better, more perfect person—or the embarrassing interviews he was forever conducting with himself in his head, and that probably constituted his main mode of self-presence. The interviews were particularly insidious. Alex himself could hardly believe how much of his mind time they took up, and yet he couldn't seem to muster whatever strength of will it might take to put an end to them.

They had been going on now for as long as he could remember. At the very least, since he was nine or ten: that was when he and his brother Gus had started watching *The Tonight Show*, on those nights when their father stayed late at the club. Even then he'd had delusions of grandeur, casting himself as a movie star or NHL whiz kid and aping the rhythms and turns of phrase of Johnny's guests. *Well, Johnny, I learned to skate on a little pond near our farm in an old pair of skates I paid two dollars for at Leamington Sporting Goods.* Things like that. Usually real things he dressed up in one way or another. Not so differently from now.

To tell you the truth, Peter, the idea goes back to a trip I made to the Galápagos in my mid-twenties.

Correct me if I'm wrong, but wouldn't that have been just around Darwin's own age when he was there?

Well, pretty close, as a matter of fact.

At least he had moved on from Johnny to Peter Gzowski, though any number of guest hosts might make an appearance over the course of a day—Liz, his academic advisor, perfect strangers, indeed anyone, it seemed, except Dr. Klein. What was most disturbing about these exchanges was that it was almost impossible anymore for Alex to formulate a coherent thought outside of them. This meant that for most of his waking life the only way he knew his own mind, as it were, was through the suspect utterances that he contrived for his imaginary public. What did it mean to have a consciousness if the only way it was ever present to him was through this infernal talking head? Who was he, really, in all that? What did he really think? How could he know? All he really knew, in the end, were the canned opinions he put together for Peter Gzowski.

It was all more evasion, of course, the mind's endless editing, exactly the sort of thing analysis was supposed to get beyond. But so far, everything he said on the couch had the feel of being as calculated and processed as his mental interviews—there were no unexpected breakthroughs, no stumbling through the underbrush into sudden clearings, just the Talk Show of the Mind made incarnate. It was as if, for all his spite toward him, Alex was just trying to dazzle Dr. Klein with the crystal clarity of his thoughts. Or worse: he actually wanted to please him. Since the start of the analysis Alex's dreams had taken on an almost parodic level of Freudian iconography, rivers and trains, rotting teeth, subterranean passageways, as if his mind were cribbing mental copies of *The Collected Works* to dredge up offerings for Dr. Klein.

Alex's father had made predictably frequent appearances in their sessions. Alex had told the story of the family dog his father had killed when Alex was four or five: this was a classic of his childhood, full of nuance and possibility. The dog, a stray they'd named Lassie after the TV dog, though it was a male, had been getting into the chickens, and his father had chased it down into the back fields and felled it with a couple of blasts of his shotgun. It would have been easy to portray his father as a villain in the matter, but instead Alex had made light of it, as if it had been a lark, merely the kind of thing everyone did in the country. But then why had he brought it up at all? It had been just another offering: see how I need you, the story seemed to say, see what a perfect Freudian disaster I am, hiding my pain.

The thing was, there was no pain in his actual memory of the event— it had indeed been a lark, a veritable family adventure, almost festive in its sense of occasion. Dogs came and went in the country; if they were pests you drove them out to a deserted concession road to let some other farmer get stuck with them, or you got out your gun. When it came to it, his father had actually liked the dog, though Alex didn't quite say this to Dr. Klein, or rather, he didn't say it very convincingly. It wasn't clear to Alex what exactly he had been trying to do, please Dr. Klein or mislead him, vilify his father or excuse him. Maybe it had just been his way of introducing the whole issue of his father's brutality, except that even there he was on shaky ground—when he tried to tally up in his mind the real instances of violence, he couldn't come up with more than a meager handful, none of them touching on him directly. What had always been worse had been the shame afterward, how his father had sulked for days or weeks after some outburst so that they'd have to keep living the thing like a penance.

Eleven minutes remaining. Still enough time, perhaps, to bring up something of import. Ingrid's letter was the really pressing thing, he knew that; everything else was just noise. In his mind's eye he saw it again, Ingrid's familiar airy script, which had always made his heart leap, and then the familiar red and blue of the airmail stripes. The letter had reached him so freakishly it seemed to have been delivered by the very hand of fate—it was that blasted article of his in *Canadian Studies* again, which somehow had turned up in, of all places, a teacher education center in Lund. By chance Ingrid had seen it, and had written him, care of the journal; by chance the journal—since he'd happened to update them when he'd moved to Montreal to keep up his free-subscription-in-lieu-of-payment, though he never actually read the thing—had had his address. What were the odds of that chain of events? And yet the letter had come. The upshot of the letter was this: he had a son.

Eight minutes. *Blah, blah, blah.* Liz this and Liz that. What he did not say was the truth: that Liz was not to blame in any way. She might be messed up, she might have lied, evaded, distorted, she might still have horrible unresolved issues with her parents, and yet he was the one, he, he, he, no one else. He was an asshole, a shell, there was no way around it; all Liz's flailing had just been her pounding against the emptiness of him, to no response. Fuck, he thought, fuck, and then, where his mind always bottomed out, *Fucking Desmond.*

He had lapsed into silence again. He heard the hand jump on the clock above the door, but didn't look over.

Well, Peter, I suppose what stopped me from bringing things up with him was a kind of superstition, the fear I'd wreck this precarious balance I'd set up.

Isn't that interesting. So you thought that by not talking about things you'd somehow keep them in check.

Something like that.

But you'd have to admit, that's pretty Freudian.

Tick, tick. Too late now to start something new. There'd be a three-day hiatus—he'd had to cancel the following day's session on account of his exam, and then came the weekend.

I want to thank you for being here, Alex—is it really Alex? Or Alessandro?
Alex is fine.

Though I guess it could also be Alejandro, since I understand you're fluent
in Spanish.

Tick. He heard the doctor shift behind him, impatiently perhaps, and then he said, in the same slightly admonishing tone he used every day, as if to underline Alex's foolish squandering of his time, "I think our time's up."

Alex sat up and started pulling on his shoes.

"Monday, then?" he said to the doctor.

"Yes, Monday."

Outside, he saw that the rain hadn't dried completely on the steps yet. He made his way down, negotiating the little puddles, feeling a bit less taken than before with the budding spring.

Alex just had time to pop up to his apartment to grab his lesson books before heading over to give his language class at St. Bart's. He was afraid he was going to run into Esther again—why afraid? what kind of monster was he?—but he got in and out cleanly, though he'd done so little in the way of prep he might as well have gone to class empty-handed.

St. Bart's was in Little Burgundy, a short walk down Guy past the new Faubourg market at St. Catherine and then the massive mother house of the Grey Nuns to where the road dipped down into the lowlands of the urban poor. The neighborhood had apparently been the heart of a thriving black community before the Ville-Marie Expressway had been carved through it. Now it blended nondescriptly into St. Henri and Point St. Charles. St. Henri Alex knew about from his Grade 13 reading of *The Tin Flute*—in the original French, no less, a feat he couldn't imagine now—though the place had changed a bit from its *Tin Flute* days. Great swaths of it had been torn down to make way for courtyard-style townhouse complexes, and many of the older streets sported here and there, amidst the peeling paint and rotting porches, the occasional façade painted over in blacks and grays or newly sandblasted, signs of the growing incursion of the bohemians and yuppies. On the side of an old warehouse near the on-ramp to the Ville-Marie someone had spray-painted, in brazen English, "Artists are the shock troops of gentrification."

St. Bart's, run by the Anglicans, was in a little square around the corner from the Sally Ann. A youngish do-gooder named Milly organized the English classes there. She was the sort of minority rightist Alex had done his best to avoid in Montreal, where the so-called minority, from what he could tell, was mainly a bunch of embittered Westmounters who still hearkened back to the days when their clubs hadn't admitted French Canadians or Jews.

The center offered English classes more or less gratis to refugees.

"They don't want to let them in in the first place," Milly had told him, "then they make sure they'll have to stay here by forcing them to learn French."

Unlike immigrants, refugees, being under federal jurisdiction, at least had their choice of official languages. But then because all the services were run by the province, they got streamed into French like everyone else. There, according to Milly, they got language labs, textbooks, professional instructors, everything state-of-the-art; the ones foolish enough to choose English ended up at places like St. Bart's. Alex could vouch that there was nothing state-of-the-art about St. Bart's: the instructors, all volunteers like himself and mainly short-term certificate students trying to log teaching hours for TOEFL, seemed to turn over weekly; the students, for their part, moved away, gave birth, lost interest, switched instructors, or had their cases decided and found jobs or were deported. As for materials, Alex generally had to manage with old handouts from his teaching days in Nigeria, photocopying them on the sly at the Concordia English office.

"It's better than nothing, which is what they'd get otherwise," Milly was fond of saying, though it boggled Alex's mind that this was the best his country had to offer its new arrivals.

Alex had started a new class a few weeks before, a mix of Salvadorans and Iranians that had quickly become polarized, each group trading what were clearly jibes against the other in its native tongue that somehow managed to leap the barriers of language to create a mood of festering hostility. Alex, who could do no more than catch the occasional lonely word of Spanish, had imagined that some heated political dispute had broken out. But then one of the Salvadorans had befriended him, a slick character named Miguel.

"Is jus' sex," Miguel had said to him, aping a North American idiom. "Is all jus' sex business."

Apparently the Salvadorans had accused the Iranians of gazing covetously at one of their women, a diminutive and not even especially attractive peasant girl who always came to class in kerchiefs and long skirts. A whole series of insults had begun, communicated, as Miguel explained, in a language outside the official ones.

"Is unibersal language. Language of the eye, of the face, of the hand. In Canada you don' speak this language but in El Salbador we know it bery well."

Miguel seemed to take the whole thing as a joke, though the irony was that the most covetable woman in the group, whom the Iranians must have been blind to overlook, was Miguel's own sister, María. Alex had picked her out at once: she was almost a caricature of voluptuousness, dark-skinned, full-lipped, long-haired, with just a slight excess of flesh, which she did not bother to rein in, that made it seem obscene merely to look at her, so much did his thoughts turn at once to the carnal. It had been a struggle getting through classes with her there, so nonchalant, so seemingly oblivious to her effect on him, though hardly ten seconds went by without his eye going to her. For her sake, Alex had incautiously welcomed Miguel's advances to him, though he was clearly someone looking for a main chance and even the other Salvadorans seemed to steer clear of him. But he was María's brother, and from what Alex knew of Latin culture he figured it would be suicide to try to do an end run around him. Not, of course, that he had a chance in hell with someone who could make his knees melt at twenty paces.

Normally, Alex's taste ran decidedly to the blond-haired and the blue-eyed. Liz, Russian Mennonite on her mother's side and Danzig German on her father's, had fit that description, as had Ingrid. Alex's childhood, when he'd been surrounded at every party and social event by mustache-lipped Italian girls, had apparently been enough to put him off the Latin type. But with María he seemed to have reverted: it was as if there had been some gene inside him just waiting to be clicked on at the sight of a María, and now every hormone and sexual instinct in him was directed toward his possession of her. This might not have been a problem if he hadn't actually liked her, but the fact was that she was as unaffected and no-nonsense as her brother was untrustworthy and slick, making up for Miguel's eagerness to get in with the teacher by making a point, it seemed to Alex, of giving him no special regard and indeed of virtually ignoring him. Unlike her brother she was friendly with the other Salvadorans, particularly the women, for whom she'd become a sort of spokesperson against the Iranians, getting off good ones that had the women laughing behind their hands and the men slapping their knees and that left the Iranians grim-faced with defeat. And unlike her brother she had an impeccable fashion sense: next to his Latin dancer's white shirts and black pants she wore faded jeans and loose-fitting blouses and flouncy sweaters, so that on the street it would have been hard to tell her from a native.

When Alex came into class today he found Miguel slouched in his usual place at one of the flimsy tables that served as desks. María's place, however, was decidedly empty, and María did not come hurrying in from the washroom or some appointment to fill it as the class got underway. Alex couldn't believe the sense of desolation he felt at her absence when he had barely exchanged half a dozen words with her and knew almost nothing about her except what he'd gleaned in class through the scrim of a foreign language.

He'd been planning to wing some conversation practice by starting up a discussion on Chernobyl, but right from his garbled introduction he saw the thing was going to be a disaster.

"Is very bad," one of the Iranians said. "Is close to Iran."

He saw a smirk appear on the faces of a couple of the Salvadorans.

"Gorbachev, is bad," the Iranian said. He was looking right at the Salvadorans now. "The Communists, always liars."

Alex didn't know where he'd imagined this could lead. Nowhere good, it seemed.

"What about nuclear power?" he said, foolishly carrying the thing on just beyond the point where he might have passed it off as casual conversation rather than an actual lesson plan. By then people were staring at him with squint-eyed, baffled looks, their notebooks spread expectantly. Alex was terrified at the chunk of unstructured class time still stretching before him. In a panic he resorted to a paired conversation exercise he used at Berlitz, but he hadn't reckoned his numbers well and got stuck pairing an Iranian woman with a Salvadoran one. Almost at once the two turned from each other back to their own compatriots, so that soon all English had given way to the usual sniping in Farsi and Spanish.

He ended the class a good twenty minutes early. Milly stood frowning at the door of the front office as his students filtered away. All Alex's hopes for his party had drained by now. In any event, he had been a fool to imagine he would ever have had the nerve to invite María.

As he was packing his things Miguel sidled up to him.

"Bad day, yes?"

Alex let this pass. He clicked shut his book bag, then said, as inertly as he could manage, "I see your sister isn't here today."

He knew at once that he'd made a mistake.

"No," Miguel said slowly. "Not today."

The bastard. He was playing with him.

Alex said nothing.

"She got son' meeting," Miguel said finally.

"Oh? What kind of meeting?"

"Don' know. Son' kind of political thing. I say, María, why you want son' political thing when they break our balls for that back home. But she say is a better way to learn things, in those meetings, than coming here."

Alex took the cut like a man, showing Miguel no pain. Meanwhile, María grew ever more remote: he imagined her part of some under-ground resistance cell, fighting for the end of El Salvador's dirty war.

"You wan' a coffee or son'thing?" Miguel said.

Alex knew he should just put him off.

"I dunno. I'm pretty busy."

"You come to my home," Miguel said. "I make you Salvadoran coffee."

Alex had to remind himself that he was indeed busy. But next to that was the prospect of seeing the rooms she lived in, of smelling her smell there, of running into her.

"Is close," Miguel said. "You come."

Somehow, Alex found himself trailing after Miguel into the crooked side streets of St. Henri. The few times Alex had been through here he'd stuck to the main roads, but Miguel was leading him on a whole zigzag-ging sweep through the place, across vistas that might as easily have been the barrios of San Salvador as Montreal. They passed dead-end streets that disappeared under the expressway, garbage-strewn empty lots, stretches of warehouse and corrugated-tin sheds behind which the sky-line of the downtown rose up like a foreign country.

They crossed an area of rubble and blight to a tiny street of old barracks-style row houses that opened out to the rail yards and the bad-lands of the canal. There was a smell here of old ice and something else, like the humic smell of thaw but a bit ranker than that, a bit sour. The houses came up so hard against the street it seemed a violation to pass in front of them, the blue of midday TVs visible through the yellowed curtains. Miguel led him through a door at the end of the street and up a tottery staircase to a flat on the second floor. The whole of the place could be held in your eye in a glance, a tiny fifties-era kitchen at the back and then two rooms connected by a double doorway, the front one blocked off by a flowered sheet that had been tacked to the door frame. Out back, through a flimsy storm door that led out to the fire escape, Alex caught a glimpse of cluttered back yards, half of them strung with laundry to take advantage of the spring sun.

"Is my home," Miguel said, smiling broadly. "Come."

The middle room seemed to be Miguel's. There was a small Formica-topped table with three battered chrome-and-rattan chairs, a worn corduroy loveseat, an unmade bed on the floor. Scotch-taped on the wall above the bed, in a fairly orderly fashion, were a Playboy centerfold of a decidedly Aryan blonde and a few smaller pictures of musclemen in various poses probably taken from some body-building magazine.

Miguel had seen Alex's eye go to the centerfold.

"You like it?"

Alex felt himself flush.

"Not really my taste."

Miguel pulled a little curtain back from a cabinet at the foot of the bed to reveal the surprise of an expensive-looking Samsung stereo. Alex didn't like to think where Miguel might have got the money for that, or for the fairly impressive wardrobe he had hanging on a metal rail in the corner—there were suits, sports coats, lounge-lizard lamé shirts, a row of immaculately pressed black pants. Yet nothing else about the place spoke of excess.

Miguel put a *Thriller* cassette in the stereo and cranked up the volume.

"I make the coffee!" he shouted, and disappeared into the kitchen.

Sunlight beckoned through the thin sheet that hung over the doorway to the front room. It took some strength of will for Alex to resist its call, though he imagined a different world there, fluffed and pillowy, perhaps, or maybe with posters of Che and Fidel on the walls. He tried to busy himself by looking through Miguel's tapes—standard pop items like Bon Jovi and Madonna and Duran Duran, half with the rough photocopied liners of bootleg editions. There was nothing that looked Salvadoran or even remotely Latino, though the liners conjured up every Third World marketplace Alex had ever been in as vividly as a smell.

Miguel had returned with the coffee. He didn't bother to turn down the music.

"Is good, no?" he shouted, though the truth was that Alex found it somewhat inferior to the house blend at his corner Van Houtte's. "El Salvador is very famous for coffee!"

Alex ought to be taking more advantage of Miguel. He liked to think of himself as someone who kept abreast of world events, yet he knew next to nothing about El Salvador except what he read in the papers— military strongmen, right-wing death squads, left-wing guerillas. That was what the country was for him, not some poor campesino on a hillside growing his coffee beans, though that was likely what the fighting was all about. And there was probably some ugly political reason why the coffee he was now drinking tasted as dull as the Maxwell House he got off the shelf at Steinberg's, though maybe the beans, bought at rock-bottom prices by some conglomerate and then specially roasted and centupled in price, were exactly the ones that showed up in the premium blends at Van Houtte's.

When he'd started at St. Bart's, he'd imagined it as a crash course in international politics. But then one of the Iranians had told him of his family's flight across the mountains into Pakistan, for which he claimed to have paid fifty thousand dollars. Alex had been staggered by the sum. He had imagined some executive exit with Mercedes and driver.

"Is very bad," the man had gone on. "Make you pay for everything, but then they steal you, no food, no clothes. My daughter she die."

Alex didn't think he'd understood. The man's tone had barely altered.

"I'm sorry?"

"My daughter die." Now Alex heard the catch in his voice. "Too cold. No food. Is very bad."

After that, Alex had tread lightly. These weren't the kinds of things you wanted to broach over coffee during break. He wasn't there to be a voyeur of other people's misfortunes; he was there to teach English. Every class he felt the same disjunction, doing past participles while out there in his students' heads were the memories of horrors he could hardly imagine, yet he couldn't figure a way around the thing. The only solution would have been to become people's friend, get into their lives, do all the hard, slow work of growing intimate, and who had time for that?

He seemed to have time for Miguel, though.

From an old Westclox Baby Ben near Miguel's bed Alex saw he had little more than an hour before his lesson at Berlitz.

"Any word on your case yet?" Alex said, though somehow it hurt him to ask.

Miguel had straddled one of the dining chairs and was bobbing to the thump of "Billy Jean."

"Eh?"

"Your case. Your refugee claim."

"Psshh. Backlog, backlog, tha's all. Meantime we get our few hundred dollars to eat and waste our time. I think maybe is better to go illegal in the U.S. Son' Salvadorans making big money there."

It felt ridiculous to be shouting like this.

"It's probably better to wait," Alex said, though what he meant was, it was better for María to wait. "They're saying there's going to be an amnesty soon."

It had occurred to Alex that his distrust of Miguel might be another case of simple animal resistance, having more to do with María than anything else. Yet there was still that aura of difference that came off him. Why did he live down here in St. Henri when most of his countrymen, even the ones who came to St. Bart's, lived up on the Plateau? For all his chumming up to Alex, Miguel had never once asked him for advice on his claim, though Alex knew this was something the other students talked about incessantly, trading stories of what worked and what didn't and building up a whole mythology of fact and superstition and lore.

Miguel was telling him about a Salvadoran he'd heard of in L.A. who was getting rich just selling *pupusas* to other Salvadorans.

"You go there, is like San Salvador, Salvadorans everywhere! Not like here."

"But you live so far from the other Salvadorans here."

"Bah," Miguel said, not missing a beat, "is jus' a ghetto up there, tha's all. Is not my style."

The song ended. Miguel, seeming suddenly bored, reached over to the stereo and hit the eject. Alex felt his ears ring with the sudden silence.

"So tell me," Miguel said, pulling his chair up closer to Alex's. "Which is the good club here for girls? The Canadian girls?"

Alex felt himself bristle.

"I don't really know the clubs, to tell you the truth. You might try some of the bars on Crescent Street."

Miguel made a face.

"Too many Jews," he said.

Alex took a big gulp of coffee. It had been stupid to come here. He cast his eyes around the room to avoid looking at Miguel, trying to find something to hang his excuses on so he could flee. By a kind of reflex his eyes went to the sheet that closed off the front room.

He felt Miguel's gaze on him.

"I'm having a party tomorrow," Alex blurted out. "If you wanted to come. You and your sister."

He regretted the invitation at once. He'd just wanted an exit line, something with finality.

Miguel's face lit up. "A party, yes, Mr. Alex! Is good!" He clapped an arm around Alex's shoulder. "I will come. I hope to see many Canadian girls."

Alex felt hopelessly dirtied now, by his own motives, by Miguel. Even his dislike of him seemed to sully him: no one Alex knew would have spoken like that, yet if he'd said, "Too many JAPS," if he'd known the idiom, Alex might not have batted an eye. Then for all Alex knew— though somehow he doubted this—Miguel was on the run from some death squad.

Miguel saw him down the stairs.

"You're a good man, Mr. Alex," he said.

At the door Alex noticed, for the first time it seemed, how small Miguel was—he couldn't have stood more than five feet. Alex completely overshadowed him. An old newspaper had blown up against the stoop, and Miguel, with surprising fastidiousness, bent to clear it away.

"*A mañana*," he said, then took Alex's hand in both of his and gave it such a firm Latin squeeze that, for an instant at least, Alex forgave him everything.

Alex had what amounted to his lunch, though it was already past four, at the Casa Italia, a passable short-order place near the Forum that for some reason was wildly popular. On the back wall, near the kitchen, was a rack that sported the signed sticks of the various NHL luminaries who had graced the place, but everything else was pure Italian kitsch, the stucco work, the plastic checkerboard tablecloths, the huge poster of the Holy Family that hung behind the espresso machine. Alex ate there because it was close and cheap and quick, though there was also the fact that the owner, Domenic, a Molisano like his parents, a mixed blessing, had taken a kind of patronal interest in him. The place was Alex's only real contact with the city's Italians. Before he'd moved south he'd lived just a couple of metro stops from Little Italy, but had seldom gone up there. It was the alienness of the place that had somehow got to him, not that there was anything there that wasn't dead familiar, the faces, the voices, the look of the houses, but seeing all of it from the outside made him feel at once how insular it was, how cut off from the wider world.

At this hour the Casa Italia was nearly deserted. Domenic was at a back table talking to a suited man in the somber, highfalutin English he put on for people of stature, in this case probably the noodle salesman.

"I'm not saying I won't change the thing if that's the law says to do it. I'm just saying the Italians we been here a hundred years, we got some rights too. You go to Chinatown you got every fucking sign it's Chinese and nobody says anything."

Domenic's beefy son Carmen took Alex's order. Domenic hadn't so much as looked over at him—it was all part of the intricate push-and-pull of insider relations, made subtle by a hundred different forces, the noodle salesman, the empty restaurant, that Domenic was from Campobasso, the provincial capital, while Alex's people were from the boonies. Fucking Italians. Yet every time Alex set eyes on Domenic, he felt a visceral tug. It was the mountain look of him, hard and stoic and plain; his mother's look. It was ancient, that look, you could feel that; the look of the Samnites, Alex thought, the old Sabine tribe of their parts. It didn't show up much in his father, but Alex knew why—his people had come to the mountains a mere few generations back, fleeing some blood feud or crime, something Alex had learned from a cousin on his last pass through Italy, along with a few other facts about his family he'd never had any inkling of.

He ought to have picked up a paper before coming in. He and Félix had more or less dropped the Berlitz lesson book in favor of open conversation, unbeknownst, of course, to Alex's Nazi boss, Mme Hertz. But now, with Félix, Alex had to go in fully armed and fully informed, lest he make the mistake of simply falling back on his usual half-baked orthodoxies. He'd almost lost it when Félix had defended Reagan's bombing spree in Libya.

"But it was all staged!" Alex had said at once, though he'd barely scanned the articles on the subject. "That whole nightclub thing in Berlin, they didn't even have any proof!"

Félix had merely shrugged his Gallic shrug, with an equanimity that had made Alex feel like the worst sort of conspiracy theorist. "So people say. Maybe it's true, but so far nobody said what's a better way."

Anywhere else in the country Alex could have comfortably relied on a knee-jerk anti-Americanism, but not here in Quebec, where they still regretted not having joined the Americans in the Revolution. Alex was sick of it, all this pussyfooting around the minefields of nationalist politics, except that Félix, for some reason, had remained his most reliable customer, making possible indulgences like this restaurant lunch.

Carmen had brought out his penne, along with some sort of seafood antipasto that Alex had never seen on the menu.

"Did I order that?"

Carmen nodded toward his father, who was still talking to the noodle salesman.

"On the house," he said, then motioned with his chin to say, Eat.

With Alex's after-meal coffee—nothing like cappuccino here, just thick-as-crude espresso—the bill came to four ninety-five. A good deal, though with the expenses of the morning he was already way over his daily budget. He added a buck as a tip, given the antipasto, despite the fact that he'd had to choke the stuff down. Ever since his overexposure to fish in the Galápagos, any kind of seafood and he'd feel his gag reflex kick in.

I guess it happens, doesn't it, one bad experience and it puts you off a thing for life.

Well, Peter, I'm not sure "bad experience" really captures the magnitude of the matter.

He popped up to his apartment again to change and get his Berlitz book, not daring to risk the wrath of Fräulein Hertz if he showed up without it. From there it was a quick dash over to University to Berlitz's beautifully corporate offices. Alex had always thought of Berlitz as some fusty Old World holdover, but politics had served it well in Quebec, where it did a brisk trade among anglophones getting francisized under the hated Bill 101 and among francophones who'd thumbed their noses at English in their youth and now couldn't get by without it. Alex had been hired at breakneck speed: three days of training and then plopped in a tony classroom at the princely sum of eight seventy-three an hour before a select handful of students toting their combination-lock briefcases and Chanel handbags stuffed with Berlitz workbooks and pads and complimentary pens.

He had to suppress a thrill of pleasure whenever he entered the Berlitz offices. The hush; the smell of the air; the sense of having penetrated, however obliquely and under whatever false pretenses, the inner sanctum. He breezed past reception to avoid a sighting of Mme Hertz and toward the warren of classrooms. Through closed doors he caught the reassuring patter of the Method: question and response, the Berlitz catechism. The order of it, the mindlessness, was a balm after the chaos of St. Bart's. A gulf divided this place from St. Bart's and yet he knew that in his toady's heart this was the work he took more seriously, as if St. Bart's was just slumming, a time-waster, a sop.

Félix was already waiting for him in one of the big leather armchairs set out in the special room reserved for executive one-on-ones. He rose to take Alex's hand as he came in, towering over him like a rebuke.

"I suppose today you give me the *coup de grâce*," he said, with the undertone of deference that always put Alex on edge, so little had he done to earn it. Alex felt the flush of conflicted emotion rise up in him that Félix always stirred, a strange mix of attraction and its denial. He was only a businessman, after all, patrician and gray, always in those suits of his carefully styled to give a hint of the casual but which probably cost three times as much as the stereo Alex had begrudged Miguel.

He wasn't wearing one today, though.

"Ah, yes, I've just come from home," he said, as if to excuse himself, though he was dressed in a cashmere pullover and plush cords that still gave him the air of the scion of some old seigneurial line.

Six weeks now, Alex had been meeting with Félix, as often as three times a week. From the outset he'd decided Félix was exactly the sort of smug, chip-on-his-shoulder Quebecois that everyone west of Cornwall thought was the norm here: it was that Gallic manner of his, like a sudden chill in the room, as if it fell to Alex somehow to carry the full blame for their coming together. Alex had started their first class with his standard opener in these one-on-ones, asking about Félix's work.

"I don't want to talk about that, it's very technical," Félix had said tersely, and right off the tone between them had been set, and Alex had seen his entire lesson suddenly give way to empty space.

All through their early sessions there had been this strange tussle of foray and resistance, as if Alex were some student wasting Félix's time for a school project. They'd chance onto a subject that showed promise, but then just when they'd reached a certain momentum Alex would manage to derail things with an ill-considered question or found himself floundering in the vast bogs of his own ignorance. Félix would grunt, he'd stare at his hands, then lapse into silence.

"Ah, well, yes," he'd say finally, with his little frown. "So." And that would be the end of it.

They got onto literature once—Alex ought to have been grateful, someone actually literate for a change—but very quickly Alex ended up in the usual cul-de-sac: all of Félix's background was in the classics, and in French texts Alex had never heard of, or had only gazed at on library shelves.

"It's normal," Félix said, in what seemed his idea of making allowances. "The schools now, they don't teach these things. At my school it was different. You've heard of it, I suppose, Jean de Brébeuf, it was

Trudeau's school, but they were all the same, those schools, very rigorous. I don't think you have that on your own side."

Arrogant nob, Alex had thought. He hadn't missed Félix's ploy of mentioning Trudeau only to dismiss him, so he could have his pedigree and eat it too—they were all the same, these bloody nationalists, always playing both sides, damning the priests and then naming the metro stops after them, holding Trudeau up as a proof of their worldliness and then deriding him as a sellout.

"Of course, my own son, he's like you," Félix said, adding salt to the thing. "Latin, Greek, it doesn't matter to him, only TV and sports."

Alex doubted, indeed, that Leamington High, where he'd spent most of his time mooning over girls he'd never had a hope in hell with and working hard to keep his marks below the eighties, had come anywhere near the rigors of a classical lycée. What he remembered most about high school now, in fact, were the stupid fights he used to get into, over every minor insult. He'd had the rage back then as well: someone would cross him and he'd feel the blackness rise up, the sense he'd do anything to cause harm, although the instant he'd struck the first blow something would recoil in him and the fight would be lost. Somehow he couldn't picture Félix in fights back at Brébeuf—he was probably one of those swanners who belonged to the tennis club and thought of themselves as the elite-in-waiting. Alex had managed to get out of Hertz that he was some sort of big wheel over at the Alcan head office: part of the *maîtres chez nous* generation, Alex figured, all those Quebecois technocrats and middle managers who'd seen getting ahead in the system as a way of sticking it to the English.

No doubt Félix came to Berlitz just to sharpen up his pronoun agreements for his business junkets to Toronto and New York, lest the Anglos get one over on him. It was not for Alex to pass judgment, of course, not in the Method, not over Félix's thin-skinned nationalism or his Reaganite socialism or his perorations on Latin and Greek. But that didn't mean he had to pander to him. He would sit there in stoic forbearance, ceding nothing, hoping language rights didn't come up or native land claims or how to divvy up the national debt.

Alex hadn't waited long, however, before putting a bit of distance between him and the Anglos by slipping in a mention of his own Latin roots.

"*Ah, vous êtes italien*," Félix said, as if registering a mental correction.

Afterward, Alex wished he had left Félix to keep imagining him an Alex Brown or an Alex McPhee—Mme Hertz didn't like to advertise surnames, given that ones like his own didn't exactly trumpet competence in English—because Félix, it turned out, knew Florence, and now Alex had to put up with being bested on his own turf, Piero della Francesca this and Santa Croce that. The closest Alex had ever got to Florence was a short stop in the dingy outskirts for gas during a family trip when he was twelve, some spindly tower rising up in the hazy distance that to this day he couldn't give a name to.

"But you must go, of course," Félix said gravely, as if Alex's humanity depended on it. "Or perhaps you are not so interested in art and so on."

"No, no, it's not that, my last girlfriend was an artist." Why had he said that? He was coming off as an ass. "Just the time, I guess."

Félix gave his little grunt.

"Well, you're still young, I suppose. Young enough."

Alex breathed a sigh of relief after their third session: three sessions at a go was usually the upper limit for Mme Hertz. She didn't like her people getting too chummy with the clientele, lest the Method lose pride of place; instructors had to remain interchangeable, like priests in the Church. But then his schedule came up and Félix was still on it.

Fucking Hertz, he thought, thinking she had it in for him, until she headed him off before his next lesson looking distinctly unpleased.

"He's asked for you," she hissed, as if he'd committed some heresy.

Alex hardly knew what to make of that. Maybe it was because Félix had found out that he was Italian.

"After our last session?"

"No. From the start."

It was probably just that he was so innocuous, the kind of blank slate people like Félix preferred because they could leave their own mark on it. But he couldn't help liking Félix a little better after that. Maybe he'd misjudged the man; maybe he'd been struggling as much as Alex to find some sort of common ground. Whether they actually had any was an open question, but Alex wasn't an idiot, he could see there was something admirable in Félix amidst all that starched dignity. Things had gone better from then on. If Alex stuck to innocuous subjects like travel and points of grammar, there was a lot less of the grunting and bristling he'd had to contend with at the outset. Félix's fondness for things Italian slowly warmed to what seemed an actual *chaleur* toward Alex, the source of that vexing deference, no doubt, though what was vexing about it was probably Alex's fear of losing it. But what truly fired the man up was English idiom: he'd show up with some irksome new phrase he'd come across and put it before Alex like a personnel problem he couldn't solve or an insult that had been flung at him, and then an entire session might pass tracing the byways of it, down through the whole sluttish history of the English language. Alex was on solid ground here, thanks to a course he'd done on the subject.

He brought in some poems in Middle English, and Félix was fascinated at how much of the Norman showed through in them.

"It's true: we don't think of it, but of course the court was all French then. It's an interesting thing, these histories. All those fights between English and French, it's like a fight between brothers. They're always the worst."

This was as close as Félix ever got to levity on these sorts of issues; Alex didn't push the point, lest he accidentally cross some forbidden border into the sacrosanct. Félix was a man of compartments, Alex sensed, everything carefully squirreled away in its separate drawer. All the weeks they'd spent together, and yet Alex had learned almost nothing about him: Félix had never mentioned his son again after that once; he'd never mentioned a home, his colleagues, a wife. Alex had learned more about Esther in an hour than he knew about Félix, though three times a week he'd been paid to do nothing but talk to him.

Félix was still standing at the window gazing up toward the McGill campus, though Alex had taken his seat and gone through the motion of opening up his Berlitz book, in case Madame checked up on him. There was an uncertain energy to Félix today, a distractedness. Maybe it was just the clothes—he looked thinner in them, more vulnerable.

"You know, why do we sit here in this terrible office?" he said. "We should go out. Come, I'll offer you a drink."

This was definitely crossing a Berlitz line.

"I'm not sure," Alex started. "I should let them know—"

"It's fine, I'll tell them. They'll get their money all the same."

There seemed no point in resisting; Félix was already ushering him out of their little executive suite into the hall. Alex's only hope was that Mme Hertz had already left for home, if she had such a thing. But no, here she came, barreling out of her office into reception, all chunky five foot one of her, coming right at them as if she'd had them under video surveillance the whole time.

She had her Berlitz death grin at the ready for Félix.

"I hope there's no problem," she said at once, by which she meant, *What is the problem?*

She was wearing a big-shouldered blazer that made her look like Napoleon, her hair boxed off around her head in an eerie symmetry and showing the effects of a recent dye job.

"No problem at all, *madame*," Félix said, a bit more icily than Alex might have wished. "I've offered Alex a drink. I've insisted on it. I hope it's not forbidden."

Mme Hertz seemed at a loss.

"No, no," she sputtered. "Of course. Not at all."

Félix let the silence hang an instant.

"I should mention that we'll be sending a few of our interns by over the summer. I hope you'll look after them."

Madame's face had frozen back into its death-grin.

"Of course, *monsieur*, of course." Alex knew he would pay for this. "I'll look after them personally."

The moment they were out the door Alex felt a lightness that was vaguely disquieting, as if some mantle had been removed from him. Out here, he was simply a young man in the company of an older one he had almost nothing in common with.

On the sidewalk Félix looked uncertainly up and down the street.

"Do you know some bar near here?"

"Well, I'm not sure, really. There's a few, I think."

He ended up leading Félix over to the Peel Pub, out of some misplaced notion that he ought somehow to expose him to his own culture. What the Peel Pub had to do with his own culture, Alex couldn't have said. He was only really aware of it because Abbie Hoffman had invited people back there a few months earlier after a talk he'd given at McGill, though Alex, too timid to take up the offer, hadn't actually set foot in the place. He was mortified to discover now that it wasn't some underground hippy retreat—though it was indeed literally underground, at the bottom of a litter-strewn stairwell that led down from St. Catherine—but just a tacky college pub. A stench of mold and cigarette smoke hit them as soon as they stepped through the door, along with the blare of a TV set over the bar that was tuned to a playoff game. A crowd of collegiate types was huddled around the TV, hooting and bantering and using up the air in a way that sent a shiver through Alex's spine.

"A bit loud, I guess!"

He saw Félix take the place in.

"No, no! It's fine!"

Félix got them drinks at the bar. A Molson's, Alex asked for, though he hated beer, and Félix, after eyeing the array of cheap whiskeys and liqueurs lined up on either side of the till, gravely ordered the same. They took a seat in a back corner. The furniture, clunky, heavily lacquered faux Canadiana, was crammed in so tightly they had to squeeze to get into their chairs, their knees bumping against each other's beneath the table. At the bar, the frat boys, glued to the set, had started to chant: *Go, go, go, go, go.*

What was he doing here with this man, Alex wondered. Félix looked ill at ease, glancing over his shoulder as if toward some threat.

"I've never been to such a place," he said. "It's like a different city for me."

"Two solitudes," Alex said, taking a stab at humor.

But Félix furrowed his brow.

"*Oui, oui. C'est ça.*"

Alex wanted only to be done with this now, to be home. It had been a mistake to risk this awkwardness, to leave the safety of Berlitz, where their roles were defined.

He could have used a cigarette but didn't want to smoke in front of Félix.

"May I ask you," Félix said, and for some reason Alex felt his heart thump, expecting he didn't know what, "how much do they pay you there at Berlitz?"

He was taken off guard.

"It's not so bad," he said, not knowing if he was allowed to reveal such things. But when he named the amount, Félix whistled through his teeth.

"Not bad for *them,* I suppose. We pay them three times as much."

Alex would never have guessed the markup was so high. Who would pay such sums, for the likes of him? He felt devalued in Félix's eyes, revealed for the Berlitz cog he truly was.

Félix had yet to touch his beer.

"Can't you make more on your own?"

"I suppose. I'd have to find the students."

"Ah."

It wasn't like Félix, this sort of familiarity.

"I have a proposition," he said. "Feel free to refuse it."

Alex felt the thump again.

"It's very simple. We continue our lessons, the same as before, except I pay you directly. Just that."

Alex wasn't sure what he was hearing. This, at bottom, was why Mme Hertz ringed her people around with proscriptions, to prevent the formation of exactly these sorts of cabals.

The alarm bells were going off in his head: if he was found out, he'd be dumped at once. But what was in it for Félix? Just saving a few bucks?

"I'd give the same fee, of course," Félix added.

"You mean what I get now?"

"No. What we pay."

It took Alex an instant to digest this.

"That seems a lot."

Félix shrugged.

"It's what we pay them, why should it be less? Then for me it means to get away from that awful place. From that woman."

Alex's greed had already reared up to shoulder his doubts aside. It didn't make any sense, really, that kind of cash, just to sit parsing phrases like *pie in the sky* and *let the cat out of the bag*. But all he could see were those dollars piling up, hour after hour.

"It's very generous of you," he said warily.

"Not so generous. It's the company that pays."

Alex was on eggshells after that, afraid of saying anything to compromise Félix's misplaced faith in him. They worked out the details, arranging to meet at Félix's home in Outremont. Twice a week; two hours a session. Alex would be making from Félix alone as much as all his Berlitz hours combined, enough to cover the whole of his rent.

"We'll say nothing to the school, of course," Félix said. "Just between us."

The clouds of the morning had returned by the time they left the pub and a light drizzle had started up. *Chernobyl*, Alex thought, but that seemed far from him now. The lights of the traffic on St. Catherine and the neon of the shops lustered against the wet.

They ducked under an awning at the corner to say their goodbyes.

"So you have the summer to relax now, I suppose," Félix said. "From your studies, I mean."

But all Alex saw was his dissertation looming before him like the wall of a cliff.

"I've finished my classes, at least. I'm having a party tomorrow to celebrate."

"Ah. *Bonne fête, alors.*"

There was a touch of embarrassment in Félix's voice, as if he felt it unseemly to speak of a pleasure he was excluded from.

"You could come, if you wanted. I mean, it's just other students and so on."

He felt foolish. He hoped he hadn't insulted the man with his presumption.

"It's very kind of you," Félix said. The awkwardness between them was palpable. "Of course, if you wish it. If it's not any trouble."

Alex had assumed he would simply make his excuses—surely he had his own life to attend to. It seemed they had fallen into another of those protocols he didn't know the rules of, and he was stuck giving a time, directions, an address.

"Until tomorrow, then," Félix said, his hand wet from the rain when it took Alex's.

Alex waited until Félix had disappeared around the corner toward the metro and lit up a cigarette. For some reason his heart was racing, as if he had embarked on some quest or joined the Resistance rather than simply signing up for a bit of under-the-table teaching work. He caught a smell in the air, something uncertain, and for a moment an insight seemed to be forcing itself on him, about Félix or something larger, Chernobyl, his son, hovering tantalizing before him but refusing to take shape. Then as quickly as it had come the feeling passed, and he tossed his cigarette out into the rain and started off home.

– 5 –

Twilight had set in by the time Alex got home. He hated coming back to his empty apartment at this time of the day, hated how the light drained away from things, how listless he felt. He missed Moses, the stray he and Liz had taken in back in Toronto. He resented how they'd just assumed that Liz would keep him after the split, though he knew that if he'd actually been saddled with the cat he would have resented that more.

His apartment was a shambles still, littered with boxes he had yet to unpack, with all the junk store furniture he'd filled it with. Half of it was ancient undergrad stuff he'd had to haul up to Montreal from his parents' basement, a cracked drop-leaf table he'd got for five bucks, the hideous floral sofa bed his parents had had at the old farm, the mattress he'd paid fifty dollars for, used, back in second year and on which he'd slept with at least a dozen different women. None of these things had the comfortable air of familiarity they ought to have had—they seemed beside the point, a charade, remnants of a life he wasn't part of anymore. Meanwhile, there was the letter in the drawer of his desk, though every time he turned his mind to it he seemed about to fly apart in a thousand directions.

The rain had stopped. He poured himself a Coke from the fridge and went out to the balcony for another cigarette. Beyond him the lit towers of the downtown sat clustered like some beast huddling up against the night, framed by the dark mound of Mount Royal and by the river and the distant hills of the Townships. He had a sudden feeling of being stranded on the island the city was, as if it were a feeble encampment against the wild, though he knew it gave way to miles and miles of featureless suburb where the closest thing to the wild was the local mall.

He thought he might read the letter again. He had already been over it so many times, though always fleetingly, as if it might detonate, that he had it practically memorized. *I write after many years*, it began, in Ingrid's Swedishly tentative Oxford-summer-school English, *to tell you of our son Per, who will be five in this coming September.* He never got any further than that before his heart was already in his throat. There were details about the boy, but no picture; there was the invitation, of course, to come, because, as Ingrid had written, as if Alex were a famous sports figure the boy had followed, "he very much would like to meet you." But then at the end: "You must have your life now so perhaps it is better not to write back, if you do not think you can be a father to him. We will manage, of course. It wasn't you who made the choice so you needn't feel guilty, though I remember you liked to."

It made him squirm now to think how galvanized he'd felt when he'd first read the letter nearly four months earlier. He'd been ready to board a plane the next day, to abandon everything. But then slowly, with each day he'd delayed, his resolve had weakened. He could hardly have discussed the matter with Liz when their relationship was in its death throes at the time; and then when it was over, and he was left covered in shit the way he'd been, he couldn't imagine trailing the noxious odors of himself into the clean, Swedish world of this innocent five-year-old. The reasonableness of Ingrid's letter had begun to feel insidious by then. What did she mean, exactly, by *be a father to him*? Every day he had turned the phrase over in his head and every day it had seemed more ominous and obscure, a kind of test. Or maybe it was just Ingrid giving him an out, holding up to him the truth of his own nature.

He had managed to dig up a few cassettes she had sent him over the years. The instant he heard her voice he felt her real and alive before him again, saw her garden and smelled its smells, felt the wonder of those first weeks they'd spent together. What was he thinking, not jumping at the chance to go back to that? And yet; and yet. There was the age difference; there was the fact that she lived in bloody Sweden; there was Jesus. Try as he might, Alex had never quite been able to take her seriously after her conversion. Of course, all that was beside the point—he didn't have to marry her to have a relationship with his son. And yet that phrase kept coming back to him, and what it might mean in her Christianized brain.

Be a father. But what was a father if not a husband? The time he had visited her post-conversion—the fateful time, it turned out—she'd had sex with him only because in some corner of her mind she had believed, he knew, that he would stay.

It had been different the first time. They had met on the Helsingborg ferry—he had noticed her from the start, an attractive blonde of the sort who made his knees go weak, with that sheen of knowingness and ease that made him think of adulterous trysts in wooded motel rooms or alpine chalets. He'd stood at the rail, backpacked and bearded and unwashed, wishing he was the sort of person who could talk to such a woman, when suddenly she was there beside him, speaking to him in a foreign language.

She was holding some sort of net on a pole over her shoulder, a fishing net maybe.

"I'm sorry?" he said, alarmed, certain she'd mistaken him for someone else.

"Oh! I thought you were Swedish."

Somehow, he'd managed not to make a mess of it. It was Ingrid, really, who'd managed it—she'd made the thing seem so natural, drawing him out, so that he didn't simply mumble some half-hearted courtesy and slouch back into his not-yet-quite-post-adolescent shell. He'd been en route to a home stay, something he'd set up with a group called The Experiment in International Living, though all he'd had in the way of direction was an address for the Experiment office in Stockholm, where he'd been planning to head.

"But you must telephone them," Ingrid said. "Perhaps they will send you to Malmö or some such. It's very far."

She made the call for him from a pay phone just outside the ferry terminal, taking the coins from her purse and carrying on an animated exchange with someone at the other end, casting looks at him the whole time as if to hold him in the sphere of the conversation. She jotted down an address.

"You see," she said, "you are very lucky not to travel all the way to Stockholm because you are going to Gothenburg."

"Oh." Alex had never heard of Gothenburg. "Is it far?"

She laughed.

"I will show you on a map. In my car."

After that, things took on a kind of inevitability. There was the question of time: it was mid-afternoon and the town was a hundred miles or more; it didn't make sense to set out and risk waiting hours for a ride. Ingrid had a guest house at the back of her garden, "a little cabin," she said. If he wanted to stay the night.

"It's not so easy in Sweden, to take rides and such. People are shy. Then they see a man with a beard—"

Nothing in this was out of the ordinary. In the month and a half since he'd set out, on the remains of a student loan from his first year at university, Alex had come across any number of people who'd been willing to look after him, to feed him, put him up, go out of their way to drop him at borders or good spots for rides.

The net she was carrying was a butterfly net for her seven-year-old, Lars. She had a daughter as well, Eva, who was nine.

"You seem too young," Alex said, but relieved somehow that there were children.

"I am thirty," she said at once. "And you?"

Alex flushed.

"Twenty. I'll be twenty in August."

"Ah." There was a pause he didn't want to read. "I thought older. Perhaps because of the beard."

She had some errands to do in Helsingborg. Alex followed her around like her attendant, oddly comfortable with her, with the way she had annexed him. In the large central square just up from the ferry terminal, a band in traditional garb was playing a polka-like march to a scattered audience of passersby who stood as grave as mourners.

"You see how the Swedes are, so serious," Ingrid said. "And then they go home and drink until they are very drunk."

Her town, Engelström, was just inland from Landskrona down the coast. To Alex it looked like something out of *Brigadoon*, with its timbered houses and thatched barns and spired church. Ingrid's house was at the far end of the town, off a little side road, a small white bungalow shrouded in shrubbery and trees. Alex expected some sort of domestic scene to greet them when she opened the door, her children, a blond-haired husband perhaps, but there was only silence.

"The children are with their father in these days," she said, reading his look, "so we are alone."

She pointed out the little cabin at the back of her garden, a steep-roofed confection with two shuttered windows and a little door low enough that Alex would have to stoop to get through it.

"So you see, it's true," she said. "You will be better there than all night by the expressway."

But she did not take him out to it, and his backpack remained parked by the front door where he'd first set it.

"Perhaps you would like to clean yourself."

He could not believe his good luck in having been taken into this place. The bathroom was small, pristine, just slightly cluttered; there was a shower stall, no bath, with a white curtain trimmed with lace. It was three days since he'd last showered, at the house of a professor in Utrecht who had taken him in; since then he'd slept in Lübeck in a kind of squat, then on the beach in Denmark after the ferry crossing from Puttgarden. He'd done the last three or four miles to Puttgarden on foot, toting a backpack laden with useless books like the *Bhagavad Gita* and *The Genealogy of Morals* that he hadn't been able to get through in his first-year reading lists.

In the shower he felt like he was scrubbing away all the grit of the past several weeks. The truth was he wasn't sure he liked traveling much, having to start every day from scratch, meet new people, make his way. It had all begun to seem a bit pointless. Yet here he was in Ingrid's house, in her shower, just because he'd been lucky enough to be standing there at the rail of the Helsingborg ferry.

Ingrid was sitting in the sun in her garden with a sketchbook and a box of pastels when he came out.

"It's only something I started since the divorce," she said. "In the way of doing something new."

They walked into town to get some things for their supper. At the butcher's shop, the butcher, a lean, stoop-shouldered man with a crew cut that made his hair look singed, gave Alex a furtive glance but then scrupulously avoided his gaze. Ingrid carried on in her usual way, forthright, polite.

"You mustn't mind this place," she said outside. "They are not so used to it here. To strangers."

They made supper together in Ingrid's kitchen, which was modern and bright, all whites and blond wood, and ate in the garden. It was

Alex's first real meal in weeks. He couldn't quite shed the terror that he'd commit some gaffe, but somehow he found things to say. Out on the road, staying in the hostels with cocky Americans and Aussies and the career backpackers who traded travel stories like currency, he often felt a pariah.

Ingrid had opened some wine.

"It's nice to have company," she said, though he still couldn't quite believe there might be something in it for her, that all this wasn't just some prize she was bestowing on him.

They stayed on in the garden after they'd finished supper. It was late June, midsummer, and the light went on and on. As the wine went down Ingrid grew more candid.

"A very typical Swede," she said of her ex-husband. He worked as some sort of engineer at the shipyard in Helsingborg. "Very conservative. Very boring."

"Like Canadians," he said.

"But you are also Italian. You are different."

"Italian and not Italian. Not really."

"Then I am like you," she said. "Swedish and not Swedish."

Before he knew it, it was midnight, though the darkness still had the dreamy crepuscular tentativeness of dusk.

"It seems so cold, to make you sleep in the cabin," Ingrid said. "Perhaps I will make a bed for you on the sofa."

Again, Alex felt relieved: so nothing would come of it. He stood by sheepishly while she arranged sheets, a duvet, on the long white sofa in her living room.

"Will you sleep in your clothes?" she said, smiling.

"No. I mean, I'll change in the bathroom."

She was still waiting for him when he emerged. All the lights had been put out save a lamp in the alcove, leaving the room in shadowy gray. Ingrid waited as he settled and then knelt beside him as if tucking in a child.

"Thank you, my young Alex, for a very lovely supper," she said, and kissed him softly.

There was still that part of him that had been hoping this wouldn't happen. What little he'd had in the way of sex in his life had always left him feeling somehow dirtied, as if he'd merely done what was expected. He didn't want to ruin things now with that feeling, not with someone like Ingrid.

They kissed again. Everything about her seemed fresh and distilled. Something shifted in him and he felt free to touch her, her hair, her midriff, her face, though it seemed incredible to him that she would allow this, that alarms didn't go off.

Her hand had slipped beneath the drawstring of his pyjamas and she was touching him, gently, in a preliminary way. He was already hard; the touch was electric. Then before he was able to distract himself, he felt a surge and he came.

He was mortified.

"I'm sorry," he stammered. "I'm sorry."

She was quiet an instant but then kissed him lightly, her hand still on him, and said, "There's no reason."

She pulled a tissue from a box near the sofa to clean them, drawing the covers down and making Alex pull down his pyjamas so she could dab at his penis and thigh. The thing felt more intimate than coming, more awful.

"Come up to my bed."

So he'd been given a reprieve. She led him up to a slope-ceilinged room with a futon bed and a skylight, the still-insistent afterglow of the midsummer sky casting the room in a kind of ghostly pallor. Alex had the sense that something had changed between them, that the stakes were higher now.

Ingrid undressed facing away from him and slipped under the covers.

"Come," she said.

But when he was lying next to her it seemed too much, this wasted luxury. She was touching him again, kneading him with a slow deliberateness, but the longer she went on, the more painful it grew.

He could feel his guts knotting up.

"I'm not sure I can," he said, when he couldn't bear it. "I'm sorry."

"Oh." He couldn't read her, if she was surprised, put out. "Oh."

"I'm sorry."

"Yes."

She had drawn her hand from him. For a moment they lay there, inert, and Alex was afraid that she would throw him out, to her cabin, to the street.

"Perhaps you can help me," she said finally.

He felt instantly ashamed, not to have thought of it. Then when he'd put his hand to her he couldn't find the spot and had to be guided, though after a minute she cupped his hand once again and gently pulled it away.

"It's nice just to be close," she said.

He felt tears welling up in him.

"I'm sorry," he said again.

He felt a wave of self-pity come over him, and was suddenly sobbing.

"You are crying!" But she said this so brightly she seemed to make the matter small. "How silly! You think I am some old witch who has only brought you here for sex."

She was kissing his tears, as if he were one of her children who'd come crying.

"How silly," she said again. "After such a nice evening we had."

"Not very nice for you."

"Don't say so. I am very happy I found you there, on that boat. It doesn't normally happen to me, to so quickly feel close to a man."

He fell asleep cupped against her, feeling her heat on him, but awoke some time later with the sense he had not really slept at all, had never lost his awareness of her lying beside him. Dawn was already showing at the edges of the blind Ingrid had drawn over the skylight. Alex felt a wonder go through him again that he should be here in Ingrid's bed. She was small, he saw, much smaller than he was. She hadn't figured that way in his mind; in his mind, he had been the small one. He felt a surge of hopefulness, as if he had seen a way that he might somehow equal her. He imagined making love to her properly, to this different Ingrid lying beside him in the gray dawn.

In the morning, when he awoke again to full light, her place beside him was already empty. He heard the sounds of her in the kitchen, the tinkling of cutlery and cups.

He went down and could feel at once that something had changed.

"Today my children return," she said, not looking at him, "and so you must go."

So this was all it had amounted to. She drove him out to the expressway beyond Helsingborg and stood with him there at the on-ramp, his backpack propped against the guardrail like a third person.

"I did not think it should be so hard to say goodbye to you, my Alex who's not Italian," she said. "Perhaps we'll meet again, who can say. I could wish it."

But she hadn't given him so much as a phone number. All he had from her was the bit of wetness in her eyes.

"You're young," she said. "You will have many adventures."

It was evening before he reached Gothenburg. His host was a middle-aged man named Stig Hörby who was as thick-necked and bug-eyed and squat as a Meso-American sculpture. He lived alone out in Västra Frölunda, a suburb of trim, identical bungalows and trim, identical trees.

"I was very worried," he said peevishly. "They called to expect you last evening."

"It was too late to hitchhike," Alex said.

"Yes." Stig cleared his throat. "I see."

And Alex vowed to himself he would not say a word to the man about Ingrid.

In Gothenburg—Göteborg in Swedish, pronounced like someone coughing up—Alex could only think about Ingrid, how he'd had her and had let her slip from him. He had no stomach for museums or tourist sites and spent his days while Stig was at work scrambling among the rocks along the seafront near Stig's house or watching American reruns on his TV. Stig was clearly disappointed in him, every day asking after his activities and every day making the same wheezing moue of disapproval at his lack of enterprise. He introduced Alex to a neighbor boy, Robert, a doctor's son who oozed confidence and privilege.

"I think you are not so happy here," Robert said. "Is very hard for Stig because he is not so good for talking."

Against his better judgment, Alex told Robert about Ingrid. He wasn't quite able to stop himself from putting the thing more favorably than had been the case.

"You slept with this woman?" Robert said.

"Well, yes."

"You know, you must be careful," Robert said. "There are women here, they try to trick you to make a baby and so on. And then you must stay with them."

Alex felt himself redden.

"It wasn't like that."

"Maybe you don't see it because you are a stranger. But here in Sweden you must be careful."

The idiot, Alex thought, bloody bourgeois Swedish prude. Yet his image of Ingrid had been sullied—why was she alone, after all, if she was so perfect? Why was she cruising young men on the ferry?

He felt he could hardly stay on after that. SAS had a special that summer, a hundred kronor, about twenty bucks, for a ticket anywhere in the country. He decided to fly up to Kiruna, inside the Arctic Circle.

There was still more than a week left of his home stay.

"But you have already paid!" Stig said. "What shall we tell the office?"

"It doesn't matter."

"I will pay for your ticket at least."

There was a change at Stockholm, so by the time he flew into Kiruna—which from the plane, beneath an overcast sky, looked lost in the landscape like a final outpost, a single rubbly peak presiding over it and then the rest just flat, endless bush—it was nearly midnight and the youth hostel office had closed. He set out hitchhiking, north, toward the Finnish border. A logging truck took him forty or fifty miles out of town but then just dropped him there in the middle of nowhere, a sea of evergreen stretching out around him on every side. He seemed truly to have reached the end of the world, not a car to be seen and the midnight sun sending a gray pall through the clouds that refused to shade off into night or to indicate in any way that time was passing.

It began to rain. Alex retreated into the shelter of the trees but the mosquitoes there were unbearable. He bundled himself inside his sleeping bag and draped a T-shirt over his head, but still they found their way through to get at his flesh, to buzz in his ears. Then the rain began to drip down through the branches in erratic splats and it was worse than being in the full of it. He felt utterly bereft, wondering what had ever possessed him to come to this place, to leave home, to imagine he was the sort of person who could actually strike out on his own like this.

He fell into fitful sleep and had an awful vision of himself as he truly was, shriveled and hopeless and small. He understood suddenly that he would never transform like a chrysalis into the perfect person he'd always longed to be, confident, charming, at home in every situation, but would probably remain forever as crippled and half-formed as he was now, closed off in his little paranoias and depressions and fears. *Citizen of the World.* That was what Trudeau had had pinned to his dorm room door at

Harvard. But Alex was not up to that standard. He couldn't even survive a bit of rejection from a Swedish divorcée.

He flagged down a car, finally, a battered Lada piloted by a couple of half-drunk Finns, and got a ride back to Kiruna, where he waited out the night at the airport and then paid his hundred kronor for the first connection south. He was back at Stig's place in Västra Frölunda, where he'd left half his stuff, by the time Stig was getting home from work.

Stig looked stricken at the sight of him.

"But you are back!"

Alex just wanted to be gone. His plan for the moment was to make for London and catch a cheap flight home.

"I just came to get my things."

"But you'll stay the night?" Stig said, seeming desperate for the matter not to lose all bounds of propriety.

It was only when they were sitting down to a painful supper that Stig mentioned the phone call.

"A lady," he said. "A Swedish lady."

Oh, God, Alex thought, his heart pounding, let it not be some idiot from the Experiment office.

"Did she say her name?"

"She left her number. From Landskrona, I think." Then, "You did not say you had a Swedish friend."

Alex's hand was practically trembling as he dialed the number. He recognized her voice at once.

"It's me. It's Alex."

"Alex." A pause. "I did not think I should mind so much, not to see you again. But you see I kept your number."

He was on the road back to Engelström the following morning. Everything had changed now. Gothenburg, Kiruna, had become just anecdotes he'd tell Ingrid instead of some sort of final judgment against him. He got a ride almost at once, from a Danish couple in a tiny rusted-out Opel whose back seat was crammed full with camping equipment and sacks of clothing and guitars but who insisted on making a place for him, offering him salami and cheese and teaching him the chords for "Fire and Rain."

They dropped him at Ingrid's front step. Alex felt a surge of fear when she came to the door that he'd made a mistake, that he'd misunderstood.

"So I was right we would meet again," she said, and kissed him so unguardedly that they seemed back at once to the intimacy of their night together.

The children had come and gone again. It was as if he had never left, as if Stig Hörby had been a bad dream: here was her bathroom, her kitchen, her little cabin; here was her garden, with its fruit trees and birds.

"It's silly, after one day, but I had such a funny feeling when you went." She smiled as if she was afraid she was showing too much of herself. "Such an awful one, I should say."

That night they made love. It wasn't quite as he'd pictured it, but everything worked, at least. They started with Ingrid and he managed better, touching her and licking her until she came, with a tremble that unnerved him. The smell of her stayed with him as he fucked her, and then for a few minutes it seemed they were truly making love, that they were truly together. She had said she was safe, though at the last instant, remembering Robert, he had a twitch of doubt, and with it of guilt.

"It was very nice," she said after, "very sweet," perhaps to reassure him. It didn't matter: he was happy to have gotten through without disaster. He had that different sense of her again, when she was there beneath him, that she was small, that she was possessable, though he could hardly say what this might mean. All he knew was that there was this barest veil between them that he wanted to strip, to see what lay behind it.

This time, he stayed on for days. He kept waiting for Ingrid to tire of him or see through him, but it didn't happen. She seemed happy to be with him, to share her meals, her bed, without requiring anything special from him. Some days, they hardly left the house. They'd have breakfast, of cereal and fruit and a yogurty substance called sour milk, then coffee in the garden while Alex smoked and read and Ingrid sketched; they might even make love, because Alex had discovered he was free to touch her whenever he wished. They had quite a lot of sex, in fact, not just at the house but in the car, once, and in the woods, and on a deserted stretch of beach, so that their awkward first night seemed forgotten. That wasn't really the best part for Alex, though—it was still when he felt most vulnerable, less from the fear of doing badly than because it seemed the most likely time for the thing to reveal itself to be a lie.

What was the best for him, really, was just getting along with her, the not being afraid he had made some mistake.

"You are suited to me," Ingrid said, and it felt true. Despite the unlikeliness of it, they seemed kindred spirits. Maybe it was just that Ingrid brought out in him a new, more balanced person, the different self that had always felt occluded in him.

Ingrid's ex came by once to drop off some papers, coming around to the patio door in back and letting himself in as if he owned the place.

"This is Carl, the children's father," Ingrid said pleasantly, as if he were the coal merchant.

She'd made no attempt to hide Alex from him. He was beefy and large, older, well-built, a veritable man. Alex expected some sort of rebuff but he looked merely put out, shaking Alex's hand as if he was actually ready to take him seriously.

"You see how he is, a bit of a bully," Ingrid said after. "You have to stand up to him is the only thing."

He had been so palpable, with his flushed face and ruddy hands. A smell of cologne had come off him and beneath that something more sweaty, more human.

"When I was young I was very taken with him, of course," Ingrid said. "To be the wife of a big engineer and so on. Silly things like that."

It was hard for Alex to fathom how he and Carl could both be connected to Ingrid, how only a few years earlier she had probably been living in a place like Stig's Västra Frölunda, cleaning house and starting Carl's dinner at five. It was as if he'd discovered some secret other life Ingrid had been hiding from him. One morning after Ingrid had gone down to start breakfast he snuck a look into the room off of hers in the loft, the children's room: two beds, both with duvets in a seaside motif; a bookshelf; a desk with some model cars on it. It surprised him, suddenly, how absent the children had been while he'd been here, how little any awareness of them had impinged on him.

On the wall above the desk was a photo of the children's father, posed in a shipyard before a massive gray tanker.

"You haven't mentioned your children much," he said at breakfast.

He felt an instant chill.

"I did not think you were so curious about them."

She brought out a photo album. The girl, Eva, was big-boned like her father, the boy more slender.

"See," Ingrid said. "You had only to ask."

"I just thought—"

"You thought what?"

But he didn't dare pursue the subject.

It was only now that he really noticed all the evidences of the children that were strewn throughout the house. Photos on the living room wall; trophies and ribbons in the alcove off the kitchen; a drawing stuck to the refrigerator—how could he have missed it?—signed by the boy, Lars, of a crude tractor and cow.

"It was from a visit we made to a farm," Ingrid said. "Two days, I think, before you came back."

It had been merely in his own mind, he realized, that the children had been out of the picture. For Ingrid, they were present in every cranny. She spoke to them nightly, something Alex had never remarked on—to keep from intruding, he'd told himself, though now it seemed he simply hadn't bothered himself about them.

He bore that awful chill of hers the entire day.

"Yes, I should say so," she said at supper. "I was very angry with you this morning."

This was it, Alex thought, when everything crumbled. It was too much for him, all of this, she could surely see that now.

"We are only playing here in these days, perhaps it's true." He could tell she had girded herself for this. "But you must never say I am hiding my children from you like a bad person."

"I didn't mean that."

"No, perhaps not."

"It's just that you sent me away before—"

"I protect my children because they are young. But I am not pretending to you what I am. I am a mother. My children are the most important to me, always. So do not say I am hiding them."

They didn't make love that night. With a few words he had shattered all the magic of the previous days. He felt the instinct to retreat, to slither back to the anonymity of the wider world.

In the morning he thought that Ingrid had reached the same conclusion.

"Tomorrow the children return again," she said. "This time I don't chase you away, maybe it was wrong to do it, but you must decide. It can't be the same for us, with the children here."

It came to him that she wasn't testing him but really wanted an answer, wanted him to decide for them. He felt terrified.

"I suppose I should go," he said, taking the easy way out, playing the youngster, as if he'd merely said what he'd thought she wanted.

She smiled, sadly, and he could see her scaling back her expectations of him.

"Oh, Alex. I should not have grown to like you so much, I think."

They spent their last day on the coast, picnicking on the cliffs that looked out to the sound. It was a day like a day from the end of time, everything poised, the wheeling birds, the pellucid sky.

"It's such a *funny* thing," Ingrid said, staring out. "All of this, the sea, the sky. I can't say it very well, what I mean."

In the morning he packed his things, early, and she drove him to the ferry. There was a mood of forced cheer between them as if to show that everything was for the best.

"So," Ingrid said. "I have stolen you from the sea and now I must return you."

She didn't wave from the pier, just stood watching him as the ferry pulled out. By the time it had settled onto its course she was gone.

He'd planned to put up in Copenhagen for a night or two with the Danes he'd met hitchhiking before pushing on to Paris. Instead a week passed, then another, and he was still holed up in a cold-water flat in Nørrebro not fifteen minutes from the ferry terminal, drinking Elephant Beer till all hours and smoking endless chillums of hash. He followed Ture, his host, on his daily peregrinations, to the community center for showers, to the Social Office for cash, to Christiania for some happening or protest or just for more hashish. Ture had the look of the blond Jesus of Alex's grade-school readers, spending the whole day sometimes in pyjama pants he'd borrowed from Alex.

One day Ture's girlfriend, Maya, came home and told Alex she'd just had an abortion.

"It's very good now, you know, we have the Free Clinic. No hassles."

That night she and Ture argued.

"It must be very boring, every day to be stoned like that." She always spoke English around Alex so he wouldn't feel excluded. "I think for Alex it must be very boring."

Maya had an actual job, something Ture avoided.

"I think he likes it or he would just stop."

"You're like a boy who has some candy or something. Even if you want to you can't stop."

Alex slipped out of the apartment in the middle of this and called Ingrid from a pay phone.

"But where are you?" As if he had called from outer space. "You must have reached Italy."

"I'm here. I'm still in Copenhagen."

"I see." He could hear the question in her voice, the quiet note of injury. "So close."

"I was wondering if I could see you again."

There were passengers in the back seat of her old Volvo when she collected him the next morning at the Landskrona terminal. This time there was no impulsive kiss, just a neutral pleasantness that reminded him of how she'd greeted her ex-husband.

"And here of course are my children," she said. "You remember them from the photos."

Alex was hardly able to take them in. They were sitting completely silent and still, blinding almost in their stunning blondness.

"They are very excited to practice their English," Ingrid said.

"I think you have come from Canada," Eva said haltingly. "We have study it in our school."

Ingrid kept up her smiling neutrality the whole way home, hardly uttering a word that didn't somehow direct him back to the children. Eva was able to manage an exchange or two, but Lars's eyes went at once to his mother at any question.

"Lars's English is not yet so good. But perhaps now he will have a chance to improve it."

This was the first indication that she wasn't going to put him back on the ferry by nightfall. At the house she had Lars take him out to the cabin—it was the first time he'd actually set foot in it. It looked like a fairy-tale place, a little desk against the wall, a little cot with a colored quilt.

"Is your bed," Lars said. He had the same Oxford inflection as his mother.

"Yes. Thank you."

For most of the day he was under Lars's commission, Lars laying out his trophies and ribbons before him like credentials. They had to pass Ingrid's bed to get to his room. It did not seem conceivable to Alex at that moment that he had shared it with Ingrid, that he was anything more than another of her charges.

Lars held out a model of a Plymouth Duster with a tiny spoiler at the back.

"My friend had one in high school," Alex said.

"Is very fast, I think."

"Yes. Very fast."

By suppertime, Lars had assumed a protective custody over Alex.

"You sit here, please," he said, pulling out the chair next to his own. He crowded the platters of food around Alex's dish as if he were to test them.

"Lars is wondering if you have such vegetables in Canada," Ingrid said.

They were having potatoes, cucumber salad. He saw Eva suppress a smirk.

"Yes. We grow them on our farm."

Lars seemed duly taken with that.

"He wants to know if you are a farmer, then."

"Well, no." Alex could see the disappointment. "My parents' farm."

He seemed such a little man, full of dignity and pride, so clearly Ingrid's son yet so different from her, so utterly male. Alex marveled at the perfection of his little body, as streamlined as a cheetah's. He hadn't thought so much of that, of the flesh-and-boneness of children, but that was what he noticed. At bedtime they all sat together on Ingrid's bed while Alex read from *Charlotte's Web*, and it was hard to separate Ingrid from these extensions of her, to sort the carnal from this other new territory of awareness.

In the living room afterward, Ingrid put a finger to her lips when he was about to speak.

"We will wait till they sleep. We'll speak in the cabin."

He hadn't so much as put a hand on her the entire day. In the cabin she took a seat at the desk and left him to the bed, which stood so low he was practically squatting beneath her.

"Alex, why did you come?"

The truth was he didn't know. Because he could.

"I don't know. I missed you."

She let that pass.

"It's not a joke now, Alex. Yes, in the beginning, it was for fun. But now when you are bored in this place or that, 'Oh, well,' you think, 'Ingrid will take me.'"

"It's not like that."

She let him stew.

"I missed you," he said again.

"And next week, or next month, when you are home, what then?"

He had no answer to that. He had not thought beyond the next hour or day, really, the next swing of his mood.

"Do you want me to go?"

He didn't dare to look at her, sitting hunched there beneath her like a repentant schoolboy.

"I don't say so. Somehow we'll manage."

And so he stayed on. He felt like a drowning man going down for the third time: each time the water grew more insistent, more familiar, the urge to resurface more dim. Maybe this was the life he'd always been headed for, with a house and a garden and the sound of children in the background.

"You need only make a place for them," Ingrid said. "You must make a house inside you for them."

She was the one making the house, of course, for him too, though maybe he could manage something more modest, a little cabin, at least.

That was where he remained, in the cabin, though soon they were making love there almost nightly after the children had gone to bed. Once Ingrid fell asleep with him on his little cot and Lars came out in the night to knock sullenly on their door.

"Do you know where is my mother?"

They were more careful after that but it was clear their trysts had not gone unnoticed. Ingrid gave no sign of apologizing for them, which with Lars seemed to have the effect of making them acceptable. Eva was harder to read—she seemed so anxious to please, to avoid unpleasantness, that she gave off the air of waiting with bated breath for some imminent catastrophe.

He lost track of the days. July passed and the end of the summer loomed and yet he was still there in Engelström, in a country that had barely figured in his thoughts when he had set out. He followed Ingrid into Landskrona to the school where she taught to help her prepare for the coming year, feeling the ghost of his childhood at the sight of the desks in their rows, the smell of the construction paper and chalk.

"Perhaps you will be a teacher," Ingrid said. "I see it in you with Lars."

It would have been the death of him to have a teacher like Ingrid— he would have built altars to her, would have pined away to nothing.

"I haven't really thought about it that much."

This was not the truth—he thought about it hourly, his exalted future, though nearly as often the actual vehicle of his exaltation shifted, as if he were still a child playing at doctor and fireman. In his mind he had already mapped out a version of himself that would fit Ingrid—he. could do a degree here, become a teacher of English perhaps. There was his family, of course, his studies, his friends, but then these were exactly the things he had fled.

One weekend they took the children's kite out to where he and Ingrid had picnicked along the coast, a deserted stretch of meadow and cliff where the wind off the sound raised the kite until it was the small-est speck.

"I think you must have kites in Canada," Eva said.

"Yes, but I don't think I've ever flown one."

"But you are so good!"

It was just the wind, any idiot could have done it, but still he took Eva's praise strangely to heart. Afterward he felt they had had a perfect day, together like that in the wind and the salt air. At night, making love with Ingrid, he could still taste the sea on her. It crossed his mind that it could actually come to pass, his remaining here. The oddest sensation went through him at the thought, not unpleasant but hard to place, like an unfamiliar smell.

But lying beside her later, he felt a sort of shame come over him.

"Is everything all right?"

It was pointless to hide things from Ingrid. She sensed every shift of mood like an animal sensing a threat.

"Just tired, I guess. I'm fine."

He lay awake after she'd gone. Everything about the day seemed to skew—they were all just play-acting, really, he saw that now, were all just putting the best face on things the way Eva had done with the kite, trying to make all this seem normal. But there was nothing normal in any of it. He was just a kid; there was no question, really, of his staying. He had known that from the start, that all this was just an excursion from his real life.

In the morning they got to talking about his friends in Copenhagen.

"It felt different there, I guess," Alex said. "Like people were trying to live differently."

"Ah," Ingrid said, clearly surprised at this. "But I thought you were unhappy there."

"That was more just personal things."

"In what way different, then?"

"I dunno—I guess that they didn't just close themselves off in their own little world. That they were trying to change things."

There was an awful pause.

"But that is what I do, is that what you say?" Ingrid said evenly. "That I close myself off?"

"That's not what I meant," Alex stammered. But he knew he'd intended exactly the meaning she had taken. "You're so curious about everything."

Ingrid forced a smile.

"It doesn't matter, you are right. I think so too, sometimes, living here in my little village."

They never got back on track after that. Someone other than Ingrid might have pretended, might have let the matter pass.

"I think tomorrow you must go," she said when she came out to his cabin that night.

Alex couldn't believe the relief that flooded through him.

"I'm sorry," he said.

"There's no need. You are young, you could not stay here."

"No," he said. "I don't think I could."

"It's a shame for both of us, is the only thing."

The children came with them to the ferry the next day. It was like having chaperones, yet Alex was grateful for them. The relief he had felt had given way to something less certain.

"I will write to you," Ingrid said. She didn't seem as stricken as he might have hoped. "I will miss you, my Italian who is not Italian. Perhaps another time."

But he doubted if he had the gumption to have to face this sort of decision again.

All that seemed far from him now, that summer with Ingrid. He'd lived a lifetime in a matter of weeks, from child to man, then had spent all his time since regressing: he was slightly older now than Ingrid had been when he'd first met her, yet he felt less wise, less grown, than he'd felt then, still awaiting some beginning to his life that would set it on course. Maybe he'd missed his chance—if he had stayed, he might have saved himself all his false starts.

He had yet to crack open a book for his exam the following day. A repeat of the interview with the prime minister was playing on the radio, though by now he would be winging his way to the Tokyo Summit, to lick the Americans' feet and beg for a place at the table. A group called the Middle Core Faction had vowed to blow the summit leaders to kingdom come, and Alex felt an instant's thrill at that prospect of apocalypse, maybe because all his private sins would seem small then.

An update on Chernobyl came on. There was apocalypse if he wanted it. Then he was back to Sweden, and his son: for all he knew it was raining fire over in Engelström. He felt anger rising up in him. At whom? The Soviets? Madame Curie? But it was simply that he was still here, so irrelevant. Already he'd missed the boy's crucial first years—that wasn't something that could ever be got over, that could ever be fixed, as enduring as a genetic flaw. She hadn't had the right to do that. She hadn't had the right to make that sort of decision on her own.

He put in some time with his notes. When he grew bleary-eyed, he switched on the TV: more updates. The winds had shifted, thankfully, blowing the cloud that had spread into Sweden back onto the Ukrainians and Poles. Better them; they were used to disaster. No images yet from the site, though from Sweden they showed the lineups at clinics for thyroid shots, long vistas of blonds who looked already bleached through by radiation.

He had to go to him, of course. Sometimes a visceral sense of his connection to him would rise up in Alex like a flood tide. But what was just as compelling was the fear the feeling might pass, the sudden real- ization that minutes had gone by, hours, an entire day, when he had hardly given the boy a second thought. The thing was slipping from him with every day that passed. Soon doing nothing would seem a real possibility, maybe the only one.

He had a last smoke on the balcony. At this hour the black hump of Mount Royal looked like a hole cut out of the city. He made a mental note to remember to call his mother the next day for her sixty-fifth. He would be the only one missing from the brood. On account of exams, he'd said, though the truth was he couldn't bear these family gatherings. They were all pleasant enough, his family, as families went, and yet the moment he was among them he would feel all the life drain out of him.

During his summer with Ingrid, he had missed one of his regular Sunday calls home. When he'd finally phoned days later and no one had answered he'd tried his sister Mimi.

"Jesus, Alex, where have you been?"

He had known at once that matters were grave.

"I dunno. Nowhere. I've been here. In Sweden."

It turned out he had ruined his parents' vacation. They had thought of canceling, then had gone on regardless but had been calling home three or four times a day.

"What was it, Alex? Why didn't you call?"

He'd been gone over two months by then. It hadn't occurred to him that anyone would care one way or the other.

"I guess I didn't think it was a big deal."

Mimi let that sit. Of his five siblings she was really the only one with whom he had what he would call a relationship.

"Well," she'd said finally, holding back all the things she might have said, "at least you're all right."

His life was full of this sort of bad family karma, much of it involving phones, which was maybe why he didn't just put himself out of his misery and phone Ingrid—he had her number, of course, it would be so simple. But each time the notion crossed his mind, he resisted: tomorrow, he would think. Until he actually called, his logic seemed to go, he still had the call in reserve as a last resort. This logic was all the more compelling, perhaps, in being so perfectly circular.

He changed, brushed his teeth, slipped into his bed. He could do it now, he could dial the number; it would be morning there. He thought of those glorious mornings that first summer, waking to sunrise at four, with Ingrid beside him.

He could do it: ten digits or so, and she'd be there. Or not now—he was tired, it was late—but surely tomorrow. Tomorrow, he vowed, he would call.

6

The English Department was a warren of dirty stairwells and windowless classrooms that occupied the back end of the downtown Y, the air there forever underlain with a chlorine stink from the Y's pool. The exam room was already a hush of fevered thought by the time Alex arrived, so that he made the mistake of sitting next to Amanda, who glanced over at him with such heartbreaking furtiveness that for some time he couldn't focus on the questions in front of him. Then the first one came clear and he felt doomed: Jameson. Of all the gobbledygook Alex had had to wade through that year, his had been the worst. It was hard to believe the man was a Marxist. If The Revolution ever did come, Alex hoped Jameson got one of the first bullets.

Exactly because he was trying to avoid her, Alex found his eye returning again and again to Amanda. Amanda ought to have been beautiful, blue-eyed and porcelain-skinned and classically, fulsomely blond. He couldn't say what it was that made her seem otherwise—the energy of her, maybe, something in her eyes, a kind of involution there that scared him, a snarling of the life force. He'd had occasion to look into those eyes at close quarters and hadn't been able to forget the pit they had seemed: *mistake, mistake,* was what had screamed through his head at the time, though by then it had already been far too late. It had been too late, in fact, from the first moment he'd talked to Amanda at the beginning of the year—about Jameson, as it happened, whom he'd actually pretended to admire—and seen the need in her, and chosen to ignore it. Or not ignore it exactly: use it. He'd always had that radar, that ability to home in on weakness and find his shelter there. Not that anything untoward had happened, not then, except for the few outings he'd made to

Amanda's International Socialist meetings, about which he hadn't been entirely candid with Liz.

History is not a text, but is only accessible to us in textual form. After a moment of utter blankness, the fog began to lift and he started to write. There was a question on Benjamin he managed to fake his way through, then some fairly basic boilerplate stuff on Derrida and Bloom and Paul de Man. Alex filled page after page, trying to cram in every possible catchword and bit of jargon to show he knew the stuff, and then subjecting it all, and this was crucial with Professor Novak, to vicious critique. There were quite a number of questions on the feminists, which threw Alex off, given that Novak, all the while professing enthusiasm, had accorded them fairly short shrift during class.

It was important that Alex do well: the year before, Novak had actually failed him on the theory part of his comprehensives. Alex had made the mistake of leaving all his theory to the end of his prep time, figuring he already had a smattering of the stuff secondhand from his Master's, but then when he'd sat down with the texts he hadn't been able to get through more than a few pages of any of them without falling asleep. He had somehow managed to fudge his way through the written exam, but at the oral Novak had been merciless.

"I'm afraid I can't pass you on this," he'd said finally. "If you want you can take my course next term and I'll put in an incomplete until then."

Alex had been livid. The incomplete was a courtesy to save risking the little scholarship the university had given him, but still Alex was tempted, out of sheer bloody-mindedness, just to take the fail and come back at the thing on his own. Except that he would still have been up against Novak, who would probably have found a way to break his balls again. Novak had it in for him, he figured, on account of that accursed article of his in *Canadian Studies*, which was a send-up of probably everything Novak held dear. In the end, Alex swallowed his pride and signed up for Novak's course. Bit by bit, he actually started to like the man—he turned out not to be the stickler Alex had taken him for but a fox, leading them into the thickets and then running circles around all their false assumptions. Then at some point he learned Novak had done work on the Victorians, and went in to speak to him about his thesis.

"Well, well. Let's take a look at what you've got."

So it had come about that a weird symbiosis had developed

between the two of them. Alex signed Novak on as his advisor, relieved to get free of the dinosaur he'd started out with, who'd had him reading Pater and Wilkie Collins for cultural context, and convinced at some level that anyone as hard on him as Novak had to be in the right. Then there was the air of political romance that surrounded Novak: he was a '68er, having left Czechoslovakia just after the ill-fated Prague Spring. In class the Prague Spring served as a metaphor for one of the central tenets of Novakian thought, the impossibility of knowing a thing when you were in the middle of it.

"The amazing thing was that people in the West probably knew more than we did—they had television, newspapers, when we were just on some street corner and didn't even know what was going on around the block."

Alex had never had the courage to put a direct question to Novak about his life then but imagined it in suitably Cold War terms, the *samizdat* presses, the petitions, the secret meetings in the dead of night. He was willing to forgive Novak quite a bit on that account—his obvious unease with young men of a certain intelligence, for instance, which he covered with banter and biting sarcasm. With intelligent young women he was worse, something that had become increasingly apparent since Alex had moved to Mackay and the weekly après-class gathering had been shifted from the Café Prag on Bishop to Alex's apartment. Novak was fond of his whiskey, which he didn't mind asking Alex to keep in supply. Not, however, that it turned him into some sort of common lout; rather, it seemed to have the effect of sharpening him like a knife. He would be off in a corner in some tête-à-tête and there would be a flash, a little gesture, a quiet word, and suddenly the ground would be covered in blood.

Alex's hand was getting sore. Novak wasn't even pretending to keep watch while they wrote, sitting up at the teacher's table peering narrow-eyed through his aviators into a text that had the fresh, unthumbed look of something hot off the academic press. He was a funny-looking man, really, spindly and slight but with a big, balding pate that gave him the appearance of a perfect egghead. And yet there was something magnetic about him, even attractive. It was the attraction of intellect, Alex figured, of seeming to see down into every sloppy syllogism or specious thought you'd ever let yourself get away with.

Novak did not look up from his book until Stephen, the first to finish, inevitably, got up, in his measured way, to hand in his paper.

"Piece of cake," Stephen said dryly, the sort of joke, for some reason, maybe because he knew everything, had read everything, he could get away with.

"Don't forget a bottle tonight," Novak said. "The good stuff, not the rotgut Alex usually has."

Alex wrote until the full three hours of the exam had elapsed. That was a·mistake, he knew, it would seem amateurish to Novak, but he wasn't taking any chances. There were big patches of sweat under his arms, the vinegary tang of which wafted up to him as he rose to hand in his paper.

"Are we still on for our meeting today?"

Novak squinted at him through his glasses as if he'd never set eyes on him before.

"Sorry?"

"About my dissertation."

"Sure. Sure. I'd forgotten all about it."

He was grateful when Novak's attention shifted at once to Amanda behind him and he was able to slip away before she'd had a chance to accost him.

The budding sense of purpose and hope Alex had had when he'd gone to bed the night before was more or less withered. He hadn't called Ingrid, of course, and wasn't about to call her now, when he felt like he'd just emptied out his insides. Instead he went down to the liquor store on St. Catherine, still fuming over Novak's crack about his whiskey, and picked out a forty-dollar Scotch, with the thought of throwing it in Novak's face. Then, realizing that whatever he did would somehow end up turning against him, he walked out of the store without buying anything.

For lunch he dug some three-day-old shawarma out of the back of his fridge, eating it cold while he thumbed through his thesis proposal in preparation for his meeting. All crap, he thought, just a hopeless rehash of the half-baked notions he had strung together more than two years earlier for his admissions application. He'd be lucky if Novak didn't just drop him. He'd be precisely nowhere then.

It's curious, isn't it? You go along all your life, expecting some plan'll show itself, then you find out there isn't one. That it's just one damn thing after another.

I suppose it's a little like evolution, when you think of it, Peter. Some things work, some don't. Natural selection.

I guess that would make you a sort of genetic dead end.

Novak's office was just up the street in the Liberal Arts Building, a Second Empire graystone where the university's Great Books program was housed. Most of the building's nineteenth-century charm had been gutted out of it, replaced by padded divider walls and acoustic ceiling tiles, but there was still a collegial air of unhurried scholarship to the place, a rarity in these days of Gradgrindian utilitarianism. Novak was at the end of the main floor, in a cubbyhole of an office that overlooked the fire exit and back alley. Despite the impression he gave of sinecured permanence Novak was actually a sessional, and so had ended up banished here to his little closet in Liberal Arts rather than over in English among the tenured. Alex was always surprised by how tidy and spruce Novak's office was, his books neatly shelved, his desk clear, the tiny couch beneath his window available for sitting. Alex supposed that all this mirrored the tidiness of Novak's mind, though it did not seem to mirror his life. Rumors about him swirled constantly through the department—the wife who had recently decamped to Toronto, ostensibly to follow a job, though the grapevine said otherwise; the son who was apparently a skinhead. Novak, however, never gave any outward sign of these disturbances, or even that he had descended long enough from the usual parapets of his thought to notice them.

The morning's exam papers were sitting on the corner of Novak's desk. Alex shot a glance at them and saw that his own was right on the top, already riddled with red but not graded yet. This was exactly the kind of childish ploy that Novak would pull, and that made Alex loathe and admire him.

"So." He sat tenting his fingers at his desk, pointedly ignoring the exams. "You have something for me?"

Alex was caught off guard.

"Well, no. Not exactly. I mean, I gave you a copy of my proposal last month."

"Ah," Novak said, though Alex couldn't tell whether he was actually acknowledging possession of the thing.

There was a silence. Novak had always asked his grad students to address him by his first name, Jiri, a privilege he didn't extend to his undergrads, though for Alex this had the effect of making him feel he couldn't address him at all.

"Why don't you just tell me what it is you really want to do," Novak said finally. "Plain and simple. In your own words."

A little spasm of terror went through Alex. This wasn't what academia was about, putting things in your own words. In any event he could hardly tell Novak that what he really wanted to do was redeem his own life.

"I suppose it's like Derrida," he started. "This idea that there's a whole structure in our minds that controls how we think. Except instead of language or binary opposites or something like that, it's genetic."

"But you're talking about biochemistry, not literature. What are you actually going to write about, what are you going to analyze? Are you going to find the genetic code in *Anna Karenina*?"

"I don't know. Maybe."

"But that's just boring. You're just stuck saying that people are ruled by self-interest or they aren't. It's too simple a mechanism, don't you see? It's fine for protozoa, but it doesn't explain much when you get to humans."

Alex was losing heart. He was ashamed at how unformed his ideas still were. Every once in a while some insight would come to him and he'd think he'd cracked the back of the thing, little aphorisms that he'd write down in a notebook he kept for the purpose, but then he'd go back and every entry would seem hopelessly banal.

And yet he remained convinced he was on to something.

"What's really behind all this?" Novak said. "I mean, it seems such a tangent. It's not like you've got a background in this."

"I did do my Master's in Victorian Studies," Alex said peevishly.

"And you probably read Dickens and Ruskin and Oscar Wilde just like I did. I doubt you were reading *The Origin of Species*."

He *had* in fact read *The Origin* at the time, but wasn't about to try to score points by mentioning that.

"So?" Novak said. "What is it?"

Alex felt cornered.

"It's nothing. I guess it was a trip I took when I was younger. To the Galápagos."

He regretted the admission at once.

"Aha. World's End." Novak had latched onto the thing like a springing cat. "Now things are beginning to make a bit of sense. Tell me about it."

Novak often made a show of inviting confidences, as if he were some benevolent *patronus*, but he was probably the last person Alex would have wanted to pour his heart out to.

"It was just a trip. An accident, really. But it got me interested in all this stuff."

Novak was losing patience.

"Look, Alex, that's great. It's good to work with something that's relevant to you. But no one's going to give you a doctorate just because you're interested in something. You have to know it like the back of your hand."

Alex could feel his blood pressure rising.

"Did you even read my proposal, at least?"

Novak gave him a look.

"Alex, all that was just the standard kind of bullshit people put in their proposals. You know that as well as I do. It was impressive bullshit but it was still bullshit. You'll have to do better than that with me."

Alex reddened. His anger crested, then spent itself on the shores of shame.

"So you're saying I should just find something else."

But Novak actually seemed taken aback.

"That's not what I meant at all. Don't misunderstand me—it's intriguing, I'll give you that. It's original. I just need you to spell it out."

It looked like he'd have to be happy with just this crumb. It was almost worse than nothing: he couldn't quit the thing now, yet wasn't sure he had the will to go on.

Novak had stood to indicate the interview was over.

"Look, Alex," he said, "you're an intelligent young man, anyone can see that. I read that paper of yours in *Canadian Studies*—I thought it was brilliant. You just need to focus a bit, that's all. Maybe scale back a bit on what you're trying to do."

For all his iconoclasm, Novak was bowing like the rest of them before that gold star of academia, publication.

"Try starting fresh. Take the summer to write something out, then bring it by."

Novak had come around his desk. He extended a hand and Alex started to raise his own, then checked himself when he saw Novak had only meant to open the door.

"Good exam, by the way. A little weak on Benjamin, maybe."

Alex couldn't shake his sense of humiliation as he left Novak's office. Somehow that felt like the point of all this, of the whole academic shuffle, not some search for the truth but just this endless jockeying for position. But then he was the one who had consecrated himself to this undertaking as if it could matter, as if some sort of expiation could come out of it.

That was his mistake in this as in everything, that he didn't simply shed his skin and move on. You got no points for wallowing. He should forget his dissertation, forget the Galápagos, should go out this minute and buy his ticket. This was the chance he'd been waiting for, a new beginning. He felt it kindle again, fickle flickering hope, then quickly snuffed it for fear it would spread.

7

Back in his apartment Alex checked the news again: Chernobyl had dropped from the lead to position three, beneath Charles and Di's visit to Expo and the fall in the prime rate to 10.5. From Tokyo, Mr. Reagan intoned, "The Soviets owe the world an explanation." Sanctimonious ass. Explain El Salvador. Explain *Bedtime for Bonzo.*

He ran himself a bath, his little refuge in moments of crisis, though this wasn't something he cared to admit to people. Unfortunately the bathroom in his apartment was a holdover from someone's bad seventies decorating idea, the walls and ceiling lined all around with one-foot-square smoked mirror tiles, so that lying in the tub Alex saw himself reflected darkly from almost every conceivable angle like a bad cubist painting.

He lay back in the water and closed his eyes. Noise, noise, noise; his head was full of it. Row out from the shore and drop your thoughts into the sea, he told himself, a technique he'd picked up from a self-help book back in high school. But it was no use, his thoughts wouldn't solidify into the necessary pebbles. He wished he had one of those sensory deprivation tanks that had been the rage after *Altered States.* Alex had become obsessed after he'd seen the movie with the notion of stripping down to his core, of climbing into one of those tanks and regressing like William Hurt to his most primitive animal self.

At the time, of course, Peter, I was thinking of it in Jungian terms, as a sort of descent into the collective unconscious. But it would have been more logical to be looking at Darwin.

That was still your Jungian period, I guess. Before you'd found out about the anti-Semitism.

Actually, that wasn't what put me off him in the end so much as all the hokeyness. But in a sense, I suppose, a Darwinian sense, Jung was right: it's all there in our genes, the whole history of the race, right back to the protozoa.

There had been an instant in Novak's office when he'd felt on the verge of the thing again, of the crucial insight, but still it had refused to show itself. Maybe time had already run out for him. He'd read about a study of Nobel laureates that showed they'd all had their big inspirations before they'd reached thirty. It was true of Darwin, just barely—his real breakthrough, his first inkling of the little mechanism that governed the origin of species, had come a matter of months before his thirtieth, while he was reading Malthus's essay on population. All the rest had been just the slow working out of that original insight, over twenty years and more and through the minutest accumulation of data from the most painstaking, most banal of investigations.

Alex sank lower into the water. Thump, thump, thump, went his heart, counting the seconds off in his brain's slow decline. Yet there was hope, perhaps, in Darwin, in his unspectacular life—apart from his *Beagle* trip he'd spent most of his life holed up in his study, sifting through bird shit and cutting up barnacles and worms. You saw it in *The Origin*, which was mainly just a compendium of the most domestic of observations, almost entirely devoid of anything resembling a grand statement. Maybe that was Alex's error; maybe he was looking too hard for the Big Explanation.

Alex had seen the study where Darwin had cut up those barnacles, on one of the few real trips that he and Liz had ever treated themselves to. It had been at a heady time for them, just after his *Canadian Studies* coup and a rave review of Liz's work in the local entertainment rag and before the whole disaster with the abortion. The trip, the calm before the storm, had gone perfectly: it had been a beautiful, rainless May and the whole of England, despite the dawn of Thatcher, had seemed laid out for their benefit, immaculately scrubbed and prettified and trim. Alex had hardly given Darwin a thought until he'd come across a display at the Natural History Museum in London on Darwin's house at Downe and been surprised to discover it was not more than twenty miles out of the city.

While Liz did the Tate he went out to see the house, by train as far as Bromley and from there by bus through hopelessly quaint Kentish farmland, along roads that were hardly the span of a human body. Darwin's village still boasted an inn where Charles had apparently taken ale; from there it was a five-minute walk along Luxted Road to his house, which was tucked off the main road along a narrow lane and lay buried in a wilderness of shrubbery and trees.

The house had a ramshackle look, a long rambling two-story manor in graying stucco tacked haphazardly with aging trellises that were just as haphazardly overgrown with ivy. At the entrance a portly custodian with the damp, tousled look of having been surprised at a nap told him in a tone of hushed apology that visits were only by appointment.

"Oh. I just came from London. I didn't know."

The man glanced over his shoulder and gave Alex a conspiratorial look, as if Darwin himself were sleeping upstairs.

"I'm sure it'll be all right if I just show you around a bit."

The place was kept up, for some reason, by the Royal College of Surgeons. The only room that was actually open for viewing was Darwin's study, which had been restored at some point after apparently serving as the rumpus room for a girls' boarding school. The room was gloomier than Alex would have expected, given the hours Darwin had spent there peering at specimens.

"You must be a student of Darwin, then," the custodian said encouragingly. "To go to all this trouble."

"Not really." In fact, Alex, having recently finished an utterly useless degree in Victorian Studies, wasn't entirely sure what exactly he was a student of. "I mean, I've read him."

"Well, you've done more than most then, I expect. A very complex man, Mr. Darwin. Much more to him than meets the eye."

The room held a couple of tables laid out with Darwin memorabilia, specimen bottles, implements, notepapers, open books. There was a cupboard in the corner with a tiny-drawered cabinet on top; there were shelves of chemicals, weights and scales, rows of books. The place did not look especially scientific in any contemporary sense; rather, it looked like what it was, the study of an amateur, of a country gentleman.

The custodian pointed out through a window toward the lane that passed in front of the house.

"He had that wall built out there, and the road lowered, quite a job in those days. To make things a bit more private." He motioned Alex over to the window. "Look just outside, next to the window frame—you can still make out where the rivets were that held the mirror in place. So he could get a look at anyone who came to the front door, you see. In case he wanted to nip away for a moment."

Darwin's special chair was pulled up to one of the tables, a worn leather armchair he'd had fitted with wheels so he could coast around the room at will. He had written *The Origin* in it, on a cloth-covered board he placed over the arms. There was a matching ottoman, which was also fitted with wheels, and which his children—"A big healthy brood he had, he did his part in that regard"—used to commandeer to ride up and down the hall. Behind a divider wall were his facilities, with a washstand and a big metal tub: this was where he had his treatments, daily dousings in icy water, for the mysterious illness that plagued him most of his life.

Alone in the center of the main table stood a framed photograph of a slightly homely girl, sad-eyed and stoic-looking, in fusty Victorian dress. Beside it sat an old pen nib, a scrap of embroidery, a lock of dark hair. A kind of eeriness came off the little island the ensemble formed, as if it had been set apart like pagan medicine, the bundles and scraps of private things used to win a lover or ward off the evil eye.

"That was his Annie. The one who passed on." The custodian paused as if the wound was still fresh. "He never recovered, they say."

Alex couldn't have been in that room more than twenty minutes, yet his sense of it had never left him. Something had struck a chord, a spirit that was almost sinister but also commonplace and familiar. Later, when he had been let loose on the grounds and had gone out to the Sandwalk, the path in the woods behind the house where Darwin used to take his constitutionals, he'd had a sort of insight: he was not so hopelessly distant from this man. That was when the idea for his dissertation had been born, when it had seemed possible to dare such a thing.

His bathwater was going cold. He ought to get up and start preparations for his party. The image often came to him, when he was in the bath, of Darwin lowering his bony rump into the frigid water of his tub: it was such a humiliating thing, to have a body, to be held in such thrall to it. These days the theorists made a big deal about the body, the body as text, writing on the body, men writing on women, but it was all just metaphor, from what Alex could tell—you only had to spend five minutes in a roomful of academics to see there wasn't a single body among the lot of them. Theory porn, was how Alex thought of it; pure compensation. He wanted something a little less metaphysical, something that might take account of Darwin's bony haunch, otherwise what was the point? Somewhere in literature's dark beginnings there had to be real blood on the page, there had to be real bodies being sacrificed or being saved.

He stared up at himself in the smoked mirror tiles on the ceiling, this unpleasant slab of pasty flesh and matted hair. He seemed such an unlikely hash in that instant, as unpredictable and strange in his lineaments as the arthropods of the Burgess Shale, with their inefficient tentacles and extrusions and frills. Why this limb here, why fingers, why a nose? It beggared the mind to think of all the billion little evolutionary mutations and mistakes that had led just here, to this freakish amalgam. He had riddled it with scars over the years as if to mark it with his own private history—a sickle-shaped ridge in the fat of his palm from when he'd put his hand through a sheet of greenhouse glass; a black dot near his knee where one of his brothers had jabbed a pencil.

He peered more closely into a mirror tile to see if he could make out the scar on his eyelid. There it was, barely discernible now, just a thin intimation of white, zigging down between his lashes. That one he'd got when he'd jumped off the back of their stake truck into the corner of a piece of plywood his brother was unloading. "My eye, my eye!" he'd screamed, clutching at it like a kid in a B movie, though meanwhile so much blood and goo was oozing from it he was certain he'd ruptured it. His father had been spreading some kind of chemical in the greenhouses and had come running out covered completely in white, head to toe, his clothes, his hair, his lashes.

"What is it? What happened?"

"My eye!"

By the time they'd got to the hospital his father had given up trying to shout some sense out of him and had started in on a litany of moaning imprecations in Italian, the increasingly desperate tone of which had done much to inch up Alex's panic. Alex knew what was going through both their heads: his brother David's accident the year before. He didn't think they could bear it, another dismemberment. He was also thinking about the little shoplifting spree he'd been on that summer—in a drawer of his desk the items had been accumulating, completely useless things like key chains and penlights and paperweights that he'd wanted, at the moment he'd taken them, with all of his being.

"What happened? How did it happen?"

Alex hadn't once dared to take his hands away from his eye.

"I just hit my eye!" he wailed.

He was dumbfounded at the air of calm that greeted them at the hospital emergency room. The nurse smiled at him and spoke slowly, though there was the life of him gushing out in his hands. Then he was stretched out in a cubicle and the doctor was with him, while his father, still ghostly white, stood by wheezing with emotion.

"It was a piece of wood or something. It was his brother who seen it."

Back when David had had his accident Alex had tried making a pact with God to bring him right—a joke, really, not just because the matter had been hopeless but because Alex was already at a point when he and God were not really on speaking terms. And yet he couldn't stop himself now from hedging his bets. If God saved his eye, he swore, he'd never steal another blessed thing his long life.

The doctor smiled.

"I guess you got a bit of a poke there."

He eased Alex's hands away and without the least hesitation put his finger and thumb to Alex's eye and forced open the lid. Instantly light came pouring through the opening.

"I can see!" Alex actually said this. "I can see!"

"I guess you can," the doctor said.

Alex's father was still wringing his hands by the bedside.

"He's okay?"

"Just a little scared, I think. He'll need a couple of stitches but nothing that we can't fix."

His father took in a stuttered breath and started to sob.

"I didn't know. From how he was screaming like that."

The doctor was still smiling.

"If you want you can wait outside while I sew him up. Maybe tidy up a bit."

Why had he had to stand crying like that at Alex's bedside? The memory of it still made Alex wince. The two of them had already been well into their period of silence by then, but his father's heart had been in his hands the whole time, any idiot could have seen it. It wasn't God Alex had made a pact with then, that bloodless Nobodaddy in the clouds, but the maddening flesh-and-bone dad by his bed who'd insisted on humiliating him with emotion. Years more had gone by after that before they'd actually had anything like a real conversation, but Alex had known all along in his gut that all this hardness he bore toward the man was for nothing.

His aunt Grace had brought him a tricycle once when he was small, a hand-me-down but utterly undented and pristine, in brilliant red and white. Right into the kitchen she had brought it, something only his aunt Grace could have gotten away with.

"*Sandro*," she'd said, which was what they'd called him then. "*You like it?*"

She'd sat talking with his mother. Somehow their attention had got turned, and then he was riding down the hall, which was vast and long, and then he'd reached the head of the back stairs. He remembered hearing his aunt still chattering in the kitchen, seeming fabulously distant; he remembered the afternoon light through the hall window. For a moment he'd sat there on that wondrous contrivance staring out at empty space and feeling a freedom he had never known; and then he'd driven forward.

There was an instant as he launched into the air when he felt what he might now call the thrill of the infinite, the sense there was nothing that wasn't permitted. Then suddenly everything was chaos and disorder: his limbs, his trike, his entire self, had passed out of his power and there was a horrible rattling and banging in which he could not distinguish wood and metal and wall from his own bones. It ended in what seemed a heap of pure pain, him lying bloodied and wailing on the concrete and the trike lying hopelessly mangled on top of him. The tricycle he would never see again; no doubt his father, who was always complaining about the "garbage" Aunt Grace unloaded on them, had simply tossed it in the ditch.

There it was still, he could make it out in the tiles, the little scar between his brows from that fall: his third eye. It was the one that had seen, as his trike launched out into the air, that he had limits. He could not simply imagine a thing to make it happen; he could not by mere force of will overcome the will of everything set against him, the walls and the concrete and steel, the perpetual downward pull of what he did not yet know was called gravity. All that he really had to get him through the whole muddle of it was the little package that held him, his body, which turned out to be hemmed in on every side by the force of the mute, unpredictable world.

The water had grown truly frigid now. He pulled the bathtub plug, watched the water swirl down, and got up to prepare for his party.

8

As Alex had more or less foreseen, the first person to arrive that evening, precisely at eight, as if she'd simply been biding her time in the garbage closet at the end of the hall since he'd left her the day before, was Esther. She was done up in the sort of woolly dress that Alex hadn't seen since the seventies, a vibrant green thing that exuded static and stuck to her curves like cling wrap.

A hint of lipstick smeared her front teeth.

"So." She'd brought a bottle of wine with her, the middling Italian red they sold downstairs at the depanneur. "We meet again."

All afternoon Alex had been busy stoking up his goodwill toward her, admonishing himself to be mindful of her, to be a gentleman.

"I'll get you a glass. I mean, are you allowed to drink?"

"Well, maybe a glass or two." She put on her coquettish air. "If you promise not to take advantage of me."

Michael had called to say he wouldn't be coming, which was bad news—Michael could work a room like a society matron, until there was hardly a corner of it that wasn't abuzz. He had a hot date, he'd said, someone he'd met on the mountain, which was worrying, probably another of his sudden passions that would come to nothing or worse.

"You know, I was reading about Chernobyl," Esther was saying. "After what you told me. All those people working there, it must have been awful."

In fact, Alex had hardly given a thought to the workers except in the most general terms. His mind had gone at once to the global, to the abstract; though not, of course, with respect to Sweden.

"They're saying only two dead," he said, as if to console her, but then felt compelled to add, in deference to truth, "Of course they're probably lying."

"Really? You really think they would lie?"

The next to arrive, as Alex had feared, was Amanda. There was nothing for it now but to face her. She looked around the room with her clouded look of disorientation.

"Oh. I'm not early, am I?"

"No, no," he said quickly. "I guess everyone's on Montreal time."

The reference seemed to go right past her. She was from one of those western cities, Calgary or Regina, he could never remember which.

Alex felt despair coming over him like a nuclear cloud.

"Would you like some wine?"

"That's okay, I brought some beer. If that's all right."

He busied himself in the kitchen pouring chips into bowls, glad now to have Esther there as a buffer. Amanda, however, hadn't seemed to notice that there was anything peculiar about Esther and so there was the awkwardness of her finding him alone with another woman, an awkwardness Esther didn't appear to be making any effort to dispel.

"So you're at Concordia too?"

"Yes, I'll be doing my Master's soon," Esther said, which was news to Alex.

It was almost nine before more people started trickling in, a few of the other women, then Katherine and, separately, Stephen, then Novak himself. Katherine had recently punked herself up to look like a street fighter, her hair shaved mental-patient close on the sides and dyed vampire black on the top. To stop people treating her like a pixie, she'd told him. Tonight she was dressed in a leather motorcycle jacket that she wore over a low-cut lacy top that made Alex's skin prickle.

Katherine was whom he should have slept with, not Amanda, but she'd slept with Stephen, fussy stick-up-his-ass Mr. Know-It-All. Alex couldn't believe it when she'd told him. Of course, Stephen hadn't turned out to be the worldly intellectual she'd imagined him to be but a typical emotionally stunted WASP. By then Alex had already fallen into the role of friend-confessor, and it was too late.

Katherine and Stephen had yet to speak.

"The thing about Lacan," Novak was saying to a group of the women, though he might as well have been saying *bullshit, bullshit,*

bullshit, "is that he repositions Freud within the discourse of *language*."

It wasn't until Louie arrived that things loosened up. Louie was a force—all year long he had held the class in thrall with a mix of menace and sheer energy. Before Alex's parties he used to take groups of them over to the East End on drinking sprees that were like Roman bacchanals, but in class it was always a mistake to underestimate him. For his term seminar he'd brought in a huge stack of clippings from publications like *Allô Police* and *Le Journal de Montréal* and had gone through them with rapier precision showing how racist they were.

Louie had skin that people in Nigeria, where they had a proper sense of the gradations of these things, would have called *black*.

"No funny business tonight," he said, putting a big, handsome arm around Novak, which made Novak look like a tiny old man. "All the women are mine tonight."

By the time Félix arrived, Alex had more or less forgotten about him. He felt a moment of utter dismay when he saw him there at the door, as if there'd been an awful mistake. Surely the man had some squash game to go to or some opera or wine bar instead of showing up here at his pathetic little house party.

He was dressed in a rakish black sports jacket that made him look as if he'd just stepped away from the gaming tables of Monte Carlo.

"Félix!" Alex tried to purge the note of panic from his voice. "It's so great that you came!"

From a plastic bag Félix pulled, of all things, two six-packs of Molson's.

"It's what you ordered. At the pub." He gave one of his shrugs, as if to apologize for his imperfect grasp of some cultural nuance. "I hope it's all right."

Somehow, the evening took on a kind of rhythm. Félix, far from sticking out, was soon in heated debate with Novak on the retrenchment of French intellectuals after the failure of '68, one of Novak's favorite subjects; Louie was holding forth on Duvalier, downing Alex's Crown Royal, which Alex smuggled back with him periodically from his father's bar, three fingers at a go. Even Esther was managing: she'd got Stephen alone on the couch, safely buffered from Katherine, and was working away at him with Barbara Walters–like determination.

"So you're saying, if I don't have the words for something, then I can't even think about it?"

"Something like that."

"But what about sex?" There was an instant's lull around them, then a burst of laughter.

Stephen blushed.

"I think she's got you on that one," Katherine said dryly.

For a moment then, the wine he'd been downing like water finally beginning to kick in, Alex looked out over his party, and was pleased. He had friends, he was able to fill a room with conversation; perhaps his life was not such a shambles. Not just friends but people who were actually interesting, Haitian refugees and Prague Spring survivors, ethnics and WASPs, francophones and anglophones, people with disabilities. This was what he had always imagined for himself, having friends of every stripe, feeling at home with them. Citizen of the world.

I suppose it was a kind of epiphany, Peter, just standing there in my living room, looking out over all that diversity and thinking: only in this country.

"I was wondering if maybe we could talk."

Amanda was at his elbow.

"Right. Yeah. Maybe not here—"

"No, I wasn't saying . . . I mean, I thought maybe we could get together or something."

Shit, Alex thought. He'd been dreading this, the after-sex debriefing. There was nothing to say except all the usual lies, so predictable he could have had cards printed up. *Just friends. Made a mistake. Need space. Circle those that apply.*

"I just thought, that night, I dunno. You seemed pretty down."

She was already giving him an out, was already allowing he might be too damaged to be held accountable, which had the effect of making him feel truly defenseless.

"I guess I was a little depressed," he granted.

"But after, you know, we never really got a chance to talk. I mean, if you wanted to."

Alex was starting to lose track of what issue it was that they were trying to avoid.

"It's just, I was thinking of staying here for the summer to do a French course," Amanda was saying. "I mean, if people were around."

"Well, if you wanted to," Alex started. "That is, if you're going to stay anyway—"

"Oh, yeah, no, I didn't mean it like that—"

The awkwardness had settled between them like a wet dog.

"Look, I'm sorry." Something had lurched in the pit of his stomach. Any minute he was going to retch right there where he stood. "I really have to use the bathroom."

He locked himself in and knelt in front of the bowl in the dark in case another spasm came on him. Why had he ever slept with her? It had all happened in a drunken haze, but that didn't relieve him of the idiocy of the thing. He wondered if he was no better at bottom than every other sex-obsessed male, ready to sleep with whatever willing specimen washed up at his door.

When his stomach had calmed he sat on the bowl. There were no windows in the room and the darkness was almost total, but he couldn't bear the thought of seeing himself reflected back ad infinitum from his mirrored tiles. People had made a lot of jokes about those tiles when he'd first started these gatherings, but not so much lately.

There was a knock at the door.

"Anybody in there?" It was Stephen. He'd have noticed that the lights were out. Alex could already see him sidling up to Novak to make some poisoned remark. *Looks like Alex has a monkey in there that needed spanking.*

"Just a minute!"

Things had definitely turned now. His paranoia had come on—he'd be going along like this in his normal deluded way and then some small thing, a gesture, a word, would seem to strip the scales from him, would suddenly reveal the world in its true malevolence. He used to think of the feeling as some kind of artist's alienation, but it was probably just a reflex, a deep insectival part of the brain sensing he was out of place, that he'd misstepped. His ant brain, Alex called it: that was how ants must feel if they stepped out of line, the alarm bells going off all along their double helixes.

He could hear Amanda and Stephen talking outside the door. There was more than a little of the ant to Amanda, Alex could see that now; he should have seen it from the start, at those International Socialist meetings she'd dragged him to, but he'd been too besotted with blondness then, too thrilled to be having those not-really-dates behind Liz's back. The meetings, of course, had been a joke: maybe a dozen people, on a good day, plotting the overthrow of the capitalist order. They were held at an old community hall down in Point St. Charles, with set talks every week on topics like "The Failure of the Union Leadership in the British Coal Miners' Strike" or "The Role of the Mullahs in Iran," talks which were actually fairly interesting but which always managed to trail off at the end into the strange illogic of The Revolution. Did these people think the factory workers in LaSalle or the paunchy transit drivers or the racist, cushily unionized Montreal police were going to storm down to University and Sherbrooke and slit some capitalist's throat?

"Doesn't it seem a little far-fetched?" he finally got the courage to say to Amanda. "I mean, who are they kidding?"

Amanda looked crestfallen.

"Well, I think they've got a good analysis."

That had more or less stalled things between them, which had been just as well. Where could they have gone, really? He'd never lied to Amanda about Liz, and so had been able to use her to shield him as soon as he'd needed to. But after the breakup he'd sat exposed. Then at the end of one of his after-class parties, Amanda had inexplicably stayed behind.

"You seem kind of unhappy," she said, putting a hand on his shoulder with a sort of sad, cheery smile.

It was true he was pretty low. At the party he'd been making dark jokes about his balcony that everyone but Amanda had wisely shrugged off.

He felt he had to offer her something.

"You know. Life and all that. My breakup."

"It's just I had a friend who used to talk that way. She used to make jokes like that."

Oh, shit, Alex thought, not wanting to know.

"Did she—?"

"Yeah."

He dipped his head.

"What a drag."

"So. I just wanted you to know. In case you were thinking—"

"It's not really something I'd do," he said, almost ready to put the matter in writing just so he wouldn't have to continue with this awful conversation.

He'd made the mistake of offering her a drink then, and by the end of the night they had polished off several bottles of leftover wine and several inches of Canadian Club, another import from his father's bar. It turned out that Alex was the one who did most of the consoling: Amanda told him the story of her dead friend, a childhood girlfriend back home who'd gone bad with drugs and slit her wrists. She ended up sobbing drunkenly there on the couch, so that there was nothing for it but for Alex to take her in his arms. Why he had started kissing her he couldn't say—some sense of obligation, maybe, or because of the alcohol, or because he'd hoped to reassure himself, after his last months with Liz, that he could still have normal sexual relations. What was more likely, though, was that he'd been driven by the usual brute male imperative: here was a woman who was available to him, blond, blue-eyed, full-breasted, satin-skinned, and in the animal discourse of flesh to flesh it did not matter so much that such a near-perfect body had got strapped to such a conflicted, not-knowing-what-it-was-striving-for soul. The sex, in the end, when they'd managed to get to it, had hardly registered, given how drunk they'd been; and yet it had happened.

Alex had read somewhere about a fish species in which the males divided neatly into two sorts: those who were perfect family men, who stuck by their wives and looked after their children, and those who acted the part during mating but were really outright cads, disappearing the instant they'd dropped their seed. Cad vs. dad was a bit of a wash in terms of surviving offspring, so that neither won out, and it was entirely likely that the cads didn't even know they were cads, just went along every time with the best of intentions until they felt the itch again, and were gone.

Cad. Dad. Circle those that apply.

There was another knock on the door, tentative: Amanda.

"You okay in there?"

How had he gone from preening like a peacock over the little social success of his two-bit party to sitting fucked up and paranoid on his toilet in the dark?

"I'll just be a minute!" he called out, a bit shrilly. "Feeling a bit queasy, that's all!"

He was still steeling himself for re-entry when a raised voice from the living room had him suddenly scrambling.

"Vous êtes raciste, monsieur! Raciste!"

It was Louie. Alex opened the bathroom door to see Félix hurrying away from him toward the exit. Alex, mortified, practically leaped after him to head him off.

"What happened?"

"I think your friend has had a bit too much to drink," Félix said gravely. "I hope I will see you for our lesson. I'm sorry to have given any offense."

He gave an official little bow like a French legionnaire, and was gone.

"The man is a racist!" Everyone had fallen silent now except Louie. "A racist, my friend!"

The charge fell to Alex now; he was the one who had brought the man here. All year long they had all labored under this fear, that Louie would expose their own racist white asses.

"But what happened? What did he say?"

"What did he say? What they all say!"

"But what, exactly?"

"It doesn't matter with them, what they say, it's what they mean. Come to my country, but keep quiet. We shoot you in the street, keep quiet. We shove our language down your throat, keep quiet!"

"But you're French!"

"What does it say, that I'm French? Why can they tell me, do this or learn that? I come here, I have the same rights as you or him or anyone. Not, you're Haitian, you do what I say. That is racism pure and simple, my friend!"

Alex had never seen him this way, so enraged. That he was drunk didn't seem to explain the matter—normally the alcohol had no more effect than water on him.

Alex felt compelled to take Félix's side.

"I can't believe he meant that. I know him. He's a good man."

"Good to you, maybe. You see your skin? It's white. Mine is black."

It took a while to calm Louie down. Alex felt sick, as if some desecration had been committed, as if someone had smeared shit on the walls.

"You don't see it, my friend. You come to the shop with me—they don't look at you, they don't talk to you, even if you are the only one in the shop. You are invisible."

"They can't all be like that."

"No, not all. But the separatists, they're the worst. And worse than that, the intellectuals."

Alex just wanted people to leave now. Everyone appeared to be waiting for some word from Louie that would set things in motion again, but he merely continued to mutter and sulk amidst the little circle of female supporters that had rallied to him. There was no help from Novak: he had gone into his anthropologist's mode, watching the whole scene without a word as if he'd just witnessed some rare dominance rite.

Just when it seemed they might end up frozen for all time in their wretchedness, there was a knock at the door. Alex was afraid that Félix had returned to have the matter out, but instead he opened the door to none other than Miguel and María.

Alex stood dumbfounded.

"Miguel." He didn't even dare to look at María. "You're here."

"Yeah, man. I brought my sister, I hope is okay."

After the fiasco with Louie people looked at them as if they were a ticking bomb Alex had brought into the room. Around María a gulf opened up at once: she stood there like a reprimand, all dark good looks and Latin-ness, dressed in the sort of party clothes—tight jeans, high heels—that most of the women in the room, fuzzy-sweatered Birkenstockers, could never have carried off.

"Is your apartment?" she said to Alex, addressing him directly for the first time since he'd met her, from what he could remember.

"Yes. I mean, I live here."

"Is very high," she said severely.

Somehow the party seemed to grind back into gear. Novak was making the obvious joke of putting Louie's outburst down to Alex's whiskey, but surprisingly good-naturedly, as if the whole incident had lightened his mood. Louie still had his circle of women but seemed to be growing bored now with their supportive coos, his eye forever straying to María. Meanwhile Miguel was just going quietly around the apartment inspecting Alex's things as if casing the place.

It was Amanda, of all people, who finally edged up to María, along with, just as improbably, Esther. They formed a strange tableau: his three women.

"So you're from El Salvador," Amanda said. "That must be interesting. I mean, with the war there and all that."

"Yes. The war."

"Oh?" Esther said. "There's a war?"

María's eye went to Esther's cane.

"You are a disease?"

Esther didn't miss a beat.

"It's called multiple sclerosis!" She had raised her voice to make up for the language difference. "I don't know if you have it in El Salvador!"

Alex retreated back into the bathroom. This time he actually peed. At some point he would have to speak to Amanda, he knew that—she'd been a model one-night stand, really, hadn't made any unpleasant assumptions when they'd woken up self-conscious and hungover the following morning, hadn't shown up unexpectedly at his door in the middle of the night to give him a piece of her mind. What was he afraid of, then? He was afraid of this: that he would sleep with her again.

He zipped and wiped a few drips away from the seat. He didn't know what to do about Félix—he couldn't see the matter clearly, could only see those dollars piling up, one nearly every two minutes. But then for all he knew the whole thing had been theater. Ever since Baby Doc had been ousted Louie had been given to wild pronouncements on every subject as if casting about for some new arch enemy.

Some loose thought was floating around at the back of Alex's brain but he couldn't get a hold of it. Then there it was, surfacing out of the murk: he'd hadn't called his mother.

Shit. He'd meant to call her before her party at the club. She might already be home by now, but it wouldn't be the same, she'd be tired or asleep, she would know he'd forgotten. He slipped into his bedroom through the ensuite door and dialed the number from the phone on his desk, then hung up after the second ring thinking it would be worse if he woke her. The truth was, it probably didn't much matter one way or the other. "'*At's okay*," was all his mother would say, in her Italienglish—not to make him feel guilty, that wasn't really her way, but just with her reflex peasant fatalism, or with acceptance or even indifference. She was a cipher, his mother—he hadn't the least notion what went through her head, what had borne her up through all her sixty-five years. But just this once, he would have liked to have been the good son.

He flaked out on his bed, unable to face the party again. María was out there, but he wouldn't go near her, not with this stink of paranoia and self-pity on him.

He heard Amanda's voice, grown sloppy with alcohol, filtering in from the living room balcony through the bedroom window. Something about the summer, and then her voice started to break.

"I dunno, I dunno. It just seemed kind of hurtful, you know?"

She must be with Katherine. So he wouldn't be spared after all, was about to be uncloaked for the jerk he truly was.

"I just feel so alone sometimes, I can't stand it."

A pause, then another voice.

"You shouldn't take it that way." Alex felt like he'd been slapped. It was Stephen. "Anyway, she probably didn't mean anything by it."

She? He felt a weird sense of affront. Here was Amanda confiding in Stephen, of all people, about something that apparently had nothing to do with him.

"Look," Stephen said, "maybe we could get together for coffee or something."

Alex tried to make out some sort of predatory note in this.

"Sure. Yeah. That would be nice."

Alex slunk back into the bathroom. There was another knock at the door. He opened it to find himself face to face with Miguel.

"Hey, man, son'thing the matter?"

"Just a bit of a headache."

"Me and my sister, we got to go. We got to see a Salvadoran friend."

So that was it, then. He had barely so much as breathed the air that María had passed through. At the door Miguel gave him a warm Latin clap on the shoulder, but María stood well away, one eye already on the elevator.

"We gonna make you Salvadoran, jus' wait," Miguel said.

Louie left not five minutes later.

"This man was your friend?" he said, heading off any attempt by Alex at apology.

"Well, my student. I mean, I know him."

"You be careful, Mr. Italian, your skin isn't as white as a Frenchman's."

The party began to break up. Katherine kept pointedly clear of Stephen, but then got stuck leaving with Novak.

"You know, that paper you did could be publishable if it was fixed up a bit."

"I'm not so sure," Katherine said, and Alex thought, *Nice try, Novak.* But then she faltered. "I had some ideas—"

"Come by next week and we'll talk about them."

It came down once more to Amanda and Esther. Amanda was drunk; the usual fog around her had become a veritable pea-souper. Alex was grateful for Esther again, who hadn't waned the entire evening, who had spoken to everyone, who was still swanning around on her cane with a pleasantly sated look.

The two women hovered near the front door but didn't make any move to leave.

"I suppose I should be getting to bed," Alex said

"Yeah, sure," Amanda said. "I just thought—sure."

Against his better judgment he leaned in and kissed her, as fleetingly as he could manage, though a familiar whiff of her beneath the booze, fresh and a bit milky, brought a pang to him.

"I'll call you."

He didn't feel relieved when she'd gone, just cowardly and ashamed. Once in his life he would like to have sex he could actually feel good about.

He'd almost forgotten about Esther behind him.

"Oh," she said, a bit coyly he thought. "You weren't—I mean, you and that girl—"

"No, no. I mean briefly, yes. But not now."

Instead of leaving, she sauntered back to the couch and settled herself there like a contented chatelaine.

"I knew it," she said. "I knew there was something."

"Not really."

"But you slept with her?"

He grew squirmy.

"Yes," he stammered. "Once."

"I thought so."

There seemed something obscene in this line of inquiry, wrong, like discussing sex with a parent or child.

"Anyway it was a mistake," he said. "I shouldn't have done it."

"But she's so beautiful."

"Yeah, well." The image came to him unbidden of Amanda's face while they were making love, of that look of tangled emotion in it, of not quite being held to the earth. He knew what she was, he knew that sense of feeling insubstantial, as if someone could pass a hand through you. "A bit messed up, I think. Or something."

Esther reached for one of his cigarettes on the coffee table so naturally that it didn't seem wrong, somehow, for him to light it for her.

"Guys," she said. "They always get so weird after sex."

He had to laugh at that.

"Has that been your experience?"

"Well, not that I've had any lately."

He began to relax a bit. He took a seat next to her on the couch and
poured himself an inch of some sort of whiskey from a leftover bottle.

"I liked Stephen," Esther said. "He was so gentle. He told me about
his son."

Alex wasn't sure he'd heard her right.

"His son?"

"He's four, he showed me his picture. I guess the mother doesn't let
him see him much."

Alex's whole vision of Stephen shifted.

"He was married?"

"Just for a year or two. She was a separatist or something."

Alex had sat just a couple of yards from Stephen for nearly a year
now, yet couldn't even have said for certain what his surname was.

"I guess you have a way of getting people's secrets out of them."

She stubbed out her cigarette.

"I guess I do."

It might have been some paradoxical counter-effect of the alcohol
that she seemed as queenly and poised now as someone out of a Swiss
finishing school, all trace of her illness gone. She had lost any hint of the
garish look she'd arrived with, so that he could imagine her just some
normal young woman with a man at the end of an evening.

She reached over and took one of his hands in hers.

"Alex," she said, looking right at him, and then she leaned in and
kissed him on the lips.

A wave of revulsion went through him.

"Esther," he said, "I don't think this is such a good idea."

She kissed him again.

"Esther—"

"Just try it," she said in a coaxing tone.

"Esther, I can't."

"Just try." More insistent.

"I really can't."

"Why can't you?"

"I just can't." His mind was casting about wildly. "I'm too screwed up right now, with my breakup and everything. I just can't."

"Why can't you just try?" Her voice had turned entirely. "It's because I'm sick, isn't it? It's because of my disease."

"Esther, that's not it."

He saw her face go through a thousand emotions.

"Oh, Alex." The anger had already drained from her. "I just thought, it didn't have to be any big deal—"

She broke into tears.

"Esther—"

He put his arms around her and she melted against him.

"You don't know what it's like. Sometimes I go months and no one even touches me. It's like I'm already dead."

He rocked her in his arms, feeling the wet at his shoulder from her tears. Maybe it wasn't so far to go, just to touch her, to make her feel human. But he couldn't shake the sense of that awful revulsion that had gone through him.

"It'll work out for you," he said. "You're so wonderful. Someone will see that."

"You see it, and you're still not having sex with me." But she laughed, a sort of snort that came out between sobs. "Anyway, I guess I can still make a joke."

He helped her back to her apartment. By now the wine and the late hour had started to show. She fumbled with her key at her door and Alex took it from her and turned the lock. He caught a glimpse of her darkened apartment, the foreign shapes looming up, the bedroom doorway fading out to black.

"Would you like me to stick around for a bit?"

"Not if you're not going to have sex with me."

His own apartment looked like a battlefield, strewn with cigarette butts and dirty glasses and empty bottles. He glanced at the bottle he'd drunk from earlier: it was one of the fancy Scotches he himself had passed over at the liquor store. Stephen had brought it. Alex would never have done that, would never have left behind half a bottle of premium Scotch.

He retreated to his bedroom, unable to face the mess. His proposal was still sitting on his desk there. He'd made the mistake of skimming through it after his meeting with Novak and had been shocked at how lifeless it seemed next to the description of it he'd given Esther the day before. On impulse he pulled out his *Canadian Studies* essay from the shelf above his desk, to take solace from it. He didn't like to think he cared that much about it anymore, yet its pages had started to darken at the edges from his having thumbed through them so often. There were passages in it that still made him chuckle. "As for me and my horse," the epigraph read—and that was the joke, a satire à la Swift of the wonky postmodern notion of "misreading" using the wonderfully grim Canadian standard *As for Me and My House*—"we will serve the Lord."

He had written the paper on a whim, one of the many brilliant ideas for projects of one sort or another that he got on a daily basis and almost invariably never pursued. That had been at the height of his cynicism, when he'd been sick to death of the ambitious young things he'd run into at conferences and the fat-cat professors who used their graduate students to write their books. But then the acceptance had come from *Canadian Studies*—and sending it there had been another whim, though he'd taken the trouble of typing his covering letter on letterhead he'd filched from the university English office—and after the initial disbelief he had begun to feel a little glow inside him. For the first time in a while he had dared to think that there might still be a place for him in the world, that he might still be a star.

In the end the article hadn't been the new start he had hoped for but instead had inserted itself in his life like a poltergeist, wreaking havoc in every direction. It had probably been responsible, at a deep, Faustian level, for Liz's abortion; it had led Ingrid to him, in seeming repayment for Liz; it had landed him in this ill-advised Ph.D. It was as if he had sold out somehow without quite realizing it, as if it had been enough just to covet this little bauble held out to him for all the cosmic forces to turn against him. The abortion, really, had been the turning point: though his mind still rebelled at the thought of their having kept the thing, he could see how different his life would have been then, how much more orderly. He'd probably be pulling in a big salary with the Toronto school board, with summers off, instead of slumming at Berlitz and growing more desperate by the hour about his dissertation; and all the problems between him and

Liz, next to the miracle of a child, would no doubt have grown small. Even the issue of Ingrid would have been resolved: he could hardly have been expected to move across the ocean if he'd had a perfectly good family of his own already. He could then have assumed the only relationship with his Swedish offspring that made any sense, the amiable but distant father kept away by completely reasonable circumstance.

He had never asked Liz to get the abortion. He had left it to her; it was her body after all. It was easy to see now what a cop-out that had been, or, worse, how it had been sheer manipulation, because deep down Alex believed that Liz would have agreed to keep the baby in a heartbeat if he'd made it the least bit clear that that was what he'd wanted. In his own mind, he'd thought it crazy even to consider going ahead: it wasn't just the practicalities, that they had almost no income and the building they were living in, a drafty old tenement on Crawford, was under imminent threat of demolition; it was also that, for the first time it seemed, they had possibilities, not just from Alex's publication but from a show Liz had been part of where she'd been singled out for praise. Now was the moment to strike out, Alex had thought, not retreat into domesticity. But of course he hadn't said any of this to Liz: he had stood back, kept mum, and let her make her own decision.

Asshole.

He should never have started thinking about the matter. He might turn it over and over in his head and never see it right, whether he should have done this or that, what Liz would have done in turn. Who had been dishonest or disingenuous or manipulative, or whether, if he had just bitten the bullet and said yes, Liz, out of sheer contrariness, wouldn't have had the abortion anyway. He thought of Liz the way Freud had thought about dreams, that there was a point where matters retreated into the unfathomable like the umbilical cord into the womb. Ever since high school there had been the same weird connection between them, long before anything like sex had come into the picture, the same weird arguments over who knew what, the same scary intimacy like a last-ditch fire they were both huddled around. There were grievances between them from back then that they had never really forgiven each other for: that Alex had turned Liz down, for instance, when she'd invited him to the Grade 13 grad. Because he didn't want it to interfere with their friendship, was what he'd said, but they had both known he was simply waiting for a better offer, not this sexless sidekick he spent all his time with, who went around draped in such an excess of clothing—scarves, gym pants, oversize sweaters, men's parkas—that she seemed to have no body at all. He had ended up going with a girl he wasn't even attracted to just because she was slightly more in, something that in the Darwinian logic of adolescence, a period clearly designed by nature to kill off the weak, had somehow made perfect sense to him.

He'd been to her house once for supper, with her reclusive sister and the crazy German father who called her a slut and the mother who was overly friendly when Alex went by after school but would shoo him away before Liz's father got home from work. "The wop," Liz's father called him behind his back, according to Liz. But at supper he'd sat smiling and laughing nervously like a harmless old immigrant.

"I know your uncle Tony there at the factory. Always joking, always joking."

Years later, when he and Liz were actually involved, he would feel a strange stab when he thought back to this time, how he'd pretended he didn't see what Liz wanted, or rather puffed himself up with it and in the same instant denied it. Who knew what it was, the smell of outsiderness that had come off her or maybe simply that she was *like him*: this was the thing he couldn't forgive, that there was no gain in it for him, to be with her. They were like two people poised at a brink; the only way forward was down.

It wasn't until the end of university, when they were both living in Toronto, that they finally slept with each other, just before he left for Africa. Gin played a part, and the titillation of being in her boyfriend's apartment while he was away. Alex awoke the next morning feeling like he'd just discovered the proper use of something he'd long taken for granted, but Liz was already going through the room as if trying to cover up a murder.

"This can't ever happen again," she said at once.

"You didn't seem to mind it."

"You know as well as I do it would never have happened if you weren't leaving."

By the time he'd left the country they were no longer speaking. He'd written her once, and received no reply, and might have been ready just to cut her from his life if he hadn't come home such an invalid, with

Desmond behind him and nothing ahead. Only a matter of days had
passed before he phoned Liz's house to track her down.

"Alex! What a coincidence!" Her mother's over-bright voice, still
with that deluded hopefulness to it, desperate and a bit chilling. "She's
actually home this weekend. She'll be thrilled!"

Within a month he had moved back up to Toronto and rented a tiny
place in the market, but was spending most of his time at Liz's. She was
alone now, she had changed her life. After wasting her undergrad years
doing a business degree, she had gone back for art, what she'd wanted.
She took him to her studio at the college and showed him her work, large,
vibrant abstracts that didn't seem anything like Liz, that were utterly
buoyant.

"So that's it," she said. "It's pretty passé even to be working on can-
vas anymore."

"They seem, I dunno—fun. I mean, I like them."

What he really felt, looking at them, was a strange arousal—that Liz
had produced them, that these bright things had come out of her.

"Fun is all right," she said. "I can live with fun."

They were already sleeping together by then. Everything happened
like that, without question, as if it were inevitable, as if there had never
been a point of decision. They fell into sex the way they had that one
night, like something they'd merely put off, then never talked about it, as
if it were some secret about themselves they needed to keep. Alex felt like
he was in hiding, like he'd holed up in a safe house; it grew rare for him
to return to his own apartment except to collect his mail. Liz's apartment
was done up with plants and checkered tiles and plump throw pillows,
everything just so—he liked that there was nothing there that was his,
that reflected him, as if he had come back after the wars to a war bride
who'd made a new life for him.

He'd had a letter from Ingrid. He had spent a month with her before
the Galápagos, but already she seemed a stranger to him. There was a
tone to her letter, as if there was still a chance for the two of them despite
the gulf between them, that he couldn't bear. "Liz is someone I've known
since high school and maybe the person I'm fated to be with," he wrote
back, then never heard from her again.

When he started his Master's at U of T he gave up his place and
moved in with Liz. The apartment grew small with the two of them

always there. Liz had finished art school and was using the living room
as her studio, taking in ad work to pay the rent. She'd stopped doing her
abstracts and gone back to figures—still lifes, disembodied hands, a self-
portrait that showed her looking back over her shoulder as if at an
assailant. She asked Alex to sit for her, reclining him nude on the couch
draped in satins and velvets, and they ended up making love on the living room floor, in their wordless way, as if it was something their bodies
did that they couldn't be held accountable for.

They lay on the couch afterward, and he could smell her sweat.

"You never said why you stopped doing your abstracts."

"I was tired of them." Then, lightheartedly, "I shopped my slides
around, and no one seemed interested."

This was the first Alex had heard of this.

"What did people say?"

"That it didn't fit their aesthetic, that sort of thing."

She was still talking in the same easy tone. Alex knew nothing of the
art world except what he'd learned from Liz, but it seemed a bordello to
him, a lawless place.

"Maybe you should try something different."

He knew at once that he'd said the wrong thing.

"What do you mean, exactly?"

"I don't know. You're the artist. Try a new direction or something."

There was the smallest pause.

"I have."

She abandoned the nude of him after that, letting it sit untouched
on her easel a few days before finally burying it somewhere. So it began,
Alex thought, all the rattle and clang of recrimination and blame that
he'd been expecting since he'd moved in. This was the pattern between
them: they grew dependent on one another and then they turned, like
animals chewing off their own limbs. Liz had slowly cut her ties with
her old art school gang, most of whom had drifted off like her into the
ignominy of hack work; Alex had a couple of friends he still saw from
his undergraduate years, but at U of T, where a cold institutionalism
reigned, he simply went to his classes and came home. Then Liz had
had another of her ruptures with her parents: she had these regularly,
like phases of the moon, though in this case it was just as well, since
before it they had lived in fear that Alex would pick up the phone one

day when Liz's mother called—always early or late, to get the cheap
rates—and they'd be found out.

They fell into a phase of crazy arguments, reckless, pointless brawls
that never had anything to do with whatever was really at issue. Suddenly,
everything seemed wrong: Liz's anal little apartment, where Alex felt she
watched him now as if he were some squatter who'd broken in to despoil
the place with his fetid maleness; their sex, which had grown perfunctory,
until it seemed just the listless work of making Liz come so that he could.

"Just stop," she said once. "I feel like I'm alone."

He might have said something useful then.

"I'm doing my best," was what he said.

"What's that supposed to mean?"

"I dunno, it just feels like so much effort with you."

She left the apartment then and was gone the entire night. By morning Alex felt an inchoate bloody-mindedness, pacing the living room not
sure if he was dreading the worst or wanting it.

She came in just past dawn and sat beside him on the couch.

"Maybe we should stay apart for a while," she said.

This was really the crux of these arguments, how far they could go
before he turned her away.

"Let's just go to bed."

At some point, Liz stopped painting entirely. Alex wouldn't let himself notice at first, the corner of the living room where her easel stood feeling like a crime scene they were both determined to ignore.

"You haven't been painting," he said finally, as casually as he could
manage.

"Just waiting for a new direction."

This was the worst thing, he knew, letting her painting become a
battleground between them.

"Don't blame me if you don't know what you want to do."

He had crossed the line.

"You'd be happy if I painted fucking landscapes as long as they got
into a gallery! You mope around like I'd have to become famous before
you'd believe in me!"

He didn't know if Liz believed these things when she said them, if
either of them meant any of the things they said or were just spilling their
worst fears as if to cast a spell against them. Yet she was right, he didn't

believe, not really, couldn't have said if her work showed talent or not or if those painstaking hands of hers, which she'd spent weeks on, had any less merit than the cheery abstracts she used to do.

It never really occurred to him that they should simply end things. She had taken him in so unquestioningly, as if they shared a doom—there was nothing she did, not even the bitterest things, that wasn't somehow just a cover for this darkness that seemed to join them.

She didn't paint again for months, each of them keeping grimly to their little tasks until their failed selves, the specters of what they would not be, were like extra presences in the apartment. Some of Liz's old art school cronies asked her to join a project they'd started, making over an abandoned house with art, but she put them off.

"It's such a gimmick," she said to Alex. "It's just all the losers like me who can't get into the galleries."

Alex held his tongue, the subject so fraught by now there seemed no right thing to say. Then Liz finally agreed to sign on, but wouldn't let him anywhere near her work until the opening. She'd had the entire bathroom to herself, and had done it over in an elaborate trompe l'oeil that seemed to extend it out to several times its dimensions, with a hyperrealism that mirrored the room's wreckage but was also vaguely off-kilter, reaching off into implausible angles like an Escher woodcut.

Alex felt the usual terror go through him—he had no idea what to make of it.

"Wow," he said.

"You think it's all right?"

"It's amazing. All the detail."

She seemed so exposed. Then the next day they went through the dailies and found a tiny review of the show in which Liz's work, in a passing reference, was dismissed as "virtuosic." Alex was crushed.

"It's just some asshole critic," he said. "He liked that sappy wall etching in the living room."

But Liz had taken on an odd lightness, as if failure freed her.

"It doesn't matter. I had fun with it."

When the weekly entertainment tabloid came out, a leftist rag that always went out of its way to attack its own, Alex was afraid to look at it. Sure enough the review was a hatchet job: "Art House Old Hat." He was ready to get rid of it at once before Liz laid eyes on it, but then his eye caught her name. "I walked into the bathroom with the idea of using the facilities"—and Alex prepared himself for it, for the jibe, the withering dismissal—"and felt like I'd stepped through the looking glass."

There was more of the same, excessive almost, self-congratulatory, yet unmistakable: she had been singled out for a rave. It wasn't long before the calls started coming in, from other artists in the show, who offered their bright, bitter congratulations, from all the people who hadn't phoned Liz in months. Liz looked positively stunned, straining to live up to the headiness of the moment as if some notion of herself that she'd held sacrosanct had been shattered.

"I couldn't believe it!" she said, sounding as false as her well-wishers. "I thought Alex had printed it up as a joke."

They had no precedent in their lives for this sort of public anointing. For many weeks afterward they moved through an air of unreality, as if they'd been entrusted with some momentous task whose precise nature had yet to be revealed. Soon someone would come to the door and hand them their new lives—that was the sense of it for Alex. He wrote his article in these weeks and sent it off, and got his acceptance in such short order that they seemed under some charm. Then they went off to England for their splurge and had sex every night, the sort of urgent, wordless sex that worked best for them, as if there wasn't a moment to spare, as if they'd be found out at any instant.

It was only when they were home again that it occurred to Alex they might simply slip back into their old lives and nothing would be different. He was mired in application forms for his doctorate but was already losing the spark he had felt that day in Darwin's study—perhaps he was headed for nothing more original than the usual drudgery of academics. At the back of his mind an anger had begun to take shape against Liz. She'd had half a dozen calls from galleries after her review and yet had not so much as picked up a brush since then, going back to her ad work as if all the rest had been some youthful folly.

They were pressed for money, because of the trip. Then the notice came of some structural flaw in their building, and the threat of eviction.

"Shouldn't you be doing something?" he said. She had fought her way into art school against all opposition, her parents, her boyfriend. Now the prize shimmered before her and she wouldn't reach for it. "I mean, while people still remember the review."

"Like what? Showing my abstracts around again?"

Do some fucking new paintings, he wanted to say.

"It just seems such a waste."

When they found out Liz was pregnant this conversation came back to haunt him. The pregnancy had been pure stupidity—she'd been off the pill when they were in England because of a throb in her leg and they'd pushed the limit on her safe days. It felt like they were being punished for their bit of abandon. They sat sullenly at the kitchen table as if there was actually something to decide, but everything in Alex screamed *no*: it wasn't the time for them, not now, maybe not ever.

Every argument he could make seemed forbidden.

It's your body, he almost said.

"Just tell me what you want to do."

She never actually asked what he himself wanted, and so showed that she knew. There followed a couple of weeks of indecision that seemed like a desert they had to cross, and out of which Liz emerged looking as drawn and worn as an ascetic.

The agony of waiting had weakened him.

"We could make it work," he said, not meaning it. "I could get my teaching certificate."

"When would you do that, exactly?"

They went to the Morgentaler Clinic on Harbord, to avoid the red tape at the hospitals. They had to push their way past a straggle of protesters waving placards with slogans like STOP THE SLAUGHTER and EXODUS 20:13. Inside, half a dozen women sat stolidly in the makeshift waiting room, some with partners, some alone. Attendants in street clothes moved patiently among them handing out clipboards and forms, with a partisan air not so different from that of the protesters outside.

"How are you doing?" Alex whispered.

Liz's voice had gone completely flat.

"Just great."

The doctor came into the reception area from a back hallway, grim-faced and hurried. He had a quick word with the receptionist, then retreated without so much as glancing at anyone. Alex knew what a hero he was, a survivor of the camps, a champion of women's rights, and yet at the sight of him, hirsute and small and slightly simian, the first thought that passed through his mind was *Butcher*.

Alex's armpits were dripping with sweat.

"I think I'm up," Liz said.

His head filled with blasphemy while he waited. It seemed now that they had not asked themselves a single question about what they were doing here—what a fetus was, for instance, or how they could know such a thing, or how anyone could; what it could mean to have one scraped out of you. Once, before she'd decided, Liz had talked about the baby as if it were alive, how taken over she felt, how her whole body seemed to be shifting to make a place for it. But just that once.

She came out still dopey with sedatives and unhappy with pain. Alex had a feeling like there was grit in his soul.

"You okay?"

"Not really."

At home he dared to ask her how it had been.

"It was awful."

"You want to talk about it?"

"I just want to sleep."

That was it, all they ever said. For a few days Liz moved bitterly through the apartment, unapproachable, but then gradually her mood seemed to lift, or she made the effort for his sake, or just put up her walls—who knew, really, who wanted to know. It wasn't any big deal in any event. People had abortions all the time. Liz went back to her work, her restaurant ads and her layouts for industrial newsletters and her two-bit logo designs for local hair salons; Alex buried himself in his applications.

There was a cat that had started hanging around their back veranda, a big gray tabby with a collar but no tag who would stare in through the kitchen window but showed no interest when Alex set out bits of salami for him. Then one morning, somehow, he was in the kitchen.

Liz had let him in.

"He must be lost," she said, though it was the first time she'd given any sign that she'd even noticed him.

The cat moved through the kitchen as if he'd memorized it, sniffing corners, rubbing against chair legs, then doing some sort of quick calculation and suddenly leaping up to a stool and onto the counter. The faucet had a leak they'd never bothered to fix; the cat leaned out to it, with unmistakable intent, and lapped his tongue at the drips. It was what he'd been staring at all these days, those tantalizing droplets.

Liz had watched the cat's progress as if he were simply some natural event, making no move either to show him any welcome or to shoo him away.

"We should put up posters or something," she said. "We should find the owner."

What Liz meant by this, it turned out—Liz, who was allergic to everything, who hated hairs on things, who wasn't the type to court any compromise to domestic hygiene—was that they were taking the cat in. She put out a water bowl, bought cat food and litter at the Dominion, spread the litter in a cardboard box in a corner of her sanctuary, the bathroom. It was nothing short of deranged, either that or one of her insidious paybacks. She knew Alex thought pets were indulgences, that it was one of his little political credos.

He put up posters, but the days passed, and no one came. The cardboard litter box grew soggy, and Alex bought a proper one.

"We should give it a name or something," he said.

Liz had put her brave face on.

"What do you think?"

"How about Moses?" Alex offered. Because of the water. Because of the little bed of dried leaves and debris that he used to sleep in on the back veranda.

Exodus 20:13.

"Moses is great."

He wanted to strangle the cat, he wanted to stick it in a sack and dunk it in a barrel. He'd be sitting at his little desk in the bedroom—it was hopeless to work there, the room was Liz's, not his, every inch of it—and the cat would jump up into his lap, where it would purr and purr like an outboard motor.

He came upon Liz petting him once on the bed, sitting cross-legged while Moses lay stretched out before her like a sultan.

"I want to go up to Montreal," he said. "To look at the universities. You could come."

She didn't look at him. He wished she would scream at him so he could harden himself, so he could think again, *It was just a fucking abortion.*

"Were you planning on moving there?"

He let that pass.

"We could think of it. If you wanted."

———

By the time they actually moved to Montreal, what he'd thought of as a new start already had the feel of a nightmarish blunder. They had a vicious argument during the move, then arrived in the dark, in pouring rain, to an apartment that had seemed extravagantly roomy and full of character when they'd rented it but now looked merely derelict. Alex slumped down in an armchair with a cigarette, numbed from the drive, from the clatter of argument, while Moses wandered arch-backed and watchful from room to room.

"I could use a bit of help here," Liz said tersely from the kitchen, and Alex thought, *Bitch*.

Somehow they got through the first year. There were moments, enough of them, that seemed strangely untainted, as if they put on workaday selves for daily use who were able to make supper, have sex, take walks on the mountain, without dragging with them every hurt and resentment. But then some tension would arise in the unlikeliest place. They audited an art history course together until Alex made the mistake one class of grandstanding in front of everyone on the subject of sexism.

"I'm sure Rembrandt wouldn't care if you found his paintings sexist or not," the professor said dryly, and everyone laughed.

He didn't want to go back after that, but Liz simply brushed the matter off.

"I'm not giving up art history just because you've become a feminist all of a sudden," she said. But what she meant was, *You made me get an abortion*.

Winter came on with a brutality that sapped Alex's spirit. They'd left a room in the apartment for Liz's studio, but she used it mainly as a sort of guest room for Moses, whose little bed she'd arranged in a corner with his litter box beside it like an en suite. They hardly went out—Alex had the people he met at school and a couple of secondhand acquaintances, but Liz had no one, nor did she seem much taken with the friends Alex brought home. What Liz did a lot of, when she wasn't working on the few contracts she'd managed to bring with her, was watch TV—talk shows, sappy dramas, bad sitcoms. She had set up her old black-and-white in the bedroom, which more or less killed the prospect of sex.

"I can't believe the time you waste in front of that thing," he said, which in their new bitter shorthand meant, *Why aren't you painting?* The

TV became another war zone after that, so that they could not even sit down to watch the news together without this sense of freightedness between them.

Alex was taking a course called "Sex and Text" that had spurred his little feminist outburst in his art history class. Liz only ridiculed the course, leafing through his readings and pulling out phrases laden with the blind self-importance of academe. But after the theory they strayed into grayer zones, to books with titles like *Big Daddy* and *I Once Had a Master* that had to be picked up from behind the counter at the gay bookstore on St. Lawrence. Some of this stuff was like nothing Alex had read: there were cattle prods, razor blades, harnesses of every sort; there was role-playing that seemed to go to the very limits of the imaginable.

Liz picked up one of these books one night and began to skim through it.

"What is this stuff?"

"It's from my course."

"It reads like something from *Penthouse Forum*."

"Maybe." He felt like he'd been caught out in a perversion. "That's the question."

She was still reading.

"What a joke. So all that theory you guys talk about is just an excuse to read porn."

The incident left a residue between them. Even in his class there was always a tang in the air when they discussed these books, an unspent charge.

"You probably like that sort of stuff," she said in bed, though not quite in judgment.

He knew that if he just put her off with "Do you?" the moment would be ruined.

"Maybe *like* isn't the right word."

When they had sex he was rougher than usual, shifting her how he wanted, feeling his blood pound when she gave way. The thought went through his head, *She likes this.*

He could never say that to Liz.

"Wow," he said after, circumspect. "Was that all right?"

Already he could feel her pulling back.

"I guess you should read that stuff more often."

The memory of the rush he'd felt stayed with him. It was there like a goad when they made love again: *She likes this.* There was nothing wrong in it—he knew now that people gave themselves over to the wildest excesses. He had learned some tricks from those books of his, things he could do, such as pinning Liz's shoulders or holding her wrists, that were enough to give them a jolt without their having to admit what they were up to. That seemed the crux of it, the not admitting. It was how their sex had always been, this looking away as if it were shameful, as if its being shameful was what drove them to it.

The books were there in the apartment when he was out. Maybe she looked at them, maybe she lay in bed and masturbated or thought of him coming home and doing the things they described, forcing them on her. Not just what hurt, the whips and electrodes, the razor blades along the skin, but the head fucks. *Get on your knees. Bend over. Fucking slut.* It was a different kind of limit, a different place. He wouldn't let himself think these things through, they were too awful, really, too delicious, yet he thought he could see the inside of her head in a way he never had. Those late nights when her father had locked her out of the house and she'd slept in the garage, her mother pretending not to know; her silent sister. All the things they never talked about, the deep, viscous places they wouldn't go.

They carried on as if things were the same, had the same arguments, kept the same routines. But it felt all for show—every day seemed to move relentlessly toward the night, everything they did until then just a stalling, a way station. If they took care not to argue, it was for that, so they should arrive there; if they picked a fight it was the same, for that, to avoid risking the thing by making it clear. It was surprising how easy it was to move from their usual pettinesses into being these profligates, these goats, each time slipping closer to violence as if to find the point where they crossed over. *Take it inside you. Turn over. Dirty bitch.*

She would bend in half to take him, she would look at him, something she never did, she would come while he was fucking her instead of in some elaborate work of fingers and hands. She came as if it had got loose from her, as if she had wet herself. He wouldn't let himself wonder what went through her head then, when he called her names, when he fucked her as if she were anyone, as if she had no choice.

She'd let him hold her afterward as if it was something she owed him.

"I'm just going to have a bath," she'd say. "You go ahead and go to sleep."

For months he'd felt closed up in their apartment as if it were all he knew, but now something was different—not better, perhaps, but different. He was glad he had never brought up the whole question of their *relationship*, though a thousand times he'd wanted to; they'd never have got to this place then, whatever place it was. A dangerous one, maybe. It was just sex, after all, not revelation. Sex was what animals did: he thought of sex and saw the rabbits they'd kept on the farm, the males starting to hump before they'd even stuck the thing in, the females squirming away. Half the time the males seemed to shoot in the air—they'd have fucked corpses, dead rats, bits of fur on a stick. And yet. He would come into the apartment and Liz would be reading cross-legged on the couch or standing at her drafting board with her hair tied up, and he'd feel the thrum in his loins again, thinking what he would do to her.

He stopped to stare at the window of a sex shop off St. Lawrence, done up like a Halloween display.

"I think this is good for you," the woman inside said, a gravel-voiced Quebecoise. She held up a harness with so many clasps and chains you might have shackled a bear in it.

"That's fine," Alex said, mortified. "That's fine."

When he gave the thing to Liz, gift-wrapped in black paper, she was on her guard at once, so out of character was it for him to bestow random gifts on her.

She pulled off the wrappings.

"Is this some kind of a joke?"

The harness had been priced well beyond anything that could qualify it as a joke.

"Not exactly."

"What, then?"

"It's just something to use. I thought you'd like it."

"It's your sick fantasy, isn't it?" He knew by then that the situation was unsalvageable. "Mister fucking feminist."

They said every manner of thing after that, whatever entered their minds—her art came into it, and this fucking city he'd brought her to, and how he had sponged off her from the moment he'd come home. Alex went to his fallback, that he couldn't do anything right, that she was deranged. But he never quite said the things he'd sworn he wouldn't say, because he didn't have words for them, maybe, or was holding them back for some final onslaught, or just because he knew he'd made a fatal mistake. He had tried to pretend what they did was a game, the way it was in his books: you got whipped, you let yourself grovel at someone's feet, but it was all to a plan, it had a limit. Sex as therapy, was what it came down to. It wasn't that for him and Liz. It was avoidance, maybe, lies, the kind of knowing and not knowing that was like walking on a knife edge, but it wasn't therapy.

It was days before they spoke again, slowly shuffling back toward civility with the tired will-lessness that always set in after an argument. Meanwhile the harness, a final sale, sat stuffed in a back corner of the hall closet. Each time Alex reached in there he'd feel a twinge, of anger or shame or regret, he wasn't sure which.

"Look, I'm sorry about that thing," he said finally. "Let's just forget about it."

She had reached the point in her anger where she was just looking for an excuse to drop it.

"I probably overreacted."

They were both worn out by then. They ended up watching a movie together, silently nestling into each other on the couch as if letting their bodies do the work of forgiveness they couldn't. They smoked a joint, from a new batch he had, and got hopelessly stoned.

"I feel kind of weird," Liz said.

They hadn't had sex since the argument. In the bedroom they undressed, together but not quite so. He looked at her naked, at her taut, Teutonic body, always more shapely than he imagined it. It wasn't quite beautiful and yet there was something to it, an uncertain quality like a family resemblance that made him quicken and squirm.

She had slipped under the covers.

"You should get that thing," she said.

Her voice sounded disembodied.

"What? Are you sure?"

"We should try it."

She wanted to please him, which sent a strange gratitude through him, since he'd imagined himself beyond such efforts. The whole enterprise was a mistake, he knew it, yet he felt too stoned to properly reason it through. She had to lie prone on the bed while he bound her limbs. There were so many straps to do up. Moses got into the room, sniffing at the leather, batting at the straps, until Alex took him roughly out.

She was bound up like a trussed pig, ankles to wrists.

"It's a little tight," she said.

It was ludicrous for them to be doing this. They weren't the people for it. He had to pick his way into her as if negotiating a thicket. With each thrust, Liz's limbs strained against the harness.

"Is it hurting you?"

They were both talking with the same slowed remove, as if imper-sonating themselves.

"No, no. It's fine."

The smell of her came up in waves. He pushed into her and felt her body giving in to him. At some point he slipped over to another territory, as if she were an island or a country beneath him.

"I love fucking you," he said. "I love you."

In his memory afterward, all of this was like what electroshock might have been, an overload, a sort of blinding of the brain. They came, some-how. Liz was already crying by the time he started to undo her.

"You okay?"

"Yeah. I dunno." She shifted awkwardly against the straps, trying to turn from him. "It's just the pot."

Behind the image of Liz trussed up beneath him was his blurting out *I love you* to her like a turn-on, like taking a gun to her head.

In the morning they both seemed determined to act as if the previous night hadn't happened. They bickered over his smoking, which he'd promised to quit, and he went out in a huff to the Van Houtte's and smoked half a pack, coming home stinking like an ashtray. They argued in earnest now.

"Half the time it feels like you don't even live here. I might as well be alone."

"I might be around more if you didn't ride me like a fucking harpy."

They were just following a script—they might as well have been trailer trash, might as well have been their parents.

It was all beside the point.

"Why don't you just leave then, if I'm so awful?" she said. "Why do you even stay with me?"

At last, the Big Question had been brought into play. It was like a probe sent up, a test rocket, something to be contradicted, but now it was out there.

The actual work of breaking up took many months, through their second summer and fall in the city and into the winter. By then he had failed his theory comp, which had put his funding in danger, and lost all faith in his dissertation, matters he kept from Liz, instead holding them against her like grudges. Meanwhile Liz didn't crumble as he'd expected. From out of nowhere she had patched together a life, had got a teaching gig in Mount Royal, had landed a couple of contracts, saw friends whom Alex knew nothing of. She had started painting again, tight, intricately patterned abstracts like Islamic arabesques or bad acid trips that seemed to say, *You are killing me.*

This was the language between them now, these were the rules. They acted like people who had nothing to do with each other, whom they had to share space with like roomers, but to whom in some other moment, some shift in the warp of things, they might have to answer. He brought Katherine home under these new rules, back when she still had the look of Anne of Green Gables, and Liz came across them having tea in the kitchen, though he never drank tea.

"Alex says you're a painter," Katherine said, and asked to look at her work. She had ideas about it, which she brought up, and Liz was animated, appreciative.

"What a bunch of pretentious crap," Liz said the instant Katherine had gone, by which she meant, *You want to fuck her.*

He was angry at her all the time now. He was angry if she reprimanded him for some oversight and angry if she didn't, angry if she let him have sex with her and angry when she put him off. He was angry about his furtive outings with Amanda, that he had this secret life but it was so pathetic. He was angry about his smoking. It wasn't as if Liz hadn't smoked her own share before this campaign of hers, but now it had become a *thing*, a moral imperative. Because of her asthma, because of her allergies. Because of the fucking cat, even, that was how low he was, willing to poison the animal for his habit. These were the kinds of accusations she made. It didn't matter that he didn't smoke in the apartment anymore, that she hadn't had an allergic reaction since he'd known her; what mattered was that he give in. Half his energies went to hiding his smoking from her, to sucking mints, finding bathrooms, carrying gum and oranges in every pocket. He'd squeeze spray from the orange peels onto himself to hide the smell from her; he'd pick fights so he wouldn't have to get near her. It didn't make sense: he was a grown man. But then none of it made sense. It didn't make sense that they never talked about breaking up except as the last screaming threats in the arguments they had. It didn't make sense that they still had sex.

The sex was like his smoking: it had its own life now, its own will, always worked out whatever logic it needed to stay alive, whatever excuse. It was most intense after they'd fought—maybe they fought just to have it, or fought to pay for it, or fought so there wasn't a chance they might have to talk about it, and so end it. Moses in his litter box was fussier than they were: at least he covered his shit, and hunched himself sheepishly to let it out, while they shat and then wallowed in it as if there wasn't any point anymore in vying for each other's good opinion.

She took an X-Acto knife to his books once, his expensive theory texts and a 1901 edition of *The Origin* he'd paid fifty pounds for in England. It must have crossed her mind then, as it did his, how thin the line might be between this step and the next, though all he could think of, seeing that knife in her hands, was how he would fuck her. How he'd make her pay.

"Why don't you go fuck Katherine?" she said. "Why don't you go read her your fucking literary theory?"

She was as angry as he was, he knew that, but he wouldn't let himself think of it, wouldn't let himself be blunted. Blunted from what? From getting up a feasible escape velocity, maybe, but also from the sex, which had to be fed, which they had to break up the furniture for, the walls, until they'd burned down the house.

Somehow they managed to carry on until Christmas. Liz was on the outs with her parents and he went home alone, feeling putrid with secrets. His parents were in their new house now, a warehouse of a place full of cold, empty rooms without uses or histories. Christmas Eve they served salted cod, *baccalà*, and Alex thought he would retch.

"Give him those bones you left for the dog," his father said, and Alex actually left the room and sat crying on the toilet as if he was five again.

He spent New Year's Eve with a friend in Toronto, without telling Liz. When he got back to Montreal the chill in the apartment was so palpable it was like stepping into a meat locker.

Liz went around the apartment furiously throwing things into a bag in a show of leaving.

"Where were you, exactly?"

"Home."

"You weren't fucking home, I called."

That would have been the best thing, if she'd actually left and never returned. *Just end it*, he thought. Instead they had one of their free-for-alls, pulling out every stop, until Liz was in hysterics, accusing him of every manner of perfidy, throwing things at him, bawling. He thought of her closed up here over the holidays, slowly going mad.

"Let's just stop," he said. "Let's stop."

But already he was thinking ahead to the sex. He took her there on the couch while she was still crying.

"Tell me the truth," she said. "Tell me you're not cheating on me."

How could she ask him that, how could it matter? It was as if she was lowering herself. It was as if they still had a chance.

Alex was in his bed. Over in Chernobyl it would be mid-morning already, and they'd be dumping planeloads of sand on the fire; in Engelström Ingrid would be making coffee in her kitchen, setting out the children's breakfasts. Even now, he could call. He had a flash of generic blondness and tried to conjure something real, something flesh and blood, but couldn't get beyond the barest intimation.

Who knew how long he and Liz might have gone on like that, if Ingrid's letter hadn't arrived. They might still be at it now, wasting away in that apartment while Moses circled them, wondering at their derangement. Ingrid's letter, with its odd, familiar stamps and script, seemed to reach him from another dimension: different rules applied there, humans were different, and what was expected of them. When he read it his first reaction wasn't at all what he later liked to tell himself, that he should go to her at once, but a kind of shrugging off like someone turning over in a bed, feigning sleep. It wasn't important, was what he'd thought. *I could ignore it.*

He put the letter in the bottom of a drawer, where Liz wouldn't see it.

Some days passed, a few or several, he lost track. It was bitterly cold, he didn't go out, he and Liz fought and had sex. He had dreams in which the boy tracked him down, and he had that sick sense of no redemption, no excuse.

Liz sensed something different in him, watching his every move, waiting to catch him out. He couldn't bear it.

See, he thought, *I have a child after all.*

"Where are you going?"

"Out, for Christ's sake. Just out."

He came home late from his theory class, drunk, and Liz was just sitting in the dark in the living room in her robe, waiting.

"You're fucking her, aren't you?"

"What?"

"You're fucking Katherine. Just admit it."

"What are you talking about?"

She sounded so certain and hard that Alex thought she might be telling the truth.

"You're fucking crazy," he said. "You're fucking nuts."

"I don't even know who you are," she said.

Alex's brain told him, *Say something stupid. Say anything.*

"The truth is I'd fuck her if I had the chance. At least it would be something normal."

"You fucking asshole!" She was hitting at him. "You fucking asshole!"

He felt a surge of adrenaline: this could be it, the end.

"Hit me! Hit me!" He tussled with her. "Get the knife, why don't you!"

They had fallen back onto the couch. He knew what would come next, they both must have, it was what happened with them, though a part of him thought he should cross a line this time, so they couldn't go back.

"Get off of me! Get off!"

She hit his lip with the flat of her hand and he tasted blood. After that he couldn't have said what exactly happened—there was just the mess of clothing and limbs, the sense of resistance, but there was always resistance. He held her wrists down, what he always did, heard her sharp intake of breath, felt her hips against his, either fighting him or rising to meet him.

He still had his pants around his ankles when he rolled off her onto the floor.

His head was spinning.

"Fuck." He hung his head between his knees. "Fuck."

He wouldn't look at her. He was trying not to think, was waiting to see how she would cast the thing, waiting to see what it had been.

He heard her turn away and pull her robe around her. Moses was watching him from the kitchen doorway.

"I think you'd better go," Liz said.

That was it, like a door closing. He jammed some stuff into a suitcase, just random handfuls that he grabbed from the bedroom, and stumbled out. When he was on the street he threw up on the sidewalk, once and then again.

two

— *October* 1986 —

So now all who escaped death in battle or by shipwreck
had got safely home except Ulysses.

HOMER
The *Odyssey*

Alex stood in the concourse of the convention center, a huge seventies-era hangar in soaring concrete and plate glass, and scanned the sea of milling delegates trying to spot María. She had insisted on coming over on her own. Around him, people were talking about protocols and polar vortices and catalytic cycles, the crowd a weird mix of science geeks and guys in business suits and greenies in jeans and tie-dye. It was the greenies who seemed to be spewing the most jargon, everyone else busy elbowing toward the complimentary doughnuts at the coffee table.

From somewhere he heard a shout of "Ah-leex!" loud and unabashed, like a mother calling a recalcitrant son.

"Ah-leex! I am here!"

She was over by the registration table, wearing her trademark pullover and tight jeans. His heart still stopped a bit whenever he saw her, at the sheer *abundance* of her, though in the three months or so that he'd been dating her, if that was what you would call it, he hadn't got any more share of that abundance than the fleeting salutational kisses on the cheek she allowed him.

He came up to her, and gave her one now that she hardly acknowledged.

"Queekly," she said. "Soon they will start. I have your card."

Somehow she'd managed to get him accreditation. She'd been in the country less than a year but already knew her way around bureaucracies, official languages, the nuts and bolts of existence here, better than Alex did.

"I don't think I can stay long," he said tentatively. When she let that pass, he added, "You'll still come by my place later? For supper?"

She had taken him by the elbow.

"Come, we must hurry."

He was an idiot wasting his time here; he should have been home preparing his lecture for Canadian Literature. The course had looked like a good idea when he'd agreed to teach it back in May, but now the workload for it occupied most of his waking life.

It was the first plenary. It remained a mystery to him that María had got involved in this Greenpeace stuff, which he'd always considered the soft end of political activism. Some kind of post-traumatic sublimation, he figured, throwing her lot in with tree huggers so she wouldn't have to think about the vicious war—he'd been reading up on it—that she'd left behind back home.

They had come to a table at the entrance to the auditorium neatly arrayed with what looked like Sony Walkmans.

"You must give your license or son'thing," María said.

"Sorry?"

"For the translation."

Instead of his license he pulled out his part-time faculty card, with the obscure intent of impressing someone—María, who couldn't have cared less? The girl at the table, who looked all of sixteen?—but then actually regretted parting with it.

The girl handed him his Walkman without so much as looking up at him.

"Aren't you taking one for yourself?"

"Is no need," María said.

He still couldn't believe he was really with her. He felt like the dog who had caught the car: this never happened to him, that he actually wound up with a woman he coveted. When María's class at St. Bart's had ended he'd assumed he'd never see her again, but then out of the blue Miguel had called and invited him to a party at their apartment.

"To return the favor," he'd said. "Is Salvadoran way."

Alex hadn't put much store in the thing. He'd figured Miguel's tiny apartment would be so crowded with Latin revelers he'd never get anywhere near María, if she was there at all. But then he'd got there to find just a tiny handful of other invitees—a shy couple just arrived from San Salvador who didn't speak half a dozen words of English; a paunchy former-hippie type from St. Bart's, Bernie, who had *loser* written all over him; another Salvadoran, Luisa, rake-thin and with a decided limp in one leg but who had a streak of acid to her, directing asides in Spanish to the others the whole evening that were clearly barbs against him and Bernie. Then there was Miguel, of course, the impresario; and María.

The place looked different from when he'd come before. In what had been Miguel's room the kitchen table had been set up with a brightly patterned tablecloth and plates of hors d'oeuvres, the porno and muscle-men removed from the walls and colored shawls placed over the lamps to dim the lighting. It all looked so civilized and formal, not at all what he had expected. Then there was the strange intimacy of the event, this odd mix whose precise chemistry Alex couldn't reckon. Before they sat down to dinner—since that appeared to be what was going to happen, though Alex, who hadn't understood this, had wolfed down a sub before heading over—they were practically standing on each other's toes, María's room still curtained off and no one making any move to colonize the kitchen. Alex, as usual, ended up talking to the person in the room he was least interested in, trading half-hearted anecdotes with Bernie about life at St. Bart's. But then they sat down to supper and he actually found himself next to María.

"Oh," he said awkwardly. "Is this all right?"

"Is your place," she said.

Once they were seated the dynamics in the room grew clearer. From the fun Luisa kept poking at Bernie and the arch looks she directed at Miguel, it was plain Miguel was setting them up. That left Alex, however; Alex and María.

He asked María about the hors d'oeuvres but then made the mistake of using the word *specialty*, botching his explanation of it so that she thought it referred to some kind of ingredient.

"Is Miguel," she said, closing the topic off. "All food tonight is Miguel."

He hadn't realized how rudimentary her English was. He was begin-ning to despair of actually having a conversation when he discovered she was fluent in French.

"I study in Paris," she said. "One year."

Alex wasn't sure what to make of that. It was what the bosses did in those Latin countries, sent their children off to Harvard and the Sorbonne.

"*C'est très beau, Paris,*" he offered.

"*Oui, oui, c'est évident.* But I missed my own country."

He had to struggle to keep up with her. It was probably the first time since he'd moved here that he'd had an actual conversation in French. He was exhausted by the end of the evening, not just from the French but from the feeling he'd been engaged the whole time in some long, irresolvable argument—over what, he couldn't have said, except that there was hardly a comment of his that María hadn't found a way to resist or contradict. He lingered behind after the others had gone, but without much hope.

They had switched back to English by then.

"I suppose I should go," he said, unable to screw up the courage to make any sort of play.

María's eyes flitted briefly to Miguel.

"Next week," she said. "Is Salvador party. You can come."

So it had begun, their series of dates that were not quite dates. After the first party there had been dinners, fund-raisers, Salvadoran art shows at tiny hole-in-the-wall spaces on St. Lawrence or Duluth, Salvadoran soccer games at Jeanne Mance Park. Once, early on, Alex had dared to suggest that the two of them go out to dinner somewhere on their own.

"Is boring, no, only two?" she'd said.

After that, he'd just gone along with whatever agenda she set, even though he couldn't rightly say he was making any progress with her, however that might be judged. Mostly, when they were together, there wasn't even a chance to talk properly: the music was too loud, or María was speaking in rapid Spanish to her other friends, or there was just too much going on, *pupusas* were being handed around or someone had started a sing-along or there was some heated argument on a fine point of Salvadoran politics. The worst of it was that he didn't really possess any extraverbal communication skills—María had quickly given up taking him onto the dance floor, though that never stopped her from finding other, more suitable partners. Seeing her move out there, with a visceral precision that seemed its own dialect, he felt like a closet WASP, as if this tight-assed, godforsaken country of his had somehow beaten him down to its own image.

They'd reverted to English as their lingua franca, the only real asset Alex brought to the table, but the switch hadn't given him much advantage in their exchanges, or deflected María from the thankless but necessary work of challenging his every utterance. If he disparaged something, she'd find a way to sing its praises; if he tried to raise something up, she'd be quick to dismiss it. Alex figured this was some sort of Latin courtship ritual, like a tango, though more often than not she caught him out. She'd torn a strip off him when he'd claimed Canadians were less racist than Americans, using the unfair advantage of actual experience.

"Canadians, they think they are very good," she said. "But in Canada, only six thousand Salvadorans. In U.S., six hundred thousand."

Never mind that all of them were there illegally and that the Americans were shipping bombs to her country as if they were Corn Flakes. Yet he had to take her point: even in the Land of Reagan some sort of place had been found for those hundreds of thousands, while the Canadians let in their piddling handfuls and thought they were saving the world.

After a few of these batterings, Alex grew more careful. Most of what passed for his worldview suddenly seemed horribly glib: he'd always thought of himself as holding the right opinions, but there was a whole order of things he'd never seen through to, that his little cocoon-life had always protected him from. He'd had an image of being a sort of confessor to María, but grew more and more uneasy about picking his way into the minefield of her personal life.

"Because of the union," she said, when he'd screwed up the courage to ask why she'd left home.

"The union made you leave?"

She actually laughed.

"Because I was part of the union. Is very hard then."

She'd been a teacher in San Salvador, he'd got that much out of her—"*dans la banlieue*," she'd said, in the suburbs, whatever that could mean. He couldn't picture it, what her school might look like, what sorts of lesson plans she might write up. All he knew of her country were the acronyms he read in the news, FMLN, FECCAS, FAPU, ERP, the splinter groups within splinter groups, the leftists who couldn't be trusted and the rightists who could. In the library he looked up articles in back issues of *The New Republic* and *The Manchester Guardian*, but the more he learned, the murkier things became: here was a country with a semblance of order, opposition parties, an elected government, but all that was the merest scrim, a rag draped over the void. In a garbage dump outside San Salvador truckloads of bodies showed up every morning in various states of mutilation, split in half, maybe, or with the heads cut off or the severed genitals stuffed in the mouth, and all this went on while American congressmen praised the progress in human rights and voted funds for new helicopter gunships. The bodies were just a sideshow: meanwhile, there was the war, whole villages burnt to the ground if the rebels had so much as begged a glass of water in them, and half the country in refugee camps, where you waited for the chance in a million that some government or church group would pick you out from the miserable rest and take you home.

At El Mozote, the soldiers brought everyone to the square and separated the men from the women and children, putting the men in the church and the women and children in some nearby houses. Over the course of a morning they tortured the men and then executed them, either decapitating them in the church with machetes or taking them to the woods outside town to be shot. In the afternoon, they started with the women, first the younger ones, whom they raped and killed, then the rest, whom they shot in groups in a house at the edge of town. Some of the children they had already hanged from trees around the playing field near the school; the remainder they herded into the sacristy at the back of the church and machine-gunned through the windows. Only two people survived, a boy who ran into the woods after seeing a baby speared on a bayonet, and a woman who somehow managed to crawl behind a bush when her own group was taken out to be shot.

It beggared the mind that humans could ever do such things, and yet Alex couldn't remember having taken any special notice of the event when it had first come to light. Even now he could feel his brain trying to shunt it off to some back corner: there was no use to it except the guilty thrill of its unambiguousness, its stark evidence that the enemy was a monster. Beyond that there was only undigestible horror, the blood and the screaming, the children hanging from tree limbs while their legs twitched. None of these things brought him closer to María—rather, he felt the weight of them like a third person between them, someone who knew, and knew, and made anything he could say pointless. He kept seeing the scrubby woods of El Mozote, the soldiers, the mud houses, like a bad dream he couldn't shake. The soldiers were just rebels with better uniforms, disgruntled peasants whom the army had got to first. People heard of these savageries and always imagined themselves as the good guys, but Alex wasn't so sure: if the captain had come to him and said, "Kill the children," who knew if he'd have resisted.

It didn't help to be off spelunking like this in the gray zones of moral relativism when he was at one of María's church-basement solidarity nights. Not a lot of the people there were disgruntled peasants, it turned out—they were ideologues, Marxist-Leninists, Trotskyites, Maoists, educated urbanites like María and Miguel who hadn't clawed their way up the continent to get there but had taken a connecting flight through Miami to Dorval. He met a mechanic who ran a hamburger joint off St. Lawrence; an accountant who'd done agitprop at a camp in Costa Rica but worked in construction now; a sociologist who'd been an advisor to the guerillas, on matters like the most humane colors to paint the detention cells where they held kidnap victims. He never met an actual fighter, he wasn't sure why: maybe they didn't survive long enough to leave, or were just having too much fun.

He could tell there were all sorts of fault lines at these gatherings, but was never quite sure where they ran. There'd been betrayals and reversals, splinterings, questions over methods, but it wasn't as if people were ready to bear their wounds to him. He got treated probably just as he deserved, as someone who couldn't be expected to understand. A scuffle broke out once at one of the pan-Latino nights, and it took him a while to figure out what had happened: a couple of Cubans had tried to crash the event, looking for women or just lonely, and had been roundly turfed out. The Cubans were reviled for having abandoned Fidel, although in the Great Chain of Latino Being they still had a certain cachet over the Salvadorans, who languished on the bottom links, well below the Chileans and below even the Guatemalans, who at least had their colorful national garb to set them off. *Guanacos,* the Salvadorans were called: hard workers, but not too bright.

María fit half the national type. She'd take him to these events—though it was more as if Miguel did, and she just happened to come along—and then she'd be off arranging tables or selling food or carting kegs of draft to the bar while he was left in some back corner with the men. It put him in mind of the courtships he'd seen in his childhood, where the suitor would come and drink highballs in the living room with the males while the women did the work. Except that there was no intimate moment afterward, with the trailing chaperones: the whole night might pass, and he'd be lucky to so much as bump elbows with María. Meanwhile his conversations at the back of the room, with men who all stood a good head shorter than he did, were never quite as compelling as he might have hoped: there was all the forced bonhomie to be got through, until his face hurt, and the problems with language and noise, the sense of sticking out like an extra appendage. It was almost worse than getting stuck with the other gringos—*las masas*, he thought of them as, the hangers-on, the milling dispossessed—or with Miguel. Miguel came and went, had his own shadowy network of associates that he checked in with like a secret service agent, but sooner or later he always turned up next to Alex.

"Is good for you, man? You like it?"

He kept trying to figure Miguel's angle. More than once it crossed his mind that Miguel was trying to marry María off to him. Alex was ashamed at how his blood quickened at the thought: he would stoop as low as that, in a pinch. Over time, surely, she'd grow to love him, which he took to mean that she would sleep with him. But then this was the sort of scheme at which María would have laughed out loud, even Miguel would have understood that.

He doubted he'd ever seen Miguel and María exchange more than a dozen words the whole time he'd known them. Yet some line of force joined them, nothing as straightforward as affection but more like an animal awareness. He thought of Miguel as her chaperone, but the matter wasn't as obvious as that—he was always there in Alex's peripheral vision, sometimes just standing alone, talking to no one, watching over things, yet Alex had the sense that if he'd been the sort to get María off by herself, Miguel wouldn't have stood in his way. But then he wasn't the sort; maybe that was why Miguel had chosen him.

About the only time Alex and María had actually been alone together had been at a mass, at her little neo-baroque church in the East End. Alex hadn't been to mass in years, and it felt to him like the primitive blood ritual it actually was.

"You are not a Christian," she said after, in her blunt way. "I can see it."

He reddened. There had seemed an openness to her in the church that he'd never seen before, as if she might be approachable, someone he might get around to touching one day.

"I was raised one. But no. Not anymore."

"Is okay," she said, making light of the subject. He'd caught sight of her room once and there'd been a shrine in the corner with a little plaster Madonna and votive candles. "Is still time."

He didn't know what made him think he could bridge gulfs like these. He thought about her constantly, obsessed with her with the sort of achy unreasonableness, the readiness to court humiliation, that he hadn't felt since high school. Yet the more he saw her, the less there was to say. She was working two jobs now, waiting tables and doing piecework for a sweatshop on the Plateau; he'd call her and dread getting her brother and suddenly hang up after the second ring, then ten minutes later call again. Then he'd manage to see her and there was always the same sense of anti-climax. The few times he'd stolen a moment alone with her at the end of a night he had stood there at her door, the blue light of late-night TVs flick-ering in the neighbors' windows, and all feeling, all hope, had drained from him. It wasn't just El Mozote and all that; it was everything, his life, the lie he had made of himself as this shambling, good-hearted white guy.

"Well." He'd lurch in awkwardly for the kiss on the cheek. "*Hasta la vista.*"

"*Sí, sí, hasta luego.*"

More and more she was just this burden to him, of knowledge, of thwarted desire. He'd joined a local chapter of Amnesty International over the summer: not for her sake, he told himself, and certainly not as anything he'd even dare mention to her, and yet she was the one who had driven him to it. Amnesty was exactly the sort of white, liberal do-gooder group he loathed, but then he came across an interview with a former death squad member in one of the journals he had been reading.

"If there was a protest from Amnesty or something," he said, "then we let them go. Otherwise, we killed them."

Twice a month now he met in an airless room in the downtown Y with a group of lonely-looking hair-shirters like himself and drafted let-ters to tyrants around the world politely beseeching them to cease their atrocities. At home, he continued the work on his new personal com-puter, a suitcase-sized portable with a flip-up plasma screen that he'd talked his father into funding—or rather, that his mother had, on his behalf—to help with his dissertation, though so far about all he'd done on it was write his Amnesty letters. "Your Excellency," the letters began, or "Your Highness," or "Your Grace." *It has come to our attention. There have been reports. We are deeply concerned.* He sent the letters out not so much because he believed in them but because he reasoned that even if he didn't, it didn't mean they wouldn't work. He had quickly learned to avoid the Salvadoran cases: too much conflict of interest, he thought, after appeals started coming in against the guerillas under the dreaded heading "Extrajudicial Executions."

Somehow he had frittered away his summer like this, mooning over María and finding every excuse to avoid whatever was truly pressing. His dissertation, for one thing, on which the only progress he'd made was drafting a new, as yet unapproved, proposal; getting his life in order, for another, making a plan, sorting out his priorities. He'd been home for a week, with the obscure intention of gleaning some sort of insight into how families ticked; though with each day that passed, it only became clearer why he abhorred them. There were children everywhere all of a sudden, nieces and nephews he'd taken for granted for so long they seemed like weeds he hadn't tended to.

"Forget about romance," his sister Mimi had said once. "Your children are the biggest love affair you'll ever have."

At the time he'd thought, *Not enough sex,* but now he hung on the notion as if it might save him. Then he went by to see her.

"I'm not even sure I *like* my children," she said now. She was about half his size, the legacy, probably, of protein deficiency back in the old country and a bout of anorexia as a teen, though now she looked wasted away from even her usual elfin self. She'd just built a new house that she hated, so that there were rooms in it she wouldn't even enter, so far did they fall from her hopes.

"My children are like strangers to me. They're like these lugs who showed up here and I have to look after them."

It was true: her children were lugs. Mimi loved books, loved conversation, had had hopes, but her boys, three in a row and big as oxen, no protein deficiencies there, spent their days in the rec room glued to the Mario Brothers. Mimi had raised them, but they hadn't turned out like her. They had turned out like her husband Nick. Alex remembered finding him alone with them once when they were little, and the smallest screaming bloody murder when Nick had tried to pick him up.

"I want Mommy! I want Mommy! I want Mommy!"

Nick had put the kid down as if he were a ticking bomb.

"Okay, okay." Not panicked, really, not angry; just baffled. He was a good man; he liked American football, he'd been to university, he never used five words when three would do.

"You might want to pop next door and get your sister," he'd said.

Alex wasn't sure what it meant, that Mimi had given her lifeblood, had given up teaching, had read Dr. Spock, only to produce these pod-kids who were nothing like her. Meanwhile Nick had stood back like a breeder watching his stock and had somehow prevailed.

"They're just teenagers," Alex said. "They'll come out of it."

"All I live for now is when they leave home. It's awful but it's all I can think about."

Alex tried his luck with his brother Bruno's daughter, Melinda. She was five, a better test case. He took her to lunch at McDonald's; he took her to the petting zoo at Colasanti Farms. It was a perfect day. In the evening they sat with her folks and went over it.

"Tell them about the lion cub," he said. "How it came up to the window."

Melinda completely ignored him, looking off to one side with a wicked little half-smile.

"She's probably just tired," her mother said. Alex got into his father's pickup and drove home, though in the driveway, finally, he turned off the engine and sat blubbering like a child because he'd been snubbed by a five-year-old.

That had been his refresher in family dynamics. Back in Montreal—who knew why he chose this moment for it?—he got out his little address book from years before, filled with the names of people he'd met in hostels or on roadsides or at currency exchange booths whom he hardly remembered, and he called Ingrid. He heard the ring tone at the other end, with its echoey European chirr, and the panic set in, at all the questions he didn't know how to answer.

There it was, her Swedish singsong.

"*Hejsan.*"

"It's Alex. From Canada."

A long pause.

"Oh. I see."

Things went downhill from there. The sureness he'd thought he'd feel at the sound of her voice, the knowing what to say, hadn't come.

"I got your letter," he started.

Her English was rusty.

"Yes. I have wondered."

"It came a while ago, actually. January, I think."

Another pause.

"Oh." Why had he admitted that? "So. Then, you are not so convinced."

"Sorry?"

"Not sure," she corrected. "What you would like."

Every word seemed so freighted. He'd been an idiot to think they could just pick things up like old times, as if all these years hadn't passed.

"It's just that my life is a bit complicated right now." But he'd grown defensive. "It's not as if I can afford to just hop on a plane."

That had been the worst thing to say. The tone was off, the suggestion of imposition, the crass sound of *afford*.

The last time they'd been together, they had argued over money.

"Yes, I see," Ingrid said, and then, with sudden Oxford precision, "But of course, you needn't have answered me."

Afterward he wondered if he hadn't intended to botch things. *It's not as easy as you think* was what had been going through his head. But she had softened finally, had sounded almost contrite.

"Maybe it's a better idea you should write me a letter. Maybe it's clearer."

For all his months of agonizing, he felt he'd come nowhere. They hadn't even mentioned the boy, not in so many words—it was as if there was some test he had to pass before they could get to that. Then the days went by, then more, and the letter didn't get written. He tried, then again, but couldn't get the tone right, kept slipping into self-pity and excuse, couldn't find the balance between what to include and what to withhold. *The boy*, he kept thinking; what mattered was the boy. He did a draft on his computer but then reverted to longhand—he couldn't bear those tight little dots that his printer spit out, as if there was nothing of him in the words, as if he hadn't sweat blood.

He could barely remember now what he'd said in the letter he'd eventually sent out. Two tight little pages: one for the past and one for the future, that was how it had seemed to him. He'd weighed every word, as if he were on probation, though there was also the other side of it, a kind of seeking permission or a waiting to be told, *This is what's right*. He could be let off the hook, still; there was that chance. He thought of that, and saw himself falling, with what felt like freedom or terror, he couldn't say which.

Nearly a month had passed now since he'd sent the letter off. With each day that went by without a response, his thoughts grew more wild. He'd been too dry, too removed, as if they were dealing with a piece of real estate to be portioned off; he'd said the expected things, the ones any idiot could guess, but not the ones that mattered. He couldn't remember if he'd offered to go to him, if he'd been as clear as that: was that possible, had he left out the most important thing? In his own mind nothing counted, really, until he showed up in the flesh. He ought to be home right now calling or writing again, offering to board the first plane, instead of sitting here at a conference on ozone depletion with a woman who was so extraneous to the main thrust of his life that to be with her was little more than a way of not being with himself.

Alex was no longer following the speakers. One after another, middle-aged white men had got up at the podium spouting rhetoric, mostly in English, though Alex had switched his headset to Spanish to help shut them out.

Tell me, Alex, because I think people will find this pretty darn fascinating: How in bejesus did you end up in the mountains of Morazán running guns for the FMLN?

Well, Peter, it was really my wife, María, who got me into it.

Beside him María was taking notes, close enough for him to feel the heat off her, though the whole session she had hardly so much as glanced at him. Ghostly redolences of sweat wafted over from her, sharp and undoctored, that made something go weak in him.

He took off his headset to make the effort, for María's sake, to follow the current speaker. But he was speaking in French.

María leaned over to him.

"Is very interesting, no?" she whispered. "Is very important, this conference."

He had spent all summer reading about the Salvadoran war, when he should have been boning up on chlorofluorocarbons.

"I have to admit I'm not quite following everything."

She tapped his headset.

"You must use it for the French."

Maybe she was right; maybe this stuff was more important than he gave it credit for. What put him off about the environmentalists was the religion they made of things, how they seemed to have come back full circle to wood spirits and river gods, but maybe they were just correcting the great life-denying aberration that monotheism had been. Alex blamed a lot of things on monotheism—his messed-up sex life, for one.

He'd put his headset back on.

"*Aleex!*"

"Oh. Sorry."

"Is finished for coffee break. We must go."

They had set out refreshments in the concourse. Alex lit a cigarette— the place was already blue with smoke—and started beating a path to the coffee table. Along the way María ran into a fellow greenie, a tousled-haired Quebecois with the flimsy T-shirt and thin-legged jeans of the St. Lawrence bohemian set, and the two of them launched at once into animated French. Alex disliked the guy on sight. He had that natural elegance to him that Alex, all hulking shoulders and fumbling hands, could never aspire to.

"Alex! Is that you?"

He turned, and there coming toward him through the crowd, his hand already outstretched, was Félix. What was he doing here? Alex felt a moment of disorientation, as if he'd been caught at something shameful.

"What a surprise! I didn't know you were involved in this sort of thing."

They'd kept up their arrangement the entire summer. The more time they'd spent together, the more unsure Alex was about what they were up to.

"You're here alone?"

The shadow that he always felt around Félix came over him. The shadow of those twenty-five dollars an hour.

"No, no. With a friend."

There were introductions. María's friend—*Rudolphe,* Alex got a snicker out of that, at least—hardly deigned to acknowledge him, turning at once to Félix.

"*Vous êtes du coté de la recherche?*"

Félix was in one of his business suits.

"*Non. De l'industrie.*"

There was an instant chill.

"*Ah, bon.*"

Rudolphe managed to hive off almost at once to a group that showed more promise, leaving Alex and María and Félix strangely islanded by the crowd. A feeding frenzy was in progress up at the refreshment table, with no chance of getting anywhere near it.

"You are with an environmental group?" Félix asked María in English, pleasantly enough.

"*Oui*," she said, and didn't offer anything more.

Alex's cigarette had burned down to his fingers but there were no ashtrays nearby to dump it in.

"Félix and I met at Berlitz," he said.

María ignored him.

"You are from a company?"

"Yes." Félix pulled a card from his pocket and handed it to her. "We make aluminum."

He didn't seem quite so pleasant now. Alex could feel it, the iciness coming off him like an October frost.

"You are against the agreement?"

This wasn't how you proceeded with someone like Félix.

He smiled.

"Not against. Just concerned. To see how it affects us."

"Is very important," María said. "Is very new, this conference."

Félix looked at his watch. He was still smiling.

"Ah, I must go," he said, grasping Alex's shoulder. "I will see you at our lesson."

Alex felt vaguely compromised when Félix had gone. A sourness hung between him and María and he had no idea how to get rid of it.

He was still holding his fucking cigarette butt.

"We must go back," María said. "They are beginning."

The day was getting away from him. He glanced at his watch, a twelve-dollar Timex he'd finally broken down and bought, and a little buzzer went off at the back of his head.

His appointment. He had completely forgotten about it.

"Shit! Sorry. I just remembered something. I have to go."

María looked unfazed, as if he was not the sort to be counted on.

"Your translation," she said. "You must get your card."

It took him an instant to understand: his bloody headset.

He untangled the thing from the pocket of his Windbreaker.

"Here, you take it. You can bring the card tonight."

He felt a pang at the thought of leaving it, but she might actually show up if his faculty card depended on it.

"You remember the address?"

"Yes, of course."

For a moment, he dared to feel hopeful. He leaned out to kiss her, impulsively, and got her almost squarely on the lips.

"*Hasta esta noche.*"

"*Sí, sí.*" She had a startled look that pleased him. "*Esta noche.*"

He hailed a taxi, his lips tingling. He still had the cigarette butt. It could be his last, he thought, suddenly full of resolve, and slipped the thing into his pocket for surety.

T he cardinal rule of Alex's therapy, which Dr. Klein had made crystal clear from the outset, was that Alex had to pay out of his pocket for any missed session. With luck he could still make the last twenty minutes or so, enough, he hoped, to meet whatever attendance requirements the doctor might have to satisfy with the Ministry of Health. Over the summer his sessions had moved from the rehab center beneath the Shriners into Montreal General proper, and he had the cab drop him at his usual entry point at Emergency, to save circling up the mountain to the main lobby. Six dollars with tip, the cab cost him, a blow, but much better than the forty-three a missed session would have run.

The Emergency entrance led into the hospital's labyrinthine basements, great engines humming away behind vented doors and orderlies in the pastel non-whites of medicine's lower orders pushing bins stuffed with laundry and waste. The hospital was divided into wings that seemed to have no communication one with the other, trailing off into perpetual dead ends, though by now Alex was able to race through the place like the seasoned regular he was.

He caught the elevators to B4, Psychiatry. The floor was divided between the doctors' offices to one side and the ward to the other, behind an intercommed metal door that read KEEP CLOSED. B4 and After. Alex always expected some scene from Bedlam to reveal itself behind the metal door, though whenever he'd snuck a peek through the little viewing window, the hall beyond was always eerily empty and quiet. If not for the door it might have been hard to tell which side was which, most of the doctors he ran into across the way looking wild-haired or wild-eyed or hunched up over their charts with the squirreled intensity of escapees.

Dr. Klein's door, as usual, was ajar. Alex, his heart pounding by then and his armpits drenched with sweat, paused a moment to collect himself, then pushed through and said quickly, "Sorry I'm late."

Dr. Klein was staring out the window. As far as Alex knew there was nothing to see out there except some kind of storage yard boxed in by the hospital's other wings. The doctor turned as Alex came in but instead of the tight, unrevealing quarter-smile he always had whenever Alex was late, his mouth opened an instant in what looked like surprise.

"Oh," he said.

"I was at a conference," Alex said, flustered. "I completely forgot."

"It's fine. It's fine."

Alex took off his jacket and shoes and lay down. After months of chafing at every reference to his lateness, he thought, *It can't be fine*. If it was fine, then it meant nothing. If it meant nothing, then maybe all of this, all these days and weeks and months—as he'd always suspected; as he'd always feared—meant nothing as well.

"Maybe it was because I was with María," he started.

He was glad he'd got María in off the top instead of having to finagle her in later. He wouldn't have predicted it, but María had ended up dominating his time here. Meanwhile all the rest—Ingrid, Desmond, Liz—remained stagnating in the usual backwater where Alex kept them.

He was waiting for Dr. Klein to pick up his cue.

"We ran into another friend of mine," Alex said finally. "Félix. It was a bit awkward."

Another pause, but then Dr. Klein said, "Félix?" with the irritating shorthand he had for flagging points he wanted elaborated, and Alex felt on familiar ground again.

"Not a friend, really. A student. From Berlitz."

And so they began.

María had come into their sessions through the sort of subterfuge Alex used to sneak in anything suspect, in this case by couching it in high-mindedness.

"It just seems so self-indulgent," he'd said, striking a new low for sleaze. "I think of my Salvadoran friend, and what she's probably been through, and then of me lying here every day talking about my little problems."

"But you're still here," Dr. Klein had interrupted, in a rare instance of unvarnished impatience, which had shut Alex up. But once María had entered the picture he found any number of ways to obsess over her, dreams she'd figured in, anxieties she'd touched off, contact he'd made through her with his Feminine Archetype. It was mostly bogus, just a way of being with her in a way he couldn't be in real life, yet often his family crept into things when she came up, oddly, since she wasn't anything like them. Not his mother, who was as phlegmatic and un-Latin as he was; not either of his sisters, whom he could not recall having ever seen on a dance floor except maybe doing the chicken dance and who would surely have looked at him as if he were deranged had he ever tried to kiss them. But then maybe María was not like María either. Despite how energy flowed out from her like heat from a stove she had a strange reserve, as if there was something important she was holding back. It made him think of the Samnites, his mother's people—they were tough mountaineers, not Latins at all. The Latins had conquered them, but they had held themselves apart. That was his mother through and through, beleaguered but unbowed.

In El Salvador, rather more recently, there had been *la Matanza*, a great massacre of peasants after an uprising that had managed in a matter of weeks what four hundred years of colonization had not: the almost total assimilation of the country's Indians, who'd been blamed for the revolt and had quickly erased every mark of distinction to save their lives. El Salvador was a country of half-breeds now, what María surely was: no more Latin than Alex, just another of the world's conquered indigenes. He took heart from this at first, as if he'd discovered some secret of birth that threw over an insuperable obstacle to their coming together.

"Yes, *la Matanza*," María had said when he'd brought the subject up, in that pointed tone of hers. "Of course is very important."

And that had been the end of the matter.

The problem with his own family, maybe, was that they weren't anything at all. They didn't eat well, as Italians should, weren't especially good Catholics, had never been especially close. The only time he could remember his mother hugging him when he was a kid was when he'd got lost once at the Heinz picnic. He could still picture the instant when they'd been reunited, how her face had lit up, as if some child in her had got loose.

He was still talking about Félix.

"It's a little surprising," Dr. Klein said, sounding almost peeved, "that you've never mentioned him before."

Alex took some pleasure at that.

"Oh? Do you think he's important?"

What he remembered most about his childhood now weren't particular incidents but an atmosphere, pleasant enough when he was small
but then growing thick with something, what he might call shame, but
that at the time had seemed more particular, like an odor his family gave
off. The worst had been when David had lost his arm—he still didn't like
to think about that. He had walked home from school after a field trip to
find his brothers and sisters home instead of at work and his grandmother crying in the kitchen.

"What happened?"

"S'ha fatte male," she said. He got hurt.

He had to piece things together. Gus sat hunched at the kitchen table;
Bruno sat in the living room, staring at the blank TV.

"It was from the tractor," Mimi said. "He must have grabbed the
power takeoff."

What was the power takeoff?

"Oh."

Later his parents returned and then the visitors came, people who at
least weren't crazy with hurt, who made the thing look almost bearable.
But at some point the wailing started and Alex left the house. He wasn't
sure where was safe, and ended up in the doghouse with the dog. The
place had a sharp, feral smell. He felt uncomfortable and false in there, in
a way he couldn't explain, and meanwhile the dog clearly resented him,
shifting and turning and finally shambling outside.

He had made his pact with God there, in the doghouse, but it was
just a rattle of desperate promises, of privations, the priesthood, if this
moment would pass. He had known it was for nothing. Whatever was
out there in the night beyond the dark, he couldn't feel it.

He had an image of his father that Sunday kneeling in church and
bawling like a child, there in front of everyone. But he could also see him,
that same service, taking a toothpick from his pocket to clean out his
ear—they might as well be animals, Alex had thought, they might as well
just shit right there on the floor of the church.

He had fallen silent. God forbid he should ever mention any of this
stuff to Dr. Klein.

"You were talking about Félix," Dr. Klein said.

"Sorry." It was the stink of the doghouse somehow that always came back to him, how insufficient and wrong it had made everything feel. "I was thinking about my brother David."

He waited for it, the doctor's flag.

David?

"I think our time's up for today."

The doctor stood hovering next to Alex as he put on his jacket.

"I'll have to cancel our sessions for the rest of the week," he said. "Something's come up."

"Oh." It felt like a punishment. "That's fine."

"So I'll see you again Monday."

The doctor was already closing the door behind him. *Fuck you,* Alex thought, wanting to kick him, to crack his skull, though knowing that Monday he'd be back.

Outside, his resolve already vanished, he lit up a cigarette at once. The sun had warmed the air to a stubborn October heat, though Alex caught a downdraft off the mountain that felt like winter crouching in wait. At least Jiri would be gone by the time he got home, he could be grateful for that. Jiri had moved in with him exactly around the time all the plumbing work had started—"Just for a couple of days," he'd said—so that the past weeks had been hellish. By a stroke of luck some sort of domestic crisis had called him away to Toronto, where his wife and son had decamped, just in time to leave Alex alone for his evening with María.

He was still making his pilgrimages past Trudeau's house. Across the way the Cuban consulate sat virtually unchanged from the spring, the upper windows still boarded and scorch marks from the firebombing still showing on the stone. Alex felt less pleased than he used to at Trudeau's intimacy with the place: all summer long he'd seen the actions coming in against Fidel in his Amnesty updates, this one jailed for some leaflet, that one kicked out of his house or his job. It wasn't the bone-crushing stuff of the big-league tyrannies, just this constant wearing away, a little message The Revolution sent to its dissenters that they were out of step. Alex knew the argument, the collective over the individual, but Trudeau had staked his whole career on the individual, then there he was pitching his tent across from Mr. Castro as if he were ready to receive the man at a moment's notice.

There was another collectivist living just up the street, Alex had learned, whom Trudeau was less likely to be inviting over any time soon: his old nemesis Lévesque. Alex hardly knew what to make of that. Even

Alex, for all his disdain of Canadian politics, thought of the battle between these two in mythic terms, Goliath to David, Achilles to Hector, Apollo to Dionysus. Now they were both ensconced in their modest retirement homes—Trudeau, mind you, true to form, in a house of Architectural Significance while Lévesque, always the poor cousin, was in a condo building with all the personality of a Howard Johnson's—not five hundred yards from one another, like the wolf and sheepdog in the cartoon Alex had watched as a kid who used every foul means to outwit one another all the day long but then punched the clock promptly at five and parted amicably. What made it even stranger was that the two of them were here on this unlikely stretch of busy road at the very foothills of Westmount, which rose up beyond Côte des Neiges into shaded side streets and cul-de-sacs watched over by private security, as if they were both, after all, still the colonial lackeys of old, begging for scraps at the gates of the Anglo establishment.

That wasn't a sentiment that Alex was ever likely to voice around Félix—there were certain places, he realized, where Félix's sense of irony wouldn't go. Whenever they got anywhere near these sorts of issues Alex could feel an East bloc carefulness coming over him.

"It isn't so much to ask, to learn the language of a place." That had been Félix's brisk dismissal of the spat with Louie. "It's not racism to say so. If I come to your country, I do the same."

There was no argument to make to this sort of reasonableness. Félix was right, surely, Louie had simply been grandstanding, yet the more time Alex spent with Félix the more he felt surrounded by the unsayable.

Félix lived in Outremont, on the other side of the mountain. The streets there were laid out in long rows of stately two- and three-story multiplexes, dark-bricked and white-trimmed and close as if the hodge-podge of the rest of the city had found here its perfect order. A hundred years earlier the place had been no more than unpeopled bush, yet Alex had the sense in its streets of an old, foreign life going on around him reaching back to the notaries and priests of the *ancien régime* and to squint-eyed officials in drafty offices near the port recording customs duties and census rolls.

He passed whole families of Hasidic Jews hurrying along the sidewalks sometimes, looking, in their strange jackets and curls and hats, as if they had just stepped fresh from the eighteenth century.

"They were very smart," Félix had said. "They bought a lot here before the referendum, very cheap. Now, of course, it's worth much more."

Alex tried not to listen too carefully to comments like these, afraid of the moment they might overstep. In any event, different rules seemed to apply out here, on the other side—the feeling he'd always had of living in the midst of a mongrel non-culture, without claims or preferments, yielded to a sense of hegemony and right. Félix's house, up toward the mountain, where the multiplexes gave way to restrained single-family homes, was a four-square place in brick and rusticated stone that conveyed a sense of generational solidity. Inside it was all rich wood hues and high ceilings and original moldings, books everywhere and polished antiques and framed posters of art exhibitions, Klimt at the MOMA, Man Ray in Paris, the Hermitage exhibition at the Musée national des beaux-arts du Québec.

They had their lessons in a room lined with leather-bound books from Félix's classical education. Félix brought out wine and crudités; he allowed Alex to smoke.

"So," he'd said, their first lesson, settling in an armchair and tucking up his pant legs like a Gentleman at Home, "maybe we should start by getting to know each other a little more. Now that we're free of Mme Hertz."

That had remained the tenor of their sessions, this sense of being slightly delinquent, beyond jurisdiction. Félix kept a notebook where he'd jot down phrases and points of grammar he wanted to discuss, but after the calculated featurelessness of the Berlitz offices, it was enough for Alex simply to look around him to find a conversation point. Photographs that Félix had taken lined the hallways, carefully matted and framed like works in a gallery. He had done a series on the street kids of Rio, brooding black-and-white shots that Alex wouldn't have expected of him, that would have required him to wander in dangerous neighborhoods, to speak to these children, to gain their trust.

"It's a hobby since I was young. Just, you know, to keep the soul alive."

There were shots of gaunt-faced uncles and aunts, of a brother in the priesthood, of weddings and feasts. In the entrance hall was a family shot Félix had taken as a young man in front of the house he'd grown up in in Longueuil, a bungalow in fieldstone and yellow brick that might have been in any fifties suburb on the continent. His family, a sprawling bevy of them, were poised on the front steps like a paradigm of the middle class, the males with their hair slicked back and the females all in bobs.

Alex had read about Longueuil in *White Niggers of America,* where it had figured as one of the lower circles of hell, a place of unpaved streets and tarpaper shacks specially designed for Quebec's suburban proletariat.

"Oh, yes, he makes a lot of fun of us in that book," Félix said, with surprising bitterness. "Those of us on the other side of the fence. We were the sellouts. But my father was getting up every morning at five to take a bus to the East End, and coming home at eleven, when that group was out drinking cognac in the cafés."

It was one of the few chinks Alex ever saw in Félix's nationalist armor. He was cut from a different cloth, it seemed, than the *White Niggers* crowd, with their manifestos and bombs. His father had raised himself up by his bootstraps, running a depanneur in the East End to put seven children through school.

"It's no use talking about independence if you can't support yourself. They don't understand, that type. They're like children who want to leave home but won't get a job."

These sorts of pronouncements were not invitations to debate. That suited Alex fine: who was he to say, in any event? He'd gone out for drinks with Félix a few times, to sleek-looking places in chrome and exposed brick nothing like the half-deserted dives in the Anglo ghetto Alex normally frequented, and he'd begun to feel as if he'd been living in some small provincial town when around the corner was this foreign city he'd never entered. People spoke French there; they wore elegant clothes; they seemed at the center of things. Félix had friends at these places, though Alex seldom got beyond the simplest pleasantries with any of them. He was afraid the talk would come around to politics and he'd commit some horrible gaffe, but that never really happened. He could always feel it, though, the moment he was left behind, as if there were little burrows people fell into, comfortable places full of innuendo and slang that he couldn't enter. Félix might translate a bit but soon enough he'd get caught up in things, so that Alex could only sit there in smiling incomprehension.

"*Ça va?*" Félix would say, and Alex would scramble to reassure him. "*Oui, oui, ça va.*"

The truth was that Alex, though he suffered guilt for this, never made quite as much effort on these outings as he might have. Perhaps he was afraid of being unmasked somehow, or maybe he just wasn't up to the work of bridging the solitudes. But there was more to it: out in the world like that, this impoverished young man next to the graying, affluent one, he felt like Félix's boy. It was clear by then, Alex wasn't an idiot, that Félix was gay—he'd known it, really, the instant he'd stepped into Félix's house, from how self-sufficient it seemed, how devoid of any feminine presence.

Alex had consulted Michael.

"Of course he's gay. What does he look like? I've probably seen him on the mountain."

"I don't think Félix is really the type for the mountain."

"You'd be surprised."

Michael, of course, claimed even Trudeau made appearances on the mountain, in the wooded enclave on the eastern slopes where gay men went for their liaisons, which was why, Michael insisted, Trudeau had bought a house not a five-minute walk from the place. His assessment of Félix was summary and sure: he was one of those deeply closeted men of a certain age who could barely admit they were gay even to themselves.

"He was trained by the Jesuits. How could he not be fucked up? He's probably having sex with truck drivers when you're not around."

All of this accorded more than Alex liked to admit with his own suspicions. If Félix was gay it was his own business, and not something he should feel obliged to reveal to his English tutor, any more than Alex was ever going tell Félix about his twisted sex with Liz. And yet. Gay men like Félix were always falling for straight ones like Alex, according to Michael—it was a way they had of feeling normal, by falling for someone who was.

"I can't imagine anyone thinking of me as normal," Alex said.

Michael gave him a look.

"Don't flatter yourself."

It was a stretch to imagine Félix having fallen for him, when he didn't seem to have a romantic bone in his Cartesian body. But there was the wine he served up and the little dishes of paté and Camembert; there was the hand that came out sometimes to touch Alex's shoulder; there was that sense, meeting here in Félix's home behind Berlitz's back, that they were up to no good. Then Félix took him so seriously, much more so than his

passing expertise in the English language seemed to warrant—they'd even
begun to talk of CanLit, of all things, it was almost embarrassing, Alex trot-
ting out stuff he'd only learned himself the week before while preparing for
his course as if he'd become some sort of gateway to Anglo culture.

Then there was the matter of Félix's son. The whole time at Berlitz,
after his first chilly mention of him, Félix had seemed to guard the secret
of him as if it were something too irksome to go into. But now, suddenly,
every lesson brought the story of some new outrage. He'd failed two of
his courses at university; he'd been caught smoking dope; he'd blown
three hundred dollars on a leather jacket he didn't need. Somewhere out
in the city this son was wreaking havoc, abetted by a doting mother who
had apparently broken Félix's balls and was now bleeding him for support, and yet there wasn't the least sign of either of them in Félix's house.
Not so much as a photograph, from him who took photographs for his
soul; not so much as a Styx poster or sweaty T-shirt. There was a guest
room upstairs that Alex had glanced at but it was in the same fussy state
of decorum as the rest of the house—books, a framed Bouguereau print,
a hand-stitched quilt in masculine colors. It was entirely possible that
mother and son were the purest invention, though the alternative seemed
more depressing, that they truly existed in some shadow strain of Félix's
world but merely as a cover for his real life. It bothered Alex how the
son—Lionel, his name was, and Alex hoped it was not after the famously
anti-Semitic Abbé Groulx—had become this cipher between him and
Félix of what was not said. It bothered him that whenever the son came
up, it seemed for Alex's benefit, the Bad Son to Alex's Good.

But it also pleased him.

In Paris, the first time he'd been there, he had let himself be cruised
by a man at the Tuileries. He had gone out to supper with him, had
returned to his apartment and gone as far as climbing into the man's bed
before he'd declared himself. He would have found it hard to explain
what he'd been thinking—he'd known from the start what was happening and yet had pretended to himself that he had not. He'd just wanted a
bed, maybe. Or he'd been lonely, and had liked the attention.

Félix paid him attention. He also paid cash.

Alex had reached the Unitarian church at the corner of Simpson.
His own church, he distantly thought of it as, on account of Darwin,
who'd had Unitarian leanings on his mother's side. The notice board for

Sunday's sermon read "What then must we do? Building a social ethic for our time." Once, seeing the church's door ajar and hearing organ music coming from inside, he had gone into the place and been surprised at how august and churchlike it was, with its dark pews and stained glass. Up at the front a mannish-looking organist in a black dress and a young woman in jeans were rehearsing an aria, Bach maybe.

A trim, gray-haired man with his sleeves rolled, as if he'd been gardening or tidying a closet, stood listening in the shadows at the back of the pews. He smiled over at Alex.

"Stunning, aren't they? That's our organist, Wilhelmina, and our mezzo-soprano."

Alex regretted at once having gone in.

"Oh," he said.

"Are you one of us? Are you Unitarian?"

"No. I mean, I'm interested in it."

"Here. I'll give you a brochure with a bit of our history. Feel free to come in any time."

Sure enough, the brochure mentioned Darwin. A potted history traced Unitarian roots all the way back to the Arian heresy against the tripartite nature of God, though this was not a debate that Alex was particularly up on. When the dust had settled, in any event, the Unitarians seemed to have ended up more or less as Alex had imagined, as a kind of squishy liberal catch-all.

Now whenever he passed the church Alex was afraid that the door would swing open and the gray-haired man would suddenly be there on the steps, beckoning. *Brilliant day! Stunning!* Alex already had his back to the place and was heading down Mackay, but he still felt a shiver. Darwin, he knew, hadn't lasted long among the Unitarians— he'd flunked out of medical school and set his sights on a parsonage with the Church of England, where he'd be free to study his beetles and slugs. But Alex had no such excuse. Who did he think he was, exactly, mister arrogant shit-for-brains, looking down on people's honest attempts at some sort of direction in life when half the time he lived his own life in the gutter?

He wondered what the Unitarians had to say about sex. *Stunning, isn't it? Brilliant!* But was it one, or was it tripartite? "A featherbed to catch a falling Christian" was what Darwin's grandfather, the cranky

Erasmus, had said about the Unitarians. Squishy liberals even then, not quite able to look squarely into the void.

He passed the Liberal Arts Building. Jiri Novak had been bedding down here after his wife's departure, on the little couch in his office, until the dean had got wind of the situation and had forced him out. Jiri was in his fifties, surely, and yet his life could come down to that, to having to curl up in the nearest warm spot like a stray. Not that Jiri was the least bit bowed; not that he'd admitted to anything. It infuriated Alex, that kind of resilience, but also awed him.

A statue of Norman Bethune stood shit-encrusted in the little delta that de Maisonneuve broke up into at Guy. Every day he was there, iconic and staunch, another Canadian hero with all the sex appeal of cat pee.

It's not that I don't think he was a great man, Peter, but it all ends up looking so bland, somehow. So nice.

I don't know if a lot of people realize this, but he actually had quite a dark streak.

Some people say you've got a pretty good dark streak yourself.

Well, I've never been one for leather harnesses and that sort of thing, if that's what you mean!

Maybe Bethune had used harnesses, maybe he'd dressed up in women's underthings. Who knew why humans were built this way, to crave whatever seemed forbidden—in Paris, after he'd put that man off, all Alex had been able to think about was what it might have been like to give in. He didn't know if that made him enlightened, or just a freak. Not that the idea ever crossed his mind with Félix: he shuddered at the thought, felt positively ill at it, never mind that with Félix, of course, there were other concerns. Alex ought to have taken better note of his suit that morning, of the fit. At home, for their lessons, all his clothing seemed to run a bit big on him, as if he'd lost weight, or was losing it.

Not concerns, perhaps: probabilities. The disease was out there in Félix's demographic; that was a fact. Alex had remained careful, however, to make a point of touching everything Félix touched, of eating the food he brought, of drinking his wine.

At his building, he caught a movement of overalled workers through the lobby windows. Certain they were up to some new mischief that would set his blood boiling, he decided to continue on to the Faubourg to fetch what he needed for the paella he planned to make for María. He checked his wallet: thirty-one dollars. It would have to do. He had a scholarship check coming in any day, but all he had to get by on until then were his sporadic hours at Berlitz and his handouts from Félix. He wished he hadn't run into Félix at the conference. All he'd be able to think of now was that Félix was buying his supper, so that the whole evening he'd be there like a spoiler, mucking up Alex's libidinal flow. Already the kiss of that morning seemed hopelessly burdened: Félix had come into it, and the Unitarians, and Norman Bethune, so that there would hardly be sitting room at the table.

He ought to have canceled the swimming with Esther.

"Do you think there's a God?" she had asked him recently, in her urgent tone, as if his answer actually mattered.

Of course there's a God, he could have said. *He's the fucking bastard who put you in this wheelchair.*

"I don't know, Esther. I don't know. I hope so."

"But you don't think so. That's all right. You don't have to say it."

María had God, even the Unitarians did, why shouldn't Esther? It would make things a lot easier. Alex thought of God as a kind of Santa Claus, something the human race would eventually outgrow, but to what end? The dark, the dark, was all he could see, like the deadness that came over him at twilight.

Darwin himself had always grown Delphic and coy when the question of God was put to him, though to his own Emma, whose fortune had saved him from the parsonage, he'd confessed his doubts. To his regret: it had been the great shadow in their marriage, Emma's fears that they should be separated in eternity. Not long before he died Darwin had taken out the letter Emma had written him years before about these fears and had scrawled at the bottom of it, "When I am dead, know that many times, I have kissed & cryed over this."

He could only kiss and cry, but not make the leap. It was the image that Alex carried of them in his head, as if people got exactly the heaven they believed in, Emma alone in the clouds with her Just God and Charles still bound to the earth in cold mineral death.

– 4 –

The first signs of the new regime in Alex's building since it had been bought up by a company called Le 1444 Mackay Enregistré were visible the instant you stepped into the lobby. What had previously been a clean, well-lit, and almost poignant monument to the failed optimism of a bygone era, with its built-in planters that had probably never been planted in, its spacious seating area that had probably never held seating, was now a perpetual construction site, forever cluttered with stepladders and drop cloths and power tools and shotgun-blast-sized holes riddling the walls and wires dangling from ceiling. Alex felt his guts clench whenever he entered the building against the prospect of whatever new devilment the owners might be up to. Many of their innovations defied understanding. They had removed the trash can that sat in the mailbox foyer, handy for the immediate disposal of useless ad mail and scrupulously emptied by the old super, Guy, so that now people had taken simply to dumping their flyers and their half-filled coffee cups and trash into the empty planters, which had become little cesspits, though under Guy you could have eaten a meal from them.

Alex checked his mailbox. The weekly specials at Steinberg's; a discount coupon from Hakim Optical; a solicitation from the Red Cross. Into the planter. But then—he could barely bring himself to actually sort it from the rest—a blue airmail envelope, with the telltale looping script. *Tunvägen 3, Engelström*. His heart was pounding. The letter had an uncommon bulk to it, a thickness, though rather than opening it at once he slipped it into his back pocket, not sure whether to heighten his anticipation or lessen his terror.

One of the elevators had been out of service for nearly a week. Still out, he saw now, the door open into nothingness, a wooden barrier set in front of the exposed shaft and a vile odor drifting up from whatever abyss it led down to. The workmen he'd noticed earlier had vanished: it was positively Kafkaesque, how often these days Alex came across bits of disorder like this abandoned *in medias res,* as if all the work going on in the building was really just some elaborate piece of theater.

He pressed the call button for the other elevator and waited a minute, then another, before beginning to itch with impatience. The air in the lobby felt muggy and close. Already Alex's provisions, which had set him back nearly seventeen dollars, seemed to be teetering past the point of freshness.

Alex knocked on the super's door across from the elevators, then again.

"Hold on to your knickers!"

The door opened and Tony, the new super, stood smiling before him in a plaid bathrobe, spindly white legs poking out the bottom of it.

At the sight of Alex his smile hardened: Alex was one of the troublemakers.

"How can I help you, son?"

Every time he saw Tony, Alex got the same bad taste in his mouth. He could see back into the suburban tidiness and faux-wood decorum of Tony's apartment, the only place, it seemed, where he exercised anything like custodial aptitude. Back in Guy's day the apartment had spewed smoke like a tire fire and the hall had been crammed with Molson empties, but the rest of the building had always looked as if Guy had just hosed it down with a power washer.

"It's the elevator," Alex said, more petulantly than he'd wanted.

"I'm afraid it's still out."

"Not that one. The other one."

"Ah. It's on service."

Alex tried to contain himself.

"How can you put it on service when it's the only one working?"

Tony put on a little frown of affront.

"Someone's moving out, son. I'd have to do the same for yourself."

The bastard was rubbing it in his face. Every departure now, Alex knew, was one more lost from the cause.

He couldn't stop himself from asking.

"Who is it?"

"Some girl on the eighth." Casually, as if it were a matter of no more than passing interest. "Lois, I think her name is."

Alex started up the stairs in disbelief. Lois was one of the last of the sane in the tenants' association—if she'd cut a deal he'd never forgive her. There had been a moment at the beginning of this whole rental debacle when it had seemed the perfect political action, local, winnable, discrete, but instead it was turning into a kind of moral goulash, so that Alex wasn't even sure anymore who the enemy was.

By the third floor he'd taken off his jacket. The stairwell was featureless and gray, like a stairwell in a gulag prison or a nuclear silo. At the fourth, he heard a racket of hammering and drilling and tried to make out whether it was coming from his corner of the building—with the water, it had been just his column of apartments that had been affected, top to bottom, as if the building had had a stroke.

That was how Alex thought of the place now, as this ailing body, though somehow the more work that was done, the worse things seemed to become. He was still clinging to the theory that this was all part of some strategy of harassment the new owners had, though it was getting harder and harder to distinguish between the malicious and the merely incompetent. Even the cash grab they'd tried when they'd taken over, sending out renewal notices with increases of fifteen or twenty percent, had seemed remarkably crude, almost naïve. Alex had felt a nice rush of socialist indignation when he'd got his own, and had gone so far as to call the Régie du logement and then to post a notice in the lobby. YOU HAVE THE RIGHT TO REFUSE AN INCREASE! He guessed a lot of people might not realize that. There was a box right there on the renewal form you could check, and then it was up to the landlords to take their case to the Régie.

Alex had more or less put the matter from his mind afterward, pleased with himself for actually having done his duty for once. But one evening a man appeared at his door in an ill-fitting sports coat and blue pants looking like a character out of a Beckett play. There was a thin film of sweat on his forehead.

"We speak in English, yes?" he said, too amenably, which at once put Alex on his guard.

Somehow the man—M. Cournoyer—managed to insinuate himself into Alex's apartment. He had come to discuss Alex's refusal of the proposed increase, he said, then immediately put up his hands to stay any protest.

"Yes, yes, it's very 'igh, of course, too 'igh maybe. But the building 'as many problems."

Alex did not like having this man in his apartment, did not like that, to avoid confrontation, he might end up making some compromise he had no wish to make.

"I'd just like the Régie to decide," he said. "I think that's fair."

"Yes, the Régie, sometimes they say five percent instead of ten, but then sometimes they say twenty-five, you don't know. It's all depend on the building, you know, on the problems."

It was just talk, of course. But it was true that Alex hadn't considered this twist.

M. Cournoyer had arranged himself, uninvited, at Alex's dining table. He took out Alex's renewal notice.

"You settle now," he said, "instead of fifty dollar, only forty. It's reasonable." And right there in front of Alex he put a stroke through the new rent the landlords had proposed and scribbled in the lower amount.

Alex shifted.

"I think I'd rather just wait for the Régie."

M. Cournoyer made another stroke.

"There. Thirty-five. That's the last."

"I'd still rather wait."

The forced friendliness was wearing thin.

"You wait, maybe it's not good for you."

"All the same."

Cournoyer put the form back in his briefcase.

"You are the one who put up the sign," he said.

"What?" But Alex felt suddenly panicked. "What sign?"

"About the increase."

Alex was taken completely off guard. How could he have known that?

"I don't know what you're talking about."

Cournoyer motioned to the fridge, where Alex had taped a copy of the notice as a sort of trophy. Cournoyer had clearly seen it from the start.

"It's not permitted," he said.

"Sorry?"

"To put up posters. It's the building's property. You can be evicted for that."

"You've got to be joking."

"We'll see it, who's joking. You sign now, it's okay, otherwise it's your problem."

Alex was practically trembling by now, though whether with rage or apprehension he wasn't sure. Some part of him was ready to give in, to cut his losses. He could offer thirty.

"I'd like you to leave now," he said.

Cournoyer stood.

"You think it's smart, what you're doing, but we see it. You don't sign, it's okay, but I don't know, maybe one day your water goes off, or the electricity, or the heat. We can make trouble for you, sir, you're gonna see it."

When he'd gone Alex felt a strange mix of outrage and exhilaration. Surely the man had made a mistake, had handed Alex a case against him on a platter. But over the next few days, stories went around of people who'd actually signed. The whole thing started to seem a lot more insidious then. They could pick people off like that, one by one; vulnerable people. Alex put another call in to the Régie, but after twenty minutes on hold he was informed, by someone clearly put out at having to speak English, that there were routines that had to be followed, forms that had to be submitted, rules of evidence that had to be adhered to. He'd been so proud of himself, putting up his little notice, but he saw now how out of his depth he'd been.

He'd asked Esther about her renewal, but her father had already taken care of it.

"He didn't agree to the increase, did he?"

"Oh, he knows about these things. He has apartments of his own."

And Alex hadn't liked to pursue the matter after that, afraid her father might turn out to be some slumlord himself or, worse, just a reasonable businessman who had seen at once that the matter wasn't worth wasting time over.

He might just have crawled back into his hole at this point if the tenants' association hadn't started up. An organizer from a tenants' advocacy group, a real Rosa Luxemburg type, called a meeting in the building and made it seem as if they were at the front lines of an all-out class war.

"This sort of thing is happening all over the city. They jack the rents up, so right away the building's worth twenty or thirty percent more than they paid for it, and then they flip it. But they have to have the signed agreements. They can't sell the place if everything's tied up at the rental board."

Everyone at the meeting had some story about Cournoyer. Alex thought someone might mention the notice he'd put up, but nobody did.

"You should keep a record of everything," the organizer said. "You've got this strong-arming, that's good, is there anything else? Anything you can use?"

Alex hadn't said a word yet.

"I think they discriminate," he said.

"How do you mean?"

Already he regretted opening his mouth.

"Just something the super said once. That he didn't let blacks in and so on."

"He actually said that?"

This was from a high-strung redhead who looked to be in the advanced stages of anorexia.

"Something like that. I mean, he put it a bit more crudely."

"I can't believe it. He actually said that?"

"I'd be careful with something like this," the organizer said. "It's not that easy to prove. You'd have to build a case."

"How hard can it be?" the anorexic said. "You know, I've noticed that. That you never see blacks here."

Alex kept his head down when they were choosing an executive. He signed up for the membership drive, but then was surprised when he went around to his allotted floors at how resistant people were to him. More of them than he would have suspected had already signed after the original notice; others had actually cut deals with Cournoyer. It was clear at the next tenants' meeting that the story was the same through the whole building. Some people had signed because they were old or they were afraid or they thought the increases reasonable, others didn't care because they were moving out. The forty or so who'd come out to the first meeting had been whittled down to maybe half.

The anorexic, Brenda, had finagled her way into the presidency.

"It's like they're getting away with it. Maybe we should push on this discrimination thing."

"I dunno," Alex said, uneasy. "That organizer wasn't very enthusiastic."

"Yeah, I was actually a little surprised at that. I mean, she was Jewish, wasn't she? You'd think she'd sympathize."

He should never have brought the matter up. For months his only relationship with the super had been to note from a distance the little subculture he formed in the building, but since Esther had entered Alex's life, Guy had become a regular presence. He had all the charm of a Rottweiler, a manner no doubt calculated to ward off frivolous complaints, though with Esther, who called him almost daily, because a window had jammed or a tap was sticking or the toilet was making a funny noise, he retained a kind of journeyman's commitment to service.

"She's a pain in the ass but she's a good girl," he'd said to Alex, in what seemed to pass for friendliness. "The Jews I don't mind, but niggers, Arabs, people like that, I don't let them in."

Alex doubted that Guy had even noticed the stony silence he had greeted this with. He ought to have said something, made his position clear, except that Esther was so dependent on Guy.

"It didn't exactly sound as if it was building policy," he said at the meeting. "Just something the super did on his own."

"That doesn't make it any better," Brenda said.

"I'm just saying it doesn't really help us much."

All the same, Brenda managed to bully the issue through, and a letter was drafted to be sent to the owners. At least Alex's name wasn't mentioned—the last thing he needed was to have Guy coming after him with a crowbar. Alex figured the matter would just end up on a back burner like everything else, but instead the owners reacted with a moral swiftness that gave him pause: within a matter of days, a reply had come back saying Guy had been let go. No denials, no defense, just total capitulation. In the same letter the owners announced the dismissal of M. Cournoyer, based, as they said, on the complaints they'd received about him. In one fell swoop, they had effectively undermined the entire case against them.

"But he was so nice," Esther said, bereft at Guy's departure. "He always came when I called."

"Maybe not so nice," Alex said, but without much conviction. Guy had certainly been nice in the terms that made any sense to Esther: he showed up. Tony, on the other hand, she might call down to twice, three times, then again, and each time get only the same cheery assurance that he'd be by soon.

The whole matter left him with such a sick feeling that he was all but ready to drop right out of the association. But that was when the troubles started. In a single week the power went out three times, wreaking havoc on Alex's just-out-of-the-box Exec. Partner portable; then the water began to go off, for hours at a stretch, without notice or even a discernible pattern. All this was so eerily close to what Cournoyer had threatened that it seemed too obvious to be intentional. And yet; and yet. On July 1, the official date for lease renewals to take effect, there was a sudden mass exodus from the building, amidst rumors of buyouts, and the outages began to seem part of a careful plan to drive out the refuseniks.

In the meantime the secretary of the tenants' association had resigned, under mysterious circumstances, though it was clear she had clashed with Brenda. Alex ought to have given the whole matter a wide berth, but he was dating María by then, and had started his Amnesty work, and he couldn't muster the complacence he would have needed to stay inert. It was logical that he should be secretary—he was an English major; he had his Exec. Partner—and it wasn't long before he was firing off letters to the building's owners in the same tone of digni-fied outrage as in his Amnesty letters. Brenda had managed to get hold of the owners' actual names, though using them made him uneasy: Ruby, Shapiro, and Schwarz.

With every letter he plodded off to the post office to send it double-registered, though all he ever got in reply was the pink proof-of-delivery card that came back, scribbled with what Alex assumed was some minor underling's signature. But one day he got a phone call.

"Is that Alex? It's Richard Shapiro here."

It was as if one of the tyrants he sent his Amnesty letters to had phoned him. Shapiro, it seemed, wanted to meet.

"I have to say your letters are pretty articulate compared to some of the ones I get."

Alex tried to gather his thoughts.

"Maybe you should come to one of our tenant meetings."

"I don't know. You know how those things are, it just turns into confrontation. I get the sense you're someone reasonable."

Alex knew it was a mistake to agree to meet privately. But then he pictured Shapiro at one of their meetings, with the madwoman Brenda and the measly half-dozen others who usually showed up.

"Nothing official," Shapiro said. "Just, you know, to get a few things on the table."

They met not in the sort of glitzy downtown office Alex had imagined but in Alex's building, in a room off the pool mezzanine that was little more than a storage closet, windowless and crammed with cleaning equipment and boxes of chemicals. Rather than some slick St. James Street type Shapiro was a baby-faced man, balding and a bit fleshy, who looked like he'd just stepped away from barbecuing in the back yard. ·

"I appreciate you coming down," he said, rising from a little metal desk to take Alex's hand.

He had a bunch of forms on his desk next to a half-eaten sub, including, Alex saw, his own renewal form, still with the strokes Cournoyer had made on it.

"So what are you, an English major?"

Alex felt put out at being so easily pegged.

"Something like that."

"I did my Master's here at Concordia, poli-sci. We were the ones who threw the computer stuff out the windows. I don't know if you heard about that."

So he was an old hippie, then. Alex looked for some sign of sheepishness in him at what he'd become, but couldn't spot any.

"All that stuff with Cournoyer," he was saying, "that was bad. We didn't have any idea."

"So you're willing to renegotiate with the people who signed?"

"We're open to that, sure. If it's reasonable."

Alex didn't know what he'd expected, exactly, what piece of his mind he'd been hoping to give to this man.

"If people can't go thirty bucks right now, maybe they can go twenty-five, whatever. We'll just have to move more slowly on the repairs."

It occurred to Alex that this was an actual negotiation they were engaged in, that any instant Shapiro was going to set his own renewal form in front of him and ask him to sign. It all seemed so banal. This wasn't some mythic battle of the forces of left and right, just two guys haggling over a matter of dollars.

"I think people would rather wait for the Régie to decide," Alex said. Alex saw his twitch of irritation.

"Well, that's their right."

Shapiro had stood. It looked like the meeting was over. Alex saw someone waiting in the hall to come in after him and realized this meeting wasn't anything special, that Shapiro was merely going through the pile of holdouts.

"We're not just some holding company, Alex—my father started out here after the war straight out of a DP camp. Most of our properties are little apartment houses the same people have been living in all their lives."

More than anyone, Shapiro reminded him of his own brother Gus, right down to the receding hairline. Gus, the lawyer, helped manage a little apartment building their father had bought when he'd sold the farm. Alex had heard him going on about the headaches of the place in the same terms as Shapiro, the rent controls, the tenants, the repairs. Alex's sympathies then didn't always lean to the tenants—the building was their parents' nest egg, their legacy, all they had to show for their years of work.

A few days after the meeting, a worker appeared at Alex's door saying he had come to fix the ceiling. It took Alex a moment to figure out what he meant: a patch of ceiling stucco had fallen in his bedroom months before, under the old owners, and he'd sent in a letter of complaint, but then had never bothered to follow up.

"It's not really a good time," he said.

The worker was a Slavic type who looked wound up with a sense of mission.

"I come back."

"No, no, do it now."

If Shapiro was trying to buy him off, it was depressing how low the stakes were. The worker heaved trowelfuls of Polyfilla up to the ceiling, scalloping it into the rococo swirls Alex knew well from the elaborate plaster work of every new Italian house in his hometown but that looked nothing like the innocuous sprayed-on stucco of the rest of the ceiling.

"I paint it whole ceiling? More same then."

"Forget it, that's fine."

Every time Alex walked into his bedroom now his eye went at once to this Rorschach patch of hyper-white swirls. It was as if Shapiro was sending him a message. *See? The building needs work.*

In August they closed the pool. Alex had used the pool, had actually got down into the not-especially-warm water of it, maybe twice in the whole time he'd lived in the building. But he immediately fired off a missive to Shapiro & Co. demanding that it be reopened without delay. This time, he had the added leverage of medical necessity: Esther used the pool almost daily. *One of your tenants, Esther Rubinstein,* he said in his letter, *who suffers from multiple sclerosis . . .* There was no reply, however, no conciliatory phone call, no attempt at explanation, and Esther was forced to go off to the Y for her swims. At least Alex had the pleasure of feeling his indignation grow strong in him again. Shapiro had played him, with his immigrant sob story.

DP camp, he'd said. Not *concentration.*

More than two months had passed now since the pool had been closed. In the interim another round of outages had started up, leading to the past three hellish weeks when Alex's bathroom had been out of service almost continuously while they replaced twenty floors of piping along his line of units, Alex carrying potfuls of water to the toilet from the kitchen each time he needed to flush. By now Alex had filed five separate complaints at the Régie, each of which had cost him many hours in lineups and twenty dollars a pop in application fees, and none of which, since the Régie didn't allow class actions, came anywhere near capturing the true scope of the landlords' villainy, reducing everything down to the pettiest sort of private grievance. There was no sign that any of these claims was nearing fruition: six months to a year was what he was told. If the landlords had tried to invent a machine for crushing tenants' spirits, they couldn't have come up with anything better than the Régie.

He passed the sixth floor. He was dripping with sweat by now. He'd drop dead soon and they'd find him here weeks from now, growing ripe along with his groceries.

He had to quash the urge to stop for a cigarette.

"Fuck," he said, fighting for breath, "fuck."

He had reached the eighth floor.

The hall was littered with a scattering of vaguely familiar objects—floorlamps, a headboard, three milk crates full of albums. So it was true. Alex had been to Lois's often enough, drafting letters and plotting strategy, to recognize her belongings. Brenda, by then, had revealed herself as the borderline psychotic she truly was.

"It would probably be really easy for us to sleep together," Lois had said at the outset, "but I think that would be a bad idea." Alex had been in her thrall after that. His own thinking in these situations was always the opposite, that sex was the best possible outcome, but the least likely.

Two scrawny guys who looked as if they'd just got out of a halfway house were trying to jam a sofa into the elevator, trading curses that sounded like the slurred trills of some forgotten insect species.

"*Calisse, c'est complètement fucked up.*"

Lois came backing out of her apartment dragging a huge potted ficus. She was dressed in sweats that made lumpish and indistinct the little package her body was, and so seemed to bring it more clearly before him.

"Alex, what are you doing here?" She looked more alarmed than caught out. "You look awful."

Her hair was tied up in a frowzy bun, leaving her neck exposed.

"You're moving out," he said.

"Alex, don't start."

"I can't believe you're moving out in the middle of all this."

"I don't really have the time to get into this right now, Alex."

Her movers had managed to get the sofa into the elevator. Lois heaved her ficus over to them.

"Don't tell me you made a deal with them."

This was how they had been whittling down the opposition, by giving them kickbacks to move out. They could jack up the rent as much as they thought they could get away with then, on the bet that the new tenants wouldn't know enough to complain.

"Look, I've been late for work twice this week because of the elevators. I can't afford to lose my job over this. I just want to be able to wake up in the morning and know that my water is going to be on, and my electricity, and that I can get to work on time."

"But it's the same for all of us. We have to stick together."

"Alex, we're not fighting the fucking Sandinista revolution. It's just an apartment building."

"That's not the point."

"What *is* the point?"

He couldn't think of a convincing comeback to that.

"Did you make a deal?" he said again.

She was still handing stuff off to her guys.

"Yes." She didn't flinch. "I made a deal."

"I can't believe it! You of all people!"

"Alex, don't."

"But you sold us out!"

"Get off your high horse, Alex, everyone knows you met with Shapiro too."

That stopped him short.

"What are you talking about?"

"Well, didn't you?"

So Shapiro was truly a snake after all: *good.* Somehow he'd found the way to turn their meeting against him.

"Who said that?"

"What's the difference?"

"Just tell me who."

"Somebody saw you, for Christ's sake."

He felt sick. It had never even crossed his mind back then that anyone would imagine he was selling out.

"I wasn't making any deal, if that's what you think."

"Then why the secret? Why didn't you tell anyone?"

"There wasn't anything to tell."

Who knew how long she'd been thinking that about him, that he couldn't be trusted. Maybe from the start.

"I made a mistake. I don't know what I was thinking. That I'd set him straight or something. That I'd solve everything. But then the whole thing was so anticlimactic I couldn't even bring myself to mention it."

They stood silent.

"Look, Alex, I'm sure you're telling the truth, but that's the thing about all of this. It's not supposed to be so fucked up."

The hallway was cleared now. The two moving guys had squatted against the wall to share a cigarette.

"I've really got to go, Alex," Lois said. "I'd watch your back if I were you. Brenda's going around telling everyone you're some kind of spy."

It was only when she'd gone that Alex realized he was stuck there, still nine floors from his apartment, elevatorless. If there'd been a window nearby, he might have jumped through it. Instead he sat down in the stairwell and lit a cigarette. All his tenants' work was shit now. He wished he'd never gone near it.

He shifted on the step and felt something press against his backside: the letter. He'd completely forgotten about it. Some parent he'd make, some dad. It was clumpy and warped now from the sweaty pressure of being in his pocket. He imagined some crucial word smudged away, the one that would have made the difference.

He wouldn't open it, not now. Not in this mood.

He had lasted all of forty minutes that morning in his vow to quit smoking. He would finish this pack and try again; the climb had decided him. But then he checked how many cigarettes remained and had to hold back his panic: only three.

He smoked the one he had going right down to the nub and butted it out on the pristine step. It left a black scorch against the gray, a sign that he'd been there.

By the time Alex had straggled within sight of the seventeenth-floor fire door, he had moved well past the point of self-pity into sheer bloody-mindedness. He'd had a chance by then to review most of his major life decisions, then to regret them, then to not care one way or the other; he'd had a chance to resolve to change in every possible way that could make any difference and then to admit that he'd never change, that he didn't even want to, that he preferred just to wallow in his iniquities like a pig in his shit. His head was pounding, his legs were jelly, his lungs felt like burst balloons. All he could smell was his own sweat, shaded by now into degrees of staleness, and then the awful seafood stench coming up from his groceries like the miasma off a swamp.

At least Novak would be gone. He had seen Jiri's bag, the same battered leather one he'd first shown up with, sitting already packed by the door when he'd left the apartment that morning. If María hadn't been waiting for him Alex would gladly have stuck around to see Jiri safely off, to his cab, to his very train. All that mattered was that he be gone, that Alex be free to have his evening with María without the sense of Jiri's looming presence, which had somehow managed to assert itself in every corner of the apartment since he'd moved in.

He had called in the first week of classes.

"Your summer all right?"

That he was making an effort at small talk had immediately put Alex on alert.

"A bit busy." He didn't ask about Jiri's summer—he'd heard all the rumors by then, about the breakup but also about some questions that had arisen regarding his relations with a certain female undergrad.

"Good, good," Jiri said. "Of course."

He'd gone on in a strained tone about a book Alex ought to look at, while Alex waited for the penny to drop.

"By the way, it wouldn't be for long, but I need a place to leave my things for a couple of days till my sublet's free. I'd go to the Y but the rooms are so awful there."

Alex wasn't sure from this whether he actually intended to stay with him until he showed up the next day with his bag. It was the worst possible time for Alex, with the problems in the building and his constant cramming for CanLit. To top it off, Liz had dumped Moses with him: they had run into each other over the summer, a bristly encounter on St. Lawrence when they'd exchanged all of half a dozen words, but then she'd called him out of the blue to take the cat while she went out of town. The request was so clearly an effort at détente he could hardly say no, even though pets, in his building, were strictly verboten.

"You'll have to be careful about the cat," he said when Jiri arrived, though without much hope that Jiri would be careful about the cat or about anything.

There was the question of where Jiri would sleep.

"There's a sofa bed, but it's a bit lumpy." At the silence that followed, Alex added, "You can use my bedroom if you want."

Jiri placed his bag on Alex's bed.

"It'll just be for a few days," he said.

Jiri wasted no time in colonizing Alex's bedroom, taking over his desk and making several trips to his office the next day to collect shopping bags full of books, which he set out on Alex's desktop and in the empty slots on Alex's shelves.

"You didn't need this, did you?"

"It's all right. I can work at the table."

That was the beginning. Several of Jiri's suits appeared over the next days, displacing Alex's clothes in the bedroom closet, as did Jiri's little manual typewriter and half a dozen boxes of files that he arranged at the foot of the bed. Through all of this Jiri came and went as if Alex were merely some stranger the Communist Housing Committee had forced him to live with. Most of their conversations were purely practical ones—where the salt was, where to find the nearest cleaners. Alex had never used a cleaners in his life except for his

Sunday suits, but Jiri took every scrap of his clothing to them, right down to his underwear and his socks, something Alex had not even known was possible.

Alex held out hope that the bedroom might at least serve as a sanctum for Jiri, keeping the rest of the apartment Jiri-free. But that hadn't been the case. Rather, Jiri, by seeming to anticipate every possible need or action on Alex's part—always up before him, always in the bathroom first, always claiming the best place at the dining table, the one that faced the windows—had somehow managed to change the apartment's usual rules of being so that what mattered were no longer the actual physical walls, which turned out to be flimsy things, but rather the psychic ones that more and more boxed Alex into the little corner of floor space occupied by his now permanently made-up sofa bed.

Even when Jiri was out, he was not gone. His toiletries filled the bathroom, including a tar shampoo that left an odor of roofing work; his strange foodstuffs filled every corner of the fridge, greenish pastes and sock-smelling cheeses and meats, thick, non-standard juices like pear and apricot. It was as if the very culture of the apartment was under siege, as if the moment would come when Jiri's had so completely taken over that Alex would be forced out like an alien. Even Moses, already out of sorts at being abandoned in this foreign place, seemed to sense that the apartment's center of gravity had shifted, skulking around in a sort of counterpoint to Jiri. Jiri showed Moses about the same amount of attentiveness he showed Alex, so that Alex was constantly on edge that he'd drop Moses from the balcony or betray him to the super or let him escape one day down the elevator and into the anonymous world. Yet a relationship had developed between them, disconcerting and strange, Moses forever circling around Jiri like a petitioner, planning his approaches, stealing quick feels against his leg. He took to curling up at night at the foot of Jiri's, formerly Alex's, bed, something Jiri actually tolerated, so that Alex was left alone on his lumpy sofa bed like a jilted lover.

The work on the water lines began, and Jiri had yet to move out. Notices had gone around about potential outages suggesting that the work would be handled with a degree of civility this time, but it quickly turned into a free-for-all, elevators commandeered, mangled pipes left in the halls, and the water going off at all hours. Jiri took to doing his toilette at the Y, where he had a membership, so that none of these disruptions seemed to leave the least blemish on him. But Alex grew more bedraggled with each day. He went to the Y as well, for Esther's swimming, but could hardly park her somewhere while he sneaked off to take a shower. Short, then, of forking out the ten dollars for a day pass to go on his own, he was stuck taking tepid bucket baths in his tub with water from the kitchen.

As the repairs inched upward Alex could hear the loudening din of plumbing work in his walls like a coming infestation. Then one morning, well before anything like a decent hour, two pasty-skinned workmen who looked as if they'd been holed up in a cellar for months avoiding capture showed up at his door.

"No one said you were coming."

"Is okay," one of the men said, "we start."

So they did. There was a lot of smashing with a ball-peen hammer to get at the pipes through the bedroom wall, then a lot of grimacing while they stared at the mess of corroded couplings and joints they'd revealed, pipes branching off in every direction. Jiri, who had already been up at work when they arrived, stood by watching all this with an intent, curious air.

"Is bad," one of the men said to Alex, clearly blaming him. An exchange ensued between the two workers full of grunts and heavy monosyllables, Jiri following it like a tennis match.

"Prablyema?" he interjected.

"Da," one of the men said warily. "Da."

It wasn't long before the three of them were down on their knees poking and prodding at the mess of pipes, to more grunts and grim pronouncements. One of the workers stepped into the bathroom and traced an ominous line across the mirror tiles above the tub.

Jiri looked charmed.

"Russian Jews," he said. "My Russian's a bit rusty, but it's better than my Yiddish."

"What's the problem?"

"It's not good. Some sort of a junction, I think."

The men hauled in matériel for their work, wrenches, crowbars, a jig-saw, and began carving channels in the bathroom walls. Much as Alex hated his mirror tiles he felt a wince each time another of them was prised away, usually in jagged bits. He could already envision the devastation these men would leave behind, the forms he would have to file at the

Régie, the months or years he would have to wait before he got anything like satisfaction.

He could barely think for the racket but didn't dare go out, afraid each time one of the men came or went that Moses would make a run for the elevator.

"Is cat," one of them said, finally noticing him.

"Yes." Alex was sure the breach would get back to Tony now, and he'd be evicted.

The workman squatted and gave Moses a little stroke on his muzzle. "Is good cat."

Jiri, through all of this, hadn't left the apartment, though his work space was a shambles, Alex's desk pushed aside and piled high with the shelving and books that had been removed from the wall so the men could smash it. He stood back watching the men's work as if it were a quaint folk ritual he'd happened upon, putting questions to them now and then in his halting Russian.

"Alex, maybe you should offer these gentlemen a cup of coffee."

It was evening before the workers had gone. The apartment looked like a construction site by then, crumbled drywall everywhere, abandoned tools, the bathtub full of broken pieces of tile.

"That's the funny thing about Russian Jews," Jiri said. "Seventy years of brainwashing but they've never forgotten they're Jews. It's like a case study for the failure of the Soviet experiment."

The work went on for days. The men might come for an hour and be on their way; or they might be working full tilt in what seemed the middle of a marathon session, then break for coffee and never return. The whole time Alex was reduced to his bucket flushes and his bucket baths, always afraid he'd catch some splinter of tile up his backside. Meanwhile Jiri, perversely, embraced the disorder like someone rolling up his sleeves at a challenge. He had grown downright chummy with the workers, Boris and Mikhail from Gomel, not so far from Chernobyl.

Back home, Boris and Mikhail had been engineers.

"Chernobyl was a lucky break for them," Jiri said. "Twenty years they'd been asking to get out, then Chernobyl happened and the approval came through in just a couple of weeks."

Even with Alex Jiri had taken on an in-the-trenches camaraderie. One evening he made supper for him, cucumber salad and schnitzel.

"This was what I was eating when the Russians marched in," he said. "At a Hungarian place in Soho, to be exact."

Alex was shocked to find out that Jiri hadn't been in Czechoslovakia at all when the troops had come, but in London for a conference. He had watched the whole thing on TV like everyone else, for all his talk in class about not knowing what the revolution was when you were in the middle of it.

"Just think of it as a teaching aid," he said. "Anyway, the point's still valid."

"So you didn't go back?"

"I thought about it. It wouldn't have been so bad, maybe—I would just have ended up in a factory or whatever like the other intellectuals. But the truth was I didn't want to have to start up the same old struggle again. Most people only have the one good fight in them. After that you start looking around for how to enjoy yourself a little."

This wasn't the kind of thing you'd hear from Jiri in class. In class it was all about laying waste to every authority and every assumption. Then there was the matter of his wife and son: that was another of his touch-stones, his seven-year separation from them, which in class always played out as a metaphor for the hole at the heart of totalitarianism. "That's the nature of tyranny in a nutshell," he'd say. "Always being defined by what's absent." But none of it looked so grand in the light of his schnitzel in Soho.

Jiri had managed to root out the Scotch that Stephen had left behind back in the spring.

"You know, I was taking a look at your new proposal," he said.

Alex wasn't sure what he was talking about.

"But I haven't even handed it in to you."

"It saw it sitting on your desk. I thought you·wouldn't mind."

In fact it had been *in* his desk, down in one of the lower drawers, though Alex felt such a strange thrill at the thought that Jiri had actually taken the trouble to go through his things that he couldn't muster any sense of outrage.

"It's not bad," Jiri said. "It's not quite there yet, but it's not bad. Your other draft, all the terminology was getting in the way. But this one seems more from the heart."

Alex took a gulp of his Scotch. This was when Jiri got most danger-ous, when he approached anything like praise.

"I guess I talked it out with someone who didn't know all the language," he said, realizing only as he spoke that he meant Esther.

"That's good, that's good. Sometimes it's important to remind yourself that all this stuff is actually supposed to mean something."

Jiri poured more Scotch.

"When you think of someone like Derrida or Lacan, they're not really doing anything different than you are. They're just drawing a shape in the air, that's all. But yours has an actual physical base—I don't think anyone's tried that before. There was Lévi-Strauss, of course, but most of that was just nonsense."

Alex's head was swimming. In a moment, surely, Jiri would tell him he was pulling his leg.

"Don't get me wrong. It's not going to be a breeze getting this past the committee. They'll want to see the language. But I think there's something there."

The rest of the evening was a haze. Alex had the feeling he used to get on acid, that he was on the brink of some tremendous revelation. Jiri was part of this feeling; Alex couldn't imagine how he had ever felt any ill will toward him.

They had drained every last drop of the Scotch.

"I'm glad you're finally buying the real stuff," Jiri said.

In the morning, Alex awoke so hungover that he wasn't sure the evening had even happened.

Jiri was already hurrying off to class.

"Bring the proposal by my office and we'll try to clean it up," he said, as if they didn't see each other every day of the week. "It's not quite up to doctoral level yet."

The workmen finished a couple of days later. They left behind exactly the carnage Alex had feared, the plaster repairs in the bedroom looking like the scar tissue on a torture victim and the bathroom such a patchwork of tile and bald wall that Alex's mind reeled every time he went in there, vainly searching for pattern amidst the ruins. In the meantime, Alex's resentment toward Jiri had built back to full force, so that every smallest infraction, his crumbs on the cutting board, his abandoned coffee cups, the spots of Ultra Brite he left on the bathroom sink, seemed set to push it beyond endurance.

Now I don't suppose it occurred to you just to kick his butt out of there, pardon my French? I mean, talk about totalitarian!

Well, Peter, the situation was a bit delicate. And then he's a fascinating character, really. I learned a lot from him while he was there.

Like how to take advantage of your graduate students, for instance.

By the seventeenth floor Alex seemed to have come to a region of the stairwell that not even Guy had ever made it up to, half the lights burnt out and a fine dust powdering the stairs that looked like it hadn't been stepped on in twenty years. He should lodge a complaint about the lights, he thought, and then he thought, *Fuck it.* Those days were done. It occurred to him that maybe his one good fight had come and gone.

He wished he was more like Jiri. Here was a man whose job hung in the balance, whose wife had left him, who was homeless, who had a skinhead son, yet he managed to carry on as if none of it touched him. The latest rumor was that his son had joined a bona fide neo-Nazi group.

"The funny thing is he looks exactly like Jerry," one of the faculty had told him. "A mirror image. Right down to his bald head."

Jerry. That was what the faculty called Jiri, the remnant, no doubt, of some pre-identity-politics self. Jiri would let the name float in the air without batting an eye, as if he was above it, as if it had been neutralized before it reached him.

Alex had reached his apartment. Everything had become a synesthetic blur, the pounding in his head, his sweat, the stink of seafood. He was seeing colors: green for the stink, strobe-light purple for the pounding.

He heard a sound on the other side of the door as he was turning his key and his first paranoid thought was that the landlords had broken in, that he was about to catch them red-handed, planting microphones or stealing his computer files or verifying some snitch's report that he was harboring a pet. But then he swung the door open and saw what in his deepest heart of hearts he had been expecting all along, Jiri's bag still planted by the entrance and Jiri himself sitting reading the paper on the sofa, which Alex, for the first time in many days, had pointedly restored to its proper use that very morning.

Moses, though he wasn't allowed there, sat purring on the sofa beside him.

Alex had to struggle to keep the tremor from his voice.

"I thought you were going."

"Hmm?" Jiri glanced up from his paper. "Back already?"

"I thought you'd be gone."

"Oh. I missed my train."

Any minute, Alex thought, he was literally going to burst into flames with rage.

"Why didn't you wait for another one?"

"The truth is I never really left the apartment. It was taking so long to get an elevator I just gave up. I thought I'd wait till tomorrow."

"There's a train at three-forty. I've taken it. There's another one at five."

"What's the difference?" Jiri said. "I'd just as soon wait."

"The difference is"—Alex tried to restrain himself—"the difference is, I had plans."

Jiri looked at him over the rims of his glasses.

"Alex, my boy, you're not saying you had a romantic encounter planned, are you?"

"What I had planned—" But there was no point being evasive. "Yes. Yes. As a matter of fact, I did."

"Good, good, I was beginning to worry about you! I can arrange to be out, of course, it's not a problem."

"Yes," Alex said, "yes, it's a problem. I don't want you to be here."

Jiri shrugged as if he did not follow.

"As I say, I can go out. The whole night, if you think it'll come to that. I'll just take a room at the Y—"

"No, you don't understand." This was the point at which he ought to have stopped himself, at which it was still possible for things to end civilly. "I don't want you here at all. I want my apartment back, I want my desk back, I want my bed. I know you're going through a rough time, I know your wife left you and your son hates you or something, but that doesn't give you the right to take advantage of me. It doesn't give you the right."

There, he had got it out. For a moment he felt a great lifting.

"Ah," Jiri said. "I see."

He looked truly crestfallen. Already Alex could feel his relief seeping away.

"Look, I'm just saying, with all the work and everything—"

"No, no, you're absolutely right," Jiri said, drawing his dignity around him. "I'll take a room at the Y until I find a place."

He had started packing papers into his briefcase.

"I didn't mean you had to go this minute."

"That's fine, it's just as well. I'll come for the rest of my things when I get back from Toronto."

He rounded up a few odds and ends in the bedroom. He'd left his paper on the dining table—not a *Gazette*, Alex saw, but a *Toronto Star*, folded to a headline that read "Man Attacked in City Park."

Jiri took up the newspaper and put it in his briefcase.

"Maybe you could dig up a couple of boxes later and leave my books in them," he said. "To speed things up a bit."

"Sure. Sure."

He added a few extra underwear to his bag, neatly folded and pressed from the cleaners, then donned his trench coat.

"So. Thank you, then. I'm sorry if I overstayed my welcome."

Whatever goodwill Alex might have earned over the previous weeks seemed cast to the winds.

"Call my office when you want to discuss the proposal," Jiri said, all business now.

After the weeks of lingering it took Jiri all of five minutes to clear out. Alex felt a chill at how abruptly the matter had ended. It seemed only now that he understood that something like a relationship had been forming between the two of them while Jiri had been there, a twisted, unbalanced one, maybe, but a relationship nonetheless. What he remembered, watching Jiri go, was the glow that had come off him the night of the Scotch, as if he were a shaman or wizard sent to guide him.

The elevator, miraculously, arrived almost at once. Jiri stepped into it without looking back, straight-shouldered and undiminished.

– 6 –

It was well past his appointed time when Alex finally managed to make his way down to Esther's to collect her for her swimming. Molly, Esther's new helper, stood waiting for him at her open door.

"Twenty minute I am waiting," she said. "You say you will come at three."

Every time he saw Molly—Wamalie, her real name was, though Alex was the only one who ever called her that, a courtesy she showed no sign of appreciating—he felt his aversion toward her surge anew.

"She would have been fine if you'd just left her on her own a few minutes."

"And what her father will say, if she tell him?"

In the three months now that Molly had been looking after Esther, Alex had yet to get a proper bead on her. He disliked her, yes, but hadn't been able to determine whether this had some basis in reality or was just him sulking over territory or being racist. He quizzed Esther on her constantly, as innocently as he could manage, since Esther worshipped her, but so far nothing he'd gleaned had established definitively whether she was an abusive power-tripper holding Esther in a kind of Stockholm-syndrome thrall or a godsend who'd brought Esther back from the brink of despair. This much he knew, that she showed up five mornings a week precisely at seven, and from then on took over Esther's life with all the force of an invading army, bathing her and dressing her and feeding her, escorting her to her doctors' appointments and to her physio sessions at the Royal Vic, attending classes with her at the university, where she worked her tape recorder for her and held open her books and for all Alex knew browbeat her professors into giving her passing grades, all of this before she left again at three with the same promptness with which she'd arrived.

She seemed to loom there in Esther's doorway, though she didn't stand more than five feet. *Molly Svengali.*

"I hope I didn't keep you from an appointment," he said coolly.

"No appointment. Only my cousin's daughter, she is coming home from school, no key."

All Alex's sanctimoniousness drained away. Somewhere in the city, probably in a gang-infested tenement in the squalid lower reaches of Point St. Charles, some innocent little Filipina was cowering alone now in a darkened hallway because Alex had been late.

"I'm sorry," Alex said. "I'm sorry about that."

"Is okay, she wait."

Esther was parked in the living room in her wheelchair trussed and prepped, her hair tied back in a ponytail, her cheeks done up with a bit of rouge to hide her pallor, a gym bag draped over the arm of her chair holding, Alex knew, a towel, goggles, a bathing cap, an extra pair of underwear, and a child's sippy cup filled with orange juice.

Her vision had grown erratic since her last exacerbation and it took her an instant sometimes to make out when someone had entered her field of vision.

"Sorry I'm late, Es," Alex said.

"Oh, Alex! Are you late?"

The wheelchair had been a shock. One week Esther had been getting around fine on her cane, her usual social-butterfly self, the next she was flat on her back in a hospital bed hardly able to move.

"I can't believe it, I just blacked out," she said when Alex went in to see her. "Has that ever happened to you? Have you ever blacked out like that?"

Alex could hear the fear in her voice. When by the third day she still wasn't able to get out of bed she began to panic.

"I can't do it, Alex," she said. "I can't stop walking. I just can't. I might as well be dead."

By then the slow procession of reality mongers had started coming through, her doctor, the hospital staff, her mother. Her mother was the one who had found her, collapsed on the floor of her apartment unable to get to the phone.

"It's still early," Alex said. He didn't want to seem on the side of the naysayers, even if in his heart he was. "In a week we'll be going out for cappuccinos again."

But a week later she was still in hospital. By then a chair had arrived, and a physio had started working on getting her used to it. Esther acted as if all of it was merely temporary, as if she was just humoring everyone. By the time she came home, wheeled up the steps at the front of the building by her brother Lenny—there was nothing like a ramp there—she was treating the chair as a lark.

"Look at my new chair," she said to people. "La-di-da."

But alone with her, Alex would see how the life drained out of her sometimes. He'd always thought of her stubbornness as an intrinsic part of her, but now he saw it was something she actually had to make an effort for. It was scary to think what her life might be like without it: there'd be only the pit then, only one bad thing to look forward to after another.

There had seemed no question of her going back to her swimming. Before the exacerbation, this had been an article of almost religious faith, her daily hour in the building's pool. In the water, Esther was transformed—it was something about the weightlessness, the way the water held her. She was strangely in control; you had to look, and look again, to see the bit of unsureness in her. The first time Alex had seen her, he'd felt as if he were looking at a stranger: this was Esther, whole. She'd done a lap, had turned smoothly, done another, just a woman in the water. It had been hard to bear the intimacy of it, as if he'd stolen a look at her naked, or as if he was the one who was standing naked.

"You didn't think it was true," she'd said afterward. "You thought you'd have to jump in and save me."

But after the exacerbation she didn't mention the swimming anymore. It was only from Lenny that Alex learned Esther's physio had actually been pushing for her to go back to it, and she was resisting. This was a new Esther, a scary one.

"I'm just so tired, Alex," she said. "I'm so tired."

"Just try it. It can't hurt to try it."

Alex stood watching from the pool deck the first time Lenny took her in again. At one point she slipped from Lenny's grasp and went under and came up hacking and panicked. Alex hurried over to help Lenny lift her to the side of the pool, crouching there at the pool edge while she clung to him, clammy as a sea thing, her coughs merging into her sobs.

"It's hopeless," she said. "I can't do it."

But she went back afterward, using a kickboard to help her, and slowly she began to get a feel for the water again. After a couple of weeks, with the board, she could manage a lap or two entirely on her own, and some of her old spirit began to return. She started using a walker sometimes to get around her apartment, though she didn't talk about fighting the chair anymore—it was real, it was part of her life. Sometimes it happened after exacerbations that people made total recoveries, Alex had read about it in one of Esther's pamphlets, but he never heard her give voice to that hope. Something had shifted in her, gone underground. She didn't use her hands much around people now, as if to avoid the embarrassment of some mishap, but the old Esther would never have cared about that, would simply have surged on like a freight train.

Then there was Molly. It occurred to Alex that you couldn't possibly help feeling like a sick person when you had someone treating you like one eight relentless hours a day, cutting your food up for you, scolding you for every little bit of initiative, forever reminding you of your limitations and prohibitions and special ailments. But a symbiosis had developed between Esther and Molly that Alex couldn't quite figure; what looked like mere bullying to him seemed to function for Esther as a sort of cult-like catechism.

"She only lets me watch an hour of TV every day," Esther boasted. "And if I want to sleep in, I have to do it on the weekend, she says my father's not paying her to watch me sleep."

When Esther returned to her swimming, Alex wondered at first if it wasn't Molly Svengali who'd somehow been behind it. But no: it turned out that Molly, pigheadedly, would have nothing to do with Esther's swimming. Alex put it down to sheer resentment, that Esther had dared to have something beyond Molly's control. But the one time Molly agreed to come to the building's pool to watch Esther swim, at Esther's repeated bidding, she hugged the walls the entire time, clearly scared out of her wits of the water.

"You see?" Esther called from the pool. "You see? Alex didn't believe it either!"

Molly stood clucking and shaking her head like an old mother hen.

"You never tell me you are a fish," she said, letting a grudging smile escape her.

Esther was beaming, happier than Alex had seen her in weeks.

The truth was that Alex's irritation with Molly was probably just his way of not admitting his abiding gratitude to her. Molly's shifts with Esther were like a daily vacation for him from any sense of personal obligation; the rest of the time, even if days went by without his seeing Esther, was all subject to appropriation, never quite his own. It was like his Amnesty work: he could have written letters every hour of every day, organized fund-raising campaigns, pitched his tent at the very gates of the world's despots, and still the work wouldn't ever be done. With Esther, five minutes quickly became thirty, which then became an entire afternoon or evening, if Alex should ever be so rash, say, as to pop his head into her apartment as he was passing. Her life was like a quicksand he fell into, full of contingencies and wants and agendas. Then, nowadays, there was a never-ending parade of other visitors he had to contend with: lifelong friends Esther had often talked about who, however, came once, were overly friendly and loud, then never appeared again; new friends she'd met hours before, people who reeked of need, and who seemed impossible to get rid of. Then there were the nurses who came by to give Esther her cortisone shots or her B_{12} or her interferon; and there was Esther's family.

Alex had had only glancing contact with Esther's family before the exacerbation. Sometimes Esther's mother had been at her apartment when Alex had gone by, this staunch, sour-faced woman, utterly unlike her daughter, with a body like a block chipped off a mountain face.

"It's all right, don't bother, I'll do that," she said if Alex made the least effort to help out. Invariably her eyes would go to the pack of cigarettes in his breast pocket—he was the one, she seemed to say, he was the tempter, poisoning her daughter with nicotine and who-knew-what.

But when Esther was in hospital he went by once to find the whole lot of them huddled in a little semicircle at the foot of her bed, her parents, Lenny, her sister Rachel, all of them standing there so silent and still he could hear the rise and fall of Esther's breath.

"She's asleep," Lenny whispered to Alex, and the whole group quietly shifted to accommodate him. For several minutes they stood there, in that same silence, making no effort, it seemed, either to bring Alex in or to close him out.

Esther's mother started to cry and her husband, with surprising gentleness, ushered her into the hall. He wasn't the brash wheeler-dealer Alex had expected but a little gnome of a man, with the same slow, measured diction as Esther.

Lenny had moved in close to Alex.

"It's great of you to come. It means a lot to us. Esther talks about you all the time."

So the door had opened and Alex had felt obliged to go through it, stuck trying to live up to the wildly inflated billing that Esther had given him. Lenny and Rachel, though they didn't have a life-threatening illness to excuse it, had the same disconcerting tendency to praise that Esther did, so that the pressure only kept mounting.

"It's so great, everything you do for Esther," Rachel said, when in his heart Alex knew that he was just a shirker. Rachel, meanwhile, who was all of seventeen, spent most of her evenings with Esther, and slept on her couch to be there when Molly arrived, and rode fifty minutes on transit every morning to get out to her CEGEP in Ville St. Laurent.

Sometimes if Lenny spent the night, Alex stayed up with him after Esther had gone to bed to share the tail end of a joint.

"I guess you didn't know that Es used to be a real pothead," Lenny said. "Mom used to find pot in her room all the time. Then one day she dropped out of school and moved out, just like that. You'd never think it was the same Es. She used to work at a jeans place on St. Catherine and hang around with this whole hippie crowd."

Lenny was an utterly regular guy, had gone to work for his father's little investment firm straight out of university and was already balding and growing thick around the middle. But there was an unflappability to him that seemed somehow more than the sum of his parts. Esther treated him like her manservant whenever Alex was around, as if he was still the menial younger brother, though if Lenny took any umbrage at this he never showed it. He used to come around after work and on weekends to take Esther down to the building's pool, though when it closed and they had to resort to the Y he'd have to take her out during the workday, since that was the only time the pool there wasn't crowded with power swimmers or screaming children.

"It's fine, he can take the time," Esther's mother said, but it made more sense for Alex to take her out. He never got any work done during the day anyway—he'd piss around until mid-afternoon and then finally admit to himself that the day was a write-off and put off to the evening any plans for real work. Thus the Y had become his particular bailiwick. Esther, of course, was thrilled at the arrangement, which made him feel, each time he showed up for her, like the Gentleman Caller, come to show the young cripple all she would know of romance.

She sat patiently while Alex released the lock on her chair and maneuvered her out of the apartment, taking care not to bang into the walls. He was hoping Molly had already gone but she stood holding the elevator for them like a reproving parent. He miscalculated his distances angling Esther through the elevator door and ended up wedged into the corner with Molly. He had long ago given up trying to make conversation with Molly. Once he'd tried to talk to her about Filipino politics and she'd looked at him as if he was insane.

"She doesn't like to talk about that," Esther had said afterward. "About politics. One of her brothers had to go to prison or something."

Fine. So she had secrets, then, she had complexities. That didn't mean he had to be nice to her. It wasn't as if she needed him—she seemed to have a whole network of so-called cousins that she was part of, women with whom she might or might not share actual genetic material but who seemed to function like a vast mutual aid society, passing children around, chasing off difficult husbands, preparing, for all he knew, for the Domestic Workers' Revolution.

"You can put her lotion after swimming," Molly said, when they'd reached the street. "I put in the bag."

He didn't dare set off until she had rounded the corner toward the metro and was out of sight.

"Isn't she great?" Esther said.

Alex tried to clear his head. Lois was still jangling around in there, Jiri, his paella. When Jiri had gone, he'd got into the shower and the water had come out a trickle—he'd wanted to scream, to take a hammer to what remained of his mirror tiles, to Richard Shapiro's head. He'd hurried down to the laundry afterward to throw in his sheets, reduced to putting dish detergent in with them because he'd run out of laundry soap, then had gone back up to his apartment to get a start on the paella only to discover that he'd forgotten to pick to up any saffron, the crucial ingredient.

"What do you think she lives for?" he said of Molly, not especially kindly. "I mean, stuck here with no family or anything."

"Oh, she has children back in the Philippines," Esther said.

Alex, irritated, wondered why he hadn't known this.

"Who would leave their children like that?"

"I know, it's awful. She showed me pictures of them."

He could see them in his head, Molly's little *chiquillos*, plump-cheeked from being overfed by their aunties and grandmas, but with that bit of hardness to them, because their mother had left them. It was depressing, that she'd had to abandon her kids on the other side of the globe to come and look after the kids of strangers. But then maybe she loved her life—she was free, had escaped her husband, her parents, her children, every expectation of what she should be.

The sun was still out, but already the air had started to cool. Alex steered past the shops on St. Catherine, trying to stay out of the shadows. He could feel distinctly now the treacherous breath of the coming cold. It was hard to believe he'd been sweating like a workhorse only hours before.

"It's beautiful, isn't it?" Esther said, inhaling. "I love the smell of the fall."

The Y building on Stanley had the not unpleasant feel of a hospital or mission house, of a place where you could not actually be turned away. Alex resisted the urge to ask at the residence desk if Jiri had checked in, knowing in his gut that he'd gone back to bunk in his office. No matter: not his problem. He handed over Esther's membership card and an attendant, this was the drill, followed them to the women's change room to stand guard while Alex and Esther went in.

He helped Esther shimmy out of her dress. She could manage most of this on her own except for getting it over her backside. Alex had to reach down the back of her wheelchair and pull while she raised one cheek, then the other. It felt intimate and wrong, all this tussling. Sometimes she stood, using her cane, though there was the danger then that she'd twist an ankle or slip on a patch of wet or simply crumple. None of these things had happened yet, but Alex felt the premonition of them.

He was always relieved when she was finally in the pool. It wasn't just that she was more in command there, but that the whole pool area was always crawling with trained professionals. That saved Alex actually having to suit up, which in any event would just have been a way of

misleading people, like aping a few words of a language you didn't otherwise understand. Unfortunately there was a new girl around lately,
maybe all of nineteen, who was a real Ilsa-of-the-SS type, with a body like
the bulked-up mutations you saw on Eastern bloc Olympic teams. Alex
spotted her at the far end of the pool as he wheeled Esther out, surveying
her dominions. Before he could look away she had caught his eye and
laid claim to him with a peremptory nod.

She took her time coming over, walking past them to the equipment
area to grab a reach pole.

"Give me a minute."

Esther, Alex imagined, was aware of Ilsa—whose name tag read
"Sandy," clearly a mistake—only as this pole, which Ilsa insisted on holding inches from Esther's face the entire time Esther was in the pool, following her with punctilious attentiveness from the pool edge as if training a
slow-witted seal. Alex had never seen Ilsa herself in the water, or so much
as a speck of damp on her sexless East-bloc-issue one-piece.

Alex went over to get a kickboard.

"You know, she can't keep coming here like this," Ilsa said, fussily
adjusting her pole.

"Sorry?"

"We're not staffed for this. Sometimes she can barely make a lap."

The arrogance of it, Alex thought. The arrogance of health.

"What exactly are you here for, then?"

"I'm just saying we can't take responsibility."

She had already turned to take up her position at the edge of the
pool. *Bitch.* At least Esther hadn't caught any of this.

"Is everything all right?" she said.

"She was just saying we're a bit late, that's all."

He helped her into the shallow end of the pool, crouching to steady
her.

"You okay?"

"Actually, I have a disease. Ha ha."

He felt an instant's panic when she pushed off, that her body would
fail her. Then, on account of Ilsa, he could hardly bear to watch as she
thrashed her way forward, though Ilsa had only said what he already
knew. At some point, a ways back now, Esther had plateaued, had made
whatever recovery she was likely to make from her exacerbation and then

had started to slide again. Surely everyone knew this, even Esther, though he could see that in her heart, which she kept secret now, she had yet to stop hoping.

There, she had made a lap. Maybe her will could still save her, maybe if she kept believing, if she kept her mind clear like some sort of Zen master, she could defeat this thing. But Alex knew that was bunk. Surely no one had believed as wildly as Esther had, as unreasonably, and still her illness had progressed.

He ought to tell Esther's family about Ilsa's warning. But one hint of it to Esther's mother, and that would be the end. He didn't want to be the one to take this last thing from Esther, this last fight.

"Pull up! Pull up!"

It was Ilsa. Esther's hand had slipped off her board, and right off Ilsa had started screaming at her like a banshee. God forbid she might actually have to get down into the water and do her job.

She'd grabbed Esther's arms and pulled her to the side of the pool.

"Sir!" Every head in the room turned to him and knew his guilt. "I think you'd better give me a hand here!"

It was like getting some huge fish out of the water, landing it trembling and wet. Alex had to struggle to avoid any sort of fleshly contact with Ilsa.

"I had a spasm," Esther said. "I'm sorry. I'm sorry."

"You don't have to be sorry," Alex said.

To her credit, Ilsa had the good grace, at least, not to allude to her earlier warning. When they had Esther wrapped in a towel and back in her chair she abandoned them with another tight nod. She was right, of course, he shouldn't be bringing Esther here, forcing others to make decisions he hadn't the courage to make himself.

Esther was sitting hunched and shivering in her chair.

"I guess we should go," she said.

"We just have to wait for the change room."

By now children of various sizes had started to come out for the after-school kiddie lessons, roving in indeterminate gangs around the pool deck or huddled up against the walls, pasty-skinned and shivering. In a matter of minutes the whole mood of the place had changed from no-nonsense adultness to the carnival air of a camp, kids squealing or flicking towels or hollering out in quick staccato to hear their voices echoing back in the cavernous chill. Around Esther, however, there remained a little island of empty terrain as if a force field protected her, the hallowed space of affliction, fascinating and terrible.

Alex wheeled her toward the change room. A scrawny boy-geek came along not watching where he was going and practically ran right into them.

"Oh!" He stared up wide-eyed into Esther's wheelchaired eminence.

"It's all right," Alex said, suppressing the urge to reach out to him.

They had a hard time with Esther's suit. He had to squeeze into her little cubicle with her, averting his eyes while he helped her.

"It's sticking. Just raise yourself up a bit."

It happened sometimes when she was tired like this that her flesh would lose all definition, become just a quavering mass.

"There. I've got it."

By the time they were out on the street again the sun had dropped below the skyline and the air had turned positively cold, as if the seasons had changed in an hour. Esther, in a flimsy sweater and frock, was woefully underdressed. Alex took some pleasure in blaming Molly for this.

"How're you feeling?"

"Tired."

He knew Esther had a show at five that she wanted to catch. She watched a lot of TV these days, after Molly was gone and the restrictions were loosed, soap operas and cheesy dramas that she guarded her addiction to like some old woman in a nursing home, saying nothing of them to anyone but growing irritable and out of sorts if anything kept her from them. Her evenings now were this regimen of favored shows, which she'd eat her supper in front of, which she'd watch while Rachel tried to piece through for her whatever assignments were due for her courses. Then around nine her body would give out as if its engine had stopped, and she'd fall into a dead sleep.

St. Catherine was in shadow now, abuzz with the queer energy of late afternoon. Alex wheeled Esther through the traffic, which seemed all to be moving against them, as if they were fighting a current. The City had recently cut slopes into some of the curbs to accommodate wheelchairs, but haphazardly, so that you could sail out into the street only to find yourself stranded at the other side.

He made a tentative stab at what they were avoiding.

"How are you feeling about your swimming?"

"All right. I don't know."

"What don't you know?"

"It's just . . . it's getting hard."

He ought to drop the matter.

"Do you think you might want to give it a break for a bit? Until you feel stronger?"

"Do you think that's a good idea? Do you think I should do that?"

"Maybe. I guess it depends on how you feel."

"I don't know. I don't know how I feel. I'm just so tired sometimes."

He should never have brought the subject up. She was actually looking to him, she was weighing what he said as if he had answers.

"Maybe I won't get stronger," she said. "Maybe I won't get better."

"You don't know that. It happens to people. They come out of it."

He didn't dare say more.

"It wasn't so awful, was it?" Esther said finally. "When I wanted to sleep with you. Was it so awful?"

Why was she saying these things to him? Who was he, that they should matter?

"No, it wasn't awful. It wasn't awful at all."

When they got back to the apartment, Esther's mother was loading Tupperwared provisions into the fridge. Her eye—Alex waited for it as he'd wait for a bullet—went straight to his cigarettes.

"Take some soup with you," she said. "There's extra. I'll split it."

"No, it's fine. I should go."

"Here. Wait."

He wouldn't say anything about the swimming. Not to her. To Lenny, maybe.

She was holding a container out to him.

"Take it," she said, as if anxious to be rid of it. "For your supper."

Supper, he thought. His paella.

"I should probably go."

"Esther, say thank you."

"I don't have to say thank you to Alex, Ma, he's like family."

Esther's mother forced an unhappy smile.

"If you want, I'll bring more soup for you tomorrow."

"It's all right."

"I'll leave it with Esther for you."

Outside the door, Alex hesitated. Esther had already wheeled herself toward the TV.

"I can take her again tomorrow if you want," he said.

"It's all right, Lenny can do it."

"No, really, it's fine. I'd like to."

For an instant her mother's eyes went to his with a questioning look he'd never seen in them.

"I'll bring the soup," she said, and closed the door.

7

A lex still had a good couple of hours ahead of him before María was likely to show up, if she showed up at all, though the certainty was building in him that she would call at the last minute with some excuse. From Esther's he went down to the laundry room to collect his sheets from the dryer, only to find them suffused with a lemony chemical smell from the dish soap, then he popped in at the depanneur on the slim chance they carried saffron. To his amazement, Ilie, the owner, pulled a dusty little clear plastic box from a shelf behind the cash. Inside were maybe a dozen crimson strands of what looked like the wriggling chromosomes in the sex education films they used to watch in health class.

"Will be six ninety-nine, sir."

"You've got to be kidding. I could buy heroin for less."

Ilie, whom Alex had liked once, until he made an off-color remark about Jews, put on the teacherly air he often donned with his customers.

"You know, this the most expensive thing in the world," he said, as if Alex should be pleased by this. "More even than gold."

He needed wine as well, and cigarettes. He thumbed through his wallet: fourteen dollars. He would have to choose. *Good*, he thought, he'd be forced now to keep his vow to quit.

The wine rack near the cash held its usual questionable array of no-name Italian and Canadian.

"Give me a pack of Player's as well."

By now his paella had run to a week's worth of regular groceries. The thought made him loath to actually start in on it, especially when the chances were the whole thing would just end up sitting in his fridge going bad. Everything felt out of joint. He had his bed to make but such a powerful smell was still coming up from his sheets that he draped them over his dining chairs to air them out, the odor of citrus mingling with the stink of cat pee from Moses's litter box in the bathroom. The apartment was a shambles. He started going through it trying to return it to its pre-Jiri state, reshelving books, shoving file boxes into the bedroom closet, though it was only once he'd moved his computer from the living room back to his desk that he felt some sense of order had been restored. For the first time in weeks, he was able to sit at his own desk in his own chair. He powered up the computer. At its blips and whirs, its familiar orange glow, he felt relief go through him like a drug.

He still had his CanLit lecture to finish for the next day. He called up his notes and felt sick at how little progress he'd made. Three hours he had to fill every week, six to nine, and this mostly with part-timers who'd been at work all day and who already by ten minutes into class had the glassy-eyed look of the undead. He couldn't blame them. After weeks of eating, breathing, and sleeping Canadian literature, Alex himself felt ready to crawl into a hole and die there.

But it's part of us, isn't it, Alex, all that Scots Presbyterian pessimism and dourness.

I didn't think "Gzowski" was exactly a Scottish name, Peter.

He could feel Ingrid's letter bulging from his back pocket. The whole afternoon he'd let it sit there getting molded to his backside. He didn't want to risk having it ruin his evening—souring his mood was what he told himself, blindsiding him if it wasn't what he'd hoped for, whatever that was, but what he was really afraid of was that it would distract him, make this whole obsession of his with María seem the sordid and foolish thing it truly was. There was nothing that connected him to María, he was coming to admit, but the simplest sort of animal lust; beyond that they were oil and water, completely unsuited. He ought to have learned from Amanda that if he couldn't have a normal conversation with a woman, if he couldn't look her straight in the eye, then the last thing he ought to be doing was having sex with her.

They were onto Atwood's *Journals of Susanna Moodie*, more in the long line of Canadian gothic. Alex, to set the tone, had been planning to open the class with Atwood's chilly hook-and-eye poem. Now, though, all he could see was Amanda impaled on that hook. He wished he hadn't started thinking about Amanda. It was too much, trying to hold her and Margaret Atwood in his head at the same time—it made him feel like some bumbling, cunt-addled oaf from an Atwood novel. He had gone out for supper with Amanda not a week after his end-of-term party, but it had been one of their typical encounters, full of awkwardnesses and convolutions.

"What happened with us," he'd finally had the courage to say, "I didn't want you to think . . . I mean, if things had been different—"

"Oh, sure, no, I wasn't expecting . . . I mean, I wouldn't want to lose you as a friend."

He started sifting through the big stack of articles on Atwood that he'd photocopied out of the academic journals, wondering if Atwood knew how many trees out there were being sacrificed so that people like him could deliver lectures on her. "Let me sum up Canadian literature for you in three words," one of his professors in Toronto had quipped. "Margaret Atwood, Margaret Atwood, Margaret Atwood." Alex himself had practically cribbed his entire CanLit course out of her *Survival,* which dredged up some two hundred years of Canadian literary history from under the rocks where it had been properly buried and divvied it up into neat little categories like "Nature the Monster" and "The Casual Incident of Death." Yes, Canadian literature existed, she'd shown everyone, and a good thing it did, too, otherwise where would people turn when they needed every shred of good feeling stripped from them by the description of one more protagonist ruined by unpardonable ambition or one more child frozen to death in the snow?

He would probably have put Amanda from his mind after their dinner if Katherine hadn't brought her up. She had come by his place, unannounced, something she never did, but his first hope that she needed solace from some romantic crisis was quickly dashed.

"I'm worried about Amanda. I dunno. She seems kind of weird."

Alex had known enough to tread lightly. Katherine had that sororal tone of hers, as if women were a union she couldn't break ranks from.

"How, weird?"

"Just weird. Paranoid, I guess. Accusing me of things. Crazy things."

He had never told Katherine that at his party he'd overheard that conversation about her between Amanda and Stephen.

"What kinds of things?"

"About Stephen. About you. That I was coming onto you."

It wasn't lost on Alex how far from the realm of the possible she'd made that seem. He had called Amanda again, arranging to meet her at a dingy shawarma place on Guy, to avoid any suggestion of a date.

She had sat chain-smoking the whole time.

"I figure, you know, it's just what you do for yourself, that's what it comes down to. Just getting my work done, that's what I'm focusing on."

Katherine was right, this wasn't the Amanda he knew. The Amanda he knew, the one he felt comfortable being uncomfortable with, was the one who would slash her wrists to show empathy for you, not this tightly wound psychobabbler.

"Have you been seeing anyone? I mean, friends or anything?"

"Oh, yeah, there's some people I still see from the International Socialists and things. I've been pretty busy though."

It was Katherine who finally took Amanda into the university counseling center, something Alex, who had mentioned nothing of his own Dr. Klein, was happy to let her do. Men were too known for this kind of thing, for screwing women over and then trying to convince them they were crazy when they took it badly.

Amanda actually called him afterward, sounding more sane than he'd ever heard her.

"I guess I just get caught up in my head sometimes. It can get a bit weird. It's great that you guys took the trouble."

Took the trouble. As if they'd brought her chicken soup while she'd had the flu.

"It's no trouble."

She had decided to spend the rest of the summer back home.

"I'll call when I get back. I mean, if that's all right."

"That would be great." Though afterward he could hardly believe that it had flashed through his mind then that they might have sex again.

He started off a new section of notes under the heading "The Double Voice." He was getting good at these sorts of labels now, nature versus culture, the garrison mentality, old country versus new. He built up whole structures this way, sprawling networks of thought that spread out against the otherworldy glow of his computer screen like mystic cities. But then he would get into class, and it would all seem just words. He could picture a sprite-sized Margaret Atwood, hook-nosed and wild-haired and sibylline, sitting on his shoulder the whole time making pronouncements against him in her famous nasal drone. *The real problem with Canadian literature*—pause here for effect—*is that it's being taught by people who don't know anything about it.* Peggy, her friends called her. Alex had always wondered about that, how you got from "Margaret" to "Peggy."

Well, Peggy, we had Alex Fratarcangeli in here the other day, and he was saying there just isn't anything out there of real quality.

That's just stupid. He doesn't know what he's talking about.

There were drawings spread through Alex's edition of *The Journals* of haunted-looking figures pasted collage-style against sinister landscapes, woman with trees, gentleman with rodent and hills. One of them showed an Ophelia-like creature who bore a distinct resemblance to Amanda floating in the riverine sediment beneath a village street. Alex had yet to call Amanda since the term had begun: he knew she was out there somewhere in the underground, he could almost feel her beneath his steps, and yet each time he tried to screw himself up to phone, the will failed him.

He would call in the morning, first thing.

He shut his computer down. Less than two months into the term and already he felt worn out by the grind of teaching—it wasn't just his ignorance, it was the whole enterprise, this closing people up in airless rooms to look for themes and image motifs when they could just as well have been home watching something decent on TV. It had begun to seem a questionable proposition to him that what happened in a classroom actually enhanced the experience of reading rather than taking away every possible good from it. What exactly that good might be, he was finding it harder and harder to put into words. Back in his undergraduate days he had thought of literature as a kind of religion, as the straight road to whatever truth might exist out there in the ether, but nowadays he couldn't pick up a novel without a great feeling of irrelevance coming over him. His bookshelves were littered with books that had markers of one sort or another showing the places where he'd abandoned them. It was as if he'd been rifling through them searching for the answer to some intractable problem: *not this,* his brain seemed to say, each time he picked up another one, *not here.*

He had gotten an idea for another of his projects, about a character, K., who woke up one morning to discover he had somehow got trapped in a novel. Suddenly the most casual objects became meaningful; conversations, rather than the wordy, meandering things they had been, became aphoristic and terse. It wasn't long before K. descended into paranoia, wondering at the menacing haze of significance that seemed to surround the smallest act. Bit by bit his life was stripped down to its most basic elements, parent, antagonist, spouse, the blood-stained dagger, the smoking gun; all the rest, the hundred meaningless people he might have met in a day, the endless clutter and mess of things, was sucked off into some vortex. Then there was the relentless clockwork of events: gone were the long mornings in bed, the endless hours in front of the TV, replaced by disorienting jump cuts and elisions, action piling on action until it seemed the whole of creation had become a flood tide whose sole aim was to raise the frail vessel of him to some monstrous height in order to smash it. Then, out of the wreckage, just as baffling as the rest, came the ray of light, the not-so-distant shore. Hope.

He managed to get everything gutted and diced but still couldn't imagine how he was going to get from the jumble of foodstuffs on his counter to his end goal. He was using a recipe he'd clipped from the back of a box of arborio rice, but important steps seemed left out of it. Already he could see María standing over him, wondering how he ever managed to feed himself.

"Please," she would say at her fund-raisers, like a command, nodding toward the tables of food that were always laid on, "you can eat."

As if eating were a skill his own culture hadn't quite mastered.

It was a mistake for Alex to show any gratitude for these feedings. That would be like saying he had such a low opinion of his hosts that he'd expected to go hungry. María, for her part, always paid him the courtesy of entirely ignoring his own largesse—the Doors cassette he'd given her, and which she had handed over to Miguel without so much as looking at the cover art; the membership he'd bought her for the local rep theater, and which she had never once made use of with him; the flowers he'd picked up on a whim at the Atwater market, a truly inane gesture, left to wilt in their wrapper on her kitchen counter and probably thrown in the trash the instant he'd gone.

The only thing she had ever specifically asked him for, ironically, was a novel, to practice her English.

"Son'thing from Canada," she'd said. "You have writers, yes?"

He had given her Atwood's *The Handmaid's Tale*—there She was again—because it was anti-American, though afterward he'd wondered why he hadn't chosen something more to his purposes than a sci-fi dystopia about sex slaves. But then that was exactly the sort of writing he couldn't bear these days, that came out for love, say, or for all those useless emotions and shades of emotion that made life such a horror show. What was the point of these emotions, why trumpet them when they were probably just evolutionary surplus, haphazard neural responses that nature had latched onto for its own insidious purposes?

"Maybe is good," María had said of the book. "Is very political."

The buzzer sounded on the intercom. It was too early for María. His first terrible thought was that Jiri had returned, but no, much worse: it was Liz.

"I'm here to get Moses," she rapped out. A small judgmental pause, and then, "You forgot, didn't you?"

Yes, he had damn well forgotten. They hadn't spoken since she'd dropped him off three weeks before.

Already his nerves were jangling around in him like loose coins.

"Come up."

He sneaked a peek at her through the peephole when she knocked, to steel himself. Her face was already set, looking menacing and skewed like a shot from a Polanski film.

He opened the door.

"A phone call would have been nice."

Already he'd set the wrong tone.

"I thought we'd decided."

When she'd dropped Moses off he hadn't invited her in, so thrown by her presence at his apartment that he'd taken the cat with barely a word and closed the door. For days afterward he'd kept going over the moment in his mind, how he should have handled it differently.

"Why don't you come in."

"I'm in a hurry, actually."

Just the same, she moved in a little from the doorway. He saw her eye going around the apartment, to the sheets spread over the furniture, the mess of cooking in the kitchen. The whole apartment was ripe now with the smell of shellfish. It had been something that had united them, their aversion to seafood.

"So. Thanks for looking after him."

He was my cat too, for fuck's sake.

"Not at all."

At some point, Alex realized, they would have to talk, they would have to try to make each other feel normal again, even if they were only pretending.

Liz had that hardness to her, like someone in enemy territory.

"I saw your show," he said finally.

There, he had admitted it.

"Oh." She went a little bit harder.

"I liked it. I liked it a lot."

He could hear how unconvincing he sounded but he was telling the truth, even if he hadn't been able to help taking the show personally. She had split up with him and almost at once, it seemed, had started painting again. It was as if she'd been saying to him, *See how you killed me.*

"Thanks," she said.

"Anyway. I hope your work's still going well."

While Liz stood waiting by the door he cleaned out Moses's litter box, dumping the contents into a grocery bag. The smell of cat pee had grown almost comforting in the past weeks. Moses had started to fret, pacing around Alex with his back up at this new disruption to the order of things. He was making a point of ignoring Liz, in his punishing way, though Alex wasn't taking as much satisfaction from this as he might have.

He had to reach around Liz to get the cat crate out of the entrance closet. Moses, the instant he caught sight of it, scuttered behind the couch.

"I'll get him," Liz said. "He doesn't like going in there."

I know that.

"It's fine," Alex said.

He had to pull the couch away from the wall and crawl in amongst the dust bunnies and filth. He managed to drag Moses back to the open but when he tried to shove him into the crate, Moses, completely out of character, lashed out.

A thin line of blood rose up on Alex's wrist. He felt utterly betrayed.

Liz shifted uncomfortably.

"You all right?"

"It's nothing. Just a scratch."

He couldn't recover from this setback. He knew Liz had been offering him a chance in bringing Moses here, and he was blowing it.

He piled Moses's things at the door.

"Can you manage all this?"

"I'll be fine. My friend's waiting with her car."

No doubt the punky lesbian wannabe she'd been with when Alex had run into her that summer. He had recognized her from the ill-fated art history class he had briefly attended, though he'd had no idea at the time that Liz had become friends with her.

"You should be careful on the way out. We're not allowed pets."

"I can't exactly hide him under my coat."

They ended on that note. Alex had been prudent enough, at least, to lower the heat on his paella, but he came back to it to find that a crust had formed at the bottom of the pot nonetheless. *Shit.* It would have that burnt taste now. Meanwhile Liz was probably already having some snarky misandrist conversation about him with her *friend.* She was the one who had mentioned the show when Alex had run into her and Liz up near Schwartz's. "It's pretty amazing," she'd said, laying the salt on. "You should check it out."

He'd been shocked then at how different Liz had looked. She'd lost weight, she'd let her hair grow, but those were the small things: it was the whole air to her that had changed, the way she held herself, the St. Lawrence chic of her clothes, this guerilla-girl sidekick he hadn't known she was friends with but to whom his eye had always gone across the lecture hall back in art history.

He and Liz had hardly exchanged two words.

"That's great," he'd said of her show, but he wouldn't let himself say he'd go see it. "That's great."

It was more than a week before he got around to tracking the show down. It wasn't at a gallery but at one of the art cafés that were becoming popular along the St. Lawrence strip—to catch the overflow of all those people who couldn't get into real galleries, he thought, feeling the old mix of protectiveness and depreciation that Liz had always aroused in him. The lighting in the place was awful; he had to lean up over tables and shuffle his way around the handful of patrons to find angles where the paintings would actually read. Liz had abandoned her pattern work to return to her first love, the human figure, though these paintings were nothing like the luscious formal portraits and nudes she used to do in their Toronto days. There was one of an emaciated man sitting cross-legged in a chair with a dwarfish-looking girl in a yellow dress standing to one side of him; there was one of a group of school-girls standing in a semicircle with their backs to the viewer as if at some game, though from the tone of the piece they might just as easily have been staring at a playmate they'd disemboweled or at a piece of road-kill. Alex found the paintings vaguely irritating and unpleasant: they were reaching for effect, he said to himself, though the truth, of course, was that they were irritating *to him*. There were nearly a dozen pieces, all fair-sized and meticulous, and all with Liz's trademark attention to every detail. What they didn't have was Liz's usual impulse to please. *Fuck you*, they seemed to say. But maybe not to everyone, only to him. At the back of his mind he had somehow imagined that Liz wouldn't actually survive in this city without him, but now it seemed she'd come into her own as if he had just been this millstone to her, this *male*.

He was down to the last stages of his preparation. The recipe called for a final baking phase to open the mussels up, but all he had in the way of bakeware was an old lasagna tray he'd got from his mother. It would have to do. He scooped the paella into it. The bit of saffron he'd used, just a few strands, had worked like a miracle, transforming the whole to an aromatic glow of orange-red like a Hindu offering. He spread all the little morsels into place until it looked like a veritable work of art, then stuck it into the oven at a low heat, thinking he would fire it up only after María had arrived.

The twilight hour had come on. There seemed something funny about the apartment: it was the emptiness, he realized, the animal sense that there was no other being in range, though he wasn't sure if it was Moses he missed or Jiri. The apartment seemed cold suddenly, but when he cranked up the thermostat there was no telltale hiss of it kicking in. The bastards hadn't turned the heat on yet. One more grievance for his list, he thought, but no, he was done with that.

There would be snow soon, a week maybe, not more. In his mind's eye he could already see it covering the sidewalks and streets, could see the bogs of slush that formed at intersections, the cars skittering up Côte des Neiges against the slippage and the great yellow arsenal of snow machines that invaded the city. *Snow was general all over Ireland.* Where was that from? There had been snow the last time he'd visited Ingrid—he remembered cooking with her in her kitchen, how comforting it had felt to be inside and warm while outside the wind was blowing and the drifts were piling up.

God, he thought. He had left her over such a little thing. Not that he found her faith any less outlandish now than he had then, but it was probably no more outlandish than his own notions of the world would surely one day turn out to have been. Liz had been as godless as he was, yet that hadn't stood out as any special marker of compatibility; rather, it had seemed merely one more part of her that was somehow debased in being such a mirror of him. That was what had put him off about her paintings, at bottom, how they had looked like images out of his own mind, as if the scarier notion was not that she had got over him so easily, but that they were still linked, that she still remained the guardian of his worst self.

He put on some Steely Dan to set the mood for María's arrival. "Home at Last": it was a nod to the *Odyssey,* he'd never caught that. Something he'd actually read. There was a detail that had always stuck with him, the twitching legs of the unfaithful maids during the great mass murder the story ended with. Who did that? Who strung people up for being unfaithful? The twitching made the scene real, as if Homer had witnessed it with his own eyes. It was the same detail the boy from El Mozote had used, the one who had survived—the twitching legs of the children who had been hanged.

Alex switched off the music. He wished he hadn't made that connection. The last thing he needed was El Mozote on the brain when María arrived.

I don't know if this is something you two feel comfortable talking about on the air, but I hear you got off to a bit of a rocky start in the romance department.

(Blushing) Well, I guess rape and pillage aren't exactly aphrodisiacs. But maybe I should let María tell the story.

Please. Is not a joke for me. Is not a story. Is my life.

It was Liz who had fucked him up, coming by like that. It would have been better if he hadn't run into her in the summer; it would have been better if he had never gone to see her show. He could have handled the obvious, a few battered women, say, or a bit of leather, but not the general creepiness of it all, which still kept tugging at him like a grapple hook in his gut. Somehow Liz had managed to get the whole of their gangrenous relationship into those paintings. Maybe a stranger wouldn't see it, some guy, say, who'd never trussed Liz up like an animal and put his cock in her; but it was there. His tying her up and his gagging her. His fucking her while she clawed at him and screamed no. His *raping* her. There. He had let the word enter his head. For months now he had not allowed himself to so much as think the separate letters of it, but then at once his heart was pounding, he wanted to smash something, he was shouting like an idiot.

"Fuck! FUCK!"

How had he got to this place? Any minute María would be at the door.

"Fucking Christ!"

He pulled out a cigarette and fumbled to light it. Surely it hadn't been like that: she would never have come here then, she would never have stomached his presence. But then he knew Liz, how her mind reworked things. How she would soften it all in her memory to try to bring it back within the realm of the normal, of the bearable.

The apartment, he suddenly realized, was blue with smoke. Not just cigarette smoke: something more savory. His paella. He rushed to the stove to discover he had somehow set the oven to broil rather than low, a cloud of smoke taking the breath from him when he opened the oven door. The paella, he could see, had not fared well—it had taken on the scorched look of a crème brûlée, the mussels he'd carefully spread on the top open-mouthed as if caught in their death throes. Alex opened a window to air the place out, but such a bitter wind blew in that he had to narrow it to a crack for fear of losing what little heat there was in the place.

In the kitchen he carefully prized away the more cauterized bits of his meal until it took on a look that could almost pass for intentional. He felt a bit calmer. Gradually his mind eased back from the precipice it seemed to have come to: in a couple of days, he thought, he would call Liz and arrange to speak to her. Who could say what had actually happened between them? Who could know?

He still had his bed to make. Instead he poured himself several fingers of the rotgut Crown Royal that had survived Jiri's stay and took it out to the balcony. He couldn't believe the cold out there. The wind, though, had abated, giving way to a stillness that had something familiar to it, some dim hint of promise. Then while he stood at the railing a fleck fell to the back of his hand, then another. Snow.

It seemed a cosmic joke. After the first few flakes a flurry of them burst out of the sky, so that for a moment it was just as Alex had imagined it, the lights of the city and the veil of white, the darkling blur where the mountain was. *Snow was general all over Ireland.* What was it that made the heart soar at the most unlikely things? It was too much, he felt tears coming up, in a moment he'd be blubbering like a child.

Down at street level the snow hadn't made any impression, maybe already vaporized by the time it had passed through the last clotted layers of atmosphere. Then, as quickly as it had started, it was done. A moment later Alex saw what seemed a familiar black head rounding the corner from the direction of the metro: María. She had come after all. In a matter of minutes, she would be at his door. He downed the last half inch of whiskey in his glass, butted his cigarette, and hurried back into the apartment to make ready a way for her.

8

María was talking. Alex had never really heard her go on like this before, so volubly. The conference had energized her—somehow, amidst all the boring white men and the splinters and factions, she had been in her element.

"I had the same feeling from my own country. From the beginning, you know, before the killings. *Everyone* was in the street in those days, everyone. Was almost a festival then. Of course, here is different, is more serious, but still you can feel it."

Alex was trying to take heart from her new openness, even if it had very little to do with him. He was waiting for the moment when the debonair side of him would kick in, the one that felt it was normal for him to be alone with a beautiful woman, but it hadn't happened yet. At least the heat had actually come on at some point, wonder of wonders, and he hadn't had to resort to keeping the oven going or burning the furniture to warm the place up. As for his paella, María had had the one reaction to it he hadn't anticipated: she had hardly noticed it. He could have cooked rice and beans, for all it would have mattered; that might at least have sparked some glimmer of familiarity from her, some comment like, "So you have learned our national dish." Instead, she had made a few distracted stabs at the paella as if it were some food substitute he'd served up—but how foreign could it be, really? it had rice; it had seafood; it was Spanish—then had seemed to lose all interest in it.

"I always wondered why you got involved with an environmental group," Alex said, not entirely innocently. "I mean, of all the possible things."

María gave a dismissive shrug.

"Is not so strange."

Alex was searching his mind for a layman's term for *sublimation*.

"It's just, I would have thought you would have wanted something more political."

"More with killings, you mean."

"Not exactly."

"You think after five years of war that I still want to hear about killings."

Alex had foolishly been looking forward to a little moment of glory on this subject, to showing María how he understood her better than she understood herself.

"I guess I meant more to do with human rights." But he was entirely on the defensive now. "I just figured something like this would seem beside the point."

"Is because you don't know. Is only one thing they fight for in my country, is the land. People don't eat human rights. If there is no land, then there is no food, no freedom, no country. So you see is very important."

He was floundering. Here she was in his apartment, finally, the whole obscene fullness of her sitting in one of his chairs and her blue-jeaned knees practically wedged between his own beneath the table, and he was picking a fight. By now the kiss from that morning seemed a fantasy he'd had.

"I saw your friend again after," María said. "Félix."

"Oh?"

"Is a homosexual, yes?"

Alex felt blindsided.

"I don't know," he sputtered. "I've never really asked."

"But he is your friend."

"Well, yes. My student. But yes, I think of him as a friend."

"But you don't know if he is a homosexual?"

Alex felt his color rising.

"It's not a big issue."

"You don't think about it?"

"Yes, I've thought about it. I mean, it's crossed my mind."

"So, such an important thing but you don't ask him. Is strange, no?"

Somehow, though he ought to have had the high ground on this one, she had managed to turn the tables on him again.

"Like I told you, it's not a big deal," he said, but then he added, rashly, "Maybe in El Salvador it's not the same."

María stiffened.

"Yes," she said. "Is not the same. In El Salvador, if someone is your friend you know what they are eating, what they are thinking, what they believe."

He had crossed a line.

"I didn't mean it that way."

"No."

"I just thought—"

"Yes. That we are backward." But she seemed to relent. "Is okay, is the truth, is very macho in my country. On the right, if you are homosexual, maybe they kill you. But on the left is more accepted."

A better man than him, more debonair, say, would have taken this rare concession from her as a chance for good grace.

"But people still hide it."

"Yes. They hide it. Like your friend."

They sat silent. By now María had pushed her food to one side, as if to be spared the sight of it. Alex thought of the work that had gone into it, of the expense. She hadn't even bothered to pick out the bits of seafood, though Alex had left his own behind as well, piling them discreetly at the edge of his plate.

He got up to clear the table.

"I guess the meal was a little burned."

"Yes," María said simply.

He scraped the remains of their plates into the garbage, quickly, trying not to think about the waste. He couldn't believe now that he hadn't planned any side courses or backups, not so much as a salad or bowl of chips.

"Can I get you anything else?" But a furtive scan of the kitchen had turned up only a bit of pumpernickel left over from Jiri and a few slices of browning Hungarian salami. "I could make you a sandwich or something."

From somewhere the thought rose up in him unbidden, *If only she would just go.*

"Is okay. Just son' bread, maybe, is good. And son' water."

Water and bread. It almost brought tears to his eyes, the thought of all his misplaced hopes.

He set two slices of Jiri's brick-heavy pumpernickel in front of her, liberally greased with Fleischmann's, and a glass of tap water.

"Do you know his company, your friend Félix?"

Alex felt his bowels fist up again. So they hadn't finished with Félix.

"How do you mean?"

"What they do. Their work."

He figured he should play it safe.

"I'm not sure, really. I guess they make aluminum. They must mine it or something."

"No, no mines. Is from the soil."

"Oh."

"They just have to take it like that, from the top. I know, from my country."

He didn't like the direction they were headed.

"You have aluminum?"

"Not so much, I think. But your friend, his company was there."

Ah. So this was the rub. He expected some horror story now of ruined farmlands, polluted rivers, of cattle dying off or children coming down with rare cancers.

"So that's why you don't like him," he said.

But María waved the suggestion off.

"Was only some months they came, to dig some holes. Then there was the war, they came home."

Alex had actually been ready to use phrases like *foreign investment* in Félix's defense, though María would have made mincemeat of him.

"Tell me the truth," María said, in an ominous teasing tone. "You play with him, don't you? With Félix. Because he is a homosexual."

Alex's blood froze.

"I don't know what you mean."

"I mean maybe you like that he is a homosexual. How he looks at you and so on."

Alex couldn't quite pinpoint the exact nature of the horror that had risen up in him.

"His being gay doesn't have anything to do with it. He's my friend. Like I said."

But María laughed.

"I could feel it. How he didn't like to see you with a woman."

Alex still wasn't sure if what she was accusing him of sounded true because it was so or merely because he was always inclined to believe the worst about himself.

"You're just not used to men being friends with homosexuals."

"It doesn't matter to me, what men do. But is true men are different here. Is very strange for me."

She had taken on the air of someone looking on at something that had nothing to do with her. *You never had a chance with me*, she seemed to be saying.

"How, different?"

"Different. Maybe is better I don't say."

It was like a challenge now.

"No, go ahead. It's interesting."

"Yes. Maybe so."

María shifted in her chair with what looked almost like pleased anticipation.

"The men here," she started, "I don't know. They are like boys. They don't know what they want. They don't know what it means to be a man."

Alex took the blow directly.

"Ah."

"Look at you, how you live. You have everything, you have education, a nice house, you are safe. In El Salvador, there are no people like you, who are so free, only the poor, who have nothing, and the rich, who are always afraid of the poor. But you have freedom and you don't use it. You're with a woman, you don't know what you want—you are polite, you don't ask a question, you don't say what you feel. Is true, in my country is different. The men, the good ones, are men. Is not macho—is because they must choose. Not like boys who want one thing on one day and a different one on the next."

Alex sat silent. He felt like a rabbit caught in the blaze of María's headlights.

"You are upset," María said, laughing.

"No, it's fine," he said. "It's fine."

It felt unseemly to make any attempt to defend himself.

"My Alex," María said, in a maternal tone that seemed truly to spell the end of any chance of carnal involvement. She rose from the table. "Thank you for your supper. You are a very nice man."

He was getting his wish: she was taking her leave. He would never be able to face her again, if they ended like this.

"You're going already?"

"I must meet with someone from my group. For the conference."

He stood by in a daze while she gathered her things. At the door she kissed his cheek lightly as if saying goodbye to some nephew or cousin.

"Maybe you can still come to the Salvadoran parties, yes? Or my brother will miss you."

When she'd gone he collapsed on the couch. This was the worst, to feel infantilized—he would rather be a prick, an asshole, a cad, than a boy. Who was she to lord it over him, coming from her two-bit banana republic with its few thousand acres of hacienda and bush and its politics out of the Dark Ages? Yet she seemed to have more sense of herself in a single toss of her hair than Alex did in the whole edifice of his pathetic life.

He turned on the radio, unable to bear the silence in the apartment. Gzowski was just announcing the lineup for the morning show repeats: a regional report from New Brunswick; a piece on Thanksgiving turkeys. In El Salvador, the rebels ran a radio station that was like the nation's lifeblood: the entire war they'd managed to keep one step ahead of the enemy, moving transmitters, generators, aerials, on their backs in the dead of night, surviving carpet bombing and special forces assaults and U.S. signal-location equipment to go on the air every evening at six for their regular broadcast. These were María's role models back home. Alex, meanwhile, had Peter Gzowski, reaching out to the nation's housewives for their secrets on turkey basting.

Ingrid had never made him feel this way, so dismissible; she had made him feel her equal, an adult. Everything else, her religion, her age, all the things he'd imagined were unworkable between them, seemed to grow small next to that. He thought again of the snow the last time he had visited: one day it had draped all the trees of Engelström in a mantle of white that afterward had glinted and dripped in the sun as if in a wonderland. Then once they had taken the ferry to the island of Ven, where Tycho Brahe had had his observatory, the island an eerie, enchanted place dotted with thatched-roofed farmhouses and smoking chimneys, seabirds forever wheeling overhead.

He knew he was romanticizing the visit now. Her conversion had changed things—reading her letters he had always felt obliged to strip away the religious bits to get at the Ingrid he actually liked. When she collected him off the Landskrona ferry it was clear that she had aged, that she had moved on to a different phase of life, yet the look of her still made him ache, made him wonder that he had ever been with such a woman.

"So you have come," she said. "My not-so-Italian."

He had been on the road five months by then, on a patchwork ticket he had put together when he had left Nigeria. He settled into Ingrid's little cabin, feeling like a stinking troll who'd stumbled into her life, dragging his worldliness and his dirt. In the house there were prayers before every meal; there was a Bible reading every evening. Alex and Ingrid were rarely alone, the entire day revolving around the children, getting them fed or off to school or through their homework or ready for sleep. He sat with Ingrid in the living room after they were in bed but Lars, a gangly adolescent now, as tall as his mother, was down every few minutes on some pretext or other.

"It's difficult for them," Ingrid said. "Our lives are so different now."

He knew from her letters that she hadn't been with a man since she'd converted. She was waiting for God to send her the right one, she said, from which he'd assumed there'd be no question of sex. But now that he was here in the flesh, he wasn't so certain. There was still the attraction between them, he felt it, and saw that Ingrid felt it too, from the way they were always skirting each other like charged particles. In practice, though, they remained scrupulously chaste, mumbling apologies if they bumped elbows in the kitchen, sitting down to eat with him at one end of the table and her at the other and the children between them like a wall. Then at night, when they talked on the couch, there were always those inches of space like an atmosphere they couldn't cross.

"It's very late, I think."

"I'll go."

It wasn't until he rode into Landskrona with her one day to her work that they were truly away from the children. She was still driving her same old Volvo. They'd made love in it once, his first visit, exactly where he was sitting. She'd been wearing a dress, as if she had planned the thing, a light summer shift that had moved sexily beneath his hands.

She had a dress on now.

"Maybe it will be boring for you at my work," she said. "If you like I can drop you in the town."

"No, I'd like to come."

She had given up her place at her elementary school after her conversion to take a job teaching language classes for new immigrants. "To change my life," she had written him, and he had imagined her in some bright, sterile church setting, with acoustic tiles on the ceiling and posters of nature scenes and happy families on the walls. But the classes turned out to be in an old community center downtown that looked straight out of the sixties, the walls painted in flower and rainbow motifs and the lounges filled with corduroy couches and furniture made from tree trunks.

"It's because of you that I'm here," Ingrid said, though she had never mentioned this. "Because of what you told me. That I shouldn't close myself off. So you see, you had a big influence on me."

Alex didn't know how to answer her.

"I'm not even sure I would have remembered saying that."

"Yes, of course." She smiled to hide that he'd hurt her. "It was only a small thing. But even still."

Her classes were full of people who seemed to have crawled out of the woodwork, for all the evidence you saw of them in the streets, brown-skinned men wearing hand-me-downs and women in burkas and kerchiefs and dark-eyed teenagers in Kraftwerk T-shirts. Alex was afraid Ingrid had made some terrible mistake: she looked so out of place, blond and blue-eyed and unblemished, like someone from a different species. But somehow the disjunction suited her. After his own years of teaching he envied the authority she had, how from the instant she entered the classroom everyone's attention was with her.

During a break, one of the other teachers, a rouge-cheeked woman whose animation radiated off her like a glare, buttonholed Ingrid in the coffee room, her eye on Alex.

"It's my friend from Canada," Ingrid said finally, in English.

"Canada! *Ah, so!*"

"A very silly woman," Ingrid said, as soon as they were away. "Just thinking to make a scandal."

The incident colored the rest of the day. At home Ingrid snapped at Lars for leaving his wet boots in the hall, and Lars sulked the whole evening.

"I don't understand," he said, when Alex was helping him with his math, and pushed his books away.

Alex had to fight to keep from losing his temper.

"Maybe your mother can help."

He slipped out to his cabin when Ingrid was putting the children to bed. He didn't think he could manage it, all this emotional footwork. But not long afterward, Ingrid appeared at his door.

"You mustn't run away from me," she said.

"Sorry. I just thought—"

"What is it?"

"I don't know. That you were angry."

"I'm angry, yes. But not at you."

They sat silent on the edge of his bed. Alex felt the weight of all the conversations they'd avoided until then.

"You must be patient," Ingrid said. "It's very strange for us to have a man with us again after so many years."

"Not much of a man," he said.

"Don't say so."

She shifted as if about to go but then leaned in to kiss him, tentatively, like someone trying something for the first time. Alex only let himself answer the kiss.

"Yes, you are right," she said. "We mustn't."

Afterward, though, it felt as if they had crossed a border. The next night, she came out to the cabin again.

"We must decide," she said. "It's too difficult, not to be one thing or the other."

But they didn't decide, not really. Instead, each indiscretion gave a kind of permission for the next, so that one night it seemed acceptable to kiss, then to touch each other through their clothes, then to lie together half-naked on his bed. At the back of his mind Alex knew that deciding would surely mean they must stop, that there was no logical way forward, but somehow it was easier than he would have thought for them to ignore this. Ingrid had made clear that she couldn't "make intercourse," as she put it, they had at least set that particular limit, but then once they had set it they seemed freed to work up to everything short of it. It took several nights of this for Alex to admit in his own mind that he wasn't really enjoying himself. He'd begun to feel the way he had back in high school after he'd felt up some girl in his car, dirtied and mean, that he'd done more than he was supposed to but less than he'd wanted. Meanwhile the children, to judge from their tense politeness at breakfast, had clearly figured out what he and Ingrid were up to, though what damage this was causing to their young Christian minds Alex couldn't say.

One night Ingrid, with what was almost her old uninhibited self, took him in her mouth and sucked him until he came. When he tried to reciprocate she eased him away from her.

"Is it difficult for you to stop?" she said.

"Is it for you?"

He regretted his tone at once.

"Perhaps it was wrong for you to come here. For me to invite you."

This was it, he thought, the end of their little deceptions.

"Do you want me to leave?"

She wouldn't say it but it was clear they couldn't continue as they were. He had made the mistake of thinking he could show up here as if Ingrid were a case study he was checking up on, instead of someone with a life, someone he'd been connected to.

"I could visit my friend Ture for a while," he said. "Since I haven't seen him."

"Yes. Maybe so."

It was December by then. In Copenhagen, he found Ture on his own now but otherwise nearly unchanged from when he'd first met him, still smoking hash, still working odd jobs to keep up his social assistance. His apartment was almost literally knee deep in mess: dirty clothes, heaps of salvage, stacks of newspapers and books. One day they drank some hash tea that Ture had brewed and spent hours roaming the city with Ture's friend Bent, a surly self-professed anarchist, ending up at Tivoli, the city's amusement park. It was closed for the season, but Bent insisted they scale the fence.

"I dunno," Alex said, hardly able to stand by then. "I don't think I can make it."

"Come on, you can tell your American friends that's how they do things in Denmark."

Somehow, they made it over. The place looked surreal in the dark, with its empty rides and boarded-up stalls, its darkened fairy-tale buildings. Bent ended up climbing one of the roller-coaster hills and screaming from the top like a madman. Two policemen came and Alex was sure they would be arrested, but they were merely escorted to the exit of the park and let go.

"Fucking pigs," Bent said, and spat.

All Alex could think through all of this was how he wanted to be with Ingrid.

"It can just be for a few more days," he said on the phone. "I feel so awful here."

He knew she was thinking it would be easier if he didn't come.

"A few days," she said. "We will try."

It was like his last visit all over again, this childish back-and-forth, except that this time he didn't have the excuse of being a child. Then, right from the ferry terminal he got off on the wrong foot, leaning in to kiss her but checking himself at the last instant, and ending up just brushing her cheek.

"Your friend is well?"

He had been so cold, as if not to promise her anything.

"He's fine. He's all right."

They stopped at the supermarket in Landskrona. The windows were tinseled with Christmas decorations.

"I was thinking how you manage for money," Ingrid said. "It must be difficult, on your travels."

"I saved some from when I was teaching. Enough to travel on, anyway."

"They paid you so well?"

"Not really. I worked something out."

In fact he had almost doubled his income by selling some of his foreign exchange allowance on the black market. But he didn't explain this to Ingrid.

"And when you go home?" she said. "What shall you do?"

"There's some money waiting. To help me resettle."

"Ah. So you are not so poor."

"Not so poor, no."

She seemed to gather this in.

"But in the meantime," she said, "you don't mind if I pay for things."

It was true—it was how he budgeted his travel, by assuming people would look after him. He wouldn't have lasted a week in Sweden on his own, already down to his last seven or eight hundred dollars, with just a few thousand more waiting at home that wouldn't even cover his student loans.

But then here he was traveling the world while Ingrid had to work for a living.

"I'm sorry," he said. "I wasn't thinking."

They had both grown awkward.

"It's not so important."

They were stuck afterward with Alex having to pay for the groceries, though they more or less cleaned him out of his Swedish cash.

"It's very silly," Ingrid said, upset now. "I shouldn't have said it."

"No, you were right."

They were silent most of the way home. Alex could still picture the brightness in Ingrid's eyes when she'd met him at the terminal, then how it had faded.

"The children are at their father's," she said finally, as if this was something she had been saving as a treat, before he had ruined things. "I don't know if there's something you'd like. Some excursion perhaps."

If only he had kissed her properly. Such a little thing.

"I'm sorry," he said. "I'm sorry."

"Sorry for what?"

"I don't know. For everything. For coming back. For starting out wrong."

"It doesn't matter," she said. "We'll start again."

They settled on driving up the coast to Helsingborg and taking the ferry across to Hamlet's castle. This was where they had met, on the Helsingborg ferry. It felt peculiar to be back there, as if they were bidding goodbye to their younger, more innocent selves. It was difficult to imagine the boy he'd been then, what Ingrid could have seen in him.

Despite the sun they were the only ones who had braved the upper deck.

"I should be very afraid now, I think, to talk to such a big bearded man as you were," Ingrid said.

"I was the one who was afraid."

"And now? Are you afraid?"

"Maybe a little."

"Then we are the same."

The castle was nearly deserted. The old foundations had been over-lain with a sprawling Renaissance construction, though from out on the battlements, looking out to the snow-covered coastline and the sea, Alex could picture the longships setting out a thousand years before, into the cold, unknown world. Ingrid leaned into him against the wind and he dared to put his arms around her.

"I'm happy you came back," she said. "I shouldn't say it, but I'm happy."

It was well past dark by the time they got home. They made a meal together and opened a bottle of wine that Ingrid said had been sitting in her cupboard since before her conversion.

"We had wine our first dinner," Alex said, hoping she'd be pleased at the memory. But her face clouded.

"Who knows what you thought of me then. What kind of evil woman I was. Or only sad, perhaps."

"It wasn't like that." But he could remember thinking of her in exactly those terms.

"I know you think it's only because of what I was that I became a Christian."

He didn't like to answer.

"I guess it's just hard to understand how someone could change so much."

"I wonder it myself," she said. "How I've been so many people. Perhaps you are right, each one only makes up for the last."

It wasn't yet ten by the time they'd finished supper. Alex lingered over the dishes, not sure things were any clearer now than they had ever been.

"I should go," he said.

"It seems a pity. The house is empty."

"I don't mind."

They were looking into the same dead end they'd already been down.

"Perhaps you can sleep in Lars's bed," she said finally.

He had to pass through her room, the first time he had been up to it this trip. It looked nearly unchanged from before, still had the same economy and grace, the sense it had all that was needed.

He could see Lars's bed through the doorway that led to the children's room, the shelves above it filled with his pictures and trophies.

"Would it be all right if I lie with you for a bit?"

"If you'd like."

This time he didn't feel that they were hiding, that they were sneaking around like teenagers. Instead of waiting for her cues he went from one thing to the next as if she hadn't a choice: that was what she wanted, he thought, not to be held responsible. She felt familiar beneath him, as if only days had gone by since they'd last made love.

Afterward he lay over her kissing her face, her eyes, the line of her hair. He kept waiting for the guilt to come.

"You all right?" he whispered.

He saw she was crying.

"What is it?"

"It's nothing. It's nothing. It isn't so easy for me again."

He fell asleep with her body curled into his. At some point he dreamt they were there, in her room, only now, for some reason, he couldn't make love to her.

"I see. Of course." She was already naked except for a bra. It was humiliating for her, the more so, somehow, on account of the bra. "I think you are very foolish. You are afraid to give anything because you think it will take something from you."

He barely slept after that. He stared at the inky lump Ingrid made beside him, as mysterious as when he'd met her. She wasn't so changed after all, not in any important way. She could just be some flake, he had thought at first, some frustrated housewife. But he would never have thought that now.

It was still dark when she started to stir.

"You are watching me," she said.

"I couldn't sleep."

"Maybe you're afraid you must marry me now," she said, so matter-of-factly he felt a thrill.

"Should I be?"

"No. Not afraid."

"What about God?" he said. "What does he think of all this?"

"I think maybe God doesn't bother so much with us, when we are so small."

She rose and slipped on her robe. He watched her move through the room in her soundless way.

"I must pick up the children for church. You can stay home, of course."

"No. I want to come. If you don't mind."

He could see this wasn't what she'd expected.

"I would like it."

He was getting in deep, he knew it. It was hard to believe only a day had passed since he'd stepped off the ferry again. He would have been on his way to Rio by now, the next stop on his ticket, if he hadn't come back. In his mind's eye he saw his double, in a different version of things, walking off into palm trees and heat, as in the last scene of a caper film where the criminal makes his escape.

They picked the children up at their father's house outside Landskrona, an imposing place surrounded by immaculate gardens. Around the back Alex made out a jungle gym and a wooden playhouse done up as a castle.

"He has his new family now to look after," Ingrid said. "Of course, he is kind enough with Lars and Eva, when they're with him."

The father came out to the door to see the children off, looking even more the burgher than Alex remembered. From the scowl that crossed his face at the sight of Alex in Ingrid's car, it was clear the children hadn't mentioned him.

Alex could feel a hundred shades of shame coming off Lars. "You are coming to the church?" he said.

"If that's all right."

Ingrid spoke in English for Alex's sake but Lars answered in Swedish, in grunting monosyllables.

"You must try in English," Ingrid said. "So Alex can understand."

"Is too difficult."

"But you must try."

"*Nej!*"

Ingrid let the silence fester a moment.

"Perhaps after. When you're not feeling so rude."

The church wasn't one of the clapboard ones whose spires dotted the countryside, but a modern building that could have passed for a credit union or insurance office. Alex expected heads to turn as they came in and whispers and glares, but when they took their place, a young couple next to them smiled over at them as if they were just a normal churchgoing family. The church wasn't much bigger than a living room, everything in white and pale wood tones. To one side of the altar was a marble baptistery that was large enough to climb into.

An avuncular man in a gray suit was standing up front talking to some of the people in the front pews. It was only when he turned out to face the room and began to address the whole congregation that Alex realized he was the pastor. A few notes rang out from a Hammond at the back and Ingrid and the children raised up their Swedish voices for the opening hymn, Lars's not-quite-broken one holding surprisingly in key.

Alex had been picturing people in ecstasies or breaking into tongues, but apart from the occasional mumbled *hallelujah,* the service had the informal air of an information meeting or a Rotary Club lecture. Afterward people milled in the foyer and Ingrid introduced him to the pastor, who took Alex's hand in both of his as if Alex had paid him some tremendous honor.

"You are welcome, you are welcome!" he said, blushing at his halting English.

Alex had thought he and Ingrid would stick out like people with scarlet letters on their breasts, but everyone smiled at him with the same shy, pleased air the pastor had had, exclaiming over his travels as if he were Amundsen back from the Pole. Alex didn't quite get it, not just this friendliness but that Ingrid was leading him around like some Christian exchange student she'd taken in, when all he could think of was that they'd been making love not twelve hours before.

"So finally we meet him, your Canadian!"

A woman had come up and taken his arm with a very un-Swedish forthrightness, a great lumberjack of a man, easily twice her size, looming behind her.

"These are my good friends Erik and Anna," Ingrid said. "My *best* friends, I should say."

Anna still had a hold of him.

"You have a very nice coat," Erik said, and everyone laughed.

Alex must have looked dazed. He stared down at his coat, a parka Ingrid had got hold of for him.

"It was Erik's coat," she explained. "He was your good Samaritan."

"Sorry. I didn't realize."

Anna hugged his arm.

"Don't mind Erik. He is only jealous that you are more handsome in it."

Ingrid had invited them for supper. The whole day Alex could still feel the press of Anna's arm against him, vaguely foreboding. At supper she sat across from him and her attention kept circling back to him like a hawk's.

"So you are a world traveler," she said. "You must be tired, after so many travels."

"I'm almost at the end now."

"Ah. And then back to Canada?"

He felt cornered.

"Yes, I suppose."

Erik had got the children onto the subject of Christmas and they began to explain to Alex all their peculiar Swedish traditions, competing with one another until they had the others in stitches at their tortured English.

"I think Alex can help with the tree," Lars said.

Underneath the table Ingrid's leg moved against Alex's.

"We'll see. If he's still with us."

He ended up alone with Anna afterward doing the dishes.

"Ingrid is very fond of you," she said.

It seemed this was the moment the evening had been leading to.

"I'm fond of her too."

"Yes, I think so. You have made her happy." He could feel the weight of that judgment settling over him. "It's some time since she was so happy."

It was easier, it seemed, to get by with one big lie than with many little ones. Every day Alex grew more ensconced in his little hovel, padding his nest out like a wintering rodent, and every day the question of leaving seemed less pressing. In the mornings, if Alex stayed home, he brewed a pot of coffee and repaired to the cabin as a monk to his cell, reading and writing his letters and filling his journal until the air was opaque with cigarette smoke; in the afternoon he'd be there to greet Lars when he got home from the elementary school in the village, and Eva when the bus dropped her from the high school in Landskrona. By the time Ingrid returned Alex would have supper going and the children would be at their schoolwork, and the lie would look so seamless and whole that it could hardly be told from the truth. Then at night Ingrid would come to his bed and there were no longer any limits to be kept to, so that it was possible to forget there had ever been.

They seldom spoke of her faith. She lent him an English Bible once and he made stabs at the Gospels, trying to get beyond the deadening familiarity of them.

"There is something, you must see it," she said. "Even you, with your education."

There had been a line in the story of the prodigal son, it was true, that had brought tears to his eyes. *But when he was yet a great way off, his father saw him, and had compassion, and ran, and fell on his neck, and kissed him.* But what he said to Ingrid was, "I admit he might have been a great teacher. It's just all the rest. It seems so far-fetched. Like stories for children."

"I see." He had gone too far. He was calling her a child. "Perhaps you read too much with your head."

"My head is all I've got. It's as if you're asking me to stop thinking."

He could hear how smug he sounded.

Ingrid gave him a controlled smile.

"Perhaps we shouldn't discuss these things."

He knew what the problem was, of course, the same one that had tortured him as a kid: the fear that the failure was *in him*, that there was something lacking in him that cut him off from higher understanding.

Later, he tried to make it up to her.

"It's just all this stuff messed me up as a kid. It's hard not to get emotional."

"So you are emotional, then."

He took her point. Maybe his rejection of these things was no less visceral and unreasoned than her acceptance of them.

"How was it for you?" he dared to ask. "How did you *know*?"

He felt as if he'd asked her to describe something hopelessly intimate, a sex fantasy or a bodily function.

"It's very hard to explain."

"You don't have to tell me."

"No. I would like to. It was Anna who did it. I had met her, I was very sad then—you should say depressed, I think—and she became my friend. And so she started to talk to me now and then about Jesus, just making conversation and so on, and of course I thought it was very silly. But she was a good friend and I didn't mind so much. Then once I went with her to the church, just to see it, and I thought, yes, it's very nice, but nothing for me. Then in the night, the feeling came. It's hard to describe it. As if I was floating. As if I was flying."

"But how did you know what it was? How did you know you were supposed to become a Christian?"

"He came to me," she said simply.

"Who?" Then he understood. "Jesus? You saw Jesus?"

"Perhaps we should stop," she said.

She was right. This wasn't something she should trust him with.

"We don't have to talk about it."

"No. Perhaps not."

He felt no further ahead than he'd been before. It all came down to that mysterious quantum leap.

"You didn't say why you were depressed."

"For silly things. Always the same, really. Worried for money. Worried to find a man."

She was about to say more but stopped herself.

"What is it?"

"It's nothing. I hadn't wanted to say. It's just that night, after I went to the church, there was a man who came, someone I knew from the town. It was nothing so special—the children were with their father, he came for supper, we had a very nice evening. Not so different, I should say, from our own evening the first time you came. And then to bed, of course. Only that. After, I asked him to go, I can't say why, and he was very surprised, he thought he should stay the whole night. Then when he'd gone, not so long, I had the feeling."

Alex held his tongue.

"You're thinking it's because of that, and so on," Ingrid said. "So you see why I hadn't wanted to say. But why this time? Why this man, who wasn't a bad man, very suited to me—he called for many weeks after that, he couldn't understand why I shouldn't meet him again. Even now, I still see him in the town and sometimes he asks to come, but when I see him I only see my old life. It's a very strange thing, as if there was something to pay. That it should happen after so many years of looking for a man, just with one who suited me."

They sat silent. There was something in the story that made Alex want to resist explaining it away.

"Perhaps you will never believe as I do, it's true. But you are looking. It's enough, I think."

He felt as if she'd bestowed a benediction.

"I wouldn't mind if I actually found something."

It must have crossed Ingrid's mind that what they were doing now wasn't so different from how she'd lived in those dark days before her conversion. Why could she bear *him*, Alex wondered, and not this man who might have continued to woo her, who might have married her, might even have found a place in his heart for her Jesus? Perhaps it was just that he'd come at the vulnerable moment. Or perhaps he and Ingrid were birds of a feather, drawn to each other because they recognized in one another the same instinct to self-sabotage.

She had seen Jesus. They had names for people like that. He didn't see how, in good conscience, he could go on with her in the face of something so fundamental, so utterly foreign to his view of the world. Or maybe her faith didn't matter. Wasn't the new Ingrid even more like him than the old one had been? She had her new job; she belonged to a solidarity group for refugees; she was raising funds at her church to build a school in Zimbabwe. It all had a missionary tinge to it, but then what had Alex been doing in Africa except following the lead of the priest-heroes of his childhood?

They drove into Lund in the week before Christmas for a conference Ingrid had at the university. Alex was surprised at how venerable the campus looked, dotted with lofty halls and ancient half-timbered buildings and gothic towers. While Ingrid was at her sessions, he wandered into the town, through cobbled squares decked out for Christmas and past bookstores and cafés crammed with students. He pictured himself living in such a place, in one of the narrow brick houses in the old quarter or some cavernous nineteenth-century apartment that smelled of plaster and old wood. He might learn Swedish, do some graduate work at the university, perhaps go on to teach. It did not seem so unpleasant or strange, such a life, not so out of keeping with what he'd imagined for himself.

Dusk was settling in when they left for home. They passed a cul-de-sac of small restaurants and shops glistening against the dark like a secret refuge.

"There must be a lot of foreigners here," he said. "To teach English and so on."

"Yes, I suppose." They were both trying to pretend this had nothing to do with them. "It's very requested these days, to have native speakers."

There was a carefulness between them now as if they had run out of innocuous things to say and had been left with only the dangerous ones. The closer Christmas got the more Alex felt he was coming to the end of an amnesty, when everything that had been allowed would be called into question. He helped with the preparations for Christmas Eve, the big day for the Swedes, but was aware that each step he took now made the way back that much longer.

Ingrid's ex came by to take the children the weekend before Christmas. There was a curt exchange between Ingrid and him at the door as the children dressed, and then suddenly they were shouting.

"You must always have your way!" her ex said in English, clearly for Alex's benefit. "What of the children? What do they want?"

Alex had never seen Ingrid so furious. The children were waiting by sullenly in their coats and Ingrid shut the argument down, though after they'd gone she was still seething.

"He is such a *stupid* man!" He had arranged a last-minute ski trip without consulting her that would keep the children away till the very afternoon of Christmas Eve. "As if he thinks of the children when it's only his way to punish me!"

Alex didn't dare ask what she was being punished for.

"Sometimes I wish he were dead. It would be easier then."

She was in a funk the whole day. Alex skulked around the house trying to keep out of her path and feeling vaguely to blame for things. It was only toward the evening that the cloud over her seemed to lift.

"You mustn't mind me," she said. "It's not so often now that we argue. Before it was worse."

When they made love that night, in Ingrid's bed, Alex couldn't shake the image of her ex-husband shouting at her in the doorway. *Carl*, his name was, it came back to him. Like a cat coughing up a fur ball. Ingrid's animosity toward him seemed more bitter now than in the past, as if over the years their divorce had gone bad just as their marriage had.

Afterward they lay silent under her skylight, the black midwinter sky stretching over them like a curtain.

"We needn't go to the church in the morning if you prefer," Ingrid said.

He could hear the hesitancy in her voice, how she was weighing things between him and her god.

"No, I'd like to."

But at the church people's smiles seemed tighter than before, their questions less leading. Erik and Anna had left for the north to see Erik's family, and without them or the children to shield them Alex and Ingrid seemed hopelessly exposed. The pastor pumped Alex's hand again after the service and grinned his shy grin but then quickly excused himself, so that Alex and Ingrid found themselves alone.

"People weren't as friendly this time," he said in the car.

"I hadn't noticed so much." But it was clear that she had. "They are only timid, perhaps. We needn't mind them."

They sat making Christmas decorations at the dining table after lunch, but the matter stayed with them. This wasn't like the incident with the busybody at Ingrid's school—Ingrid seemed to feel betrayed, as if she had trusted people to accept her, to be *Christian,* and they had turned away from her.

Why was he still here, Alex wondered, why hadn't he left Ingrid to her life? He pictured accusation sessions in the dead of night at her church, the two of them exposed and brought to the scaffold while someone hung their bloodied sheets. Or somehow her ex would wrest the children from her and she and Alex would end up in Lund living in a version of the life he'd imagined but feeling banished and embittered like Vronsky and Anna Karenina.

He was making a paper chain using the children's school glue, not very adeptly.

"You should try the tape," Ingrid said, eyeing him. "It will be quicker."

He wondered why she had ever given in to him. It was as if God had been merely a place holder until the proper man had come along.

"It looks better with the glue," he said.

"Ah." She let the silence stretch as if he were Lars. "In the meantime, you are getting glue all over the table."

There was always this suburban streak in her, he thought. *She always has to have her way.*

"You're always doing that. You make it sound as if you're concerned for somebody but you're just trying to make them do what you want."

He regretted the words as soon as they were out.

"Maybe you'd prefer if I'm rude, like you are! That it's more honest!" Her anger fell as quickly as it had risen, and she sat fighting back tears. "How can you say such a thing? How can you say it?"

"I didn't mean it. I'm sorry."

This was it, he figured. He had broken immunity. Now the flood-gates would be opened, now she would throw in his face the thousand ways he had failed her.

But she looked abject.

"Perhaps you think badly of me for letting you come, is that it? For letting you be with me."

"It's not that." But she had touched the heart of the matter.

"What, then?"

"I don't know. I'm just not sure sometimes what we're doing. What you're thinking. If you think I've been sent by God or something."

He was still waiting for the barrage.

"Yes," she said finally. "Yes, it's true. It's very difficult."

Somehow, out of the blue, they were at the crossroads.

Ingrid had taken his hand.

"I think you must go soon," she said. "You will stay for Christmas, yes, but then you must go."

It took Alex an instant to admit that the suffocation he felt, the sense of his insides being sucked out, was mainly relief. All the hundred ways he had tried of looking at the matter had come down to this one, that he would go.

"We will try with the glue," Ingrid said. "Here, I will help you."

Somehow, they got through Christmas. The children returned Christmas Eve and after that things were a blur—there was the tree to fetch and trim, the Disney Christmas special on TV, the dinner and gifts. Alex felt like he was walking underwater, waiting for the moment when he might surface again for a breath. For their gifts they had been limited to things they had made, though when Alex came to Lars's he was at a loss: it was a crayon drawing of a tractor and cow, done in the crude hand of a five- or six-year-old.

Alex looked to Ingrid.

"You must ask Lars," she said. "It was his secret."

The title "From our visit to the farm" was written across the top in a more mature hand.

"It was from the last time," Lars said. "When you went with us to the farm."

It began to come back to him. The picture had been taped to Ingrid's fridge his first visit. It was a miracle that Lars had held on to it. But the way Alex remembered things, the visit to the farm was something that had happened before Lars had even met him.

He shot another glance at Ingrid.

"Of course," he said. "I remember."

"You drove the tractor, I think. You knew from your farm in Canada."

He seemed so sure of himself that Alex felt a moment of doubt. He barely remembered Lars from his first visit. Yet clearly in Lars's mind, Alex formed some important subplot to the story of his life.

"Thank you, Lars. I can't believe you kept it. Thank you."

Ingrid crossed over to Copenhagen with him when he went to arrange his flight. It felt odd to be boarding the ferry with her rather than leaving her behind—almost at once she seemed different, more than he deserved, like the stranger he had yearned for from a distance five years earlier on the ferry to Helsingborg.

They spent their last night together at Ture's apartment. Ture gave up his bed to them, a loft that was like a floating seraglio or tent, curtained off and festooned with colored Christmas lights. The ashtrays had been emptied and the sheets changed; the squalor of the rest of the apartment seemed far from them.

They made love and he fell asleep with the glow of their sex still on him, then awoke to a feeling of deadness. Ingrid had to return home that morning to collect the children from their father's. He ran a hand over the curve of her hip and wondered how it was that he hadn't memorized every inch of her body, every rounding of flesh and hollow of bone.

"I think I must go," she said.

He saw her to the ferry station, past where the city center gave way to the port lands. For the longest time the station was deserted, but then suddenly there was a crowd, and the boat had pulled in, and people were boarding.

Ingrid had his hand.

"Tell me," she said. "Did you ever think you would stay? Was it possible?"

She ought not to have asked. She ought not to have given him this power over her.

"I don't know. I don't know."

"So." She squeezed his hand. "If one day you know."

She gave him a fleeting kiss.

"Don't wait," she said. "Just go."

That last kiss had stayed with him. Even now, sulking in his apartment after his abortive dinner, he could feel it, light as a waft of air or the flit of a wing. He often wondered if Ingrid had known then, in some wordless, animal way. It was their last unguarded roll in Ture's bed that had done the damage, surely—she was at the end of her period and they had forgone a condom—though it had seemed every risk had already passed by then, that they were at a point in their story that would properly have been the denouement. Structurally, then, the pregnancy was a mistake. It didn't seem right that in life, any more than in art, something so random and flukish should end up claiming so much emotional space.

It was late. Alex sat staring at his computer screen, watching the cursor throb like something panicked. He had managed another paltry page and a half of notes: Persephone and Demeter. Death and Rebirth. Meanwhile poor Susanna Moodie was still trapped beneath the streets of Belleville, waiting to be resurrected as Margaret Atwood.

He saved his work and shut his computer down. He had the strong sense that there was something he'd forgotten, though his hand went to his pocket before his mind did: the letter. He pulled it out. The pillowy thickness of it had been flattened now to the matted warp of something that had been rescued from a flood. He couldn't find where Jiri had put his letter opener and began rummaging through his drawers looking for it, growing more and more irritated. He should never have let Jiri stay with him, never have put himself in Jiri's power in the first place. But then he should never have moved to Montreal, never have shacked up with Liz, back and back. When he got to Ingrid, though, he stumbled: it still wasn't clear what his mistake had been, to have gone to her or to have left.

He gave up on the letter opener and shredded a crease of the envelope with a pen nib. The pages inside had stuck to the envelope glue; he managed to prize free a few sheets of onionskin, but another thicker sheet remained welded to the back of the envelope. At least the onionskin was still legible, filled edge to edge with Ingrid's elegant script. "Dearest Alex," she started, but then he couldn't bring himself to take in more than snatches of phrases. "Very angry," he read, and "your cold, cold letter to me," and "finish the contact."

He couldn't have stayed with her, he knew that. He'd been only twenty-five then, five years younger than Ingrid had been when he'd met her. With a baby in the picture he wouldn't have lasted a month—he would have thrown himself into the Öresund, he would have drunk himself to death, he would have ended up strung out on junk on the streets of Copenhagen. It had just been a dalliance for him, the older woman, the children, the house, like one of those science fiction scenarios where you tried on a different life. Who knew what he'd been working out, what deep Oedipal patterns? It hadn't been lost on him that Ingrid's ex and Ingrid and he and Eva had formed a nearly perfect helix of descending ages, a tidy boy-girl symmetry in the shadows of which Lars the young Hamlet no doubt awaited the moment for a final bloodletting.

Alex lit a cigarette and started the letter from the top again, more slowly: there was hope, maybe, the tenor wasn't quite what he'd thought. The few references to his own letter were mildly encouraging—she mentioned his humor, for instance, though he couldn't remember having been especially funny. "I can see this has somehow been also for you a difficult time," she wrote, and he felt humbled that she could still give him a place. He couldn't have stayed, it was true, he hadn't had it in him, but he had a sudden sense of what he had missed.

She gave an account of her life, harrowing in its concision, from when he'd left her at the Copenhagen pier. Her discovery that she was pregnant and then the series of Hardian misunderstandings between them, the letter she'd sent, the dismissive one he'd sent back.

"I knew if I told the truth, you would come, but I thought, he must come only if he truly wishes it. Then your letter arrived, your cold, cold letter to me. I cannot say how awful it was, how I wished I had never met you! I was so very angry then, that you wrote to me about a woman as if you thought I was a person to tell your love stories to. 'She is the one I am destined for,' you said, or some such thing, and I thought, he is a child after all. Next week it will be a different one and then a different one again. Perhaps you think I was hard on you but you must understand what it was to hear such things as I was then."

There was more—about the shame, for instance, which she said had been a test (a test of what? what sorts of diplomas were granted for these things?), about how with each month and then each year that had passed it had seemed harder to break her silence. All of this stung him in a peculiar way he couldn't quite name. There was the guilt, yes, but also a sort of hopelessness, that this child existed, wasn't a figment, that his own loss of him—all the years he hadn't known him, all that he could never be to him—was something real.

"I say all these things not to punish you, but only so you understand why I acted as I did." This was where she softened him up for the letdown, he figured, where she told him how extraneous he was, how he couldn't expect to go waltzing into her life like a callow bohemian again. "Now, however, I think I was wrong to keep the truth from you. I was thinking only of myself, and not of you and your son."

His throat went tight at the phrase *you and your son.* It was as if she was offering the boy to him, handing him back.

"I am sorry also for my first letter to you, which perhaps frightened you to think you must do as I wanted. But it is not for me to decide what sort of father you are to your son. It was a very funny thing, not to know that one day he must grow curious of you. I feel I have been sleeping here all these years in my little village, and now he has woken me. You mustn't feel guilty as you will because it was not so unpleasant, to be asleep, to be here safe in my home with our son."

He felt as if he'd been threading his way through an impossible maze of narrow passages and had emerged, unaccountably, into light. Where had this forgiveness come from, what turn had he made to reach it? It seemed to loom before him even more ominous than accusation: there was no wall in front of him now, only empty space.

"We hope you will come, your son and I, we hope you will stay with us for a time. Not as before, perhaps, not the same, but still as our family."

She'd ended not with the sort of blessing she always used to include, the divine invocation, but simply "With love." God had hardly been mentioned, only the "test" she'd referred to, but then she might have failed it, might have cursed the Great Examiner and sent him packing. There would be no obstacle between them then. No excuse.

There was a postscript that made reference to a picture. "He did it himself, of course, but I thought I must send it, it was such a surprising thing. Perhaps you still have the other." It was that sheet still stuck to the envelope. He pulled it free to reveal a child's drawing of some sort of vehicle, a tractor perhaps, big spiky wheels at the back and smaller ones, a bit lopsided, at the front. Across the top, in Ingrid's hand, was the title "From Our Visit to the Farm."

For an instant he couldn't make sense of it. There was Lars's picture, yes, packed away now in some box in his parents' basement, but this seemed merely some parody of it, some practical joke. Then his eye went to the bottom corner, and the tears welled up in him. "From Per," it said, in a child's simple lettering, "for Father."

It was past one. He felt exhausted, drained, as if he'd lived a lifetime in the space of a day. But for the first time in months the fog over him seemed to have lifted. María, Liz, all the rest, felt suddenly manageable: he would put his lands in order.

He thought of calling Sweden. They would just be rising now. He could say he would catch the first flight. He could say a millstone had been lifted from him. But it felt too soon: he wanted to relish this last bit of his old life, before he turned into someone new.

He fell asleep almost at once, dead tired now, but awoke some time later to a sound of ringing. The phone: it was Ingrid. A panic went through him. He clambered up from his bed, groping toward wakefulness, and his first lucid thought was, *He's dead.*

The horror of phones in the night: car crashes, drownings, sudden death. He had to stumble around in the dark, disoriented after his weeks on the couch.

"Hello?"

There was a sound at the other end that he couldn't make sense of, heavy breathing, maybe, or someone underwater.

"Who is it?"

Someone was crying.

"It's me. It's Katherine."

His heart sank. He realized at once who he'd hoped it was, who could have called him in tears at two in the morning without having stepped from the realm of the expected.

"What is it? What's happened?"

It was an eerie sort of crying, breathless and reedy.

"My God, Alex. My God."

At every instant, some theory went, every timeline divided into an infinite number of other possible ones, each one infinitesimally different from the next. Which one would he end up in?

"Katherine, where are you? Tell me where you are."

But he knew.

"It's Amanda," she said. "I'm at Amanda's."

He had imagined this moment a dozen times, but in imagining it had somehow believed he had headed it off.

"Just stay there. I'll come. Just stay."

He had to scrounge for quarters, dimes, whatever, to gather up cab fare. Somehow he got to the street and managed to flag one down.

He gave the address.

"Cold night," the cabby said, in unaccented English.

Everything felt very small suddenly, a pinprick, as if the universe was shrinking back to the sucking black hole it had been at the start, the nothing in nothing.

"You wanna take Sherbrooke?"

"It doesn't matter."

Out of the black beyond the windows another whirl of snowflakes descended and speckled the windshield of the cab with drops of wet.

"Winter, eh? I couldn't believe it. Next week all the Frenchies'll be heading to Florida."

Alex hunkered down into his seat and tried to will his mind into blankness, feeling the cold coming off the window as the bits of snow wheeled out of the dark and back into it.

three: galápagos

Hence, both in space and time, we seem to be brought somewhat near to that great fact—that mystery of mysteries—the first appearance of new beings on this earth.

CHARLES DARWIN
The Voyage of the Beagle

By the time Alex boarded the weekly flight out of Quito for the Galápagos—a place he'd never had any intention of going to, that he couldn't afford, that he wouldn't even have been able to place on a map before he'd met Anders on the Inca Trail—it seemed that everything that could possibly have gone wrong since he'd left Ingrid had. It started on the connecting flight through London, where the woman sitting next to him, a high-strung American somewhere near the detonation point of her biological clock, talked him into sharing a hotel room with her that set him back some fifty dollars out of the paltry few hundred he had left. In Rio he spent New Year's Eve in a hostel in the Catete district listening to the reveling outside with a strange dread, the whooping and the shouts and the endless salvoes receding into the distance that might have been fireworks or submachine-gun fire, for all he knew, the rat-a-tat of swaths of street children being mown down in honor of the coming year. In the morning he walked out through neighborhoods that looked as if a marauding army had passed through them until he got to the beach at Ipanema, where he stared out at the apartment blocks and hotels that circled around to Dois Irmãos and thought, *What am I doing here?*

Their plane was a noisy sixteen-seater that rode the air pockets out of Quito rising and dipping like a leaf, so that Alex envisioned ending up in one of those tabloid stories where people were wrecked in the remotest mountains and ended up resorting to cannibalism. At Guayaquil, on the coast, they stopped to pick up a handful of locals, flying in low over a muddy delta that was spilling every manner of flotsam into the Pacific, car parts and bits of building and whole palm trees with clumps of earth still clinging to them as if they were little islands putting out to colonize the seas. After that there was nothing but the roar of the engines, which at least drowned out the Americans at the back of the plane, and then miles and miles of empty ocean that stretched to the very curve of the earth.

At some point Alex slumped into sleep like a dead man, his body worn out from a week of illness on the Inca Trail. In his dreams he tried to work out quadratic equations that looped through a dozen variables he had to pound one by one into place, only to have them revert at once to chaos. He woke just as they were making their final descent, though what he saw beneath them was not the Edenic world of white sands and blue lagoons that Anders's descriptions had led him to expect but an island that looked like a lesion on the skin of the sea, a patch of rock and scabrous earth completely barren except for the occasional cactus.

Taxiing into the terminal, they passed an area of sunburnt streets laid out amidst the waste in a tidy purposeless grid, empty squares of concrete coming off them as if a pleasant suburb had once stood here that had been vaporized by some nuclear blitz.

"It's the old GI base," he heard one of the Americans say, the know-it-all, a real collegiate type. "I guess the locals picked it apart after we pulled out."

We. As if he'd been here in the flesh, fighting at Iwo Jima or whatever.

The only sign Alex saw of the wildlife the place was supposed to be famous for was a lone bird that looked like the commonest sort of sparrow, standing vulturish and bored on a post near the entrance to the terminal building. Inside, they had to pay what they were told was a park fee, something Anders had failed to mention. A WANTED poster depicting a mustached man who looked like the archetypal *bandito* hung on the wall behind the ticket counter with the warning PELIGROSO PARA LA SOCIEDAD.

They were ferried across a channel to a second, much larger island. An old army bus sat waiting for them at the dock. The land rose up with a monotonous regularity to a single peak that disappeared into cloud, the sole mark of human incursion the road that cut up the slope as straight as a seam. The landscape was freakish, barren near the shore but slowly giving way to gray half-soil studded with gray scrub, the vegetation spaced out so evenly it looked sinister, crisscrossing the slopes with the same eerie symmetry as the abandoned streetscape they had passed near the airport. As the bus rose higher, the scrub turned to bush and the bush to spindly forest, row on row of desolate telephone-pole trees that stood completely naked except for their bits of crown.

At the crest of the slope, in the space of a dozen yards, they passed from brilliant sun into impenetrable fog. For half a mile or so it went on, until they came out at the other end of it into what seemed a different country. The landscape was within the realm of the familiar now, messy and dense and multispecied and soon enough dotted with signs of civilization, roadside shanties and smoking fires and little half-plots of field carved out of the bush. It was as if they had passed to the normal world by way of its underside, its infernal blueprint.

Alex felt exhaustion clotting his brain again by the time they reached Puerto Ayora. He had to walk the length of the town to get to the hotel Anders had recommended, the Black Mangrove, past the string of gloomy restaurants and shops that lined the harborside like a false front. Ahead of him, the Americans had all turned in at the Angermeyer, a two-story place with a gallery up top like a frontier saloon's and a rubbly courtyard where people had pitched tents and stretched out sleeping bags as if the place was a free-for-all. This was clearly the favored establishment for travelers of his ilk, though the thought of having to face the whole Byzantine world of backpacker culture right then made him shudder.

The Black Mangrove, set back in foliage amidst a snarl of unprepossessing outbuildings, had the air of something out of a Graham Greene novel. The lobby was deserted except for a great lizard who sat sunning himself on the patio, which gave onto a scraggly backwater of overgrown cove. Alex rang a bell, and by and by a young black woman with hips like bludgeons and a look of ancient affront shuffled out from a back room.

"You have reservation?"

"I didn't think I'd need one."

She leafed through the register with an air of impatience.

"Come."

Though the place looked empty, she skipped all the oceanfront rooms to give him one with just the barest sliver of a view onto the harbor. Now that he was settled, Alex had nothing to distract him from the folly of his having come here. Fucking Anders. Alex still wasn't sure if he had been some kind of saint or just a head case. He had saved Alex's life, it was true, but the more Alex thought of him the more his memory of him seemed to skew.

He stretched out on his bed and fell asleep at once. Night had fallen by the time he awoke, but instead of grabbing something to eat, he went out to the bathroom to take a leak and fell right back into bed. This time he didn't wake until morning. When he opened his eyes he felt the fear go through him that he was still on the trail, in the rain and the cold. He had been so horribly ill. His body felt like an engine that had been run without oil or coolant: too late to do any servicing, the damage was done.

He had breakfast on the patio. His lizard was there again, a demon-ish, black-skinned creature, along with his black warden, who took his order and then brought out items that seemed to bear little relationship to it. Afterward he set off into town. What one did here in the Galápagos was charter a boat: that was how you got to the interesting game, or whatever it was that was out there. He had picked this up not from Anders but by eavesdropping on the know-it-all from the plane. It would have made sense to have cozied up to the Americans so that he might have joined them and split his costs, but the prospect of spending days and days on the high seas with them like some sort of Canadian pet was too depressing for words.

He stopped in at a cruise office he had passed the day before, a tiny hole-in-the-wall, frigid with air conditioning. The agent, a young man immaculately dressed in pleated trousers and a pressed shirt, looked him up and down.

"You are alone?" he said, frowning.

"Well, right now I am, yes."

He spread a map of the islands in front of Alex. It was the first time Alex had really looked at one. He was surprised at the distances involved, hundreds of miles.

"You see? Many islands. Many days. You pay the food, the boat, the guide, is very expensive."

"How expensive?"

"Five hundred. Six hundred. Eight hundred. Like that."

Alex winced.

"Isn't there any other way?"

The man shrugged as if to abjure any responsibility for him.

"There are the fishing boats. But very dangerous."

Alex returned to his room to brood. He couldn't believe Anders had left him so woefully underinformed.

"You must visit, of course," he had said. This was on one of the first clear nights since they had started out, when Anders had made a fire and Alex had had an inkling of how it might feel to be warm and healthy and dry again. "It's something, I can't describe it to you. Being there with the animals, with nature, it makes you think, maybe this is the way. Maybe it's possible on this earth to have paradise. At least you can dream it, when you are there."

Alex wasn't sure why this little encomium had so mesmerized him at the time. The lingering delirium of his fever, maybe, or just the altitude. It was the altitude that had first brought him under Anders's auspices: he had literally passed out at the side of the trail from the rarefied air and had opened his eyes to see this gawky bird of a Swede staring down at him. Lucky for Alex. It might have been days before anyone else had passed. The trail was usually closed that time of the year, because of the rains.

He tried his luck at the wharf. The Americans were there, with a strapping Aussie in tow, already loading their stuff into a sleek-looking motor launch. Alex couldn't have said what it was that he had found so objectionable in them the day before.

There were a couple of women among them, attractive, earthy types who smiled at Alex when he approached.

"I was on the plane," he said. "I'm trying to get out to the other islands."

The know-it-all gave him a look as if he'd never laid eyes on him before.

"Gee, I'd like to help you out, buddy, but we already cut a deal. It's too bad we didn't hook up on the plane."

He made a few half-hearted inquiries amongst the locals, mashing his Italian into bad Spanish. Everyone had a scheme, an uncle who had a fishing boat or a friend who ran private tours on his yacht, but it all sounded too expensive or too dodgy. He checked in at the Angermeyer and found an actual sign-up sheet in the lobby, but there weren't any names on it.

"It's bad time," the woman at the reception desk said, a wattled bleached blonde who looked like she'd descended here from outer space. "Because of the rains."

The fucking rains.

He was left to his surly keeper at the Black Mangrove. Mara, her name was, he'd got that out of her in the way of making conversation, though afterward, to judge from the new level of contempt he had graduated to, it was as if he had tried to steal her mumbo-jumbo from her or her soul. It was six more days before there was another flight out. Mara would have broken him by then, would have him tied to a post in the yard to do her nails for her and pumice her feet.

From the patio he watched a fisherman gutting fish on the back of his boat and the pelicans flocking around him like bothersome children to get the innards.

Fucking pelicans, he thought. *Fucking Anders.*

On the Inca Trail, he had barely acclimatized himself to the altitude before he had fallen ill with some bug he had probably caught from the domestic fowl he had shared space with on the train out of Cuzco. The rain had come by then, every possible species of it, cloudbursts and soul-sapping drizzles and torrential downpours that sent muddy rivers gushing down the slopes. Alex had been on the verge of splitting with Anders, who had grown entirely too maddening, smiling away at everything like a simpleton but hoarding his food and his gear with an irritating fastidiousness and carrying on with his own little itineraries as if Alex had hardly registered on him. But now he found himself at Anders's mercy again.

He had thought of Anders until then as an argument against the virtues of travel. Anders had an arrangement with the high school where he taught in Uppsala to take two-thirds pay so he could get every third year off to travel the world. But Alex felt forced to conclude that the only upshot of all his journeys—he had done China, India, Africa, Eastern Europe—had been to make him entirely unfit for normal human intercourse. He had his smile, which served as a sort of transition point between himself and the world, but beneath it he seemed as insular and unknowable and fixed in his ways as an insect. Back home, he'd told Alex proudly—and there was no mention of anything like children or a wife, though he must have been pushing forty—he got by without so much as a telephone, to save his kronor for his travels. What sort of person didn't want a telephone? Someone like Anders. Someone who had no one to call.

Once Alex had fallen sick, however, with a violence that made his altitude sickness feel like a mild head cold, the whole dynamic between him and Anders began to shift. Bit by bit Anders's finicky self-sufficiency ceded to Alex's helplessness, until he was giving his tent up for him, his food, was practically carrying him on his back to make headway along the trail, up rain-slicked switchbacks and through nightmarish passes and along narrow cliff edges that gave way to nothing. The landscape passed by like images from a dream, jungled valleys rife with flowers, ruined cities that floated in the clouds or clung to the slopes in impossible terraces. Anders tended to him as if he were a child, feeding him bits of food that he retched up almost at once, wiping the sweat from him when the fever came on, which it did in staggering waves. At night he built fires whenever the rain allowed, and sometimes, uncharacteristically, he talked. That had been Alex's undoing. The fire, the Incan dark, and Anders waxing poetic about paradise on earth.

By the time they had reached the Gate of the Sun to gaze down on Machu Picchu, Alex felt as if he had been torn apart by wild animals and stitched randomly back together again. But if Anders had never happened along, he might not have been stitched at all. At the height of his illness he had begun to take Anders for Ingrid, to turn himself over to him as he might to a parent, with that same feeling of being safe, of being looked after. An image had kept coming back to him then that he could never place, that had felt like a home he was moving toward but not his own, maybe Anders's or Ingrid's: there was a lake and a road, snowy or wet and with a smell of mountains, none of this like anywhere he had been to or that even existed but that had a particular reality in the mind, itself and not itself, the meeting point of some inexpressible skein of emotions, but also just a lake, a road, a smell of mountains.

They had walked down into the ruins. The sun had refused to show itself and the place was shrouded in fog, bits of cloud, really, so that they had to make their way almost by touch, not knowing if three feet ahead of them the path they were on would give way to empty space. At one point they climbed up the steps of a sort of pyramid and came to a massive slab of stone with a rough pillar rising up in the middle of it. The Hitching Post of the Sun. Around them the fog stretched, so that they seemed to be floating in it.

"You must put your face to the stone," Anders said. "Or so they say. To see the spirit world."

"Will you?"

Anders grew sheepish.

"No, no, I mustn't, I think. They say you only see what's inside you. Perhaps I shouldn't like that."

As if to make light of the matter, Alex put his cheek to the stone. It was damp from the fog, and surprisingly cold. The cold seemed to cut into him like a brain freeze.

He came away a bit too quickly, perhaps.

"The spirit world seems pretty cold and wet," he said. "A lot like here."

But it had stayed with him, that instant. What had he seen? The way he remembered it afterward, only the blank wet face of the stone staring back at him.

Alex emerged from his room the next morning girding himself to wrestle Mara for his breakfast only to find her busy at the front desk with a new arrival. Someone from the research center, Alex figured, because he was wearing a rumpled blazer and had actual luggage, a duffel bag, a battered valise, a funny black case that was almost a perfect square. A local boy trailed him hauling more luggage still.

"Careful with those!"

A fucking Brit. Alex knew the type. Probably some low-level bureaucrat back home but the last bastion against the wogs in the colonies.

He handed the boy a coin.

"Go on, then."

He must have come in on a cargo ship, to judge from the look of him. His hair had the matted sheen of having gone unwashed for many days; the tail of his shirt was poking out beneath his blazer. There was a general air of unwholesomeness to him that made Alex think of damp, chilly rooms and of fish and chips that tasted like they'd been cooked in petroleum.

He was relishing the thought of how Mara would deal with this man.

"One night," he said loudly, and then added, in an execrable accent, "*Una noche.*"

"*Sí, sí,*" Mara said irritably, but turning from him as if not to look him in the eye.

She picked out a key and started toward the rooms.

"You can bring the bags in after," the man said, taking only his valise and the funny black case.

Alex had already vowed to himself to have nothing to do with this ass, though he sat waiting there on the patio taken with the spectacle of those abandoned bags, which Mara proceeded to collect one by one and carry off in the direction of the rooms. Then before Alex had even had a chance to order his breakfast the Brit had come out and plopped himself at his table, still in his blazer and untucked shirt.

He actually snapped his fingers to get Mara's attention.

"Would you get me some eggs or something? And coffee. And don't break the yolks."

In a matter of minutes he'd got more service from Mara than Alex had managed since he'd arrived.

"I suppose you're going out to the islands," the Brit said grudgingly, as if this were a question Alex had forced him into.

"I dunno." He ought at least to be civil. "I was going to. I can't afford a boat."

"You should come out with me."

He threw this out with such an obvious absence of anything like real intent that it was clear he was merely trying to switch the topic of conversation to himself.

"You've got a boat?"

"I'll get one. Soon enough."

"Oh."

"Research trip. A little project I'm working on."

So Alex had been right. And yet he didn't want to satisfy the man by pursuing the matter.

"American?"

For some reason Alex flushed. "Canadian, actually."

"Ah. The last dominion."

Their breakfasts arrived. Mara set the Brit's eggs before him, perfect, intact, then lingered beside him an instant as if for further instruction. He ignored her.

"It's Desmond, by the way. Desmond Clarke. University of London."

"Oh." Alex wasn't sure how impressed he was supposed to be by this. "I'm Alex."

"So I guess they didn't warn you," the Brit said, between mouthfuls of egg. "Everyone tries to gouge you here now, not like the old days."

"You've been here before?"

"Mmm. Once or twice." He mopped up a bit of yolk. "Out of money, is that it?"

"Not exactly. A little low is all."

The Brit gave him a quick once-over.

"I could use an assistant," he said cagily. "Carrying equipment and so on. If you're up for it."

Alex's resolve to avoid the man weakened before the prospect of passage.

"How long are you going out for?"

"How long have you got?"

This wasn't a question Alex had an answer to.

"A couple of weeks, I guess."

"That sounds about right. Three at the most. You'd go batty out there, any longer than that."

The guy probably had some whopping research grant. He might even be meaning to pay him, though Alex couldn't bring himself to ask.

It was either this or five more days with Mara.

"It's not as if I'm doing anything else," he said.

The Brit wiped up his last bits of egg. Now that Alex had more or less turned himself over to him, the man seemed to have grown weary of him.

"Just show up here tomorrow morning," he said. "Crack of dawn."

Alex changed his mind about the matter a dozen times over the course of the day. He was exhausted, worn out, he ought to go home; except that he couldn't, not until the next plane. Then he had spent all that cash to get out here. His mind was always doing the accounts, the profit and loss: he hadn't *learned* anything here yet, hadn't so much as an anecdote to take away to show he'd got value. But then he wondered if the guy had even been serious. There was something odd about him, with that funny black case of his. He might be a terrorist or spy, who knew in this place? *Desmond Clarke.* It had the sound of a code name.

Alex showed up in the lobby the next morning just after dawn, still hedging his bets. There was no sign of Desmond yet. Alex checked out, had breakfast, a second coffee, then another.

He wasn't sure of it, but Mara seemed a bit less glacial this morning.

"Have you seen that man who came yesterday? Mr. Clarke?"

"He go this morning."

"He checked out?"

"He pay," she said, looking almost displeased at this, "then he go."

So the creep had left him in the lurch.

"He didn't leave any message?"

She shrugged an African shrug.

"He leave some bag. Take only one."

Maybe all was not lost. Now that Alex had experienced the letdown of thinking he'd been left behind, there seemed no question of his not wanting to go. He set out for the wharf in a huff, determined to track Desmond down and give him a piece of his mind. He spotted him near one of the boats and hurried over, but Desmond gave such a cursory nod at the sight of him that he was pulled up short.

"So it's our Canadian," he said, hardly glancing at him.

"I thought we were going."

"Right." As if they'd never agreed to anything. "Just finessing the price."

The boat was an ancient fishing trawler in blue and white, of the sort that crowded the harbor, with the look of something that had been cobbled together from the discarded lumber of some other, realer construction. There was a cabin up front of warped plywood, and plywood patches spotting the hull.

"I got him down to two hundred American," Desmond said, which sounded outrageous to Alex. The boat didn't so much as have a name on it. "Split between us, that's a hundred."

So there was something to pay. Not a job, then, not in that sense.

It crossed Alex's mind that Desmond might be the sort to bump the number up to cut his own share.

There was no sign of the owner.

"It's a bit steep for me," Alex said.

"What have you got?"

He was foolish enough to take out his cash in front of Desmond, not sure what remained after the extortionist exchange rate Mara had charged when he'd settled his bill.

He was down to a hundred American in traveler's checks and a hundred and thirty and change in cash.

"A couple of hundred," he said vaguely.

"There you go." As if the matter was settled. "You've got your ticket back to the mainland, haven't you? That leaves you a hundred."

Alex felt it would be petty to quibble. At least he wouldn't have to be the guy's lackey, not if they were splitting the cost. But when they went back to the hotel to collect their things, Desmond stuck him with half of his luggage for the walk back to the wharf.

"It'll save us an extra trip," he said.

There was a man on the boat when they returned, a bearish hulk in soiled overalls with boulder-sized hands, the skin on them hardened and cracked like old leather. He was wearing a New York Yankees cap, his face beneath it bronzed to the color of roast pork.

"*El capitán*," Desmond said, with what seemed to pass as bonhomie. "*Es mi amigo* Alex."

The man looked down on them stone-faced.

"*En la cabina*," he said of the luggage.

Some sort of discussion ensued between the captain and Desmond while Alex was left to load their things.

"There's a problem," Desmond said. "He wants another forty dollars for the extra passenger."

"But didn't you tell him?"

"Of course I told him. Tell you what," not missing a beat, "I'll split it with you."

The captain wanted all the cash up front. Alex felt a moment of terror as he peeled off the bills. Here he was at the end of the world with not enough money left in his pockets to last through a week.

"You'll want to pick up supplies," Desmond said. "Don't worry about food. Our man Santos'll take care of that."

Alex hadn't even thought about food. He decided to pick up a bit of fruit, at least, and maybe a few carrots, but at the lone grocery store in town he saw shelves piled high with canned goods of every sort, but no produce.

"*Fruta?*" he said to the owner. "*Vegetales?*"

"*Verdura*," the man said. "*Sí, sí, verdura. No verdura. Mañana.* In the morning, only. Early, early."

Sold out. Alex had to content himself with two cartons of Marlboros and a jar of Nescafé, which set him back a whopping twenty-three dollars.

"*Mañana, mañana*," the owner repeated.

The boat was deserted when he got back. He waited fifteen minutes, half an hour, afraid he'd get left behind, then finally started searching the town. He found Desmond casually having his lunch at a nearby eatery.

"Aren't we going?"

"In good time, my boy, in good time. Might as well wait out the heat."

It was nearly sunset before they put out. By then Santos, *el capitán*, had spent the better part of the afternoon loading the boat with every manner of gear, frayed nets and great hoops of fishing line, sacks of salt, a little brazier of corroded iron, a strange blackened contraption with a bolted lid that looked like some sort of hand-fashioned pressure cooker. The bulk of the load, however, was fuel. Alex lost count of how many canisters Santos brought aboard, but surely enough to blow them all to kingdom come. They were stuffed down into the engine well and strapped to the rails and wedged up against their luggage inside the cabin. Already the smell of them was overwhelming.

Desmond was studying some maps on the wharf, crude, photocopied things patched together with tape.

"Where are we supposed to sleep, exactly?"

Desmond nodded toward the boat.

"In the cabin."

The only accommodations Alex had seen there were the two narrow bunks along the sides, little more than benches, really, that they'd stuffed their luggage under.

"What about the captain?"

"I guess he'll manage, won't he?"

The last thing to be loaded was a little dinghy Santos strapped to the roof of the cabin. All that remained clear of the back deck by then was a narrow aisle around the hatch into the hold and the hatch lid itself, which Desmond promptly claimed as his throne. Santos had crouched into the engine well to fiddle with the engine. It sputtered briefly then died, then sputtered and died again. Alex had a flash of every bad trip he had ever been on, the engines that wouldn't start, the papers that weren't in order, the ten-minute delay that turned into an hour, or three, or whole days.

Now the engine caught, definitively.

"*Es bueno*," Santos said, the first sign he'd shown of anything like good humor.

The sun was setting behind the top of the island when they put out. The orange light made the headland they skirted around, an escarpment of black rock and cactus, look surreal. Coal-colored lizards stared out at them from the rocks. Soon the light gave way to twilight, then almost at once it was night. Alex could see nothing more than the hundred-odd twinkling lights of the town and beyond that a darkness so big it startled him.

He edged out a spot for himself next to Desmond. A strong odor was coming off Desmond, at once animal and vaguely medicinal.

Alex figured he ought to make an effort. This might be his only company for three weeks.

"You never told me what you're researching."

"It's a bit technical, to be honest. Not fit stuff for laymen."

Fuck you, too, Alex thought.

Desmond seemed put out that Alex hadn't insisted.

"My actual specialty, if you want to know, is *Mollugo flavescens.* That's carpetweed to you. A pioneer plant. Fascinating, really."

Alex couldn't come up with a logical next question.

Three weeks, he thought.

Desmond rose, working a kink out of his neck by twisting his head around like a crotchety gull.

"Think I'll get a bit of shut-eye."

Alex glanced at his watch.

"But it's only seven."

"You can forget about your watch out here, my boy. There's day and then there's night. Only what nature intended."

He was left alone. His stomach was grumbling, but there didn't seem to be any plans for supper. He smoked a cigarette, then another, while hundreds of gallons of diesel fuel sloshed around him. He had a moment of panic at not having brought any water, but surely Santos had taken care of that. He could have used some at the moment, but lacked the will to track it down.

His stomach grumbled again. Not half an hour out of the harbor and already he was feeling privation. It occurred to him how long the night would be, with no food, no company, not even a pinprick of light to read by. *Three weeks.*

For a time a shadow of shoreline was still visible in the distance beneath the moon, but then it vanished and there was only the sea.

Alex awoke to pitch black, his ears ringing with a sound that it took him an instant to realize was silence. The engine had stopped. A small light flicked on: Desmond was crawling in the space between the bunks shining a flashlight among his bags. He pulled out what appeared to be an old shoe bag, lumpy with jangling things, then the black case.

"*Vamos,*" Santos said from the door.

There was a sudden scraping, then a splash. Alex couldn't piece together what was happening. His head ached from the diesel fumes, his throat was parched, his stomach felt hollowed out. He didn't know how long he'd been lying there on that awful board, an hour, five, fighting the motion of the boat to keep from tumbling off it.

"*Rápido, rápido!*"

A thunk, then a slosh of oars. Desmond and Santos had gone off in the dinghy. Alex, panicked, scrambled up and peered out through the clouded windshield. Sure enough, he saw the dinghy gliding across the water in the moonlight toward a great shadow ahead of them, humped and strange, like a monstrous tortoise or whale.

It was one of the islands. They were making toward it at a steady clip, though the shoreline seemed a wall of impregnable cliff. The dinghy grew small and indistinct, then rounded some sort of headland and disappeared entirely.

Alex waited what seemed hours, imagining every sort of possibility, that he'd been abandoned, that he'd been made a pawn in some nefarious scheme. His hunger and thirst gnawed at him but he didn't dare take his eyes from the sea, afraid he'd miss some crucial clue. Then finally the dinghy reappeared, a tiny shadow against the massive one of the island.

Desmond was already rising, clutching his case, as the dinghy slid toward the back of the boat.

"*Cuidado!*" Santos said.

Alex reached out to take the case.

"Just leave it!" Desmond said. "I'll manage it."

He clambered aboard, nearly losing his footing, and headed into the cabin at once to stow the case.

"What's going on?" Alex said. "Why did we stop?"

"Just picking up a few specimens." As if none of this had been out of the ordinary.

"But why did we stop in the middle of the night?"

Desmond wedged one of the diesel canisters up against his case to secure it.

"Let's just say it seemed prudent." He looked pleased with himself. "There's the little matter of permits."

Alex wasn't sure how much more he wanted to know. He'd been an idiot to set out with this man, who was now revealing himself to be some sort of outlaw.

"Why didn't you get a permit through your university or something?" But Desmond turned on him.

"I don't know about Canada," he snapped, "but where I come from, you don't sit around twiddling your thumbs while some Third World bureaucrat decides whether or not you can visit his little island."

Desmond crawled back into his bunk. He had managed to rig a sort of hammock, which he folded himself into like a worm in its cocoon. Alex wasn't sure what Santos had made of all this, though from the look of him, not much: he was standing in the engine well cursing under his breath, yanking at the pull cord again and again before the engine finally growled back to life. The boat set off with a lurch that nearly knocked Alex to the floor. His thirst was still on him, but now didn't seem the moment to be scrounging for water. The only source of it he'd seen so far was the personal supply that Santos hoarded at his feet, in a dirty jeroboam that looked as if it doubled as a drain for engine oil.

Alex passed a wretched night, turning and tossing on his board, feeling the vibrations of the engine through the wood like a jackhammer in his brain. He was aware of Santos at the controls, hand on the throttle. Didn't the man need to sleep? It must surely be dangerous to be driving full-out like this through the night, with only the moon to guide them and the single running light that flickered from the head of the cabin. A dozen times Alex thought to ask Santos to stop, give him water, give him food, turn the boat around and take him back to what now already seemed the incredible luxury of the Black Mangrove. But then somehow he fell asleep, and didn't wake again until it was day.

Santos was still at the controls.

"*Agua*," Alex said.

Santos took a swig from his jeroboam and handed it to Alex.

"*Bebe.*"

All Alex's inhibitions had gone. At the first swig his body seemed to unfurl like a fist opening.

"*Gracias.*"

They were just entering some sort of bay, a perfect circle of guano-washed cliffs. Out on the deck it was surprisingly cool, the air strident with bird cries. A low line of clouds sat on the horizon, but otherwise the sky was clear.

Desmond was sitting on the hatch, peeling an orange, still in the dandruff-flecked blazer he'd been wearing since Alex had first laid eyes on him.

He tossed the peel into the water.

"Darwin Bay," he said. "The irony is, Darwin never laid eyes on it."

Alex eyed his orange.

"Is there another one of those?"

"Personal supply." Desmond pried off a wedge and popped it into his mouth. "You should have stocked up."

Alex felt ready to knock him over the rail.

"I thought Santos was supposed to supply the food."

"The basics, yes. Not the goodies."

"Are the basics going to be making an appearance any time soon?"

Desmond downed another wedge.

"I expect once we get to the beach."

It took a good while to get across the bay to the sole stretch of beach that broke up the ring of cliffs. Here, at least, was a bit of bluish lagoon and whitish sand, though beyond them the black cliffs rose up, topped with bush that had the gray, dried-out look of a failed crop. Santos anchored the boat. He stuffed various bits of cooking equipment into a sack, then climbed down into the hip-high water without so much as removing his boots and began wading into shore. After a moment Desmond followed, cringing like a cat, though unlike Santos he had taken his socks and shoes off, holding them aloft as he sloshed toward the beach.

"Fuck, fuck, fuck!"

He had stepped on something. Alex, taking his cue from Santos, kept his sneakers on during the crossing. He could feel the bony unevenness of the seabed through his soles: they were walking on coral.

Desmond squatted on the beach to inspect his foot.

"Fuck it! I've cut myself. Damn it to hell!"

Santos, entirely ignoring Desmond, had started collecting up bits of wood and brush for a fire. Alex followed his lead. Desmond could fuck himself, for all Alex cared.

"Bloody hell. I'm bleeding like a stuck pig."

Santos had a fire going within minutes. He had brought his odd pressure cooker with him and he dunked it into the sea to let water gurgle in through a nozzle at the top, then set it on the fire on a little tripod of rocks. From his sack he pulled out a length of crudely coiled metal tubing, fitting one end of it over the nozzle and inserting the other into an empty jeroboam.

He saw Alex watching him.

"*Agua*," he said, seeming to puff up a bit. "*Es muy importante.*"

Alex twigged. It was a still for their water. He stood looking at it, trying to express a proper level of gravity.

Santos grunted.

"*Más leña*," he said finally, more wood, their moment of communion over. Alex could already see how this was going to go: he was going to be everyone's bum boy, while Santos played the captain and Desmond, who was still fretting over his foot, managed to shirk every responsibility.

He went off to look for more firewood, past an outcropping of rock further along the beach. A couple of tide pools had formed there, a number of odd gray lumps stretched out next to them. Alex went nearer to see what they were but started back when one of them raised itself up and let out a bark. Seals, half a dozen of them. He expected them to waddle off at the sight of him, but apart from the one, a massive brute whose hide was covered with scars, they didn't pay him the least attention.

A mother was suckling her pup, pale white droplets spilling from her teats.

"I'd watch out for the bull." It was Desmond, limping up behind him to take a seat on the rocks. "He might think you've got designs."

Alex moved inland to scrounge for wood in a patch of mangrove. Big blue-snooted birds sat roosting in the branches, clutching to them incongruously with their red ducks' feet. They seemed as incurious as halfwits, not even bothering to shift their weight when he approached. He saw their nests in the foliage, assemblages of twigs that looked like they'd been slapped together in the most careless manner. Some had eggs in them or huge fluffy hatchlings, who stared out at him dopily between the leaves, close enough to touch. It gave Alex the strangest feeling, walking among these things so unregarded. What brutal beasts the animals back home must have thought humans, that even the sparrows and squirrels scattered at the first sight of them.

Back near the fire, a few large white birds with blackened eyes were nesting in hollows they'd fashioned in the rubbly earth, little depressions of cleared ground surrounded by a nearly perfect circle of birdshit.

"Masked booby." Desmond again. He hadn't moved from his perch. "Two eggs at a go, and the first one to hatch kills off the other. There's a way to start off your life. The tourists come here and think it's lion and lamb, but it's nature all the way, make no mistake. Red in tooth and claw."

Alex tried to ignore him. Santos had managed to snag a fish with a hand line, a big reddish-orange thing that had glinted brightly as he brought it up from the water but almost at once grew dull. He knocked its head on a rock to stop its writhing and in under a minute had it scaled and gutted. He threw it directly into the fire. There was another pot going there now, into which Santos poured a few handfuls of dirty rice.

"*Pescado*," he said to Alex, nodding toward the fish. He seemed to have taken it upon himself, like Desmond, to be Alex's tutor.

"*Qué tipo?*" Alex said.

Santos actually laughed, though it was more a guffaw, as if Alex had a lot to learn.

"*No importa*," he said. It doesn't matter.

The still, in all this time, had produced about a cupful of water. Desmond limped over to the bottle and drained it.

"Bloody brackish," he said, scowling. "We'll die out here if we have to survive on this."

They ate in grunting silence, sitting squat-legged on the beach. The rice was oversalted and tasted of sea; the fish wasn't salted at all and was laced with tiny bones. But Alex couldn't get enough. They ate without utensils on army-issue tin plates, scooping their rice up with their hands. Alex had thought Desmond would be finicky, but he was quick to grab the lion's share of things, thumbing around in the fish head to scrounge what extra morsels he could from it.

Around them the masked boobies sat on their nests while great redbreasted birds wheeled overhead.

"That's better," Desmond said.

A boat appeared at the mouth of the bay as they were finishing up. At the sight of it Santos and Desmond sprang into action, stowing the rice pot and heaping sand up around the fire, ready to douse it.

"Who are they?" Alex said.

"No idea. Just clean away that fish mess."

They waited tensely until it grew clear that the boat wasn't headed for the beach but for a spot across the bay, though all Alex could see there was the same wall of cliffs.

"Aren't we allowed to cook here?"

"It's just nonsense," Desmond said. "Some of these ball-breakers will turn you in if you so much as fart here."

None of this concerned Alex as much as it might have, now that his belly was full. Maybe it was better to be renegades like this, to come and go as they pleased. The agent he had talked to had said the official tours were required to use guides from the research station, who probably ushered people around like cattle.

They waited on the beach until the still had run dry, then covered their tracks so that there was hardly a sign that they'd been there. Santos sprinkled seawater over the embers from their fire to douse them, then collected them up in one of the cooking pots.

"Charcoal," Desmond said. "Waste not."

This time Desmond kept his shoes on when they waded out into the lagoon. There were more nests in the shrubs at the water's edge, crumbling little guano pads sitting completely exposed to the sun, scrawny buzzard-like nestlings cawing unhappily from them. Everything seemed just slightly out of whack in this place, as if nature had not quite got things right. Yet Alex felt a peculiar sort of calm here. He didn't know if he'd ever enjoyed a meal as much as he had their breakfast, even with these lugs for company, eating grunting there on the beach, just three animals amongst other animals.

Desmond was dragging himself through the water like a cripple.

"*Rápido!*" Santos called out.

They set out again. The boat skirted the cliffs, which were swarming with birds of every sort, until it came to a crack in them. The other boat was there, a ways off from shore, a massive yacht with tinted windows and half a dozen aerials and whirring instruments projecting from it.

"I hope they're not here all bloody day," Desmond said.

Santos maneuvered the boat until it was practically up against the rock face and idled the engine. Somehow, using a grappling hook, he managed to steady the boat against a little outcropping that afforded a landing.

"*Ándale, ándale!*"

Desmond was suddenly scrambling among his bags.

"Hold your bloody horses, you big oaf. I have to get my stuff!"

A wave lifted the boat and Santos had to struggle to hold his position.

"*Váyanse!*"

"What's going on?" Alex said.

"Go! Go! We're getting off here."

"What about Santos?"

"Don't worry about fucking Santos!" He had started tossing bags into the rock cleft. "Just go!"

Alex leaped. The boat lurched at the last instant and he ended up tumbling into the rocks. He felt a stab of pain in his shoulder.

"Quickly, for Christ's sake! Grab the case!"

Desmond was holding it out to him.

"Don't drop it!" He leaped after the case without the least thought for his injured foot, making the landing in a graceless flurry of limbs. "Here, I'll take it. You grab the rest."

He was already hauling himself up to higher ground.

"Back before dark!" he shouted back to Santos. "Not fucking *mañana!*"

Alex watched their boat disappearing into the bay, at a loss again as to what was happening. He was stranded here with Desmond, wherever here was, and on whatever questionable mission Desmond had made him an accomplice in. He didn't care, really, what Desmond was up to or even where he took him—what difference could it make, when his ignorance of the place was more or less absolute?—but he hated being shuffled around like some sort of cabin boy.

Desmond had taken only his satchel and his case. Two hefty duffel bags bulging with unknown implements were left for Alex. He hoisted them both onto one shoulder, his other aching still as if someone had pounded a nail into it.

He scraped his way to the clifftop to find Desmond sitting again, nursing his foot.

"He could have brought out the dinghy instead of just dumping us on the rocks, the fucking baboon."

He'd removed his shoe. His foot did indeed look injured, a livid gash near the heel oozing red. He wrung out his sock, wet from the lagoon, and the water dripped brown with blood.

Alex wondered what happened out here in the case, say, of an infection. Words like tetanus and gangrene came to mind.

"Where is Santos going, exactly?"

"To get his bloody fish, I imagine. Don't expect any special treatment from him, I'll tell you that. We're just extra cargo as far as he's concerned."

It seemed entirely possible that Santos might decide just to leave them here to rot. They should never have paid him up front. Alex looked out to the gleaming cruiser in the bay and considered whether he should place himself at its mercy.

"Did you bring any water, at least?" he said to Desmond.

"You didn't bring a supply?"

Alex was tempted to toss Desmond's bags over the cliff.

"It's not like I had a lot of time to think about it."

"You'll be fine. We'll be finished up here in a couple of hours."

They started along a narrow path choked with branches toward the other side of the island. A single tree near the start had held a smattering of yellow blossoms, but otherwise all they saw was a gnarl of leafless bush fading back to darkness, skeletal and vaguely menacing and giving off a narcotic smell like someplace bewitched. Alex was still saddled with the two bags, which shifted against him with each step and caught against the bushes, so that soon his good shoulder ached as much as the injured one.

Part way along they heard footsteps, voices, snapping twigs, and then a column of trekkers came into view ahead of them wearing sensible headgear and khaki, canteens and binoculars and impressive cameras with foot-long lenses slung from their shoulders. It was the group from the yacht. They were a strange sight, in this forsaken bush, tanned and hale like a misplaced species.

"Bloody krauts," Desmond said.

The leader stood a good six foot five. He towered over Desmond, smiling down on him like the sun itself.

"You are come for the boobies, I think. It is very good here, many nests."

"Actually, it's more the flora I'm interested in," Desmond said dryly. "Plant Biology, University of London."

"Ah, so."

People stood aside to let them pass. An older group brought up the rear, professorial types holding guidebooks and walking sticks who greeted them politely as they went by.

"*Ja, ja, sieg heil,*" Desmond muttered.

To Alex the troupe seemed like a little pocket of the known world amidst this alien one. It wasn't too late; he could just abandon Desmond and go after them. But then the sound of them diminished—they were laughing at something, at Desmond, maybe—and the moment seemed lost.

"Fucking Germans," Desmond said. "They'd buy the place if they could."

The bush ended suddenly, as abruptly as if it had been razed, and a wide expanse of stony earth opened out to the sea, bare except for the occasional bit of shrub and for the hundreds upon hundreds of masked boobies squatting at intervals in the chalky rubble. They had come to the nests, which stretched out a mile or more across the flats, each with its little acreage, like the ghost houses of the old army base near the airport. The birds sat placid in their little domains, rising sometimes from their eggs to do a waddling circle around them before settling again. Alex couldn't make out any sign in them of the bloody battle to come, though at some of the nests a single chick tottered nearby, hardly able to stand but no doubt gathering its forces. What would the parents do when the time came for their offspring's awful deed? Cheer it on, perhaps, though maybe for a booby it was exactly the moral thing to kill your sibling, otherwise there were years of therapy ahead and bad relations all around for the family.

The path curved to continue along the seafront, to one side of a great rift beyond which nothing grew except a few lonely clumps of tiny cacti. Desmond, without a word, set down his satchel and case at one of these clumps and suddenly vaulted over the rift. He crouched and without hesitation pulled up one of the cacti, inspecting the little tangle of roots and the bit of soil beneath.

"Pitch me that satchel, will you?"

It was surprisingly heavy. Alex tossed it over and Desmond fumbled with it and nearly lost his balance but didn't even pause to catch his breath, pulling a battered camera from it, the cheapest sort of Instamatic, and kneeling on the rock to snap some quick close-ups of the cactus's soil and roots.

He tossed the cactus into the rift.

"Catch," he said, heaving the satchel back.

They followed the trail until it petered out at a promontory, just beyond where the nests ended and the fissure gave out. The terrain further on was rough and untrammeled, just rock and ragged scrub, with a sheer drop to the sea. The birds circled over them, boobies, pelicans, a dozen other sorts Alex couldn't have named. Sometimes they would drop out of the sky like stones to plunge headfirst into the water, their beaks flashing silver an instant when they came up before something disappeared into their gullets.

Desmond cast a furtive glance back along the trail.

"Let's keep going," he said.

"It's a bit rough here. For your foot."

"Never mind that."

They set out across the rocks. Desmond stopped at every shrub, putting a hand down to finger the sprinkling of soil at its base.

"Here," he said finally. "This'll do. Give me those bags."

He set to work. Alex thought he'd be gathering more specimens, but he began to chisel at a little hollow in the rock with a hammer and pick, breaking pieces of stone away and then pounding at them in the hollow until he'd formed a little bowl of powdery earth. He scrabbled a few handfuls of dirt from a nearby shrub to add to it.

"There's a few hundred years of effort I've saved Mother Nature," he said.

He unlatched the black case. Alex didn't know what he'd been expecting, a state-of-the-art mini-laboratory or maybe the blue glow of some nuclear device. Instead Desmond folded back the lid, which split open into halves, to reveal merely a crude sort of plant box, already crammed with a mass of tangled tendrils and vines. The thing looked like a child's science project, lined with sheets of foggy Plexiglas held together with caulking and tape and sectioned off with dividers that seemed made of floor tile.

"The work begins," Desmond said, reaching in and carefully cupping one of the plants under the roots to set it in his bowl of dust.

Alex was beginning to think that maybe Desmond wasn't so much an outlaw as simply nuts.

"What are you doing? I thought you were collecting things."

The plant Desmond had set out was just a jumble of spindly vine, half-dead from the look of it, with the barest hint of tiny leaves and an even barer hint of some sort of flower or bud at the tips. Bits of nascent earth clung to the roots.

"Patience, my boy," Desmond said, gently bedding the roots in his dirt. "All things will be revealed."

"Isn't this dangerous or something? I mean, doesn't it mess up the ecosystem or whatever?"

"Not if you know what you're doing."

When Desmond had settled the plant he pulled a plastic spritzer bottle from his satchel and sprayed a fine mist over it, as frugally as if he were applying an expensive perfume.

"I thought there wasn't any water."

"Not for drinking, I'm afraid. Strictly reserved for the plants."

They proceeded along like that, Desmond limping across the terrain to smash up bits of rock at intervals and set out his plants. There were two types, the spindly vine and then some kind of succulent whose foliage ranged from yellowy green to brilliant red. These he planted near the cliffs, at a spot where a sucking hollow in the rocks below acted like a kind of geyser, sending wafts of sea spray to the clifftop whenever a big wave broke over it.

"Also called carpetweed," Desmond said of these, doling out his bits of information. "Entirely different plant, of course, though the same order, believe it or not. Theoretically, they could interbreed. What you would call a wide cross. This one likes salt, hence the sea spray. So you see nature looks after its own."

He was almost bearable when he was like this, in his element, seemed almost legitimate, even if it was all madness—his precious transplants would surely be dead by tomorrow. Alex knew from the farm how finicky plants got when you messed with them this way. And then in this sun: it wasn't especially hot, but they were on the equator. Even up in the Andes, a few hours of this sun had been enough to fry him like bacon.

He hadn't thought to wear a hat.

"Shouldn't we get back soon?"

"Just a few for insurance. The second egg."

He had no idea what Desmond was expecting, maybe to come back one day and find that his plants had taken the place over the way rabbits had done in Australia. If Alex had thought there was any chance of this he might have been more concerned, but as it was he ended up on his knees next to Desmond, pounding along with him to help make his dirt. It was bone-rattling work but there was a kind of satisfaction in it, as if they were taming the hinterland.

Desmond kept about half of his specimens back, some of each type.

"Best return before our Virgil decides to ditch us."

Walking back past the nests, Alex found the trail blocked by two boobies facing each other at a distance, one clearly intent on getting the other's attention, prancing and flexing its wings while the other stared off with a kind of put-on indifference. The first pointed its beak skyward and let out a piercing lament until the other came forward to peck at its beak. The first plucked up a twig to set before the other, then a stone.

Desmond came limping up from behind.

"Get on with it, you two," he said irritably, shooing the birds from the path and clomping over their gifts.

The sun had started to drop. As they approached the bush again a honking rose up from the nesting ground and one by one boobies began to wheel in from over the sea to descend tottering amidst the nests. All across the plain a great shift change was occurring, the new arrivals patiently circling their nests, waiting to take over, while their partners honked at them and ruffled their feathers and flapped their wings before giving way, parading their martyrdom.

"Like bloody humans, you're thinking, isn't it?" Desmond said, though he had hardly seemed to be attending to any of this. "Except that it's the other way around. The bogeyman of anthropomorphism, my colleagues would tell you. As if there's any difference between us and them, except that we shit a bit further from the nest."

Alex didn't like to admit it but he was starting to feel a sort of grudging respect for the universality of Desmond's disdain. Probably his tooth-and-claw routine was just a way of justifying what a bastard he was, but at least he was consistent. If Alex wasn't careful out here, far from more-edifying influences, he was going to start thinking like the man. He remembered those films he'd seen back in Intro Psych where people were ready to zap test subjects with near-fatal shocks just because somebody told them to. They giggled, maybe, they squirmed, but then they cranked up the voltage. Here was Alex, meanwhile, messing with the very machinery of evolution at Desmond's say-so, with no idea to what end.

There was no sign of Santos when they got back to the steps. The yacht had gone, but another boat was coming toward them across the bay, a small, robust-looking cruiser painted military green.

"Damn it!" Desmond said. "It's the fucking Park Patrol."

He grabbed the bags and frantically dragged them behind a clump of bushes.

"Get down, for Christ's sake! Don't let them see you!"

It was too late. A small figure was already hailing them from the prow of the boat.

"Fuck," Desmond said. "Fuck, fuck, fuck."

They waited on the clifftop while the boat made a beeline to them and pulled up at the landing. It looked a bit sorrier from up close, just a sort of fortified speedboat with a little doorless cabin, the hull spotted with rust. Two men in fatigues and caps were aboard, small and earnest-looking, one mustachioed and seeming the senior, though neither of them was much more than a boy.

They were both sporting revolvers at their hips that looked like remnants of the Wild West.

"*Buenas tardes, señores!*" the mustachioed one shouted up.

Desmond smiled broadly and waved.

"Yes, yes, hello, you bastards."

"*Dónde está su barco?*"

Desmond put a hand to his ear and shook his head.

"What was that? Sorry! No Spanish! No comprenday!"

The two men exchanged a look.

"You boat!" the younger one called out. "Where is you boat?"

"I'm afraid you'll have to speak up!"

"Boat! *Barco!* You ship!"

On cue, a boat suddenly rounded the line of cliffs at the mouth of the bay, a speck of blue and white. It was Santos.

"Our boat! Yes, of course! Here it is now!"

Santos slowed as he entered the bay and began the long journey across it. Desmond, meanwhile, retreated to the shade of a nearby tree as if the matter was out of his hands now, so that the wardens had no choice but to idle there until Santos's boat drew near. Santos maneuvered casually up to the landing without the least regard for the patrol boat, though he was practically knocking against it.

"*Señor! Podemos hablar, por favor?*"

There was an exchange across the sterns, the wardens growing more and more animated and red-faced as Santos, nearly twice their size and surely more than twice their age, grew more taciturn. Finally Santos put his back to them with an air of having done with them and began to pull his boat into the landing with his hook. The ploy seemed to work—the mustachioed one grimaced, then tilted his head at the other in a signal to go. The boat eased away from the rocks and sped off in a wash of spray.

"What was all that about?" Alex said.

"Just the usual nonsense. They try to fine you if you haven't filed an itinerary. It's just their way of getting bribes."

But their manner hadn't quite jibed with the language of bribery.

"Won't they just come after us again?"

"They've got thousands of miles of ocean out there to look after. It'd be like finding a needle in a fucking haycock."

They waited until the wardens had cleared the bay, then reloaded Desmond's gear. Santos pulled the boat away from the landing and headed toward the beach they had eaten at that morning. His fishing lines were wet now, and an odor of sea was emanating from the hold. Above them a frenzy of birds had filled the sky as thick as a horde of insects.

Alex looked at the huge ring of cliffs that formed the bay and it suddenly struck him what they were.

"It's a volcano."

"Of course it's a fucking volcano," Desmond said. "They're all volcanoes. That's the point."

Alex felt himself color. He hadn't meant to speak aloud.

"Tell me this, I'm curious," Desmond said. He had that self-satisfied look again, now that his day's work was done. "Why do you lot come out here exactly, you rucksackers? It's not as if you have the least idea

about the place. From a tourist's point of view it's about the last desti-
nation I'd pick."

Desmond was right. Alex ought to have stuck to the beach at
Ipanema like everyone else.

"If it's any consolation, Darwin didn't think much of the place
either," Desmond said. "Here, why don't you read up on it."

He rummaged in one of his bags and pulled out a battered hardcover.

"*Voyage of the Beagle*. Best travelogue you'll ever read. And don't just
skip ahead to the Galápagos like everyone does, you'll miss the effect."

The gesture was so out of character for Desmond that Alex was at
a loss.

"And I'll thank you not to drop the thing in the fucking ocean. It's
my study copy."

It was nearly dark by the time they got to the beach. Desmond made
Santos take down the dinghy this time—the panga, he called it—to save
them wading through the shallows. Alex helped with the fire again, and
with the still. Desmond, meanwhile, sat jotting notes in his journal,
pulling up to the fire as if it had been made for his express benefit. For
supper there was fish again, though this time a big bulldog-faced one,
speckled brown, that Santos had pulled up from the hold. While it
cooked, Santos brought over more of them in the panga, spreading them
out on a tarp near the fire and beginning to gut them.

"*Quiere saber qué tipo, no?*" he said to Alex, with his grunting laugh.

The last thing Alex needed was Santos taking the piss out of him.

"*Es bacalao,*" Santos said, with emphasis. "*Bacalao.*"

Baccalà. What they had back home every Christmas Eve.

"Cod?"

"Not cod," Desmond said. "Grouper. They only call it that. Generic
for poor man's fish. Whatever there's lots of."

Santos threw out some guts and something swooped out of the dark
to take them up the second they'd left his hand.

"Fucking frigates," Desmond said. "Bloody pirates. They'll knock a
fish right out of your gullet."

They had their supper. Alex's face burned from the day's sun, his
shoulders ached, his throat itched from the briny water. Yet already his
body seemed to be adjusting itself to the different order of things out
here, lowering its expectations.

Desmond had spread out his maps and Alex made out what island they were on from the shape of it. "Tower," the map read, but then beneath this, in brackets, as if to make the place seem one you might actually want to visit, "Genovesa."

"You're probably wondering what it is I'm doing out there," Desmond said.

Alex did indeed wonder, though mostly because he didn't want to end up in an Ecuadorean jail.

"It's not really any of my business."

"But you must be curious. It would only be natural."

He was going to make Alex pay now for the book he'd lent him by forcing him to put up with his talk.

"I suppose."

"Not that I should say. For all I know you're some Canadian do-gooder who'll turn me in the first chance he gets."

Alex thought he should probably just let him believe that.

"I'm not going to tell anyone, if that's what you're worried about."

"Hmm. Yes." He grew coy. "It's a little complicated, really. As I was saying. About the wide cross."

"You want the plants to interbreed or something?"

"Oh, they won't do that here. Or they might, in a million years, but I don't have that sort of time. I'll do it myself, back home. I just need it to *look* like it happened here."

The scheme was starting to sound crazy on levels Alex hadn't even imagined.

"I don't understand."

"It would be a new species, don't you see? Unrecorded. Mine. It would shift the whole landscape. I get my doctorate and a certain professor who shall go nameless, and who claims, for instance, that there is no sesuvium on Tower, sees his life's work go down the pan."

"Your doctorate? I thought you were a professor already."

"I never said that."

"But you go around telling everyone you're from the University of London."

"Imperial College, to be exact. And so I am."

"But you don't teach there?"

"Not at the moment, no. But soon enough."

Alex regretted that he hadn't gone off with the Germans when he'd had the chance.

"Why are you doing all this, exactly?"

"Why? For science, my boy! For science!"

Alex saw from the maps that they had crossed the equator the previous night. They ought to have keelhauled Desmond then, or whatever it was that sailors did to each other to mark the passage.

Tower was miles to the north of the central cluster, virtually off in its own hemisphere.

"Bindloe next," Desmond said, "due west. All part of the plan. The winds always reverse themselves, you see, whenever El Niño comes along, which by my calculations should be any day now. Hence the eastward dispersal. It all makes sense."

It makes sense. It was the sort of thing madmen said.

Santos was rowing back from the boat, a black shape against the black of the night. This was Alex's only surety against Desmond, this leviathan. He emerged out of the dark carrying a big plastic sack of what turned out to be salt, which he started packing in handfuls into the gutted insides of his fish.

"*Bacalao,*" he said again, with his unpleasant smile. "*Qué tipo, muchacho? Le gusta?*"

Alex had lost all his reading material to the rain on the Inca Trail, which left him to Darwin's *Beagle.* He didn't hold out much hope for it, but he pulled up next to the fire as far from Desmond as he could manage and started in. Darwin, it turned out, hadn't had it much better than Alex did—his own captain was not only a tyrant but a depressive to boot, and had apparently brought Darwin along, at Darwin's expense, just to keep from slitting his own throat.

A couple of lumps dragged themselves onto the beach and plopped themselves down, followed by a bigger one, the bull, who took up a position peering out to sea against the threat of rivals.

"Looks like we're sharing," Desmond said.

Alex stretched out his sleeping bag for the night, trying to avoid the booby nests, the guano pads in the bushes, the ubiquitous gulls with the red circles around their eyes who ambled about the beach hunched up like old men. He was getting value out here, at least, he'd have to grant that; he was pushing the boundaries. In Africa he'd taken trips through the bush where the wild had seemed to loom on every side ready to swallow him, but here it felt as if they'd already crossed over, as if there was no us and them anymore, no certain distinction. He would awake one morning to find he'd sprouted flippers and fins and would take to the oceans his forebears had abandoned a billion years earlier, eating *bacalao* until the sea cows came home. Out on the beach, meanwhile, the bull was still at his vigil, while his brood lay around him dreaming, for all Alex knew, of becoming human. It was getting hard to say anymore, out here with the likes of Desmond and Santos, in which direction progress lay, or whose fate seemed the better.

They awoke to a haze that had blocked the sun, not so much cloud as a thickening of the air, and to a sticky breeze that revealed itself, the instant they'd cleared the bay, to be a stiffish wind.

"Right on time," Desmond said. "The trade winds fail, and all that hot water that's been pushing up against Asia comes sloshing back."

The wind wasn't especially strong but was insistent—it didn't gust or blow about but came on straight and warm like a wall. Alex and Desmond took refuge in the cabin with Santos, who had the throttle down full, though still the boat seemed to be inching forward at a crawl. Alex felt concerned, all of a sudden, at what passed for the boat's navigation system, now that navigation might actually be called for. Apart from the throttle and the tiller, the one bolted to an old two-by-four that served as the dashboard and the other consisting of a wooden pole sticking through a hole in the floor, the only instrumentation was a cracked compass on the dash, the face of it so clouded that it might just as well have been a Magic 8-Ball.

Alex tried to read his Darwin, but Desmond couldn't stay put, poring over his maps, making notations, peering out through the guano-caked windshield into the haze.

"Where the fuck is it? We should be seeing it by now." He was crowding up into the little space that formed Santos's command post. "Bindloe, for Christ's sake. Isla Marchena. *Dónde?*"

Santos kept his eyes on the ocean.

"*Sí, sí. El viento.*"

"The wind, my arse. You've probably passed the thing. You just want to get out to your bloody fishing fields."

A smudge finally appeared in the distance, a patch of darker gray against the gray of the sea and the sky.

Alex saw Santos's eye slip to the compass.

"It's about bloody time," Desmond said.

He got out a pair of binoculars, puny things that looked like a lady's opera glasses.

"Fucking haze," he said, fiddling with the focus wheel.

There was a tension in the air, but Alex couldn't read it. Santos glanced down at the compass again. Desmond had squeezed in past him with the binoculars to get up close to the windshield, practically edging him away from the tiller.

"I don't get it. There's a cinder cone out there."

All Alex could make out was the barest streak of land, beneath a streak of cloud that hung over it separate and low like its own private weather system.

"It's not right. It's not fucking right."

Something seemed to click suddenly in Desmond's head.

"It's fucking Pinta! It's not Marchena at all! It's Pinta, you bloody idiot! You've fucking missed it!"

Santos stared out, stone-faced.

"*El viento*," he said.

"Yes, *el* fucking *viento!*" Desmond looked fit to be tied. "It was a bloody straight line to the place, a child could have found it! You'll have to go back! *Regreso!*"

Santos kept his hand on the throttle.

"*Es el mismo.*"

"No, it's not bloody *el mismo!* Everything's different, the wind pattern, the soil, everything! If I'd wanted Pinta I'd have asked for Pinta! You have to go back, for Christ's sake, or I'll take the fucking rudder myself!"

He seemed ready to do it. Even Santos looked momentarily cowed, though he could have snapped Desmond like a twig.

"No gas," Santos said finally, in perfect English, as if playing a trump.

Alex had no idea what he was getting at—they were up to their ears in gas, they were swimming in it. But he seemed to have given Desmond pause.

"We'll get more bloody petrol if we need it," he said finally. "We'll stop at Villamil or whatever. I'll get it from Mrs. Wittmer if I have to, the old witch."

Santos had slowed now, but was still holding his course.

"You pay," he said.

"Yes, I'll fucking pay. Just get us back there."

Santos turned the boat.

It looked like Santos had actually screwed up. Maybe it was just Desmond's El Niño—already it was beginning to seem like a poltergeist who was dogging them, a mischievous Ariel. Santos had hardly turned the boat around before Marchena suddenly appeared out of nowhere in front of them, and it was hard to see how they'd missed it. Like Pinta it lay under its own little bubble of climate, shrouded in what from a distance looked like mist but turned out to be a fine drizzle. It came down on them as straight as a curtain as they drew into shore, no sign here of El Niño's wind.

The island looked dismal even by Galápagan standards, just a low swell of rubbly hills like the scattered slag heaps of a smelting operation. Santos brought them into a little bay that gave onto a somber-looking beach, almost black in the rain and entirely devoid of vegetation.

"We'll have to hurry," Desmond said. "Bloody day's almost shot now."

"Aren't we going to wait for it to clear?"

"You'll be waiting till August, my boy. Time and El Niño wait for no man."

Santos anchored and dropped the panga while Desmond gathered his things, limiting himself this time, apart from his satchel and his precious case, to a single duffel bag. All he had against the rain was a dime-store poncho of flimsy plastic.

"No rain gear?" he said to Alex.

Alex wasn't sure why he didn't simply refuse to go along.

"Not really."

"Here, take this." He handed Alex a little zippered pack with another poncho inside. "We'll just be an hour or so."

Santos stood on the back deck in the drizzle holding the panga ready. Desmond boarded and Alex, despite himself, followed. But Santos stayed on the deck.

He threw down the rope.

"*Me quedo aquí.*"

"Bloody hell you will," Desmond said. "You're rowing us in."

But Santos didn't budge.

"Fine. Suit yourself."

Alex wondered why he was following this man around like his pet. It was better than just going stir crazy out here was what he told himself, but it wasn't just that. Somehow, the more time he spent with Desmond and the more reasons he amassed to detest him, the more he felt in his thrall. He wasn't sure what sort of pathology might lie behind this, if he was drawn to him because he thought them so different or because he thought them the same.

"I hope you know how to row this thing. They must teach you that up in Canada, don't they?"

Alex was already half-soaked beneath his flimsy poncho by the time they reached the beach, then had to wade through the shallows up to his knees to drag the dinghy ashore. Desmond kept his place until the dinghy was safely on terra firma.

"Bloody superstition is all it is," he said. "He doesn't want to land here because it's Dead Man's Beach."

Dead Man's Beach. Alex felt it best not to ask. No doubt Santos just wasn't so stupid as to come out in this miserable rain, which was coming at them with the same maddening tedium as the wind had that morning.

They had skipped lunch again. Desmond pulled a strip of jerky from his satchel and bit into it.

"You got any more of that?"

"Oh." Alex had caught him off guard. "Sure."

He quickly gnawed off another length of the strip, leaving a tattered remnant.

"Here. Why don't you have the rest."

Here as well they had to cross to the other side of the island, though there was nothing like a path, just rock and scattered growth. They followed the seashore until the beach gave way to impassable rock, then moved inland. The ground, which from a distance had looked nearly barren, turned out to be carpeted in prickly vegetation, cactus leaves and desiccated brush and thick clusters of thorny vine that rolled out over the rocks like barbed wire. They had to pick their way through this tangle step by step, scrambling for footholds on the drizzle-slicked rocks. At one point Alex looked behind him and realized he had lost the sense of any landmark to gauge their progress by, the boat, the beach, the shore all hidden from sight behind the endless hummocks of rock and brush they had zigzagged across.

"How far is it, exactly?"

"Well, we wouldn't have had to do this at all if that ox had come up on the other side like he was supposed to."

Alex wasn't sure of it but he thought the light had dimmed. He'd stopped wearing his watch after Desmond's crack about time, but now with the cloud cover they'd have no way of telling the time of day.

Little red-necked lizards darted from under their feet. Overhead, a hawk traced wide, slow circles around them.

"Aren't we going to get lost out here?"

"It's not as if we're out in the fucking northland. The whole place is the size of a postage stamp."

They came to a wide clump of shrub they had to push their way through, of the same cadaverous bush that had lined Genovesa but that was stunted and small here, scratching at them with every step. *Palo santo*, Desmond called it, holy bush, though it looked like a cursed thing. There was a clearing in the middle of it, a patch of beaten earth that looked like some sort of gathering ground. The remains of an animal lay at the edge of it, shriveled and ancient-looking but still with much of the hide stretched over the bones.

"Goat," Desmond said. "One of the last of them, looks like. Park Service actually managed to hunt them all down here, probably with those six-shooters they carry around with them."

"They shot them?"

"And a bloody good job, or they'd have made a quick meal of my mollugo. They'll eat a place down to the rock if you let them."

The light held until they reached the far shore, where the land flattened out to ease down to the sea. The rain, mercifully, had stopped. The ground here was worn down to a gravelly marl, spotted here and there with patches of growth.

Desmond had bent to finger it.

"Is this the place?" Alex said.

Desmond scowled. He looked out across the water, but there was nothing out there except the gray of the sea and the sky.

"I can't fucking tell where Tower's supposed to be. Anyway the soil's too old."

He moved from spot to spot, squatting down to grub at the earth. The light was definitely fading now. Alex couldn't say how long they'd been walking to get here, an hour at least, maybe two.

He looked around them and couldn't even have said what direction they'd come from, every hillock and patch of bush indistinguishable from the next.

Desmond was on his hands and knees now, pawing through the scrub along the shoreline like someone looking for his keys.

"We have to get back," Alex said. "It's getting dark."

"There's no point doing this if the conditions aren't right."

There was no way they'd manage the trip back in the dark.

"Then I'll start on my own."

"For Christ's sake," Desmond said churlishly. "Fine, fine, just give me a minute. Bring that bag, will you?"

He settled for a little outcropping rising out over the sea, arranging what remained of his succulents there. He didn't bother this time with smashing rocks up, just cadging what soil he could from the surrounding plants.

"It'll have to do. I was supposed to have the whole day here to map the place out. This fucks up everything."

Somehow the light had continued to hold, as if by the force of Alex's will. But once they had started back he felt the twilight creeping up behind them. It was only a matter of minutes now before it would be dark.

"Do you have a flashlight at least?"

"A what?"

"A flashlight. A torch."

"Well, I would have if we'd brought the other bag, but I thought I'd spare you."

They hadn't gone more than half a mile before it grew too dark to pick their way through the brush. They retreated to the shoreline, where they could at least keep from going in circles. The tide was out and there was a bit of a shingle to walk along, greasy with sea slime but relatively flat. They were able to scramble along it by clinging to the bank that ran along the shore. Even so, they went at a snail's pace. Alex, in the lead, Desmond's duffel bag flopping against him at each step, heard the waves lap at their feet and wondered how long it would be before the tide turned.

The only thing keeping his panic down was his rage at Desmond.

"Slow down a bit, would you, I've got this bloody case to look after."

They came up against an outcropping. Alex tried to edge around it but quickly found himself up to his thighs in water.

"We have to cross over," he said.

It was like traveling blind. There was rock, which he slithered over, though it jagged out like broken glass, then some sort of thicket, which he shouldered through on hands and knees, keeping his head low. He couldn't hear Desmond behind him anymore. If Alex was lucky some rogue wave had hauled him out to sea.

"Fuck, fuck, fuck! Give me a hand here, would you, I think I've broken my ankle!"

This was it, Alex thought, this was the end. They would surely die out here now, that was the way of these things—the smallest mistake, an insect bite, a missed turn, a lost shoe, and suddenly nothing else mattered. He felt a sick sense of how little he amounted to, that he could die out here so stupidly with only this asshole for company.

He crawled back through the brush until he stumbled up against flesh.

"Watch it, for Christ's sake!"

"What happened?"

"I've twisted my fucking ankle."

"I can't believe this," Alex said. "I can't fucking believe this."

"Don't start going gutless on me," Desmond said, without the least hint of sympathy or remorse. "It's just the dark, not the bloody end of the world. It'll be over soon enough."

He was right. Even if all else failed, at some point morning would come. It seemed unlikely they'd be killed before then by marauding boobies or goats.

Alex heard Desmond fumbling around in his satchel. Something came at him in the dark.

"Here." It was a piece of Desmond's jerky. "It'll take the edge off till we get some of that bloody fish into us again."

They made a little hollow for themselves in the brush. There was nothing to do but wait. A couple of stars showed themselves through the clouds and it was actually possible to make out the outlines of things.

Desmond tore off a strip of his plastic poncho to bandage his ankle.

"How is it?"

"Big as a fucking melon."

Alex lay back, using the duffel bag as a pillow. He could stay calm this way, just staring up through the brush into the night.

"Not what you bloody bargained for, I imagine," Desmond said. "Stranded out here in the bush."

Alex hoped they weren't headed toward some sort of apology. He wanted to keep his dislike of the man hard in him.

"I've had worse."

"I'll tell you what's worse. A Council flat in East London with fucking Pakistan outside your door. I'll take this in a minute."

Alex might have tried to sleep but Desmond chose this moment to wax philosophical, going on with a kind of pleased virulence about the Pakis and the blacks, the mucky-mucks at Imperial College, the fucking Ecuadoreans, who seemed to think these islands belonged to them.

"If we'd left it to them they'd have turned them into salt mines or something, or bloody Acapulco. Then they have the balls to try to kick us out, though there's hardly one of them that knows a Darwin's finch from a parakeet."

Alex grew dimly aware of a distant rumble. It grew gradually more insistent, until Alex understood with a start that it was real. Through the bushes, out along the shore, he thought he glimpsed a pinprick of light.

Desmond was suddenly on his feet.

"It's a boat! It's a fucking boat!"

All his stoicism was gone.

"Over here!" he shouted, screaming like a schoolgirl. "Help us! I've broken my ankle! Over here!"

Slowly a boat drifted into view along the shoreline, a pale headlight gleaming above the cabin. It was Santos.

"It's about fucking time! He could have figured we were stranded out here. Over here, you moron!"

Santos had retrieved the panga from the beach. He rowed it out to their little promontory to fetch them. The shingle they'd walked on earlier had completely vanished.

Desmond made a great show of leaning into Alex as he struggled into the boat, raising high his injured ankle.

"I'll bet you were wishing you'd seen the last of us," he said to Santos.

A look passed between Santos and Alex. Santos put a finger to his head and gave it a discreet turn. *Loco.*

"Get on with it, then. I hope you've got some supper ready."

There was indeed some supper waiting: fish again, and rice, picked over and long cold, though Desmond lit into them with his usual animal vehemence. Santos had set the boat off without a word, heading straight to open sea. It looked like they were in for another long night. Already their awful journey on the island in the dark, the fear Alex had felt, seemed unreal.

Desmond searched through his literature—he had a big bag of it— and fished out another book.

"There it is," he said, shining his flashlight. "What we'd have looked like in a couple of months."

He'd opened to an old black-and-white photo of the beach they had landed on that afternoon. A rowboat in an early stage of decay sat near the water, a figure lying next to it curled up on some sort of tarp. Further up the beach was another figure, stretched out on the sand as if he'd fallen asleep there. *December 1934.*

"Rudolf Lorenz and his crew," Desmond said. "One of Mrs. Wittmer's victims. We'll stop in on her if we get a chance."

So that was what it was to die out here. The two of them looked so well preserved, like the goat on Marchena: nothing to eat them, Alex imagined.

"One wrong turn," Desmond said sententiously, as if it had been some prowess of his that had saved them. "That's all it takes out here."

He crawled up into his hammock. Alex had to figure out how to rig one of those. For now, he removed his shoes, not even bothering to peel away his moldering clothing, and stretched out on his plank to sleep.

Santos's preferred fishing grounds turned out to be at the far end of the archipelago, beyond the headlands of Isabela. A peculiar silence reigned there, creation seeming still poised at the moment of its birth, awaiting the spark that would set it in motion. To one side were the blank walls of Isabela's coastline, great fingers of rock at the tops of which hundreds upon hundreds of blue-footed boobies nested; to the other were the black lava runs of Fernandina, which looked as fresh as if they had been formed days before. "Like pitch over the rim of a pot," Darwin had described them, and it seemed nothing had changed since then, nothing had moved, all the years in between the merest heartbeat.

When they had entered the channel they had seen a shadow move on the water and suddenly a great hump of silver-blue reared up in front of them, not ten yards from the boat, flashing an instant before dipping quietly back into the sea. Santos had pushed back sharply on the throttle. If the beast had breached beneath them they might have been tossed over like a feather.

Alex thought of the inscriptions on the old maps: *Here there be monsters.*

"Off to find their krill," Desmond said. "Big ones eat the little ones."

But Alex had seen the flinch in him too, the instant's panic as if some nightmare thing had come for them.

Their days took on a sameness. The weather continued as before, with the same haze clouding the sky, the same hot wind, the bouts of drizzle when the wind died and the rain came down straight as falling pins. They passed a single tourist cruiser and a couple of other fishing boats, which Santos steered well clear of, but otherwise they were alone. Each day they grew more scruffy and rank, the cabin taking on a feral odor like an animal's lair. Desmond, despite his oranges, which he'd sneak in his bunk now, the smell of citrus wafting over to Alex, had taken on a scurvied look, his skin flaking and red and oozing pustules flaring up on the back of his neck. They used the rain for their water now, Santos collecting it in plastic vinegar jugs from the runoff on the cabin roof—though once when Desmond tried to use it to wash himself, Santos seemed ready to strike him.

"*Es para beber,*" he said harshly, taking his jug from him. It did not occur to any of them to wash themselves in the sea—there seemed to be an agreement among them that it was off limits, as if some absolute boundary existed between what was above it and what was below.

Santos rose well before dawn to start his fishing, hauling in two or three catches before they had their breakfast. Desmond railed about his sleep and his schedule—he was working obsessively, spending the days combing the wastes of Isabela as if to map every last ragged strand of his mollugo—but ever since Marchena, Santos had ceased to make any effort to appease him. Alex had become a sort of token between them: in each other's presence they vied for his allegiance like suitors, as if it were proof of the other's derangement, though if he was alone with either of them they quickly reverted to their usual bullying.

Early on, to get free of Desmond, Alex had made the mistake of spending a day alone with Santos while he fished. Maybe he'd imagined

that the crust would fall away from Santos, that the two of them would
bond in some deep peasant way, though once they were alone Alex felt
only the usual icy blankness coming off him. Santos's methods were
gruntingly primitive: there were no fancy reels or nets or hydraulics, just
a long, greening rope that he rolled out by hand from a wooden spool
and dangled hooks from at intervals. The hooks he baited with bits of
octopus and squid and with little crabs he stored live in a burlap sack
that dragged behind the boat and stabbed whole onto the hooks, their
limbs writhing. At longer intervals he tied off a pair of the same battered
jugs he used for their water, one lidless so it sank and one capped so it
floated, the series of them holding the line suspended along its length
some twenty or thirty feet below the water's surface.

Santos pulled out a bottle of something when he'd set the first line
and took a long draw.

"*Te gusta?*"

He eyed Alex grimly, top to bottom, with a look that sent a chill up
Alex.

"*No, gracias.*"

Santos reeled the line in barehanded, fist over fist. It came up heavy
with flopping grouper, big, vicious things that wrestled with every fiber
in them before Santos swung their heads against a tackle box to quiet
them. It seemed a sort of magic trick to Alex, that with that bit of line and
bait Santos had managed to lure up all this writhing flesh. Santos,
though, was grumbling: some of the hooks had come up untouched.

"*Conche tu madre.*"

The next line came up the same. Without a word Santos set about
gutting his catch, the birds circling at once, pelicans and boobies and
greedy frigates who perched vigilant on the roof of the cabin. Alex
dragged the salt over and began packing it into a fish the way he'd seen
Santos do.

"*Así no.*" Santos took the fish from him. "*Hazlo así. Entiende?*"

He was worse than Alex's father. He could salt his own fucking fish,
for all Alex cared, though still he kept at it, until his hands were raw and
he was covered in fish slime.

It wasn't yet sunset when they went to fetch Desmond at the little
cove they used as their anchorage, a ruined caldera on the Isabela coast
just across the channel from Fernandina. The cliffs ringing the cove were

veined with graffiti: ALBATROSS, MOANA, ST. GEORGE, the names of other ships that had put in there. Desmond had shown off the oldest: PHOENIX 1836. The year after Darwin had landed. Alex had gone up to the little cinder cone that Darwin had described from his stop, a "beautifully symmetrical one" cupping a tiny lake to which Darwin had hurried down hoping to slake his thirst, only to find it was salt.

The lake was still there.

"On time, for once!"

Desmond was waiting for them at the bottom of the gully that served as a landing. A couple of seals waddled up behind him from a rock ledge and gave him a start.

"Fuck! Bloody hell!"

Santos was watching beside Alex from the boat.

"*Maricón*," he said, with a leer. Faggot. His hand reached up, so quick Alex wasn't sure if he'd only imagined it, and cupped Alex's balls. "*Él va culearlos, no?*"

It was the first time Alex was actually glad to see Desmond. Santos retrieved him in the panga and he limped onto the deck with his things, looking harried, one hand gripping his kneecap.

"Put my fucking knee out." His ankle by now was long forgotten. "I hope the Old Man in the Sea didn't try to bugger you."

All night long Alex's balls itched from the feel of that big callused hand on him. Maybe it had been nothing, just the usual sort of locker room horseplay, but then who knew what could happen out here, what people were capable of? The whole trip was starting to seem a bad dream, the sort where you did some foolish, irreversible thing you couldn't get free of.

He lay in his bunk the next morning waiting until Desmond had stirred before he dared go out to the deck. Santos was there in his Yankees cap, baiting a line.

He shoved an empty gas canister toward Alex with his foot, hardly glancing at him.

"*Rellénalo.*" Fill it. Alex was at a loss—maybe this was part of some test, some freakish rite he was going to put Alex through.

Desmond had yet to emerge from the cabin.

"*Con agua.*" Santos motioned toward the back of the boat with his chin. "*Agua de mar.*"

He wanted him to fill the canister with seawater. Alex lay on his stomach at the back of the boat, one eye on Santos, and let the sea gurgle into it until it was so heavy he was barely able to lift it to the deck.

Santos tied an end of his line to the canister and swung the canister over the rail, letting it drop down into the sea until the line pulled taut against the cleat that anchored it.

"Depth line." Desmond had finally come out. "To find out where the fishies are biting."

They waited. The whole operation seemed oddly fraught. The line thrummed, then again, and Santos began to haul it in, putting his weight into it. Then suddenly the line went slack, and Santos stumbled back against the hatch.

"*Hijo de puta!*"

He jerked the rest of the line up with a few angry pulls. The end came up free, the canister gone. Santos was furious. Alex could see he blamed him, though he was the one who had tied the thing. To top it off he hadn't hooked a single grouper, just a few small, colored aquarium fish and another rogue species, ugly and mean-looking, that he tossed at once back into the sea.

"Poor sod," Desmond said. "Looks like El Niño has been at it. Fucks up the currents."

"Shouldn't he know about that?"

Desmond was looking cheery.

"He's a mainlander, sadly, that's why I chose him. Less territorial about the place. I suppose he hasn't worked out all the tricks yet. Probably quit his job in the merchant marine thinking he'd come out here to make his fortune, and now all the fish have gone home."

Santos's mood turned black. He set his line deeper than usual, down to seventy or eighty feet, the nylon cutting into his palms from the extra drag when he hauled it in. But still half his hooks came up empty. He couldn't be bothered to cook any breakfast and just thrust some leftovers at them from a couple of days before, the rice already going sour.

Desmond put on his highest dudgeon.

"If you're not going to feed us properly you can at least let us off the fucking boat."

It was nearly midday before Santos finally pulled up to shore, not at the cove but at a rocky promontory jutting out among the mangrove lagoons of southern Isabela.

"I'm not getting off in this swamp," Desmond said. "I haven't finished the north end yet."

But as soon as they were within heaving range of the rocks, Santos grabbed one of Desmond's bags and tossed it onto them.

"That's my equipment, you fucking ape!"

Desmond was already clambering down the ladder after his bag, his case in hand. He stepped off into the water but sank down to his chin before he touched bottom.

"Bloody hell! He wants to fucking drown me!"

He had to bob his way to shore, pushing the case across the water with the tips of his fingers.

If Alex didn't hurry, he'd end up stuck on the boat with Santos.

"*Me quedo aquí.*"

Santos tossed out another bag.

"*Como quieras.*"

He waded out from the ladder before he could change his mind, making the rocks just as Santos tossed out their sleeping bags.

"*Regreso mañana! Por la noche!*"

Desmond stood dripping among his scattered belongings looking like a castaway.

"*Mañana?* Have you lost your mind? What are we supposed to do for food, exactly?"

Santos grabbed a sack and tossed a couple of fish from his morning's catch into it, then went around adding whatever came to hand, a pot, a jug of water. He heaved the sack onto the rocks.

"You cook!" he said.

Desmond seemed ready to shit himself.

"I don't believe this! I don't believe this!"

But Santos had already gunned the engine.

"Can you believe that gorilla? I don't fucking believe this!"

The boat bucked like an old horse and began churning out to sea, quickly growing small. Alex collected their things. Little crabs scuttered away from him on the rocks.

"We should never have paid him up front, I'll tell you that. Bloody fucking gall!"

They had to thread their way through the mangrove to get off their little landing, Desmond complaining of his knee again and Alex stuck with the bulk of their things. When they came out to open ground they found themselves at the foot of a wide slope spiked with the usual smattering of *palo santo* and rising up in the distance to the rim of a massive crater. Here and there the brush was cut through with barren runs of dark lava rock.

Alex wasn't sure, but he thought he made out a plume of smoke drifting up from the crater into the canopy of cloud above it.

"Well we'll just have to make the best of it," Desmond said. "It'll give us a chance to get up to the crater at least."

Any relief Alex had felt at being off the boat was quickly dissipated under the strain of their trek and of Desmond's company. The terrain was as tangled and inhospitable as Marchena's had been, but sloped parabola-like ever more steeply upward. Alex could see the crater ahead of them rising almost sheer, like a big top hat, and wondered how exactly Desmond was planning to scale it. Meanwhile the sun had come out, for the first time in days, through a hole in the cloud cover that seemed trained directly above them, so that Alex could feel it beating down on the top of his head with all the force of midday. He made the mistake of complaining about it and got one of Desmond's lectures.

"The source of life, my boy, don't knock it. The Egyptians had it right, all that sun worship, before the Jews came along and fucked things up with the Invisible Man."

He'd started dragging his plant maps out, big topographical things in some impossibly large scale. Now that he was at his work everything else seemed put aside, Santos, his knee, their being stranded out here with two stinking fish and a jug of rain.

The maps were ruled off into tidy grids, little markings in what seemed a kind of code strewn across the areas he'd already covered. Some of the marks were in red, though surprisingly few: his mollugo.

"What if you miss some?" Alex said. "It's kind of hard to be thorough."

"Who's going to contradict me? I don't see a lot of competition around."

As they passed, surly iguanas scattered into holes in the underbrush in their exhausting little spurts, clumsy, prehistoric things much more outlandish and baroque than the demonic black ones that matted the rocks by the sea. Somewhere in one of Desmond's books Alex had read they had a third eye on the tops of their heads. It sounded freakish, but maybe no more freakish than having eyebrows, say, or fingers and toes. In any event freakish seemed the norm here—off the Isabela coast they'd passed penguins basking on the rocks like happy vacationers, and flightless cormorants, with stunted thalidomide wings, gliding through the water with the grace of sea lions.

Now, from the recent rain, there were actually greenish buds on the *palo santo,* tiny as dewdrops but giving off an odor as vegetal and rank as a rain forest's. The higher they went, though, the more ragged the scrub got and the more bitter the terrain, until they were down to thorny weeds struggling up through a rusty alluvium of volcanic scree that gave way beneath them with each step. Alex could already see what was going to happen: at some point the whole slope would just crumble and they'd end up buried alive beneath tons of volcanic scurf.

At least Alex had the water with him.

"Fucking dust," Desmond said. "Give me that jug, would you?"

Desmond had grown vigilant: they were in mollugo territory. Alex had actually glanced at a few of Desmond's articles on the stuff, hopelessly footnoted things that Alex had nonetheless managed to glean a few essentials from. What a pioneer plant was, for instance: one of those that was the first to take root in virgin rock and begin the eons-long work of breaking it down into dirt. Looked at in that light *Mollugo flavescens* took on a kind of nobility, of romance. The beginnings of life. Two billion years ago or whatever, before the first fishy half-thing had crawled up from the deep, this was what the world was, this dead rock, waiting for the likes of mollugo to make it over.

"Bloody crap." Desmond was scavenging irritably amidst the bits of growth. "Fucking goats have been here. You can see the tracks."

"I thought they'd killed them all."

"Not here. The battle still rages."

Desmond didn't stop his foraging until the scree had given way entirely to solid rock, sharp as nails and nearly impassable. They still had a ways to go to reach the summit. They swung around to the southern end of the slope to find better ground and soon the rock turned to scree again and then to scattered brush. The first of the goats appeared here, a rotting lump much more putrid and fresh than the one on Marchena. Further on there was another, still with a bloodied hole visible behind the ear where a bullet had gone in.

Desmond kicked it.

"Hasn't been here a week. The last thing we need is to run into the bloody Park Service."

The vegetation grew rapidly denser. In the space of a few hundred yards they passed from near desert to lushness, the *palo santo* replaced by grasses and by shrubs in full leaf and these by woods so overgrown you would have had to hack your way through them. All down the southern slope the green stretched, a different world. Almost despite himself—it was just a matter of winds, after all, he'd learned that, not some miracle—Alex felt a surge.

Part way down the slope, the woods opened out to scattered clearings. *Fields.* It was the first sign in days of anything human.

Desmond had hardly given the view a second glance.

"We'll have to speed up a bit if we want to make the crater before dark."

"Are there actually people living here?"

"Eh? That's Villamil, on the coast. We could be there in a couple of hours if you wanted. Awful place, of course, though it would serve Santos right if we just fucked off on him."

They started up toward the crater. Alex couldn't get over the thought that there were people so close, houses, streets, electric lights. It seemed almost incredible that these things still existed, that he hadn't actually stepped back into some Precambrian world. He could set off at dawn, he thought, and be there in time for breakfast—eggs, maybe, anything but fish. From there he'd beg his way home if he had to, whatever it took to be free of this place.

"You're lucky to get up here, I hope you realize," Desmond said. "It's not exactly on the usual tourist run."

They scrambled forward, up rubbly inclines and over crags tangled with growth. They passed more of the goats lying dead here and there, one hanging grotesquely from the limbs of a stunted fruit tree it had somehow toppled into. Then in a clearing they came across a whole killing field of them, maybe a dozen or so, weighing the grasses down, fresh, from the looks of them, and sending up a stench.

Desmond scowled.

"Looks like they've sent out the whole bloody posse."

They were close to the crater now. The air had grown misty and the terrain too steep to hold anything more than scraggly vines. Alex's bags pulled at him like clinging animals. Then just when it seemed they couldn't go any further against the slope, they came to a narrow rift in the cliff face that snaked up like an old streambed, bubbled with twisting rock from some recent lava flow.

"This way," Desmond said.

"Do you know where this goes, exactly?"

"We'll find out soon enough, won't we?"

Alex was just able to squeeze into the crack with his bags, clinging to whatever handhold he could grab and balancing back and forth against the pocked latticework of mangled rock at his feet. Within a few steps all he could see were the snarled walls of the rift on either side, towering over him to where they disappeared into cloud.

With each step the passage seemed to narrow.

"We should go back."

Desmond, in the lead, kept blundering forward.

"Just a bit further, I think."

Alex's hands and elbows were raw, his ankles ached, his sneakers seemed on the verge of splitting. Then suddenly the walls of the rift folded back and they came into a little pit about the size of a swimming pool, beyond which a vast green plain lay spread before them, cupped in an oval of hills that held it like a stadium of the gods.

They had passed through the rim of the volcano into the crater. Alex had imagined it a lifeless pit, more heaps of ash and scree, not this hidden universe, a kind of heaven and hell of lakelets and scrubby meadows and bush interspersed with great moonish stretches of scorched rock. Here and there shafts of smoke drifted up, flattening out like mushroom clouds against the mist overhead.

"Better make camp," Desmond said. "I hope you know how to cook."

They camped down on the crater floor, where they found a clump of grass that provided some cushioning against the rock. They'd spotted a herd of goats to the north, maybe a hundred or more, grazing peacefully there while their comrades lay rotting on the other side of the crater.

Desmond had already claimed the thickest patch of grass.

"Gather up a bit of firewood, would you? I've got to finish my notes."

Alex couldn't even be bothered to resent this sort of behavior anymore. He set out to scout through a nearby stand of *palo santo* but part way there came across a mud pit, huge grayish mounds rising out of it like giant toadstools. Tortoises, about half a dozen of them. They were the first he had come across. At his approach, one of them stretched its brontosauran neck in what seemed a kind of tired affront, but almost at once a second one came charging at it with a surprising burst of speed, head raised high as if to strike. The first beat a hasty retreat into the muck and the victor preened an instant, gazing this way and that, before giving Alex a look that made it seem as old as Adam.

"There's turtles over there," he said back at camp. "Tortoises."

"Too bad you can't make a nice soup. It'd be a change from that fucking grouper."

Twilight was coming on. Alex made a fire and threw one of the fish in, then dug some rice out of their sack and made a stand for the pot with a circle of stones. The wood burned with a smell like incense, vaguely calming and soporific. Alex lit his last cigarette—after the landing he had had to dry out the few he'd carried with him. His cigarettes were his life-lines here, those and his coffee, though already he was well into the second carton of his cigarettes, and his jar of coffee, thanks to Desmond, who treated it as his own, was down to a few paltry fingers.

Alex had been sure their little blanketing of cloud would rain on them at any moment, but a few scattered stars appeared above them as the dark set in, then a crescent moon.

Desmond started in on the fish.

"Amazing place, isn't it? Think of those tortoises out there—hundreds of thousands of years, and nothing's changed. We humans think we're so special, with our big brains, but we've got nothing on them. A flash fire is what we are. One day, poof, we'll be gone, and they'll still be here."

And good riddance, Alex thought, if Desmond was anyone to go by.

Desmond was off on another jaunt through his long list of grievances and peeves.

"What's consciousness, for fuck's sake, what does that mean? Don't tell me my cat isn't fucking conscious when he waves his bloody arse at me. Darwin said it all a hundred years ago. But most of these idiots—and I'm talking scientists here, not bleeding evangelists—still go on about how unique we are, as if God just came down from his cloud one day and sprinkled us with fairy dust. When was that, I'd like to know, was it *Homo habilis* or *Homo* fucking *erectus*? Bloody nonsense!"

So he owned a cat. Alex wasn't sure he wanted to think about this, any more than he wanted to think Desmond had a mother somewhere or maybe even some sniveling brat-child, whom he dispensed bullying parenting to and told to mind his manners.

Where was that cat now? Alex wondered.

"And then the fucking Labour Party, still holding their breath for The Revolution. They could do with a course in natural history. People are still bloody apes on the plains—you can shove Marx down their throats till they choke on it, but you won't change their DNA."

Desmond was right, of course; this place was amazing. There were the goats out there in the distance, and the tortoises in their mud, and the stars coming out, one by one. That it was Desmond who had brought him here conferred a measure of redemption on him. The truth was Alex was getting tired of holding himself hard against Desmond—it was too much work, all this spite, it was too much commitment. Then who knew if Desmond's view of things wasn't actually the right one, or if what he was up to was any more suspect or strange than the Park Service carving a blood trail through a nature reserve.

Desmond had crawled into his sleeping bag.

"Time for a bit of shut-eye. I hope you brought some of that coffee along."

Alex already knew that he wouldn't be sneaking off at dawn to Villamil. If nothing else, he wanted to see how all of this ended, if Santos got his fish, if Desmond got his mollugo. It was always these nightmarish trips, the ones he cursed the whole time he was on them, that he remembered most viscerally—in this, too, though it pained him to admit it, maybe Desmond was right, that Alex was lucky to be along, instead of off on some pointless drinkfest with the Americans or killing the hours at the Black Mangrove under the thumb of Mara.

Alex sat by the fire to finish the last of *The Beagle*. He'd come to the biographical note at the end: it seemed Darwin had become somewhat of a recluse after his voyage, shutting himself up in his house at the edge of his little village and keeping an eye out for unwanted visitors. He'd had that ailment of his, never properly diagnosed, that had made him retch and convulse and that had required, on doctor's orders, daily dousings in cold water. Somehow, it all seemed to go back to the Galápagos—it was as if some bit of volcano dust had got lodged in his being then, some metaphysical worm that kept eating away at it.

Alex settled down to sleep, feeling suddenly worn out from the day's climb. The crater held a circle of stars above them as if they were closed up in a snow globe, a private cosmos. He thought of Darwin sleeping out on the Pampas during his *Beagle* trip, a middle-class white kid traveling the world, the first of the backpackers. It was only afterward, really, that he had made any sense of what he had seen. Alex wondered what, in the fullness of time, he himself would make sense of, what small, crucial detail might be lodging itself in his brain that would shake his life to its foundations.

He awoke the next morning cold but dry. The sun was peering above the rim of their crater, the private cupola of cloud that had hung over them the previous afternoon completely dispersed and the blue stretching away as far as they could see. Alex would have felt cheered if not for the thought that they'd be going back to the boat.

Desmond was already making his rounds.

"Get a fire going, boy! Busy day ahead of us!"

Desmond wanted to descend by way of the far side of the volcano. The way out of the crater proved less harrowing there than the way in had, but very quickly the ground grew treacherous, the slopes brittled over with prickly lava fields. They had to make their way by whatever path they could pick out, shifting up and down the slope, clinging to rock and scrub, shimmying along rivers of scree. By mid-morning the water had gone, and soon Alex felt as if he'd eaten a fistful of dust. He regretted the sun now, even more insistent than it had been the previous day, the black rock sucking it in until the whole landscape around them seemed to burn.

Desmond was looking particularly demented, acned and sunburned and caked with dust and still clutching that case of his as if it were the Grail. Plants had come and gone from that case, according to some scheme Alex hadn't quite been able to figure, except that it seemed to involve making a mockery of a certain professor's field research. But somehow the case itself had taken on a kind of life. Every morning Desmond performed his rites upon it, lifting back its portals to sprinkle it with his holy water and bare its mysteries to the God of the Sun.

Past noon a cloud front, massive and dark, began to move in from the west. The wind had died again, with that ominous sense of the stillness before an onslaught. From the slopes they could see out to the bay

Santos usually frequented, still smooth as silk but with no sign anywhere of his boat.

"The bastard's probably halfway to the Philippines by now," Desmond said.

Below them the coastline seemed an endless labyrinth of tiny green-encrusted inlets and lagoons. Alex couldn't have said for the life of him which of them they'd landed at the previous day. From the shifty looks Desmond kept casting out in that direction it was clear he was no wiser.

"Well we didn't come up this fucking route, did we?" he said. "At least I don't see any of the breadcrumbs you left to show the way."

They had to continue to the south in the hope that the ground would grow more familiar. They lost a lot of time in this, and in Desmond's cursing, and meanwhile the afternoon slipped by and the clouds kept pushing in. They'd end up stuck out here in some hurricane, Alex thought.

Each time Desmond turned his eyes coastward he looked more rattled.

"Fuck, fuck, fuck. Bloody bastard probably dropped us here on purpose."

They were back into *palo santo*. Looking for any distinguishing marks in it was like looking for a particular grape in a vineyard. Then finally they came across a patch of weeds that looked as if a truffle pig had been rooting through it: Desmond's handiwork.

"Christly hallelujah. Thank God I leave my mark."

They were able to trace their way back, reaching the coast just as the clouds were rolling into the bay. They found where they'd picked their way through the mangrove and came out to their little landing to discover Santos already waiting for them in the boat. He slid the panga over to them.

"*Vámonos*," he said, as if he'd dropped them there moments before for a pee.

"*Buenos* fucking *días* to you, too," Desmond said.

It had grown as dark as dusk over the bay, the sky slowly closing above them like a vault. Santos eased out of the inlet and veered north toward their cove following the jagged line of the coast. Then he rounded a spit and a boat appeared out of nowhere heading in their direction, done up in the telltale military green of the Park Service.

"Shit," Desmond said. "Bloody fucking bastards."

The boat was still a couple of miles out but was headed right for them. For an instant Santos didn't react, but then as if on some impulse he pulled hard on the tiller. The boat rocked and swerved and Desmond toppled back.

"What the fuck are you doing? They're going to think we're bloody pirates!"

In a twinkling Santos had ducked the boat back behind the spit. It was hard to say if the patrol had seen them. Santos cut sharply into a little mangrove-shrouded backwater, reversing the engine to keep them from ramming headlong into the bush. The water frothed and churned behind them until finally the boat glided to a stop against the trees.

Santos killed the engine.

"Bloody idiot!" Desmond screeched, dashing around to stow his things. "They weren't going to waste their time on us with this fucking monsoon on the way!"

Alex could hear the whine of the speedboat as it grew nearer, then the sudden drop in pitch as it slowed.

Desmond was casting around frantically for a place to stow his case. He flung open the hatch and practically crawled down into the hold in an effort to cram it in amidst Santos's fish.

"*No, allí no!*" Santos bellowed.

But it was too late: the patrol boat had appeared at the mouth of the inlet. Desmond clambered out of the hold and kneed the lid into place.

"We're just bloody tourists, you understand? Not a word about my plants!"

The boat came toward them with the caution of a reconnaissance patrol in a guerilla zone. Once again a boyish recruit was at the helm, but a small, much older man was standing in the bow, done up in starched khaki like a drill sergeant.

He had a hand on the butt of his pistol.

"*Identifíquense!*"

An exchange ensued across the rails that involved barking demands from the ranger, who seemed ready to shoot them all on the spot if they crossed him, and Santos's laconic replies.

"*La tormenta,*" Santos said tersely, the storm, in the way of explaining their flight.

Alex was surprised at the sheaf of documents Santos was able to hand over, battered little booklets and cards, huge folded sheets coming apart at the creases and covered in signatures and seals and colored stamps. The ranger looked each of them up and down with a painstaking thoroughness, then again.

He grimaced.

"*Su itinerario.*"

Alex could see Santos had taken the measure of the man. This wasn't some child he could put off the way he'd done at Tower. There was a particular tension between the two that Alex couldn't quite place but that might have had something to do with Santos's being a mainlander.

"*No tengo,*" Santos said finally.

The ranger let the admission hang.

"*Es obligatorio.*"

"*Sí. Lo sé.*"

The ranger bundled the documents back into a tidy stack. Maybe that was the end of it, maybe he was just one of those self-important types who would bristle at everything but let them pass.

He slipped the documents into his shirt pocket and drew his revolver.

"*Revise la barca,*" he said to his underling. Inspect the boat.

The deputy clambered over the rail and went about peering in tackle boxes and poking at bags without the least notion, it was clear, of what he was looking for. One of Desmond's lumpy duffel bags was poking out from beneath his bunk through the cabin doorway.

"Jesus bloody Christ," Desmond muttered, then nudged the lid of the hatch with his shin where it sat a little askew.

The ranger caught the movement.

"*La bodega! Apúrese!*"

Desmond blanched. The deputy lifted the lid and leaned down into the hold, the stench of grouper wafting up.

"*Es bacalao, capitán,*" he said sheepishly.

"*Busque!*"

The deputy made a half-hearted show of rooting around in the fish. But then something caught his eye.

"*Es una caja, señor.*"

"*Traela, imbécil!*"

The deputy brought up the case. Things happened quickly then.

"It's mine, you idiot, leave it!" Desmond snapped, grabbing the case, and the ranger cocked his gun and trained it with both hands at Desmond's head.

"Drop it!" he said in perfect English. "Drop it or I will shoot!"

Desmond threw up his hands, dropping the case as if it had bit him.

"It's full of plants, for fuck's sake! It's bloody plants! Get that thing off me!"

"Stand back!" the ranger shouted. "Stand back!"

"It's just my fucking plants!"

The deputy was fumbling for his revolver. In a moment they would all have a bullet in them.

"Stand back! Everyone stand back!"

The deputy's gun was pointing waveringly toward Alex's midriff. Alex didn't dare budge. All he could see was that barrel staring at him, not two feet away.

"*Ábrela!*" the ranger shouted.

The deputy squatted to the deck and pulled the case over to him with his free hand, his gun roaming erratically. It took him an instant to figure out how to prize open the lid and Alex actually felt a squirm of suspense, as if some dreadful secret was about to be revealed. But there, after all, sat Desmond's plants, in sad disarray now from their fall, dirt and broken tendrils everywhere and all the careful labels Desmond had affixed to them hopelessly tangled.

The deputy stared down blankly.

"*Son plantas, capitán,*" he said finally.

"*Sí, imbécil, no soy ciego.*"

Alex suspected that if the ranger hadn't still had his revolver trained on Desmond, Desmond wouldn't have been able to restrain himself from leaping on the case again.

"You can see for yourself, for the love of Christ, it's just plants, now take that thing off me!"

The deputy was sorting through the plants with the barrel of his gun. He fiddled with the little dividers.

"*Nada, capitán,*" he said. "*Solo plantas.*"

The ranger finally uncocked his revolver.

"*Traígalas aquí.*"

They came back to earth. Slowly the color returned to Desmond.

"You'd think it was the bloody atom bomb!" he said under his breath.

The deputy brought the case over to the rail and the ranger gave it a cursory look. The whole drama, it seemed, had put him out. His business had been with Santos, not this gringo, but Santos was pretty well forgotten, standing arms crossed by the cabin door with what seemed almost an amused look. Alex sensed that he and the warden might even have shared a joke at this point if they hadn't been so inimical, some mocking jibe about the gringo and his plants.

"*Mollugo flavescens*," Desmond said. "If that means anything to you."

The ranger made an effort to restrain his contempt.

"You are a researcher?"

"Imperial College, University of London."

Now that he wasn't under the threat of imminent death, Desmond had returned to his old self.

"So you have a permit, then. For these plants."

"Yes, I have a permit," Desmond said, not wavering an instant. "Back at the research station. I'll be very happy to show it to you when I return there."

A spasm of irritation crossed the ranger's face. It was clear he would have preferred simply to be done with the matter.

"You must carry it," he said. "It's required."

"Well, I didn't know I'd have to wear it on my bloody sleeve."

The ranger motioned to his deputy to close up the case.

"*Traigalo.*"

The deputy made to climb back over the rail with the case, but Desmond looked ready to spring on him again.

"You can't take those! That's weeks of work in there!"

"You must follow us to Villamil," the ranger said dryly. "There we will see. In any event there is the storm."

Santos, having apparently got the gist of this, stirred uneasily, but Desmond pre-empted him before he could make any protest.

"Those specimens are extremely fragile, you're not carting them off to some storage shed! If anything happens to them you can be sure your superiors will hear about it! They'll probably be very anxious to learn how you and your assistant nearly gunned down two researchers from the University of London!"

The ranger scowled. He might simply have pulled his revolver again to finish the job if the storm hadn't chosen that moment to unleash its first fat drops.

He looked skyward.

"*Qué pendejo*," he spat out, which Alex would have guessed meant something along the lines of "fucking asshole." He gave an angry nod toward his deputy. "*Déjelo.*"

"*Capitán?*"

"*Déjelo!*"

The deputy, still at the rail, set down the case. Desmond snatched it up practically before it had touched the deck.

"*Vamos!*" the ranger barked. "*Rápido!*"

Santos's papers were still bulging from his shirt pocket.

"*Mis documentos, señor!*"

"*En Villamil!*" the ranger shouted, and they moved off.

There seemed nothing for it but to follow them. As soon as they were out of the inlet the wind gusted and the first timid smattering of rain became a downpour. Alex and Desmond huddled up in the cabin, Desmond sitting hunched over his case like a distraught parent. Santos looked like he would gladly have thrown the both of them overboard.

"I guess they'll find out you don't have a permit," Alex said.

"I guess they bloody well will, won't they?"

The wind was lashing them now and the windshield had become a steady wash of rain. Ahead of them the patrol boat bobbed in and out of sight amidst the waves. It was the first rough weather they'd had. Santos's boat seemed suddenly insubstantial in the face of it, tilting with every swell, the tiller straining against Santos's grip like an animate thing.

"Fuck, fuck, fuck!" Desmond pulled a broken vine from his plants. "Half these things are ruined."

The dark of the storm gave way to the dark of night. They saw only the thin haze of Santos's headlight against the rain and the little running lights of the patrol boat ahead of them, gone and then there again. The waves were crashing up to the very windshield. One caught them hard, and Desmond, working in the beam of his little flashlight, nearly went sprawling off his bunk.

"Shit!" He inspected the plants for further damage. "Bloody casing's cracked, on top of everything."

There was no telling how long the trip to Villamil would be. Santos had the throttle at full, but it seemed they barely made headway against the waves. Ahead of them the patrol boat was inching away from them, bit by bit its lights growing smaller and the intervals when it dipped from view growing longer, though now and again Alex could make out the silhouettes of the ranger and his deputy against the light of the little doorless cockpit that served as their cabin. Then a long moment passed when it seemed the boat had disappeared entirely.

Santos cut his light suddenly and eased off on the throttle. It was as if he'd given them over to the waves—in an instant the boat had lost all momentum and was being tossed like a twig, up and then down again. They sank to a valley and then seemed to get sucked up in the maw of a wave, the whole boat twisting and tilting so wildly Alex was certain they would capsize.

Alex felt Desmond's bones crunch against him in the dark.

"What the fuck are you doing? You're going to sink us!"

Santos pulled on the tiller hard and gunned the engine again. For a moment it felt like they were hanging against the wall of the wave, about to be swallowed in it, but then the boat seemed to catch against something like a gear clicking in, and they wrestled upright again. Another wave caught them, but differently, as if the wind had shifted or the sea had changed its direction.

Desmond, suddenly energized, pulled himself up and flung open the door of the cabin.

"They're behind us! The fucker turned the boat around! He's running them!"

It was true: every few instants the lights of the patrol boat reappeared behind them, getting smaller. But what was Santos thinking? They would truly be outlaws now.

"My man Santos!" Desmond said, as if this had all become some grand adventure. "There's balls for you!"

The patrol boat had slowed now, and begun to turn in a wide arc. It had noticed their flight. A powerful beam of light pierced the rain from its deck searching them out, moving back and forth across the waves. Somehow it managed to miss them, once, and again, but then a crack of lightning lit up the sea and held them frozen there on the waves.

The searchlight swung around to them, but Santos kept the throttle at full.

"He's still going to run them!" Desmond said, as excited as a school-boy. "It's bloody Butch Cassidy and the Sundance Kid!"

It was madness: already the patrol boat was gaining on them. Alex made out the ranger standing in the bow in the lashing rain, maybe shouting at them, though whatever he was saying was lost to the wind and the waves. Then he drew his gun.

"Fuck me!" Desmond said, ducking behind Alex.

The ranger aimed the gun skyward and fired a single shot. It came out muffled and strange in the rain, the merest clack. Alex hunched, waiting for more, but the ranger just stood there, bobbing up and down with the waves, looking rain-swept and maddened.

He turned away and a moment later the patrol boat began to circle back in the direction of Villamil. Desmond was still cowering.

"They've stopped following," Alex said.

"He's not aiming that bloody pistol at us, is he?"

"No. They're going back."

Santos turned on his light again. They continued in silence, the fren-zied energy of their escape giving way to exhaustion. It took an hour or more of hard slogging before they made their cove, and then another half hour's maneuvering to get the boat into it without smashing against the rocks. The cove, at least, was calm, with only the rain and the slightest heave of the sea to tell of the storm not fifty yards away. Santos lined the side of the boat with his jugs and his lifesaver to keep it from grinding against the cliff face and leaped out into the rain to tie the mooring lines to the rocks and trees. They were all drenched by then, even Desmond, who stood flinging ropes inexpertly to Santos from the deck.

There was no sign that Desmond's newfound respect for Santos was in any way mutual.

"*Aquí, mujer, aquí!*"

The only thing Desmond cared about was, of course, that Santos had saved his plants. Alex still couldn't figure out what was in it for Santos, though he was coming around to the opinion that at bottom he simply wasn't very bright. He wanted his fish, as Desmond had said. Everything else was an inconvenience.

They'd gone beyond mere madness by this point.

"Quite the adventure, isn't it?" Desmond said. "Looks like you're getting your money's worth."

The rain was battering the roof of the cabin. Through the cabin door, Alex saw Santos put a jug up to the little funnel he had rigged to catch the runoff, then a minute later another. They had water enough to last them. Alex suspected they would need it.

They retreated to the far side of Fernandina, where there was only the ocean between them and the Chinese coast. Alex kept expecting the cavalry to arrive at any moment, choppers and gunships, SWAT teams that would storm them on the beaches, but the days passed and they saw only the lizards and the birds. Fernandina was another planet, what he thought Neptune might be, or Uranus, a place of black sand and purple scoria fields and highways of bouldered lava rock that rose up to the rim of a single massive crater. A green lake lay at the crater's bottom, placid and remote, little conclaves of ducks drifting across it that looked as if they had strayed there through a warp in space.

They had days of drizzle and gray, more storms, then sudden cloudless mornings when the sun beat down on them like a tyrant. Santos was up every day in darkness, baiting his lines, but the fishing here was even more erratic than it had been in the bay—half-catches, with half the fish undersized, and half the rest just bastard interlopers that ate Santos's bait, then had to be chucked. Day by day Santos grew more impassive and sour. Alex kept sneaking looks at the hold to try to gauge what remained of their exile, but the time passed and the hold seemed no closer to filling.

He avoided being caught alone with Santos. That left him to Desmond, who after the first thrill of their escape had had to come around to the fact that they were stuck out there now at the remotest reaches of the archipelago.

"We're in virgin territory, my boy," he'd said at the outset. "Time to stake our place in the history books."

But they scoured the slopes for his mollugo, through glaring sun and bitter rain, across lava fields that were like climbing through a landfill and along precarious ridges where the ground threatened to give way with every step, and found no trace of it.

It wasn't long before the bloom had gone off Desmond's brief infatuation with Santos.

"Might as well be in fucking Alcatraz. The Mongol should never have given them a reason to come after us."

If the merest speck appeared on the horizon Santos at once hid the boat in some mangrove clump along the coast until it had passed; if they camped on the beach they had to cover every trace of themselves lest someone come looking for them. It all seemed pointless: surely Santos's boat would be impounded the instant he pulled into a harbor, and Desmond's specimens probably crammed into a baggie so he could be brought before some international tribunal on crimes against nature. Desmond and Santos avoided each other now like partners in a murder who couldn't bear being forever reminded of their villainy. The sheen they had seemed to have of being survivors, above every obstacle, when they had set out from Puerto Ayora had completely gone—they looked beleaguered and small now, men with a mark on them.

Desmond kept cooking up plans for his escape, schemes that involved sneaking off in the panga in the dead of night or hailing a passing freighter to hitch a ride to the mainland. Alex didn't want to hear about them: the more he knew, the more chance he'd get dragged into them. He would rather take it up the bum from Santos than set out in a rowboat on the high seas with the likes of Desmond.

Desmond never let his case from his sight, dragging it up and down the island like a dead child he couldn't part with, stopping obsessively to give his plants their daily doses of light.

"Bloody gunslingers put them back a good month, at least. If the fuckers don't go to seed they're completely useless."

It looked to Alex like the plants were on their last legs.

"Maybe you should throw them out," he said. "Destroy the evidence."

"Over my fucking corpse."

Alex, to fill the hours, had begun to sneak glances at Desmond's *Origin of Species*. He was surprised—put off, really—at how unassuming it was, with its talk of visits to the neighborhood pigeon fanciers and of the varieties of primrose and cowslip. He kept skipping ahead, looking for the Big Pronouncement, but it all went along like this in the most tentative way as if it was just a polite accumulation of the musings of a Victorian gentleman. Maybe that was the chilling thing: here was a theory that had turned the established order on its head and it seemed to depend on nothing more than the difference between pouter pigeons and fantails.

Back in university, Alex would have put this sort of book aside as hopelessly mired in minutiae. Yet it had a kind of suspense to it, as if poor Darwin was being driven despite himself toward an awkward conclusion. He wouldn't say it, he spent the whole of his book finding ways not to say it, and yet there it was, the unacknowledged elephant: the chance, the possibility, that all of creation made no sense. There was no end point in his version of existence; there was an order, but it was a sort of order without Order, that carried on blind. Alex had never quite understood this. He had always seen Darwinism as just another of the grand schemes for making sense of the world—like Marxism, say, or Freudianism, or the New Criticism—that proved all was right with it.

These were the sorts of thoughts that ran through Alex's head while he was out traipsing after Desmond across the wastes of Fernandina. Meanwhile he had the primordial world in front of him like his own Darwinian science kit, an outcrop of rock that had heaved itself up to the light of day just an eye-blink ago, in geological time, and the paltry offerings of life it had managed to scrape together in the interim. There were those same Jurassic iguanas as on Isabela, with their crazy third eye, and their black-skinned brethren by the sea that massed together on the rocks in tangled heaps; there were the hawks that circled patiently over them, day after day, waiting for some fatal error. A margin of green ran around the island's coast and another mirrored it around the rim of the volcano, but in between there was only gray and black, though in ten million years, or a hundred million, the place might have got around to being vaguely habitable. Who could say what new freaks of nature would have sprung up by then, three-armed or fully amphibious or with a second set of eyes in the backs of their heads? There was no telling, really, that was the thing: there was no Plan. Things went on and on, this happened, then that, and it was all merest chance.

With a symbolism that wasn't lost on him, Alex had dropped his watch into the sea. He had taken to wearing it again after the near-disaster on Marchena, but one day he was leaning over the rail of the boat and it simply slipped from his wrist. Plop, he heard, then felt the lightness. Now he was reduced to following the sun to get his bearings, which usually had vanished behind El Niño's veil by mid-afternoon. By that time, Alex had invariably smoked the last of the three cigarettes that were all he allowed himself on their excursions these days and his only thought was to get back to the boat for his next one, the minutes hanging like hours, now that he had no means to measure them. Somehow, in his head, the dwindling of his cigarettes was linked in an inexplicably cosmic way to his lost watch, and to the sun inching hidden across the sky, not really inching at all but actually hanging there ninety-three million miles from them in the middle of absolutely nothing. He began to feel as if with each cigarette he smoked he was somehow bringing them all closer to calamity, the instant when whatever laws there were that held everything just so would cease to function.

His cigarettes were all that were left to him, his coffee long gone by now. He couldn't face the horror of running out, and just shoved a blind hand down into his remaining carton when he needed a new pack without daring to count how many were left. Then one morning he rose early and went out to the deck to find Santos baiting his line with a cigarette drooping from his lip. The sight of him smoking so cavalierly, as if they'd somehow been transported back to the cigarette-rich civilized world, sent an instant's thrill through him. But then the alarm bells went off: the only cigarettes he'd ever seen Santos with were the ones he'd cadged from Alex.

Alex was suddenly sure, with the rock solidity of instinct, that Santos had pilfered from him.

"*El cigarrillo,*" he said hotly, hardly able to stop from wrenching the thing from Santos's lips.

Santos didn't even bother glancing up from his work.

"*Qué quieres?*"

"*El cigarrillo. De dónde?*"

Now Santos looked over at him.

"*De dónde?*" An acid grin spread across his face. He pinched the cigarette between his thumb and middle finger and took a drag, held it. "*De dónde, muchacho? Qué tipo?*"

He exhaled.

"*Es un cigarrillo de bacalao,*" he said, with his laugh, and flicked the butt into the sea.

It was war after that. A single pack, it turned out, was all Alex had left—he did the math, what he would have smoked, say, at fifteen cigarettes a day for some twenty days, a generous estimate, and came up about two packs short. He began to watch Santos like a hawk, was up when he was, would spy on him from the shore with Desmond's binoculars to try

to catch him sneaking smokes while they were away. At the smallest
opportunity he made covert searches of the boat, the tackle boxes, the
engine well, the little wooden chest that Santos kept near his feet at the
helm, looking for half-finished Marlboro packs, foil, cellophane wrappers,
anything incriminating. He found not the least evidence to support his
suspicions—the little chest, for instance, held a map, of all things, and a
small pile of neatly folded clothing some woman must have laundered for
him. Yet he remained convinced of Santos's guilt. At the very least he'd
been hoarding his own secret supply, crime enough in Alex's eyes, and
surely justification for raiding it if he sniffed it out.

He had cut down to a lone cigarette after breakfast and then a final
tantalizing one before bed. The sudden drop in his nicotine intake
seemed to have whittled away at what little remaining patience he had
with Desmond. When Santos set them ashore in the mornings now, Alex
left Desmond to fend for himself, taking with him only a little shoulder
bag with his own bare necessities, his Swiss Army knife and his lighter
and his remaining cigarettes, which he had taken to keeping on him at all
times, then a jug of rainwater and whatever leftover fish and rice he could
scrounge, stored in a little tin pot with a handy latching lid to which he
had helped himself out of Santos's supplies. If it ever came to it—and to
this end he always kept his moneybelt with him, tucked in his pants, his
documents and cash safely sealed away inside it in Ziploc bags—he figured he could leave Desmond and Santos to their fates and make his way
on his own, cooking up lizards and crabs for his meat and rigging a still
for his water with hollowed-out crab legs.

The first time Alex had left the boat without taking any of Desmond's
equipment, Desmond had stood on the deck looking as if he'd been left
in the lurch by an incompetent bellhop.

"I can't lug all this stuff on my own. Not with my fucking knee."

Alex sat waiting in the panga.

"Then just take what you can manage."

Desmond looked like he'd been betrayed.

"Fucking hell, then. If that's how you want it."

It was too late, though, for any fundamental shift in the order of
things—their roles were too ingrained by then, the hierarchy too established. Short of sulking alone on the beach, Alex was stuck following
Desmond on his rounds, which at least gave a shape to the days, something

to hold back the amorphousness they were slipping into. All that Alex's newfound independence amounted to in the end was a constant prickliness that Desmond went out of his way to inflame.

"Grab that satchel, would you?" he'd say, putting Alex in the position of looking petulant if he refused. Now that Alex had made his aversion to him plain, Desmond seemed determined to give it no quarter. Alex felt he had lost his trump card, the one thing that had afforded him any sort of power over Desmond.

"There's no point moping around like fucking Achilles," Desmond said. "Not many people get this sort of opportunity, you should be grateful for that."

"Opportunity for what, exactly?"

"Don't be an ass. Something like this changes your life. What's that worth to you? Or would you rather go back home like some bloody jock just to say how many girls you've fucked?"

It would have been easier to keep strong against Desmond if Desmond hadn't actually had his number. Desmond was willing to say anything, to speak his cesspit mind, which meant he often strayed into the truth.

"In a week," he said, "you'll get on a plane and go back to whatever it is you do up there in Canada. But you'll have this. You'll thank me for it. A day won't go by when you don't remember it, I'll guarantee that."

Desmond didn't say where *he* might be in a week—probably winging his way back to England, having somehow wormed his way out of this mess. Alex was surprised at how much he actually took heart from the thought. He'd been hatching his own escape plans, carting around his little survival kit and thinking he might simply hike down to Punta Espinosa one day, where the tourist boats stopped, and head for the nearest police station. But what he really hoped for was a clean escape for the lot of them, Desmond with his mollugo and Santos with his fish, if only because he didn't want either of them on his conscience, didn't want to have to think of Desmond stuck in his East London flat teaching English to foreigners all his life or Santos shipped back to some Third World hell on the mainland, sans boat and sans fish and with the woman who laundered his shirts on his case every day and who knew how many hungry *niños* at his heels.

Alex had continued scouring the battered suitcase that served as Desmond's library in search of more reading material. It was crammed with every manner of arcana, thousand-page reference books and hand-bound monographs and photocopied journal articles with titles like "Effects of Seed Dispersal by Animals on the Regeneration of *Bursera graveolens*" and "Cacti in the Galápagos Islands, with Special Reference to Their Relations with Tortoises." Most of these were replete with Desmond's crabbed annotations, as impressively unreadable and obscure as the material itself. But once Alex dug through to a folder buried at the bottom of the suitcase filled with articles by a certain Prof. J. M. Bowinger of Imperial College. Here the annotations were easier to make out. "Bollocks!!" Desmond had scrawled across one of the articles, and "Bloody crap!!!" on another. But try as he might, Alex couldn't see anything in Bowinger's leaden prose and ponderous thoughts that made him any worse than the rest. In fact, one of the articles talked about pioneer plants in terms that might have come from Desmond himself. It was almost heartbreaking to see Desmond's vindictiveness, his sense of injury, exposed so baldly. Some sort of contest had been fought, it was clear, and he had lost. Perhaps there was a sort of dignity in that, in hard-won bitterness. Alex had had his own share of it.

They gave up their search for mollugo across Fernandina's slopes and descended for the first time into the island's crater. This one was of a different order than the one they'd been in on Isabela, almost entirely barren, runneled cliffs of ashy gray stretching down half a mile or more to the lake on the crater floor. They had to test every step, inching their way down along capricious footholds that seemed firm one instant and the next as soft as sand, the crater gaping in front of them at every turn.

It was a couple of hours of knee-busting work before they got down to the lake, a pocket of life amidst the waste. There were the ducks, entirely ordinary-looking creatures of dullish brown that were boating casually along on their green element as if it were a wetland in Muskoka; there were clouds of insects, gnat-like things that hovered above the surface of the lake like a miasma it gave off. Now the lake's preternatural green was explained: the water was a thick algal soup, as viscous as creamed broccoli.

"The thing goes as clear as the Mediterranean when there's an eruption," Desmond said. "Then it starts over again. God's little laboratory."

Alex could feel the spectral stillness of the place, the isolation. The only ripples on the lake were the wakes of the ducks, quelled in an instant by the carpet of algae. Maybe this was as close as you got to the beginning of things, a bit of water and dust and then His Big Finger reaching down for the spark.

Desmond had picked up Alex's shoulder bag from where he'd dropped it.

"I'll take a bit of your water, if you don't mind. Mine's out."

They found a scattering of stubborn plant life in the nooks and crannies around the lake, grasses and vines and tiny flowering weeds. But no mollugo. Desmond was surprisingly sanguine.

"All this is just birdshit, most likely. Brings the seeds over. Ergo, no mollugo. A certain colleague of mine maintains that birds are the major factor, but that's just nonsense, it has to be wind. It's a pioneer plant, for Christ's sake, it's not going to wait for the bloody birds to show up."

"Is that what all this is about?" Alex said. "You and Bowinger?"

"Bowinger? What the fuck do you know about Bowinger?"

Alex felt a thrill. He had struck a nerve.

"I saw his articles. In your things."

"You were fucking snooping! I don't believe it! You went through my things!"

There was a genuine outrage in this that threw Alex off balance.

"I was just looking for something to read."

"My bloody arse you were! You're a common sneak! So Mr. Fucking Goody Two-Shoes from Canada finally shows his true colors!"

Alex felt like he'd blown another crucial advantage.

"So is that it? This wind thing?"

"Yes, that's part of it. The 'wind thing,' as you so articulately put it. You can bet it bent his nose out of shape. Though he was smart enough to pick on something else when my dissertation came up. But never you mind. I'll fix all that, once I get these fuckers home, which I'll manage even if I have to eat them first and shit them out on the other side. That'd be a fine bloody irony."

They crawled their way back to the rim before nightfall, both of them gray as ghosts from the dust. Alex thought he'd never be rid of the taste of it, ferrous and bitter like burnt bone. Clouds had massed over the crater and they had to make their way in the fog a good ways before they got clear of them. But higher up in the sky, another layer of cloud stretched to the horizon.

They reached the shore just as the first rain began to fall. Santos's boat was not ten feet from where they'd left it, as if it hadn't moved. Alex had begun to suspect that their gas had run low.

"Bloody home sweet home," Desmond said.

Santos rigged a canopy over the engine well and cooked up some fish on the brazier. They ate in the cabin, in silence. Alex's clothes clung to him like mud from the dust and rain. He thought of their first meal together on the beach in Darwin Bay and how different the silence had seemed then.

The fish was one of Santos's discards, barely edible. He wasn't wasting his grouper on them anymore.

"He might throw on some crab for a fucking change," Desmond said. "Bloody nigger'll be feeding us rat shit next."

Santos rose and in one movement grabbed Desmond's dish and hurled the remains of his dinner out the cabin door.

"Fucking hell! What the fuck did you do that for?"

Santos sat back down without a word.

"You fucking bloody oaf! You fucking monkey! I ought to split your skull, you fucking spic!"

Desmond made a stab for Santos's plate but Santos lunged at him, lightning quick, and pinned him against the cabin wall, a hand at his throat. Santos looked massive suddenly, murderous, the smallest shiver away from snapping Desmond's neck.

"Go on, you fucking animal!" Desmond screamed. "Why don't you kill me? Go on, or I'll kill you first!"

Alex cast an eye around wildly for something to strike Santos with if he needed to.

"Stop, for Christ's sake!" he shouted. "Stop it!"

A long second passed, but then something seemed to give in Santos and he let Desmond go.

"You fucking cocksucker! You fucking coward! I hope they lock you away, you bloody pirate, it's what you deserve!"

An awful silence followed. Santos hunched over his plate, then finally took it out on deck and flung the remains of his meal after Desmond's.

He set about erecting the tarp outside that he slept under when it rained.

"Did you see him, that fucking murderer?" Desmond said. "If he touches me again I'll take a hatchet to him, I swear it!"

By morning the rain had stopped, and the sun rose blood-red over Isabela against a cloudless sky. Santos set about his fishing as if Alex and Desmond didn't exist, offering no breakfast and making no move to bring them ashore. Desmond, bloody-minded, unleashed the panga and angled it off the cabin roof on his own. It slipped from his grasp and looked as if it would plunge nose first into the water, but somehow it righted itself and landed, with a thunk, almost perfectly square.

Santos watched all of this with a steely glare.

"Give me a minute," Desmond said, conspiratorial. "Then we'll get the bloody hell out of here."

He dragged three of his bags out of the cabin.

"We don't need all that stuff," Alex said.

"Just keep your fucking mouth shut."

There was a beachhead not a few hundred yards from the boat, but Desmond made away from it, rowing around a curve in the shoreline until Santos's boat had disappeared from view. Alex already felt sick with the thought of what Desmond was up to.

"We've got the panga, don't you see? If the weather stays clear we can set out tonight and be free of the bastard."

"Set out for where, exactly?"

"I'll row the thing to the fucking mainland if I have to."

Something had to be done, maybe, before they ended up slitting one another's throats, but sneaking off in this cockleshell was not it. It was madness. It was suicide.

"I'm not coming. I'm staying behind."

Desmond didn't even trouble himself to take this seriously.

"With that animal? You've got to be joking."

He could still make a go at Punta Espinosa. It was half a day's walk, at most, he'd seen it the previous day from the slopes, an oasis of green and tiny lakelets.

"I left all my things behind. You didn't exactly warn me."

"Well, we didn't want to rouse his suspicions, did we?"

Alex ought to have set out on his own the minute they hit the shore. He had his moneybelt with him and his little survival kit, complete with a cupful or so of leftover rice. Yet he was still clinging to the notion that things would come right in the end, that there was still hope. Hope for what, he couldn't say, maybe simply that all this was not an unmitigated disaster, was just another lark, something he'd laugh about in the fullness of time and add to his repertoire of travel stories. Hope that, despite the longing he always had to be made over, he'd somehow come through all of this unchanged.

"Why wait for night? Why not start rowing now?"

"Don't be daft. The bastard would just come after us. Anyway, I want to go back into the crater. There's something there, I'll bet my mother on it, I can feel it in my bones. Always follow your instincts, my boy."

Follow your instincts. What could that mean, coming from Desmond? If Santos had followed his instincts the night before, he would have snapped Desmond's neck.

None of Alex's alternatives seemed things that someone like him would actually do: taking to the ocean with Desmond or setting off on his own with his cup of rice or even returning to Santos, who would probably force some unspeakable act on him the second they were alone and then drop his used corpse into the sea. It was as if he had strayed into someone else's crisis, someone else's life. He wasn't used to facing choices like these, ones that really mattered.

"We'll hide the boat up shore a bit," Desmond said. "In case he comes looking."

Desmond dragged the panga up the beach, not even waiting for Alex's help, and stowed it behind a clump of bush. They left most of Desmond's things with it, including his water—to save for the trip, he said—though by the time they had struggled up to the rim of the crater, they had polished off most of Alex's, as much from hunger as thirst.

Desmond, the whole way up, had gone on about getting their story straight.

"They'll believe us before they believe that triceratops, I'll tell you that. That is, if we're consistent."

"But what about your plants? They've already seen them."

"Well, we'll just have to hope we don't run into the same cunt as before, won't we?"

They started down into the crater along the path they had used the previous day, though part way down Desmond veered off into a rift that snaked back upward. It brought them to a narrow shelf, from which Desmond shimmied down along a bank of scree to an even narrower one below, barely a few feet across.

"Hand down my case, would you?"

It looked to Alex as if they were painting themselves into a corner. Beneath Desmond the cliff face dropped off almost sheer all the way to the crater floor, with no hint of a navigable trail.

"Where are we going, exactly?"

"You can stay behind if you don't think you can manage it," Desmond said.

Alex got onto his belly and snaked his way down the slope to where Desmond waited. He was just filling time now, was just stalling, following Desmond in the hope his mind would clear before he had to make a decision. At the bottom of the slope he leaned his weight cautiously onto the ledge until he was sure it would hold, but felt his head spin when he stood—just a step away was empty space.

"We need to make that ridge," Desmond said, nodding to an outcrop that rose up just beyond where their ledge tapered away to nothing beneath a hill of scree.

The only way over to the ridge was across the scree. For perhaps two lethal yards it sloped out uninterrupted over the cliff edge—one false move then, and they would go sluicing down to the crater floor.

"This is crazy," Alex said. "We should go back."

But Desmond had already started out.

"Just dig in your heels. Something to tell the folks back home."

Somehow Desmond managed to slither across. At the ridge, he reached out to the rock and a piece of it broke away in his hand. Alex was sure he was about to lose his traction, but he managed to inch himself upward and get a solid hold. He swung his case up onto the ridge, then pulled himself up after it.

"Piece of cake," he said breezily. "Come on, I'll give you a hand."

For one awful instant when Alex was hanging on the slope all his volition failed him, and a tickle ran up his spine like the scratch of death's very fingernail. But then he had somehow grabbed hold of the ridge. Desmond's arm failed to appear, and he had to heave himself up on his own. Behind him he caught a glimpse of a cloud of debris spraying out into the crater.

Desmond was standing well back from the edge.

"Didn't want to risk the extra weight."

They were on a wide shelf jutting out from the crater wall, uncommonly lush with growth.

"Saw the place with my bins," Desmond said. "Looks like it must have escaped the last eruption."

It was a strange spot, only a few hundred feet from the rim but not accessible from it, the crater wall towering over it so forbidding and sheer it seemed about to topple onto it. The only access to it seemed to be the way they'd come by, the rest of it cut off by the cliffs. The dusting of green that covered it was mostly grasses, though here and there were patches of leafy trailers and of tiny plantlings as pale and insubstantial as cloud.

In front of them the crater yawned and yet the place had an air of separateness and seclusion like a cavern.

Desmond was already on his haunches scrabbling amidst the growth.

"More fucking ash," he said, sour-faced. "I feel like a bloody chimney sweep."

Despite himself, Alex felt something droop in him on Desmond's behalf. It would all come to nothing, all his busy chasing across the islands and ferreting out.

He wandered off on his own, doing his own little half-hearted investigations.

"Careful!" Desmond snapped. "Don't muck up the waters."

Toward the crater wall the rock dipped away into an old satellite cone, maybe a dozen feet across, the floor of it a lifeless bed of rippled lava. But in the scree along one of its slopes, Alex spied a little field of spindly growth, spread as even and thin as a mesh.

He felt a flutter.

"There's something here," he said.

"Eh? What is it?"

Something in him wanted to keep the find from Desmond, for a moment at least.

"Some plants. Maybe you should look at them."

Desmond rose up irritably. "Don't touch them! Give me a minute! They're probably nothing, mind you, it's too shady over there for anything good."

He climbed to the edge of the crater and stood next to Alex, looking down at his find.

"Jesus bloody Christ." It seemed the first time he had ever been this still, that he hadn't seemed to hum with noxious energy. "I don't fucking believe it."

There was such a tone of reprieve in his voice, of thankfulness almost, that Alex actually felt a twinge of embarrassment for him. He became all business now—he brought his case over and in a matter of minutes had sorted through his plants and tossed out a good half of them, as if all the attentions he had lavished on them for days and weeks had been nothing.

"Wish I'd brought some of my fucking tools." He'd started brushing away scree around the edges of the plants. "We'll just have to manage by hand."

He worked with the painstaking carefulness of an archeologist. He had his toothbrush with him in his satchel and he used it to sweep away at the base of the stems, uncovering twisted taproots with the slenderest filaments branching away from them like the translucent cilia of tiny sea creatures. He took up two, three, half a dozen of them, making a place for them in his case. They were already in flower, tiny white-petaled blooms radiating out from the little stemlets like constellations. When Alex had come upon them they had seemed such scrawny things, but under Desmond's ministrations they grew weirdly intricate and substantial.

"I could fucking smell them here," Desmond said. Alex's role in their discovery seemed already well on the way to oblivion. "This is bloody research, not sitting in your fucking office by the green while your bumboys review the literature for you."

Alex took a seat at the edge of the cone while Desmond finished his work. He wondered if the excitement of the moment would seem silly in a week's time. They had found a bunch of weeds was all; hardly anything worth risking your life for. Maybe in the entire world there were a dozen people who could even have named them. That Desmond was one of them cast a shadow over the entire lot.

At the bottom of a hill of chalky rubble near where Alex was sitting was another little web of spidery plants.

"What're these things?"

"Just leave them, I've got my bloody hands full at the moment."

Alex went down for a closer look. They seemed the sibling outcasts of the stuff that Desmond was digging at, flowerless and practically leafless.

Desmond was suddenly standing over him.

"I told you to leave them, for fuck's sake."

He squatted to the plants and pulled one up as carelessly as if it were a dandelion or a bit of clover.

"Just runts, like I suspected. It's the fucking ash."

But something had caught his eye.

"Fucking root." He touched a finger to one of the tendrils branching away from the taproot. "That's odd."

He pulled up another of the plants, more cautiously this time. It came up the same, with a taproot leading down, though some of the tendrils led off a couple of inches or more through the ash, fine as cobwebs.

Desmond held the thing against his palm.

"Look at those roots." Alex wasn't sure what he was getting at. "It's fucking odd."

He retrieved his case, seeming taken over now.

"Look at the difference." He laid one of the plants from the satellite cone next to the newer one. All Alex saw was that the second was a sort of laggard version of the first, its leaves stunted and small and its buds still tight as tiny fists.

"I can't believe it," Desmond said. "Look at the roots. Look at the laterals. It's fucking obvious, once you see it."

The second's roots were a little more scraggly than the first's, but not in a way Alex would have called obvious.

"It's a variation, don't you see?" Alex didn't think he'd heard this tone in Desmond before, so absent of guile. "Out rather than down."

Alex still wasn't sure if he followed.

"It's not mollugo, then?"

"It's fucking mollugo, all right. Only different. An adaptation. Probably some bastard seed that normally would have just died out on the rocks but wafted over here instead, and liked what it found. A bloody chance in a billion."

"So it came from the others?"

"It doesn't fucking matter where it came from, don't you see? A bloody mouse could have carried it over, or maybe Bowinger's right and some bird shat it out from bloody Peru. That's not the point—the point is it's an adaptation. It's fucking adapted to ash."

He began to pull up another, working with his toothbrush again.

"There they are, you see? Those laterals at the base of the stem. That's new, I tell you, I've never seen it." He ran a fingertip along one of the tendrils as if petting some frail alien pet. "This is what it's about, boy. The origin of species. The fucking evolutionary jackpot."

He was busy again. This time he dumped out his remaining sesuvium—what had been the linchpin, Alex thought, of his grand scheme, of his magic wide cross—and then slowly replaced it with his new mollugo, which he extracted from the ground as if it were nitro-glycerine, tenderizing the ash with his toothbrush and then gently blowing it away from the roots. When he ran out of niches in the case he began to throw out mollugo as well, what was left of the older ones and even some from the satellite cone, until the little clump in the ash had been practically halved.

"Mustn't take too many," he said. "The fucker'll take over the whole island in a few years, if we're lucky. Quicker than fucking crabgrass."

But he kept at it, one more, then another, until his case was crammed with specimens, three or four to a niche. There couldn't have been a dozen plants remaining in the ground when he was finally able to bring himself to stop.

"That should do it." He looked uneasily at the sorry remnant he'd left behind. "If it doesn't make it I'll come back and reseed the thing myself."

Alex had stood by during all of this still not quite comprehending—it was just a matter of a few extra root hairs, surely what any self-respecting plant could have managed in a twinkling to handle an extra spot of drink. Yet Desmond was acting as if the skies had opened, as if Darwin himself had come down from the clouds and anointed him his holy son. Alex didn't think evolution happened like this, overnight—it took millennia, eons, while whole continents shifted and mountains rose up and decayed.

Desmond was packing up. Alex needed to know if he was truly a madman, now that decisions had to be made.

"You never finished telling me about your dissertation," he said warily. "What they actually failed you on."

"Why in Christ would you bring that up now?"

He had to push on before Desmond beat him down.

"I was curious. Wondering if this will help."

"It's not actually any of your fucking business," Desmond started, but already relenting. "If you really want to know, it was a frame-up. Fifteen words. Fifteen bloody words. A fucking sentence. Bowinger claimed that I lifted it from his stuff."

He'd grown gloomy with remembered bitterness.

"Did you?" Alex said.

"As if I'd bother. You could have put an armadillo in front of a type-writer and eventually he'd have come up with the same thing. But it was enough to sink me."

"But had you actually read the sentence somewhere?"

"Of course I'd fucking read it! I'd read everything, even that arsewipe. Especially him. So maybe the thing stuck in my head, who the fuck knows, these things happen. But once he had that, he made a whole bloody argument. Probably fed my dissertation through a fucking computer, I wouldn't put it past him. Three words here, some bloody turn of phrase over there. And because he's such a mucky-muck, everyone kow-towed. Plagiarism. They might as well just have hanged me from a tree."

He fell silent. At once Alex regretted having brought the subject up. He saw it all now, everything he hadn't wanted to know. The dingy base-ment flat with the books everywhere and the moldering walls and the stinking cat litter in the bathroom; the mother, even, who came over Sundays to do the dishes and bring Tupperware meals and to whom he'd said nothing of his shame, guarding her illusions. He could see the whole of it, could practically smell it, the stale odor of Desmond's life.

Desmond clicked shut his case.

"This'll change all that, though," he said quietly. "This'll change it."

It was not much past noon yet, to judge from the sun, though the first pale wisps of El Niño cloud had started drifting in.

"Might as well set out before the weather changes," Desmond said. "Let the fucker come after us if he wants. My guess is he'll probably be glad to be rid of us."

This was it, then, Alex thought. He would have to decide. Somehow their find seemed to make his choices more ambiguous. He cast a glance back at the paltry shred of mollugo they'd left behind in the ash. A new thing on the earth, for all Alex knew. Its fate lay in their hands.

Desmond waved off Alex's help at the ridge, clutching his case in one hand and somehow managing to lower himself over the edge with the other. He disappeared from view and Alex heard gravel trickling off into space. After a long moment Desmond reappeared on the ledge below him.

"Be quick about it! I don't like the look of those clouds."

Alex began to lower himself down. His shoulder bag shifted and nearly threw him off balance.

"Don't monkey around up there, for Christ's sake, you've got the fucking Grim Reaper behind you."

By the time Alex made the ledge his limbs felt like water.

"You'll have to give me a boost here to get the case up," Desmond said. "Then I'll give you a hand once I'm over."

Alex was too jittery to argue. He just wanted off that ledge. It was maybe ten feet to the one above them, up an ashy slope that reached a few feet short of it.

Desmond insisted they get the case up first.

"Just give me a boost and I'll shove it over."

But Alex's feet kept slipping against the scree under Desmond's weight.

"Just leave it!" Alex said. "I'll hand it to you! You need both hands to get over!"

"Fine, fine! Just don't fucking let go of it till I've got it!"

Desmond clambered up the slope. There was a heart-stopping moment at the top when he had to stand nearly vertical against the cliff face to clear the last few feet, but then he was over. In a flash he'd turned and was on his belly, leaning out for the case.

"Let's have it, then! Just don't drop the bloody thing!"

Alex gauged the slope. It would be awkward getting traction with only a single hand to pull himself up. He leaned his whole body into the scree, bracing one foot against it and pushing off from the ledge with the other.

He heard a whoosh behind him, like an intake of breath, and saw Desmond's face twist.

"Jesus fucking Christ."

Alex froze.

"Don't go back, for Christ's sake! Keep coming! Keep coming!"

Another sound reached Alex, a distant rain of debris like a handful of pebbles reaching the bottom of a well.

"Keep moving, dammit! Move!"

All Alex could see now was the image in his mind's eye of the slope giving way to air beneath him. His body was in the grip of an unfamiliar sensation, as if speed was pumping through him or a thousand volts.

He felt a warmth at his groin.

"For the love of Christ, move, goddammit!"

He eased his hand forward, surprised his brain could still send messages to such distant outposts. It was a matter of moving ahead inch by inch, only that. One inch, then another.

Desmond was leaning out over the cliff edge, arms outstretched. Alex felt something like gratitude flood through him.

"The case, for fuck's sake! Hand up the case!"

The fucking case. That was all it came down to.

For a second, then, Alex almost gave up his grip. It would be so easy, a crossed signal in the brain, a tiny misfire, and then the almost instantaneous electrical surge through his nerves that would shut his muscles down. He would slip over the cliff edge and into the air, and a moment later nothing. Mineral death.

"Hand up the fucking case, for God's sake!"

It would serve him right, Alex thought.

He heaved up the case.

"Thank fucking Christ!"

It seemed almost as an afterthought that Desmond held a hand out to him to help him up.

"Pushed off a little hard on that one, eh?" he said, with grotesque cheeriness. "You must have been pissing yourself."

Alex's heart was still pounding, his hands were shaking, but suddenly none of it seemed to have anything to do with him.

The ash had covered the wet at his groin.

"We should go," he said.

He went ahead, following the trail they'd come by. He was trembling still but wouldn't show it, keeping up a brisk pace so that Desmond had to struggle to keep up. Then they reached the rim and saw what they hadn't seen from inside the crater, a line of dark cloud that was pushing toward them from the horizon.

Alex was pleased.

"Fuck it!" Desmond said. "Bloody hell! This fucks up everything."

The clouds moved in while they descended. By the time they had reached the coast the sky had closed over and the wind had started to pick up. Santos's boat was already waiting for them offshore.

Alex hadn't spoken since they'd set out.

"Fucking perfect chance shot to hell," Desmond grumbled.

There was nothing for it but to drag out the panga and row back to the boat. Santos was battening things down with a look of dark intent.

"*Regresamos a Puerto Ayora*," he said, without preliminaries.

So he'd had enough: they were heading back to port.

Desmond's face screwed up as if he was about to lay into him, but he seemed to think better of it.

"That's just crazy," he spat out.

"*Sí*," Santos said. "*Loco*."

The matter didn't appear open for discussion. Alex couldn't see what Desmond had to complain about: he had his mollugo now, his mission was done, and the storm would likely get them past whoever might be watching for them at Villamil. Alex didn't really care. He just wanted to be free of these men.

Santos wasted no time in setting out, heading around the far side of Fernandina. Within minutes they were in open sea; within minutes more the rain was coming down in sheets and the waves were washing over the bow. In the dark of the storm Alex could barely make out Fernandina's shore. One wrong turn and they might end up in Fiji or on some uncharted atoll, with only a cracked compass to guide them.

Desmond had grown muted. He was picturing his vindication, Alex imagined, his revenge, close enough to taste.

"Think I'll rest up a bit," he said, climbing into his hammock, though by now the boat was tossing in the waves.

Alex stared at the storm from his bunk, not wanting to think. With each swell he had to brace himself to keep from cracking his skull against the beams. The waves rose out of the dark again and again like an unstoppable legion. Each time the boat dipped beneath them Alex thought it must founder, but somehow it rose again.

He still had the smell of piss on him. He couldn't believe how they had lived out here all these days, wallowing in each other's filth, smelling each other's shit. Desmond had stopped bothering even to duck behind a bush when he shat, so that more than once Alex had seen the logs fall from his scrawny ass, viscous and thin. It turned his stomach to think of it. They'd become animals out here, except that animals had lines they wouldn't cross, a sort of integrity they couldn't betray.

Night came on, a sudden deepening of the dark. Alex couldn't say how long they'd been plowing the waves, two hours, maybe three. Desmond was snoring in his hammock, turned to the wall, tilting this way, then that, yet maddeningly still. Alex had never quite managed to rig a hammock of his own and had made do with his bunk, unable to bring himself to ask Desmond for help.

For a scary moment the engine sputtered and seemed about to die, then rumbled to life again. Alex caught a glimpse of the hard set of Santos's face in the crooked light from the headlight. They went on for a time in a kind of suspension, but then the engine faltered again, and went dead.

In an instant they were tossing on the waves.

"What in Christ?"

Desmond had awoken. There was no order now to their movement, the boat swinging in every direction.

"Fuck it! Bloody hell!"

He'd smashed his forehead against one of the beams above his hammock.

"What in fuck is going on?"

Santos had gone out into the storm. Alex heard him banging around with increasing fury among the canisters on the deck.

"Looks like we're out of gas."

"You're not bloody serious!"

Santos lurched back into the cabin dripping like some monstrous sea thing and began kicking at the canisters wedged under the bunks. One of the ones under Desmond gave a liquid thunk.

Desmond was caught up with tending to his head.

"Find me a plaster or something, I've split my fucking skull."

Santos disappeared into the storm again. A minute passed, then another, the boat pitching wildly. Then suddenly the engine stammered back to life and Santos resumed his spot at the tiller.

Alex caught a flash of wetness from Desmond's forehead. It looked like he was bleeding in earnest.

"I don't suppose he has a fucking first aid kit."

The boat took on a kind of rhythm again against the waves and Desmond crawled into the aisle between the bunks, rummaging among his things.

He managed to lay hold of his flashlight.

"Fuck it. Bloody battery's gone."

He groped around in the darkness. Santos, at the tiller, hadn't taken his eyes from the sea.

"What in hell?" Quietly at first, as if he had made some sort of mistake. Then the note of panic came into his voice. "It's not here. Where the fuck is it?"

Alex thought of ignoring him.

"Where's what?"

"My specimen case! My fucking case is gone!"

He began scrabbling madly under the bunks.

"It's not here! It's not fucking here! Where the fuck is it?"

"It probably just shifted when Santos took the gas."

As soon as Alex had said this, though, the same suspicion seemed to dawn on both of them.

Desmond leaped up.

"The fucker took it! The fucking cocksucker took it!"

He flung himself at Santos's back.

"You fucking bloody motherfucker, where is it? Give me my fucking case!"

He was grabbing at Santos trying to get a purchase.

"Where's my bloody case, you fucking ape? You fucking savage! Give me back my fucking case!"

Santos fended him off with one arm as if he were a yapping mutt. Desmond tried to come at him again, but Santos swung out at him and sent him sprawling. Desmond grabbed for something on the floor. Santos's jeroboam.

"You bloody cocksucking motherfucker! I want my case back!"

Before Desmond could swing the bottle up, Santos had let go of the tiller to take hold of him by the scruff of the neck. The boat rolled to one side and the two nearly toppled full force onto Alex, but then it pitched sharply back and Santos flung Desmond hard against the cabin door, where he crumpled in a heap.

"*Basta ya!*" Santos shouted, as if for Desmond's own good. "*Está con los pescados!*"

It was with the fish. So he had actually taken it. Alex, now that it was clear the matter had come to this, felt an unexpected sense of violation.

It couldn't be true, he thought, the man wouldn't simply have tossed the thing into the sea, not with those plants in it.

Desmond was still sitting collapsed against the cabin door, the jeroboam cradled in his lap like a child.

"You fucker, you fucker, you fucker, I want my fucking case! You have to go back for it, I'll pay you! Turn the fucking boat around! You might as well have killed me when you had the chance!"

He was beside himself. He tottered up, and for a second stood there looking dazed, at a loss, then he opened the cabin door and stumbled out into the storm.

Santos gave Alex a look.

"You fucking bastard," they heard him intone, "you motherfucker, you fucking cunt! You should have killed me, you should have killed me."

Alex heard him thrashing around out there amidst the cargo and wondered if he shouldn't go after him. *Let him stew a bit,* he thought. It wasn't as if the world would be a poorer place if he actually fell into the sea. For all the gall of what Santos had done, there was a bracing fitness to it.

More banging and thrashing.

"Fuck, fuck, fuck!"

Santos shot Alex another glance.

"*Está loco totalmente.*"

A wave hit the boat and Alex caught a muffled "oomph" from the deck, then silence. So he had finally worn himself out. Any second he would come through the door drenched and defeated, broken maybe. Dealing with a broken Desmond, it occurred to Alex, might be worse than dealing with a whole one.

The seconds piled up and Desmond didn't appear.

"I should bring him in," Alex said.

The silence still hung behind the noise of the storm.

"*Como quieras.*"

Alex stepped out to the deck and the rain lashed into him. The only light was the backward wash of the headlight. Alex couldn't so much as make out the rails or the deck, only looming shapes and then the rain and the sea.

"Desmond!"

No answer. A wave hit the boat and washed over the deck, then another.

"Desmond!" He heard his own voice, full of panic now, as if it were someone else's. "Desmond, come inside!"

Nothing.

He got down on his knees, fighting the tilt of the boat, and crawled around the deck, grabbing whatever handhold he could find. The rain and the sea made a river of the aisle that circled the hatch. There was so little space to search, for someone to wash up in.

In desperation he jerked open the hatch and shouted into the hold.

"Desmond!"

Silence.

He staggered back into the cabin.

"*No está aquí! No está aquí!*"

Santos caught his tone at once.

"*Qué pasa?*"

"*No está aquí!*"

They both seemed dazed by the shock of seeing what they'd imagined actually come to pass. Alex still hadn't let the reality enter his head, but his body knew it—his blood was racing, he could hardly form words, he felt ready to retch.

Santos motioned for him to take the tiller.

"*Agárralo!*"

He pulled a flashlight from under the dash and lunged out to the deck. The tiller wrestled against Alex like a raging animal. He felt the same deadness coming over him that he'd felt on the cliffs, the urge to let go.

Santos came back into the cabin.

"*Él se cayó.*"

He has fallen. There was fear in his voice, the first time, it seemed, that he'd shown an open emotion.

"*Regresamos.*"

He had to make a wide circle to get the boat turned, fighting the waves. There was no mistaking what had happened now.

Alex was trembling from head to foot.

"We have to get help," he said.

"*Dónde?*" Santos snapped, as if speaking to a child.

They made their way back, peering out into the storm. With the rain and the waves they couldn't see ten feet beyond the bow.

"This can't be happening," Alex repeated to himself, then fell into a bated silence. He kept seeing shapes in the water, though each one dissolved into black the second he fixed on it. When they had gone a ways, Santos circled back again, in the same wide arc, but it was impossible to tell if they had even crossed the spot where he'd fallen.

For much of the night, they circled. One spot, then another, in ever-widening turns. In the storm and the dark it was like drawing a map in thin air. With each hour that passed, Alex's hope drained to what he thought must be the dregs, and yet it was there still, pooling in the bottom of him like a poison, so that the same agony hung in him. Twice he retched, his stomach so empty that all that came up was a blackish bile, awful to taste; every nerve in him ached, as if he had lost the ability to filter out what mattered from the useless barrage of sensation coming at him. What seemed the worst, though, was that morning might come, that the darkness would end: it was something, at least, to circle around and around in the dark as if it wasn't too late, as if time had stood still.

In the end he grew groggy and feverish, and could no longer tell the projections of his mind, the faces staring up, the bits of flotsam that appeared and then vanished, from what was actually before him. Gradually the storm died away, and the sea went flat like something erased and the rain settled into a sluggish drizzle. The sudden calm felt like a mockery, a little pocket of hell they'd slipped into where there was only their crime to think of.

Santos kept circling in the dark, then finally pushed back on the throttle.

"*Es inútil*," he said, and killed the engine.

They ought to have eaten, but instead they just sat in the cabin like dead men, waiting for light. When it came, it grew clear they had gone off course. There was no sign of land in any direction, only sea and more sea, leaden beneath the overcast. Santos made a show of checking his map and set off to the east, toward the islands or Tierra del Fuego, for all they knew, but it didn't matter: not twenty minutes later, the engine went dead. Santos rattled around among the canisters again, sullenly at first, then with growing rage.

"*Mierda!*" In a fit he heaved one of the canisters into sea. "*Mierda! Cristo cabrón!*"

It didn't matter. Alex wished some cataclysm would come, some whirlpool, some monster, and suck them into the deep.

Santos was sitting hunched in the engine well in the drizzle, head in his hands.

"*Vida de mierda,*" he said.

For the longest time they sat like that, Santos on the deck and Alex in the cabin. The drizzle stopped; the sky cleared. The sun shone down on the water, glaring, and still not a speck showed on the horizon, neither land nor ship, not so much as a gull.

We have to eat, Alex thought. *Eat or die.*

He had left the lid of the hatch askew when he'd checked the hold in the storm. Santos, stone-faced, burrowed down through the fish to reveal them practically steeped in the bilge that had collected there from the rain and sea. They did relays with a bucket to try to get some of it cleared, but short of emptying the entire hold they couldn't make much headway. They both stank of fish now. Water had got into the charcoal as well, and Santos had to pick out the drier bits piece by piece to get a fire going on the brazier.

Whatever little Spanish Alex had managed until then had completely left him.

"What do we do?" he said.

"*Nada.*" Then in English, "We wait."

"Wait for what?"

"*Un barco.* We wait for boat."

The sky remained clear through the rest of the day and then all through the next. The wind had died to nothing; the sun flamed off the sea like a nuclear blast. Without landmarks, it was impossible to say if they were drifting or sitting still. They were becalmed: the word, with its deceptive allure, came to him out of childhood adventure stories trailing images of wasted corpses, of men driven mad. Periodically he scanned the horizon, saving the task like a bit of food he'd hoarded, standing on the hatch and turning inch by inch through the whole of the compass, dreading and hoping for rescue. Each time it was the same, nothing but sea, but it comforted him in some way to know that he'd made the effort, that he couldn't be faulted.

He and Santos fell into a wordless rhythm that seemed at once evasive and complicit. All Alex's old animosity had fallen away. Because his mind turned sometimes to the thought of blame, because he saw how easy it would be for him to twist the matter to his own advantage, he felt a perverse sense of obligation toward Santos, of humility. The second night, Santos pulled a rumpled pack of cigarettes from under the dash— it had been in plain view, practically, Alex couldn't see how he'd missed it—and offered one to him.

It had been days since his last cigarette.

"*Gracias.*"

They were a local brand, acrid and sharp. Santos drew his rum out from the engine well, down to its last couple of fingers, and they finished it off.

"*Te gusta?*" Santos said.

"*Sí, sí. Bueno.*"

On the third day, Santos set a line, using grouper for bait because his bait bag had gone missing in the storm. He pulled in a shark, a stubby, vicious thing that reared suddenly as he drew in the line, seeming about to leap up onto the deck. Instead of cutting it loose Santos scrambled to fix the line and grabbed a machete, hacking wildly at it as it tried to twist free. The shark lunged and writhed, refusing to die, going at the blade again and again as if it were some baffling new sort of enemy. Then finally it went limp and dull-eyed against the line.

The water around it was clouded with blood.

"*Carajo malnacido!*" It had a death grin on it, its teeth bared three rows deep. "*Vaya al diablo!*"

Santos sat down heavily on the hatch. His shirt was speckled red.

"*Llévatelo,*" he said to Alex. Take it.

Alex made the mistake of grabbing the shark by the flank as he pulled it in, and its scales cut into him like broken glass.

"*Cuidado!*"

Santos didn't fish again after that. They ate the shark bit by bit, like a kind of penance, letting it lie there on the deck packed in salt and cutting slabs of it away with the machete. The flesh had a dense, meaty taste, strange and off-putting, like something too close to their own species. The sun continued hot and blinding, and they spent entire days holed up in the cabin; the nights, when they tossed and paced, one keeping watch and the other stretched out on a bunk or just sitting sleepless, seemed to go on without end. They were down to their last few jugs of rainwater, with no more in the offing: they had Santos's still, they weren't facing death, not yet, though Alex wondered if they had the will to avert it.

One evening the sun grew strangely flat as it dropped behind the line of the sea and a lozenge of bluish green appeared above it that almost instantly shattered and shot skyward. The green flash: he had read about it in one of Desmond's books. It was like a portal to the beyond, with just that one second to slip through; or like the light of miracles, perhaps, of Saul on the road to Damascus. Except that it was just a matter of physics, no more something to make into a traveler's tale or a moment of truth than the rest of it. None of this would be something to tell: already he could feel himself building containment cells to shut it away, drilling mine shafts into the deepest cortices of his brain to bury it.

At some point a smell started coming up from the hold, faint enough to ignore at first but turning rapidly pungent. The fish had begun to go off, from the heat, maybe, or the rain that had got in, or just whatever curse it was that hung over them. Santos did a culling, tossing a few dozen of them over the rail and massing the rest on the deck in great heaps to give the hold a proper bailing. Afterward, he went through the remaining fish one by one, packing more salt into them. The salt had gone hard from the storm and he had to spread chunks of it beneath a plank to crush it with his boots. Alex watched him and then did as he did, smashing salt beneath his feet till his soles ached. The work filled the day and then much of the night, but they went at it unstintingly, hardly bothering to keep a watch out for ships. Then they reloaded the hold by the light of Santos's hurricane lamp, layer by layer until it was full once more nearly to the brim.

By morning, the smell had returned. Santos flung open the hatch and began tossing more fish out, erratically, as if he'd given up on any system. The castoffs floated around the boat, staring at them one-eyed like pleading beggars before finally turning belly up; a couple of sharks circled around at the smell of them, but Santos hit out at them so furiously with an oar that they shied away. Then, after a time, following some unknown chemical law, the fish began one by one to sink below the surface.

All day, in the blistering sun, Alex could feel the warmth radiating up from the hold as if something were cooking there. Santos laced buckets of seawater with salt and poured them down the hatch, but still the smell kept building, a tangy, layered scent like the smell of garbage left out too long in the heat. With no wind to disperse it, it hung over the boat like a fog. There were hundreds of fish in that pit, thousands of pounds of them. The more they rotted, the more they seemed to grow diabolic and weighty.

Santos stayed out on deck well into the night, untying hooks from his lines, stringing his jugs together, checking his ropes, with the obsessive methodicalness of someone about to murder his family with a hatchet or put a gun to his head. Alex tried to sleep but the smell of the fish had got into his pores. Then he nodded off and fell into a dream of being stranded at sea, with someone dead, and awoke with a start.

Santos was already banging around on the deck, though it was barely light. Alex went out to find him tossing fish from the hold again.

"*Qué pasa?*"

But Santos kept at his work.

The stench now was like a separate atmosphere they were in. Beyond the rails the fish lay practically heaped on the surface of the water, spread out in a skin that seemed to shimmer and move like something alive. An optical illusion, Alex thought, then he realized they were crawling with vermin: maggots. The fish were covered in them, teeming mats that seethed like a single organism. They were on Santos's hands, they were crawling up his arms. Alex thought of the dead goats on Marchena, so free of pestilence, and wondered how out in this nowhere, this end of the earth, these worms had managed to infiltrate.

Another shark started to circle, a big one, but nosing toward them timidly, as if it had been forewarned. Santos took up a vigil. The shark seemed enfeebled or old, drifting around half-heartedly in the open water like a great ambling mutt, but then suddenly it reared up into the fish open-jawed to take in a huge mouthful of them. Santos was ready for it: he heaved out another of the empty canisters and hit it squarely on the snout. The shark buckled and thrashed in the water before disappearing back into the depths.

"*Diablo!*" Santos shouted after it. "*Salga, diablo!*"

Santos had to climb down into the hold now to get at the rest of the fish, dumping slithering armfuls of them onto the deck, one after another, then coming up at intervals to pitch them into the sea after the rest. He carried on without stint until he had cleared the hold down to its last rotting codling. There were maggots everywhere, on the deck, on the fishing lines, in the foul soup still sloshing around at the bottom of the hold.

Santos reeked. He stripped off his shirt and threw it into the sea.

"*Dios me ha jodido*," he said. God has fucked me.

The fish spread out around the boat like a sinister island they'd run aground on, sending up their acrid stench. The sun beat down; sometimes a lucky breeze would bring a pocket of bearable air, but then the smell would be there again. Then, just as the others had done, the fish began to sink down. A few through the afternoon and into the evening, but then all through the night they must have kept dropping away because by morning the sea had returned to its inscrutable blankness, every one of them gone. To where, Alex wondered, what hand of nature or God had dragged them down? Somewhere, now, they were resuming their place in the food chain, being broken down by microbes, who would be eaten by plankton, who would be eaten by minnows, who would be eaten, in turn, by grouper. What could it mean, this stupid cycle? What comfort or purpose was in it?

It wasn't until sometime the following day that the fish began to resurface, carcasses so bloated they were hard to recognize at first, and giving off such a sulfurous smell now that they seemed to have come back from the very bowels of hell. They rose up randomly and widely scattered but then somehow converged on the boat like entranced acolytes, with their slit bellies and clouded eyes.

"*Ándale, ándale!*" Santos shouted, trying to push them back with his oar, but still they continued to gather. Then in the night came another plague, out of the same nowhere as the worms, some invisible pest that took bites out of Alex while he slept and left him covered in welts the size of silver dollars. At dawn he saw that the archipelago of putrid fish they floated in was haloed now by great clouds of tiny insects. A swarm of them surrounded him at once on the deck and he tried to swat them away, but might as well have swatted the air.

It seemed truly possible that they wouldn't survive, that the line between their lives and their death had grown hopelessly thin. Alex was aware of his body and of how it grew hungry then balked at food, but none of this seemed any more real than the strange twilight place he'd retreated to in his brain. What was it to be dead if not that, to step outside of your body? It seemed months, years, since he'd walked on the earth in any normal way.

He lost track of the days. Santos dangled a single hook into the sea from time to time, pulling up fantastical fish with a dozen fins that yielded only the barest mouthfuls of meat, or tiny herring-like things that they ate whole, not even bothering to skin them. Their water ran low, then ran out, and they drank briny cupfuls from Santos's still; their charcoal dwindled and Santos tore strips of wood up from the boat, from the tackle boxes, the cabin wall, to make their cooking fires. They shat in a bucket, still with an odd regard for propriety; they exchanged, in the course of a day, maybe half a dozen words. A wind came up and blew off the fish and the flies, but then another day—the next one? several later?—they found themselves in the midst of them again. Finally another cycle of rain started up, a soulless drizzle that went on and on and wore at them like the churr of an insect. Alex couldn't have said how he spent the days: they were a wash, a blur, as blank and as featureless and without hope as the sea.

He kept seeing the mollugo he and Desmond had left behind, like the last thing you remembered after an accident or a blow to the head. Half a dozen plants, maybe, not more. Little homesteaders. How had they come there, how had they made themselves over from what they'd been? He couldn't remember how it was exactly that new things appeared out of nothing, as big as houses or tiny as dust motes, living on for hundreds of millions of years or dying out in a heartbeat. On the farm they had waged a constant chemical war against the bugs that had afflicted them and yet the bugs had persisted, getting wilier year after year, growing new armor. They developed resistance, people said, as if they were Nietzschean *über*bugs. *That which does not kill me makes me stronger.* Was that actually true? How could you know? The question went around and around in his head, how things lived, how they died, how they grew stronger. He pictured his father walking up and down the rows of their greenhouses in the tropical heat, his forehead beaded with sweat, checking the undersides of leaves: little white dots, little black ones, little red spiders. One year a whole crop had been wiped out. The insects had been stronger than his family was—his family didn't change, had always the same arguments, the same fears, while the insects, from one year to the next, managed to shift their very DNA.

Those fucking mollugo. The first, maybe last, of their kind. A butterfly flapped its wings, and the whole world shifted. In a matter of years those plants might have overrun the place, might have changed every smallest relation of insect and weed and rock, the dates of eruptions, the drift of continents. It was beyond fathoming, that sort of randomness, of cosmic whimsy. A head could not hold it, all of space could not. If everything made such a difference, then nothing did.

The bites from the fish flies itched like acid now. Alex scratched at them until they festered, until his body was covered in open sores like a scurvied sailor's.

Fleas, he thought. *Adam had 'em.*

He had kept up his watch. The occasional bird went by, including a flock of high-flyers who began to circle the boat way up in the ether and then suddenly swooped down to it like falling stars, maybe spotting the bloated fish. Massive things, at least ten feet across. Albatrosses. They circled the boat like gunships, riding the air, then seemed to think better of alighting and rose up again without once having flapped their wings. They might have been the angels God had chased from heaven, seeking allies: not these, they'd decided, not so low have we sunk. The blue of the sea reflected off their bellies as they rose. For a long while afterward the air seemed bruised by them, by their unflapping weight, the whispering crush of their descent and then their silent retreat.

It was Alex who spotted the boat. It was dawn and overcast and his sightlines were fogged with El Niño haze, and yet it was there, to the west, the smallest dot but growing larger. His first urge was to say nothing. He wanted to turn the matter over in his head, understand what it meant, if it could be real. To savor it, maybe, or turn away.

"*Un barco*," he said. "*Veo un barco.*"

Santos was there in an instant.

"*Dónde?*"

"*Allí*," he said, pointing.

It came right at them. Santos didn't have so much as a pair of binoculars; Alex might have rummaged for the ones he knew were in one of the bags under Desmond's bunk, but didn't. Santos stuck one of his shirts, a dulled crimson, at the end of an oar and waved it incessantly, fixated now. His whole manner had changed: he'd become more himself.

"*No digas nada*," he said. "*Hablo yo.*"

Don't say anything. Alex didn't know what he would have said in any case. There was nothing to say.

The boat was a tanker, massive. It might have been a ghost ship, for all they knew, might simply have kept churning unstoppably forward until they were crushed underneath it.

Santos continued waving his flag.

"*Socorro!*" he yelled, long before there was the least chance of anyone hearing. "*Socorro!*"

Somehow the ship managed to slow, gliding over the water like a great seabird. Alex could make out movement on the long highway of deck, tiny specks of men who shifted this way or that or stood at the rail.

A shout in a language Alex couldn't decipher, then, "*Qué pasa?*" strange to his ears, like someone calling out to a friend across a street.

From the moment they boarded, hauled up a hullside ladder by a flurry of arms, Alex felt as if they had left the real world for some weird simulacrum. The boat had been real; but here, people spoke, moved their lips, seemed flesh and bone; yet it was all a charade, a horrible caricature.

Santos, grotesque, bowed and scraped before the crewmen with a manner Alex had never seen in him.

"*Mi barco,*" he said. "*Aseguren mi barco, por favor.*"

Secure my boat. Still watching his interests. The crewmen, small and dark like Polynesian tribesmen, seemed amused to have found them here, lost at sea.

"*Sí, sí, amigo!*" they said. "*No se preocupe! Tranquilo!*"

They were taken down through a warren of passages and companionways to a sort of mess room, windowless and tiny. A small television in a cupboard was playing a grainy kung fu film.

Some sort of officer had come, Japanese, from the look of him, but it seemed he spoke neither English nor Spanish.

"*Horrible, horrible,*" Santos was saying to one of the crew. "*Él se cayó. Fue cosa malísima.*"

He was shaking his head like someone traumatized. So this was the line, then.

"You look for him? *Usted lo buscó?*"

"*Sí, sí! Toda la noche! Pero al fin, el gas se acabó.*"

It was all simply the truth. Alex, as he'd been ordered, said not a word, though the crewmen, Filipino, they must have been, spoke a passable English.

"We call the shore," one of them said. "*Las autoridades.* To look for him."

"*Sí, sí.*"

It couldn't have been more than an hour before the islands came into view. They had been that close. Alex had gone back up to the deck—no one seemed interested in him, this silent white man, not the crew nor the officers, who seemed to have bothered to assure themselves only that he and Santos weren't pirates or drug runners. Santos's boat bobbed along from a hawser at the stern of the tanker entirely dwarfed by it, a toy, not at all the life-and-death amphitheatre it had seemed all these weeks.

A patrol boat was waiting for them just beyond the Puerto Ayora harbor. They were being handed over like criminals, Alex thought, but then they climbed down into the boat and one of the men there, not in a Park Service uniform but in standard police garb and cap, put a hand on Santos's shoulder as if he were an old and trusted retainer.

"*Un asunto desagradable,*" he said. A bad business. "*Haré todo lo que pueda para ayudar.*"

He was offering help. So Santos was known here.

Santos gave a deferential bow.

"*Gracias, señor. Muchas gracias.*"

Things went as they had on the tanker. Santos talked, with the same air of innocent affliction; Alex kept silent. The policeman asked Santos about him, if he was the lost man's *amigo,* but Santos quickly put him off.

"*No, no, señor. Es canadiense.*"

"*Ah,*" the man said, as if that explained things.

They towed Santos's boat into the harbor and were taken to a grubby police station well off the sea, along a market street. The policeman offered Santos a cigarette, then put questions to him in a gentle, leading tone while a younger policeman scratched notes on a pad.

"*Un accidente,*" the older one said. He had the smiling, open face of someone used to having things go his way. "*Fue solo un accidente.*"

The question of blame seemed to hover in the air, a threat, and yet never arise. Alex recognized the play of forces, patron and client. There would surely be a tribute to pay, not now, maybe, but soon enough.

"*Sí, sí.*"

Santos covered it all, from what Alex could tell, even the contraband plants, his papers, their flight, the whole time watching the younger officer's pencil scratch on its notepad as if for his cues and changing the facts of things so minutely that it would have been difficult to say he wasn't telling the truth. By the end, though, everything looked different from how it had felt: they had only acted as anyone might have. Even their flight seemed excusable, on account of the storm.

The older policeman seemed to know the ranger who had stopped them off Isabela.

"*Es un verdadero pendejo, aquél,*" he said. "*No le caemos bien.*"

He doesn't like us. Us mainlanders, he probably meant.

Santos bobbed his head warily.

"*Sí, señor. Es posible.*"

The policeman had the younger one take them to a hole-in-the-wall up the street for a meal. They were served a stew with big chunks of meat in it, most likely goat. Alex had dreamed of this, his first meal ashore, but now he could barely keep it down.

The young policeman made some sort of joke about life at sea and Santos forced a laugh.

"*Siempre bacalao. Día tras día, bacalao.*"

"*Sí, sí,*" Santos said quickly. He seemed resentful that the man had assumed the same familiar tone with him as his superior had. "*Siempre bacalao.*"

Someone had typed up a report by the time they got back to the station. It was the merest paragraph, a jumble, from what Alex could see, words crossed out and written over in pen and barely a capital or period in the lot. Desmond's name had been spelled *Desman*, with a blank left for the surname.

Alex's name didn't appear.

"You must sign," the older man said. "I can translate."

It was just a heap of words.

"That's fine," Alex said, and signed.

They had to bring up Desmond's bags from the boat. The policemen went through them, lingering over items of particular interest, the binoculars, the battered camera. It seemed unlikely that any of the stuff would ever leave this place.

"Do I need to stay here?" Alex said. "On the islands, I mean."

The man smiled as if at some needless courtesy.

"Is not necessary," he said.

A boy came into the station, barefoot, not more than ten, and handed the policeman a manila envelope wrapped in elastic bands. The policeman handed it to Santos.

"*Sus documentos,*" he said.

There was that casual flourish in his gesture of someone conscious of having done, generously but without breaking a sweat, the remarkable.

"*Muchas gracias, señor,*" Santos said, with his deferential bow, deeper this time and maybe more heartfelt. "*Muchas gracias.*"

They walked back to the boat in silence. Alex grabbed his pack. Desmond's *The Voyage of the Beagle* was sticking out from one of the pockets.

Santos had already set about putting his goods in order.

"*Vaya,*" he said, as if to be rid of him. "*Vaya con Dios.*"

Alex couldn't bear the thought of facing Mara again and took a bed in a fleabag place in the upper town, his window hard up against the street. There was a plane the next day. He awoke early to catch the bus out to Baltra, expecting the whole time he was waiting for it that some-one would come to tap his shoulder. *I'm sorry. There are still questions.* They hadn't even taken his address, if family wanted to reach him.

Neither had he offered it.

Santos's boat was still in the harbor but he turned away from it and never looked back.

The same WANTED poster hung in the airport, staring out. The same moonscape waited outside. Alex tried to feel some relief when the plane left the tarmac, but relief was for children, it seemed now, for innocents.

In Quito, for the first time, he had a problem with his ticket.

"*Es inválido,*" the woman kept saying. "*El boleto es inválido.*"

He lost his temper and began to shout, in a bastard mix of Italian and Spanish and French.

"*Qué pasa?*"

A soldier was suddenly standing beside him, a submachine gun draped over his shoulder. Now they'd arrest him, he thought. Now they would shoot him.

"*Tranquilo, señor,*" the soldier said. "*Tranquilo.*"

Some sort of supervisor came out and puzzled over the ticket.

"Very sorry, sir. Is no problem."

Three hours later he was on a plane heading home. He had enough money for a bus from Toronto, for a decent meal. Everything had worked out. The plane rose over the mountains and came out to the sea, which stretched out like a maw to the end of the earth.

four

— *April* 1987 —

. . . it is difficult to imagine that access to the possibility of
road maps is not at the same time access to writing.

JACQUES DERRIDA
Of Grammatology

Stephen's son was playing down by the water. Alex couldn't remember the last time he'd been here, to the lake—with Liz, maybe, in their first days, back when they'd made a point of walking on the mountain.

"You have to look at what the place would have been like without him," Stephen was saying. "More like Haiti than Florida."

Alex had learned by now that it was usually best to cut his losses early in these arguments with Stephen, who had the disconcerting habit of bringing actual facts to bear on them.

"Don't you think Ariel's a little too close to the water?"

"He's fine. The water's barely a foot deep. And he can swim." But then he called out, "Ariel, careful by the water please!"

Ariel didn't so much as twitch to show he'd heard or in any way alter the frog squat in which he was hunched, rather precariously, Alex thought, over the curb that encircled the lake. He was an elfin child, as ethereal and pale as a changeling, polite enough, in that adult way of children, and yet never quite present, as if following some train of thought only his own five-year-old brain could know the mysteries of. Alex couldn't figure how Stephen, man of reason and order, had given life to this fairy creature.

"I just don't think he's some kind of hero, that's all," Alex finished up lamely. "Even with all the health care and stuff."

He had seen quite a bit of Stephen since the fall. Despite the history with Katherine, he'd found himself warming to him more and more— he'd thought him a prig, with his lofty manner and his fussy little finger movements, but instead had discovered in him an unexpected humanity.

His mind seemed to Alex like some pleasant city in Northern Europe, pristine and well aired and well swept but full of promising turnings and cobbled alleys. Then there was something else that drew them together: they'd both slept with Amanda.

From health care, they had somehow veered off into nationalism.

"We're the big success story, not them," Stephen said. "They've never gotten over the Big Lie. You can't be a slave state and say you're founded on freedom."

The topic depressed Alex—it made him feel unpatriotic, deficient, clichéd, because he felt, like most everyone else, that his country was boring.

"If we're so great, why isn't everyone flocking to come here?" he said, thinking of all the people he'd met traveling who'd treated him like a quaint halfwit the instant they'd found out where he was from.

Stephen paused, warming to the kill.

"If you mean the five percent of the world with disposable incomes who'd rather go to Paris for their holidays than Regina," he said, "then I suppose you're right. About the only thing keeping out the other ninety-five percent is Customs and Immigration."

That Stephen had slept with Amanda had only come out through Katherine, to whom he'd confessed. Alex doubted if, in the awful aftermath of things, he himself would ever have done anything more with the information than let it fester. But a few weeks after the event, Stephen had phoned him.

"I think it might be good if we talked."

Amanda had taken an overdose of Tylenol. It had seemed just the sort of thing Amanda would do, Tylenol, of all things, so scattershot and prosaic, though the method turned out to be a lot more common than Alex would have suspected. Just a few extra pills of the stuff with a bit of alcohol, apparently, and you sent your liver into toxic shock. All over North America, people with a bit of medical expertise but no access to handguns were reaching for their headache pills and a bottle of Scotch when the black dogs circled. What troubled Alex was whether Amanda had known that. Maybe the whole thing had just been a stupid mistake.

Though Amanda had drawn him and Stephen together, it was rare that she actually came up between them.

"Sometimes I think people should just stay in their own countries," Alex said. "At least they'd be warmer."

It was warm today, though. The sun was out, the snow had melted, and some of the flowers around the lake were poking out their timid heads. A young woman went by in a skimpy sweater and Alex found himself staring after her, before the thought police intervened.

Stephen was looking too.

"Like the man said." He pulled his cigarettes out of his blazer. "April is the cruelest month."

It was Katherine who had found her, that night she had called. They'd had a date for drinks, and Amanda hadn't shown up. After waiting for her and trying again and again to get her on the phone, Katherine had gone by her place. She'd had to get the super out of bed to open Amanda's door. There was already a smell by then, though no one in the building, a run-down low-rise on one of the seedier stretches of St. Denis, appeared to have noticed.

By the time Alex arrived, Amanda had already been taken away and Katherine was sitting alone outside the apartment on the dirty hallway floor. She looked broken, completely unlike herself, her clothes askew and her face puffy from crying.

"Tell me this isn't my fault," she said. "Tell me I couldn't have known."

Under his horror, Alex felt a small, shamed relief that he wasn't alone in this.

"It wasn't anyone's fault. We did what we could."

The super stood hunched beside the elevator in his pyjamas and slippers, puffing furtively on a cigarette. The apartment was open. Through the doorway, Alex saw a couple of policemen nosing around inside.

"I should have called her," Katherine said. "I should have called."

It was all too familiar, this black anguish, this circling back and back to find the right moment, the one that would change things.

Each thing he told her, he knew, was a lie.

"You couldn't have known," he said.

The policemen took down their numbers when they'd finished. They were polite, in their broken English, but didn't seem much interested in them after they learned they weren't family.

"We 'ave to call, eh? For de body. It's only dey who can say."

The super was still slouching unhappily nearby as if waiting for some sort of instruction from him and Katherine, though Alex couldn't think what it might be. He felt compelled to go inside the apartment but wasn't sure why, if it was just morbid curiosity or the need to know this thing, to face up to it.

The smell hit him at once, an odor of rot and of something more foul, more forbidden. He'd never been in the place: it was tiny, just a single room, though it looked as if a great wind had whipped through it, a bookshelf knocked over, broken dishes scattered on the floor, food spilled on the counter and moldering. There was a mattress in the corner, the sheets a tangle; there was a little desk in gray metal under the single window. He expected a chalk outline somewhere, as in a police show, but there was no sign of where she'd been found, curled up in her bed or sprawled frozen in some death throe across the floor.

There were smears on the wall and on the bedsheets of what looked like blood.

"She must have cut herself," Katherine said. She stood at the doorway but wouldn't come in. "You get delirious in the end. That's what they said. It might have gone on for days."

It was too horrible to think about. It felt obscene, somehow, to be looking at the place, like watching a snuff film.

It occurred to him what the super probably wanted from them.

"We'll clean the place up," he said. "For when her family comes."

The super shifted, looked heartened.

"It's no hurry, eh. She still got 'er last month."

They brought boxes the next day to pack the place up. They both seemed to be hoping for a purging, a revelation perhaps, but all the place betrayed of Amanda's life was the strange poverty of it. There were no photo albums; no journals. The only books were her course books, barely a novel or a grocery store flyer outside the required texts, though most of these were carefully underlined and annotated, with notes like "compare to Derrida's notion of difference," behind which her real self seemed hopelessly occluded.

There was a stack of photocopied journal articles on her little Salvation Army–issue desk and next to them a yellow writing pad with a few heavily corrected paragraphs of what looked like the start of an essay. "Julia Kristeva, in her article 'Woman's Time,'" it began, and went on in that vein, jargon-laden and hanging always at the edges of intelligibility but not in any remarkable way for its subject matter. No sudden turn into delusion or strangeness, no final Kurtzian scrawl, just a trailing off in mid-sentence as if the kettle had boiled or someone had knocked at the door. He couldn't picture it, how the thought might have formed from that trailing away, *Now I will do it.*

"It was the last thing we talked about," Katherine said. "That paper. It makes it all look so stupid."

"Maybe she was having problems with it," Alex said, but at once the thought felt banal. You didn't kill yourself over an essay.

Amanda had crossed out a word and replaced it, then crossed out the replacement and gone back to the original. Nothing that he hadn't done. In the margin she'd written, "Check references to Joyce."

"We should finish," Katherine said. Already there was an edge to her, a hardness. The night before, he had held her, but that seemed forbidden now. "So we don't have to come back."

They had left the door open to air the place out. There was a knock, and three people were standing in the entrance, an older couple and a young woman, dark-haired and stocky. It took Alex a moment to recognize Amanda in them.

The man was broad-shouldered and tall, towering over the women like the mast of a ship.

"The super said you'd be up here." He motioned out awkwardly. "We've just come to see about her things."

The father took a seat at the kitchen table, but the mother stood at the counter, half-turned to it as if to some chore there. She was the smallest of them, a wisp. They were like Russian dolls in not quite the right order, mother, daughter, father.

He and Katherine had got the mess cleaned up, at least—they hadn't had to see that.

"You're the ones found her, I guess," the father said. "We thank you for it."

There seemed no clue here. Alex had hoped for some ogre, not this gentle giant. The mother stood, still half-turned, avoiding their gaze, clutching her hands together as if she held something fragile in them. It was too much, the weight of these people, it seemed to press down on him like a continent. And yet there was a strange decorum to them, not so much of something suppressed as of something contained.

The sister was watching him and Katherine with a feral awareness. She had Amanda's look but none of her aspect, clear-eyed in a way Amanda had never been.

"She tried it once before, back home," the father said, and it came to Alex, with sudden sureness, that the story she'd told of her dead friend the night they'd slept together had been of herself. "We never quite knew what was best for her. You can't bear it sometimes, letting go, but you have to."

The blame was spreading. It was like a pool rising up around them, taking them all in, up to their ankles, up to their knees.

The father stared at his hands.

"I used to come in once a month or so. Not her mother, it was too hard on her, but I'd come. Last time, I said, 'I'm worried. You look happy.' And we laughed about it."

There was a freighted silence.

"I should make tea or something," Katherine said.

"You won't find any tea. Didn't drink it. Only coffee. But I'll take a cup of that."

Afterward, the visit felt like a secret shame between him and Katherine.

"All I could think of was how I'd found her," Katherine said. "That was what kept going through my head."

Alex didn't dare to ask, but he wanted to, he wanted that image, he wasn't sure why, even if he would only have ended up playing it over and over in his head the way Katherine was. He had a picture of her slumped by her bed, slack-faced from the pills and some last thought or horror written on her, but it was like an image from a movie, it wasn't the thing itself. Maybe it was simply a matter of needing to gaze on the body, the way people said, of wanting the image of it seared into his brain like something he could believe in, that he couldn't forget. But it was Katherine who went out for the funeral, not Alex. Because of the money, he told himself, even though Amanda's father had offered to pay; because of the time; because of the guilt. Because the dead should bury the dead, whatever that meant, when he had the living to look to, and should be seeing his son. He had all his reasons lined up, but it came down more to the feral look her sister had given him, to her mother twisting her hands at the kitchen counter.

At Katherine's insistence they had paid a visit to the therapist Amanda had been seeing. It was futile, Alex thought, just another way of spreading the blame, but he didn't say this to Katherine. The therapist was an older woman in a business suit, her hair tied back so tightly it stretched her face back as if it were a mask.

"You understand I can't tell you anything about what we discussed in our sessions," she said.

"She's dead." The words dropped from Alex like a rock that had been dislodged from him. "What difference could it make?"

The therapist looked down at her desk.

"It doesn't change things."

It turned out Amanda had quit seeing her weeks before. To Alex, the one time he'd asked, Amanda had said only, "She's great, she's really great."

"Shouldn't that have been some sort of a flag, her dropping out?" Katherine said. She was better at this than Alex was, she went straight for the systemic. "I mean, otherwise, what's the point?"

The woman seemed to soften.

"Look. You feel angry, you're hurt, you feel a hundred different things. Mostly, you feel guilty. That's what happens. But don't be so sure there's an answer out there. I shouldn't say this, but the truth is the subject never came up between us. Not once. People do that, they come in here and lie all the time. Especially here. But we can't force people to come in and we can't force them to tell us the truth. They make their choices."

"It's like you're saying there's no help," Alex said.

"Maybe I'm saying that, yes. Sometimes there's no help."

It seemed too easy, this sort of blanket forgiveness.

"If you want," the woman said, "you can come and see me. Just to talk."

Alex felt tempted despite himself. For all the hardness of the woman she seemed to have shown more insight in five minutes than Dr. Klein had in five months.

"Let me know. I'm here."

Katherine left town to stay with a friend in Toronto. It was already clear that Amanda's death would only divide them—she would come by and they would lapse into silence, unable to talk about it anymore and unable to talk of anything else.

"I'll stay if you want," she had said to him. "It's just, I need to get out."

"No, it's fine. I'll be fine."

For a week, then another, he barely left the apartment. He canceled his classes; he called in sick to Dr. Klein. Whenever he thought he saw a way through, the old Galápagos hole would open up in front of him: back then, he had managed to turn himself around by vowing to change, to keep the matter close, like his cross to bear, and yet it hadn't been long before the guilt itself had become a kind of prophylactic, what allowed him to think well enough of himself to fall back to the old complacence. He had buried the experience, that was all; there had been no conversion, no makeover. It would be the same with Amanda, he'd slide back and back, telling lies to himself until there was nothing left of what was true.

He found himself wishing that he had fallen that time on Fernandina, that he had let go.

So, how does it come to that, really? I mean, not that it hasn't crossed my mind once or twice.

Well, Peter, I suppose it's sort of like someone taking a pickax to your brain. They keep picking away like that, and you'd like them to stop.

It was only after Stephen had called and they had met to talk that the fog started to lift. It shouldn't have mattered so much that Stephen had slept with her, but it did: it wasn't just the sharing of the guilt but that things had gone, from what Alex could gather, more or less as they had with him. Too much booze; then regret.

It came out that Stephen had seen her just a matter of days before Katherine found her.

"We didn't sleep together then, if that's what you're thinking." But he'd grown hesitant. "There was something, though. She seemed different. Calmer, I guess."

He fell silent.

"Her therapist said that sometimes you can't stop these things," Alex said.

"Well, that lets her off the hook pretty nicely."

The blame seemed spread out so widely by then that it was growing thin.

"I have my son on the weekends," Stephen had said. It was the first time he had mentioned him to Alex. "Maybe we could catch a game or something."

There hadn't been much in the way of games—a couple of outings to the Forum, where Ariel had a habit of wandering off through the stands, and then one ill-fated excursion to a monster truck competition at Olympic Stadium, where he had recoiled in terror as soon as the first engine had revved and they'd had to make a quick exit, after forking out twelve bucks a head to get in. Thereafter they stuck to playgrounds and parks, mainly, and to libraries on the bitter days. It comforted Alex to be with Stephen: because he was not the sort to keep wringing his hands over things; because of Ariel. Corn-child that he was, Ariel was still a link for Alex, a kind of expiation. Alex didn't say anything about his own progeny—he considered it, then it seemed too much time had passed, then he was glad he had not. It was his secret. Instead he watched Ariel and thought, *Perhaps I could do this.*

Now, at a distance of months, Amanda's death already felt Peyton Place–ish and remote. So much had happened since then. There was only the chill at the back of his neck that never quite left him.

Another girl went by, in a school uniform, and Alex's eye followed her until he registered, with a start, that she was probably all of fifteen.

"It was pure revenge." They had got onto Stephen's ex-wife. "Fathers are nowhere these days as far as the courts are concerned. So he ends up spending half his time in daycare because she works all day."

Alex had formed a mental profile of his ex from the various snippets of information he'd gleaned about her over the months, as a no-nonsense *séparatiste* who dressed like someone from the Red Brigades and went around the city scrawling slogans on buildings and defacing English signs. Stephen himself was vague about her, referring to her almost exclusively as "Ariel's mother" and alluding darkly to her infiltrations into the corridors of power, from which Alex supposed she was part of some secret cell of intellectuals ready to seize the reins of state at the opportune moment. About their breakup Stephen was silent, except to bemoan his custody rights and his legal bills, though to judge from his recent philandering Alex suspected there had been Cause in there somewhere.

Stephen's spirits had fallen. He was staring at Ariel now not with a parent's vigilant eye but as if at something not quite in his reach.

"He'll probably get back at us by turning into a neo-Nazi or something, like Jiri's son. The joys of parenting."

Another boy had come up near where Ariel was still crouched, Haitian, from the look of him, peering into the water with feigned disregard

for Ariel and yet clearly edging himself into his territory. A moment later
the boy's father, raven black and as thin as a rake, came trailing up behind
him on the sidewalk.

They were both dressed in parkas despite the warmth, bundled up
like Michelin men.

"*Gee-mee! Pas près de l'eau!*"

It took Alex an instant to make out the name: *Jimmy.*

"*Gee-mee, viens!*"

The boy paid him no attention. He was smaller than Ariel but had the
sureness of someone older, standing fearless at the edge of the curb. He
picked up a rock and heaved it out into the lake in a long, high arc, then
picked up another.

"*Tu veux jouer?*"

Do you want to play? He had made his approach. Alex felt Stephen
tense beside him. Ariel, poking at something at the bottom of the lake
with a stick, didn't look up.

"*Hé, toi! Tu veux jouer?*"

The boy squatted onto his haunches next to Ariel. Stephen was on
high alert.

"Ariel," he called out, with forced calm.

It was too late. Ariel, looking transformed, suddenly turned on the
boy as he settled and shoved at him with all the force of his little limbs.
Alex was horrified. He pictured the boy cracking his skull on the curb or
falling into the lake and ending up waterlogged to death by that monstrous coat of his. Instead the boy, with lightning quick reflexes, shot a
foot back to steady himself and swung his fist against the side of Ariel's
head. He still had the rock in it.

Ariel was screaming.

"Shit!" Stephen said, already in motion. "Shit, shit, shit!"

He was next to Ariel in an instant. The blood was pouring out of
Ariel's head.

"I'm bleeding!" he screamed. "There's blood in my eye!"

Stephen's hands were already covered with it.

"It's okay, you'll be okay." He managed to pull a Kleenex out of his
pocket, but it was drenched in an instant. "Shit! I need some help here,
somebody!"

But there was only Alex and then the boy and his father. The boy, at the sight of the blood, had pulled back in a kind of wonderment at what he had wrought.

It took the father an instant to realize what had happened.

"*Qu'est-ce que t'as fait?*" With each instant he seemed to grow more amazed with the magnitude of his son's crime. "*Qu'est-ce que t'as fait? T'es fou? Qu'est-ce que t'as fait?*"

"*Il m'a poussér,*" the boy said defiantly.

"*T'es fou?*" The father picked a rock up and hurled it at the boy, who dodged it, retreating further. "*Je vais te tuer! Je vais te tuer, sauvage! Je vais t'abattre!*"

Ariel was still howling. The blood wouldn't stop.

"We have to get him to a hospital," Stephen said. He had the cuff of his blazer to Ariel's head. "Rip my shirt or something, we need some kind of a bandage."

Before Alex could comply, the boy's father had flung his coat down and stripped off his own shirt.

"Take it, mister! Please take it! Quickly!" Seeing Stephen hesitate, he ripped a strip from it and held it out. "Here, take it!"

Stephen took the proffered strip. He mopped the blood away so they could see the wound, a nice gash near the temple, but still the blood kept flowing.

Ariel looked truly panicked.

"You're hurting me, Daddy! You're hurting me!"

"Fucking hell." Stephen grew more assiduous. "I'm just cleaning it, that's all. It's going to be fine. You're going to be fine."

Jimmy's father had taken over now. With a few quick pulls he shredded the rest of his shirt into strips, wadding one of them to put against the wound.

"Mister, I can do it!" He looked positively Biafran stripped down to his undershirt like that, his arms thin as sticks. "Leave it! Let me, please!"

The blood was still coming. Stephen, with a helpless air, stood aside. In an instant the man had tied a strip around Ariel's head and pulled it tight, then another, which he pulled tighter still. Ariel, his wails dropped to sobs, didn't dare to protest.

The bleeding had stopped. Stephen checked the bandage with a kind of dazed relief. He looked like an ax murderer, completely spattered with blood.

He took Ariel up in his arms and Ariel clung to him like a tree frog.

"We have to get a cab or something."

"No, no!" the father said. "We take my car! It is very close!"

They hurried out to the parking lot beyond the end of the lake at a half run, the father pulling his parka back on as he went and Jimmy trailing uncertainly behind them.

"*Je vais te tuer, toi!*" his father called out. "*Tu vas voir! Je vais te casser la tête!*"

The man's car turned out to be an ancient blue Datsun that looked like it had done time in a demolition derby, battered on every side and leprous with rust. One of the back doors was held shut with a fraying bungee cord.

"We can just grab a cab," Stephen said uncertainly, though there was none in sight.

"No, no, impossible! I will take you!"

The man worked the bungee cord and Stephen crawled into the back with Ariel.

"*Jimmy, viens, idiot!*" The boy was still lagging behind. His father chased up to him and gave him a swift backhand across the head. "*Je vais te charcuter!*"

He dragged him to the car by the wrist.

"*Papa, ça me pince! Ça me pince!*"

"*Tais-toi, salopri!*" He gave him another backhand.

Alex had got into the back with Stephen and Ariel.

"We should go to Montreal General," Stephen said. "It's closest."

"*Oui, oui, monsieur, je le connais!* I know it!"

Ariel's bandage was holding. There was dried blood all along his cheek but nothing oozing from the pad against his gash. He'd grown quiet and still. Stephen hadn't wasted time looking for anything like seat belts and was still clutching him to him. It was the first time Alex could remember seeing Stephen hold his son.

"It's going to be fine. We'll be there in a minute. You're going to be fine."

Some question was on Ariel's lips, but he was holding it back.

"Will Momma be there?" he said finally.

Stephen tensed.

"I'll call her. As soon as we get there."

They had come out to Côte des Neiges. The man was driving at breakneck speed, weaving wildly through the traffic.

He had been talking the whole time.

"*Je suis très, très désolé, monsieur, je suis très désolé! Il est fou, là!* My son is just crazy!"

"It wasn't his fault," Stephen said. But then Alex could see him doing the math of what it might cost him with Ariel to take the blame. "It wasn't anyone's fault. They were just being boys."

"No, you are wrong, *monsieur*! You are wrong! It is not Port-au-Prince here, to break someone's head because of nothing! He must learn that!"

At the intersection with The Boulevard the man swerved into the oncoming lane to get around the cars stopped at the light, leaning on his horn. He eased the car into the intersection in lurching increments until the cross-traffic had screeched to a halt.

"They are crazy, these drivers! They don't give a chance!"

It was only a matter of minutes from here.

"Daddy, there's blood." A trickle of red was coming down from the bandage now. Ariel's eyes had taken on a panicked look again. "The blood's still coming out."

Stephen pressed on the pad.

"We're almost there."

"It hurts when you press, Dad," Ariel said, his voice heartbreakingly small.

"I know. I know."

Alex went past Emergency almost daily on his way to see Dr. Klein but had never once popped his head into the ward. It was a busy day. Two laden stretchers blocked the hall and an indiscriminate mass was clustered around the reception counter. Beyond it people milled listlessly in the dingy waiting room, a small TV in an upper corner tuned to Phil Donahue. Despite the unhappy crowd there was an air of calm to the place, a relief after the panic and blood.

Jimmy's father broke the calm in an instant.

"Please! Please! This boy is bleeding, we must pass!"

Somehow he managed to get them through to the triage nurse, a big-boned matron who stood stone-faced at her counter like Hecate at the gates of hell. She looked them over, taking in Ariel's bloodied bandage, Stephen's bloodied clothes, without batting an eye.

"He's cut his head," Stephen said, then seemed to feel foolish at stating the obvious.

The nurse peeled up an edge of the makeshift bandage to take a look. She seemed almost on the verge of sending them back to the end of the line.

"It hurts, Dad," Ariel whispered.

She glanced at her chart.

"Go on," she said finally. "Curtain Four."

Stephen was pulling money from his wallet, holding it out to Jimmy's father.

"For the shirt," he was saying. "*Pour la chemise.*"

"*Ah, vous parlez français! No, no, monsieur, vous êtes fou?* No money, *monsieur,* impossible!"

Stephen headed down the hall toward the cubicles, Ariel still clutched to him.

"I'll make it up to you. Leave your number with my friend."

"No, no, I wait to see if the boy is okay!"

They disappeared around a corner. As soon as they'd gone the man's energy seemed to drain from him.

"*C'est mal, ça,*" he muttered, pacing the waiting room. "*C'est mal.*"

Jimmy was already working the room, thumbing through magazines, watching the traffic coming in through the doors.

"How old is your son?" Alex said. "*Quel âge?*"

"Ah? Jimmy? He is six. A good boy, a good boy. But sometimes very wicked."

A gloom had come over Alex. It was all this fathering, maybe, the pitfalls of it. All that blood. Alex had never been much good in a crisis. His nieces and nephews were forever getting hurt in his care—once, one of Mimi's kids had got his foot jammed in a grate on the farm and had gone totally limp in Alex's arms when he'd come to free him. Alex was sure he was dead. He came to in a matter of seconds, of course—he had some sort of fainting disorder—but afterward Alex couldn't shake the feeling he'd had when the boy had gone limp, the immediate urge to get rid of him, to hide the evidence, to put this broken thing out of his sight.

The image kept playing in his head of Ariel grown suddenly vicious, of Jimmy swinging his rock. It was hard to believe those had been the same children as the tiny-voiced one in the car, as the one roaming the waiting room, now all innocence and wonder. They'd been nothing but animals then, bundles of instinct. The most dangerous creatures on earth, he'd read somewhere. He wondered how he could ever be trusted with that, how he'd ever be up to it.

A woman burst into the ward looking as if she had just stepped out of Holt Renfrew, high-heeled and silk-blazered and coiffed, her shoulders padded out like a linebacker's. She made straight for the triage nurse.

"*Je cherche mon fils*," she said loudly.

All eyes were on her now except the nurse's, who finished the form she was working on, checked her charts, took a sip from her coffee cup, without so much as looking up.

"His name?"

Alex waited for the inevitable language war, but the woman shot back in perfect Westmount English, "His name is Ariel. Ariel Macleod."

The nurse had already turned to the next person in line.

"Check Curtain Four," she said, to the air.

Alex couldn't believe it: it was Stephen's ex. A moment later Ariel's voice rose up from the cubicles, in a breathless tone Alex had never heard from him.

"*Maman! Maman! Je suis blessé!*"

"*Mon trésor, mon trésor, mon trésor!*" As if they had been separated for weeks by some holocaust. "*Filleul, qu'est-ce que c'est passé?*"

"*Je suis blessé, maman! L'enfant noir m'a agressé!*"

All of this could be heard clear as a bell in the waiting room. Even Phil Donahue seemed momentarily hushed by it. Alex wondered if it sounded as bad in the original as it did in translation: *The black boy attacked me.*

Jimmy's father seemed oblivious.

"It is the boy's mother, no?" He looked suddenly revived, as if the day had been saved. "She has come!"

The voices behind the curtain had been lowered. Alex edged toward the cubicles until he could make them out again, Stephen's guilty murmurs and then his ex's barely restrained barrages.

"I can't believe this. I can't believe it. And you wonder why I don't leave him with you."

It was not going well. To worsen matters, Stephen had had Ariel that day only on special dispensation. It had been bring-in-a-toy day at his kindergarten, and Ariel didn't like sharing his things.

There were a few muted exchanges Alex didn't catch, but then Stephen's voice rose up suddenly sharp.

"It was his own fault, for Christ's sake. He pushed the kid!"

There, Alex could almost hear it, the death knell of defeat.

A pause, before his ex staked her flag.

"Well, I'm glad you're taking your son's side, at least. It's so typical."

It was some time before Stephen emerged. The doctor had come; there'd be a few stitches, maybe a scar.

"You guys might as well go." He looked utterly worn out, deflated. "It'll be a while still."

Alex didn't like to leave him alone with that woman.

"I thought your ex was Quebecoise," he ventured timidly.

"On her mother's side. On her father's she's pure Westmount WASP."

Jimmy's father had fallen asleep in an armchair in the corner and Jimmy had wedged in next to him to watch the TV, an arm draped unthinkingly over his father's, as if the volley of threats in the park had never happened. They were both still in their parkas.

Jimmy gave his father a thump to wake him.

"*Ah! Je m'excuse, je m'excuse!*"

There was the whole ritual of leave-taking to be dealt with, more apologies and assurances, money proffered again and again refused. Alex followed Jimmy and his father out and was on the point of accepting a ride from them when he glanced at his watch and realized he would hardly get home before he'd have to come back for his appointment.

"I'll be all right," he said. "I have a friend here to visit."

The man scribbled his number in a matchbook.

"You will call, yes? You and your friend, we can have a drink. No children, ha!"

Alex looked at the matchbook: *Emil.* He could already feel the guilt settling on him of knowing he would never call.

"*Tu es chanceux, toi!*" the man said to his son, cuffing him playfully and pulling him to him as if, against the odds, he had managed to come out on top of some difficult contest. "You are lucky! Next time they throw you in prison!"

Then from across the parking lot came the clatter and roar of their car speeding off with the same urgency with which it had arrived.

$\mathcal{A}$lex hadn't lied about having a friend to visit. For almost three months now, Esther had been a more or less permanent resident at the General. She had come in during an exacerbation late in January and had emerged since then only for a disastrous week when she had smashed half the dishes in her apartment trying to look after herself and had fallen from her wheelchair getting into the bath and broken her wrist. From there, she had deteriorated rapidly. Alex could hardly bear to look at her now, so much a shadow of herself had she become, though his sessions with Dr. Klein had fated him to almost daily visits, something that had raised his already overinflated stock with her family and made him feel ever more the impostor.

He had nearly an hour to kill until his session and decided to squeeze in his visit before it. Esther's room, in E-Wing, was accessible only from the main lobby, four or five floors up from Emergency over on the mountain side of the building. He climbed around by the outdoor staircase so he could fit in a cigarette, though he was thoroughly winded well before he had reached the top. He had to quit, he told himself, for the hundred millionth time; though this time he was determined. Already he had managed to go most of the morning without one: he didn't like to smoke around Ariel, even if Stephen didn't seem much concerned. Children noticed these things, Alex thought. It was like litter, or suicide: set the example, and your children followed.

From the mountain, the hospital presented an entirely different face than the grim, institutional one it had from Côte des Neiges. It was several floors shorter, for one thing, more human-scaled, and instead of rising over a snarl of traffic it gave on to the wooded slopes of the mountain and the spa-like gardens of the Shriners. The lobby, however, had been under renovation for as long as Alex had been coming here, so that the pastoral calm of outside quickly gave way to the disorder of a work site, exposed duct work everywhere, dangling wires, unpatched drywall, an array of cement-caked scaffolding forever standing either half-built or half-dismantled like some giant child's Meccano set. It was a lot like entering his own apartment building, in fact, with about the same likelihood that the lights would be dead or one of the elevators would be out of service, as if here, too, the owners were trying to wear down the residents until they fled the place and the rents could be jacked up. Meanwhile the lobby itself was slowly taking on exactly the urban chic of a condo conversion, the front entrance opening out to a soaring expanse of stained glass and a trendy-looking coffee bar going up smack dab in the center of the space complete with marble counters and hi-tech trim.

Esther was on the top floor, in chronic care. Up here the *ancien régime* still reigned, as if nothing had changed since the fifties, the same floors in checkerboard cream and brown linoleum, the same pastel green walls, the trolleys stacked with chrome bedpans and with packets of gauze and surgical gloves. There were the bleachy linen closets, the funny hospital hush, the ever-present medicinal smell—what was it? antibiotics? some kind of cleanser?—that lay over everything and that immediately conjured up every hospital visit he'd ever made as a kid to their endless web of wounded or dying relations. It ought to have been off-putting, all of this, but it wasn't. Instead it had the feel of an old-style institutionalism, familiar and instinctively comforting, almost Soviet in its air of worn-but-serviceable paternalism. What his visits most reminded him of were the hours of reverie he used to spend in church as a kid—things didn't necessarily get better in these sorts of places, but at least they seemed put off for a while.

Esther was alone. Her father had paid to have her moved to a private room, which was probably costing him a small fortune, though she didn't seem in much of a position to enjoy the luxury of it, asleep most of the day or lost in a kind of lethargy that might have been the effect of whatever drugs they were giving her or just her body's slow shutting down. It had been several weeks now since she'd been able to manage anything like a conversation. Initially this had been because of some medical complication that had reduced her to just a hoarse sort of aspirating, but now she didn't even make the effort much. Writing was out of the question—a lot of her muscles had seized, and her hands had frozen into claws that made holding things nearly impossible. About the only way in or out now was through her eyes, though these so often had a trapped look that Alex didn't like to dwell on them.

Her bed was surrounded by appliances of various sorts. The main one, oddly, which her father had had to buy, since the hospital didn't stock it, was a device whose stubborn, phlegmatic purpose was to keep her body temperature constant. Its technology was of the most basic sort: there was a big monitor at the foot of the bed, and then a water-filled pad that stretched out over her mattress and heated or cooled as her temperature fluctuated. Esther had complained of it: it was like lying in her pee, she'd said once, then her laugh.

Esther was asleep. The curtains at her window were drawn, and the room was dim with the crepuscular graininess of filtered daylight. For a long time Alex just sat there watching her, the heave of her chest as she breathed, the digital flicker of her monitor as her temperature rose a tenth, then fell again. Just a single sheet covered her, the hieroglyph of her body clearly outlined in it, legs splayed but relatively straightened, thanks to the cuts they'd made behind her knees after her muscles had started to lock. She was wasted almost to nothing now. Her cheeks were sunken, all the blush on them gone; her hair had thinned to the wispy sparseness of an old woman's. How many times he had thought of this body since that night she'd come on to him, how many shades of feeling it had brought up in him. So much strangeness seemed invested in it even now, that it should house this person and *be* her and also turn on her like something alien. In Alex's mind Esther had become utterly inseparable from her body, so much did it define her and his relationship with her, and yet always he felt this as a betrayal, a failure to see past her surface and know her in some more essential, uncorrupted fullness.

No one had ever quite put it in these terms, but they were on a death watch now. The smallest infection, a virus, a cold, and she could turn. Each time he stepped into her room he felt a chill, not knowing what killer might cling to him.

"It's great that you come," Lenny said, his constant refrain. "Her mind's still working, I know that. I know the real Esther is still in there."

It had all happened so quickly. Alex knew that people lived with MS for years, into old age even, half of them probably total defeatists, with none of Esther's determination and spunk. And yet the illness had ridden roughshod over her as if her will had counted for nothing.

When she'd gone back into hospital after her terrible week home she had told him she wanted to die.

"It's like the old Esther's gone," she said, holding back tears, and he could almost see it before his eyes, the Esther who was bent on fighting, who would walk again, who would never give in, taking flight. "Is that awful, to want to die? Am I awful?"

"It's not awful." She had reached the moment he'd dreaded, when there was nothing before her but the truth. "It's hard right now, that's all. In a week you'll feel differently."

She didn't let on that she didn't believe him. It occurred to him that she might actually be asking something of him, to help her along when the moment came, to pull the plug, but he wouldn't get into that.

"Would you hold my hand?" she'd said. "Would that be all right?"

And he had sat there, holding her hand in both of his until she passed into sleep. It had still been supple then, warm and soft and alive; he could feel it even now, sitting next to her while she slept again. *Her life in his hands.*

They had reached the moment, surely, when plugs should be pulled, if one had a mind to. He watched the monitor flicker, down a tenth, up again, but couldn't believe that turning it off would make much of a difference, except in some long, drawn-out way. It remained to the Great Bastard in the sky to shut the machines down, if he had the heart to.

Back when she was still talking, she'd told him a dream she'd had.

"I dreamed I went to heaven," she'd said, "and everybody liked me."

Alex's copy of *Les Misérables* was still sitting on Esther's bedside table. He had taken to reading to her from it during his visits, choosing it because it was long and because he remembered the readings his Grade 8 teacher, Mrs. Jackson, had done from it, making them lay their heads on their desks like Grade 1's and teasing out the last languid hour of the afternoon with it. "This is so great of you," Esther kept saying, in her hoarse whisper, "it's so great," though the opening chapters were so leisurely and long-winded that Alex was afraid this would just turn into another of his failed enthusiasms. But then they came at last to Jean Valjean, and there was no turning back.

The story seemed to bring out the same wonder in Esther at the world's outrageousness as it had in Alex back in Grade 8.

"Was it really like that back then? Just for stealing a loaf of bread? We're so lucky to live when we do."

For a few weeks the readings became the highlight of Alex's day. He would sit there at Esther's bedside with the guilty afternoon light slanting in through the window, the light of sick days and special reprieves, and be back again with his head on his desk in Mrs. Jackson's classroom. The story drew him on like a drug. It was the worst sort of philistinism in his circles to care about something as barbarous as plot, yet for the first time in months or even years Alex felt himself taken over again by a book. The story was as pumped up as an opera, the penitent prostitute, the innocent child, the good-hearted criminal who couldn't escape his past, and yet it had such a scope to it, was so full of twists and new beginnings, that it seemed to carry a kind of Scheherazadian hopefulness.

He looked over once, and Esther was crying.

"What is it?"

"I don't know. I don't know." Her voice was the barest rustling by then. "It's just the story. It's so beautiful. It's sad, but it's beautiful."

Occasionally Esther's sister would come, or her mother or Molly, and they would sit and listen with her until the window had grown dark and there was only the glow of the bedside lamp. Alex would have the feeling he had in airplanes sometimes, of not wanting to land. What was it, this power stories had, that moved Esther to tears, that he had forgotten? They might have been cave dwellers then, gathering around the fire. *Come, I will tell you things, I will hold back the dark.*

Then suddenly it was over. Esther got a cold, from him, maybe, and was put on a new round of drugs that drained the life from her. She never really recovered after that. He kept doing his readings for a while, but she'd fall asleep in a matter of minutes or would seem to grow irritable in a way that was completely unlike her, wincing at the light or shrugging away from him suddenly as if something unpleasant had touched her. For a couple of weeks now, he hadn't read to her at all—they'd managed to get to the midpoint, as far as Little Gavroche, thanks to a few judicious excisions, but Alex hadn't the heart to go on again. Maybe it was the same with her as it was with people in comas; that you ought to keep speaking to them in some normal way, but all he could think of was this new wincing impatience in her, this twisting from him as if to say, *Can't you see that I'm dying?* So he sat silent, mostly. If she was awake he would take her claw hand and mumble awkward niceties, trying to hold her eyes, to make a connection there, which happened sometimes, for seconds or minutes, longer than he could bear, really, and sometimes not. That was worse: she would look at him, and see him, and turn away. Not as if she hadn't recognized him, but as if she couldn't be bothered. *Let me be. Let me sleep.* It surprised him how much this cut him—he was her hero, her champion, her star. He could do no wrong. She was utterly mistaken in him, of course; God knew, he had tried to make her see that. Yet it seemed that if he lost her good opinion of him, if it was not something unshakable and eternal in her, he would somehow lose the possibility of ever becoming that better person.

Esther's sister Rachel appeared at the door.

"Oh! Alex." She looked flustered. Seeing that Esther was asleep, she dropped her voice to a whisper. "You're not usually here now."

"I can leave if you want. I mean, I have an appointment to go to."

He regretted at once having mentioned the appointment.

"No, no. She wouldn't want you to leave. I was going to wash her, but she's asleep. I'll just go to the lobby and do my homework for a while."

She was gone before he could stop her. It seemed odd at first, but then it dawned on him that they actually kept track somehow of his comings and goings, that all this time they'd been working around him, giving him his place. Giving Esther her time with him.

There was another sister whom Alex hadn't known about. Maybe Esther had mentioned her in the beginning, back when a lot had got past him, but afterward, when he'd become the family mascot, he would surely have noticed if she had come up. Then one night Lenny had invited him back to the house from the hospital. It was the first time he had been there. He had always thought of Côte St. Luc as a distant suburb, but it was tucked just north of NDG, not fifteen minutes from downtown. They passed under a railway bridge into a neighborhood of modest bungalows faced with siding or brick.

"We moved here from Park Extension," Lenny said. "I never liked it here because of the tracks. All those trains passing at night."

The tracks ran right behind the house, not twenty yards from the back fence. Alex could see them from the window of Esther's old room. Esther had mentioned them too, but differently: she had liked the trains, the sound of them passing, going somewhere. It was what she had wanted, to go.

The tracks bounded the whole of the neighborhood, no way in or out without crossing them.

"It just always seemed spooky or something," Lenny said. "Closed in."

Esther's room was used by Rachel now. The walls held a couple of laminated posters, a Reubens and a Monet, but were otherwise bare.

"It hasn't changed much, if you can believe it," Lenny said. "Those were her posters, from when she went to New York once in high school."

The house was a modest split-level, with the bedrooms upstairs and then a living and dining room covered in hourglass wallpaper and below that a den that their father had built, with a fireplace and birch paneling. Alex could have been in one of his cousin's homes in the subdivisions around Leamington, the same heavy furnishings, the china cabinet full of mementos and the good dishes, the ceramic tile in the kitchen and hall.

It was late, past nine, though Esther's father had stayed behind with Esther.

"You haven't eaten yet?" the mother said, like a reprimand.

"No, not really. No."

"Then you'll eat with us."

There was a family portrait over the dining table, everyone in overtight seventies dress, and he noticed the extra sibling. He was afraid to ask, in case some other tragedy lurked.

"It's Sarah," Lenny said. "You wouldn't have met her. She lives in Israel."

The mention of her seemed to change the room's mood.

"Does she ever come home?"

"We don't see her so much," their mother said heavily. "She has her life there."

And the subject seemed closed.

In the car, driving Alex home, Lenny said, "Don't mind Mom. She's a little funny about Sarah. She feels like she deserted us."

"Didn't they get along?"

"It was more Esther, really, to tell you the truth. I guess Sarah always felt she was in her shadow or something, even though she was a bit older. Esther left home, so she had to stay. Esther dropped out of school, so she had to finish. Then one day she just left, right after Esther got sick. She became a citizen over there, she did her army service, she joined a kibbutz, the whole experience. It's like she turned into Esther. I've been to see her and she seems pretty happy, really. She's even got a kid, a little boy. But the whole thing drives my mother nuts. She refuses to go over there."

"Does she know how sick Esther is?"

"More or less." He was silent a moment. "Families, eh? What a nightmare."

He thought of Sarah as a sort of mirror planet whose orbit had kept her always hidden. Behind Esther there was this alternate in his mind now, this different version, someone she might have been, someone more like himself, in fact. He wondered if Sarah would come, how the boy figured in, if the father was still in the picture. In the family portrait, Sarah was dark and wary-eyed and lean.

So tell me, Alex, how does a good Roman Catholic boy end up living on a kibbutz in the West Bank, of all places?

Up a tenth, down again. Esther stirred and turned in his direction, her eyes drifting open and then closed again. It was hard to know anymore how well she saw things. Sometimes her vision blacked out or grew hopelessly blurred, depending on what meteor storm happened to be raging against her optic nerve.

She seemed to mouth something in her sleep, but whatever it was was lost.

"Time to turn." One of the nurses had come in, the stocky one, who had all the finesse of a bouncer at the bad end of St. Catherine. "We don't want those bed sores festering."

She had already muscled past Alex.

"She's asleep. I think her sister's coming to wash her."

The woman seemed to take this as license for special aggression, grabbing Esther by an arm and a leg to pull her toward her and then flipping her onto her belly like a slab of meat. Esther grumbled and twitched in her sleep, hunching away from her.

The nurse straightened the sheet with a sharp tug.

"Her sister will have to change the dressings. I hope she knows that."

There didn't seem much hope of a connection today. Esther had curled up under her sheet like a slug, shrugging the world off. *Let me be.* He wished Rachel would come. He wished Esther's sister Sarah would. Sarah, who had been the one to stay home, doing her math, while Esther had gone out with her friends to the Orange Julep. Who had saved her money. Who resented how Esther said out loud the things she only thought.

Now Esther was paying for it.

"There were so many places I wanted to visit," she'd told him. Apart from New York, the only big trip of her youth had been to Spain with a friend when she was twenty. "So many places."

Blip. Blip. For an instant the monitor dipped an entire degree, then righted itself.

She wouldn't have been Sarah, not really, or at least not the phantom adventurer Sarah he had imagined. In Spain, she had told him, she had stayed in the nicest hotels, had gone shopping, had met Spanish boys in the tapas bars. Not for her the rough-and-tumble of backpacks and roadsides, of crowded local buses leading off to mud villages. She had gone on a holiday, that was all. It had taken her two years at Jean Junction to save for the trip. In Montreal she had put in her hours at the shop, had spent the nights on Crescent Street, had dated this one or that. No plans. She might have gone on like this, become a manager, perhaps, married a Jewish boy and moved back to Côte St. Luc. Might have been unremarkable. Maybe it was just a way of wringing hope from despair to think this way, that it was her illness that had marked her, that had made her stand out, as if it were a gift.

For Alex's money, she would have been better off marrying the Jewish boy.

There was a sound at the door. He turned, expecting Rachel, but instead felt a flash of disorientation like a whack to the head.

"Alex. It's you."

It was María.

Alex hadn't exchanged more than half a dozen words with María since their ill-fated dinner at his apartment. He had seen her often enough, across crowded rooms or through the window of the café where she worked on St. Lawrence; he had even got her on the phone once or twice when he was calling Miguel, back when they were still living together. But since the dinner it had seemed understood that there wasn't much point, really, in their continuing to have anything to do with each other. For some stupid reason he had kept following Miguel around to Salvadoran fund-raisers and solidarity nights, maybe to prove to María that his intentions had been honorable, but if he actually saw her at any of these he would just smile stiffly from across the room or turn his back to her, pretending to interest himself in Miguel's inscrutable friends.

At the sight of her in Esther's doorway he rose up so abruptly he practically knocked his chair over.

"María!"

"So you are here," she said, without batting an eye, as if running into someone expected but disappointing.

It was a moment before Alex was able to gather his faculties. She must be visiting a friend, he thought, a sweatshop colleague who'd lost a finger to some machine or maybe a wounded guerilla who'd been medevacked here by supporters of the cause.

"Are you looking for someone?"

"Not looking, no." She was dressed in tight black pants that held her backside like a taunt. "I am come to see Esther."

"You mean—Esther? This Esther?"

"You can remember, no? It was in your house that I met her."

Of course he fucking remembered. The image was etched in his mind like a woodcut, of the strange triumvirate she and Amanda and Esther had formed in his living room. But he had had no idea they had ever set eyes on each other again.

"It's just—she's sleeping," he stammered.

"I will sit with her. You don't mind?"

Without waiting for anything like permission, she took the chair he had vacated and started pulling things from her purse, a Bible, then a rosary, setting them in her lap like an old village woman come to say her novenas.

All this had the air of established routine.

"Have you been coming here? Have you come before?"

María put a finger to her lips.

"Shh. She's sleeping."

He was stuck standing there at the foot of the bed while María fingered her beads and mumbled her prayers. It was too strange, all of this, that she was here at all, that she was whispering her Jesus prayers over this Jew as if in some death-bed conversion. He hoped Rachel didn't walk in. It was hard to believe he had ever pursued this woman—she seemed so alien all of a sudden, from a different century.

"You must give this to her from me," she said when she'd done, setting her rosary on the bedside table. "To remember me."

It took him an instant to process this.

"Are you going somewhere?"

She put a finger to her lips again.

"Come. We will take a coffee."

He had thought of María differently since their dinner. Less charitably, mainly—it might have been simply her dismissal of him or the dark screen Amanda's death had placed in front of everything, but more and more he'd felt that she and her people were just spinning their wheels, that even those freedom fighters down in Chalatenango or wherever, the men he didn't measure up to, were just boys with big toys. That might have been the real reason he kept going to those fundraisers, merely to feed his own cynicism, to get some sort of bitter revenge. María, he began to notice, now that the fog of infatuation had lifted, wasn't quite so above it all as he'd first imagined—she had her enemies, her detractors, her cliques. He could see the battle lines now at these events, the slow drifting to one side of the room or the other, the huddled groups, the burst of laughter in a corner at which a head would turn in the corner opposite. The big earthquake in San Salvador in the fall had brought people together, but after a few weeks of stoic solidarity all the old controversies had surfaced again.

There was a big split between those who favored negotiation and those who opposed it. María, Alex knew, he had his informants now, was a negotiationist, which put her at odds with a lot of the men, so that almost by default it was to the men's side of the room that Alex gravitated, wanting María to see him there amongst the enemy yet feeling like a fraud. He would sit listening for the umpteenth time as the world was divided neatly into peasants and imperialists, the vocabulary so familiar by now he didn't need a translation, and the whole while he'd be hearing a little voice at the back of his head saying, *Bollocks.* It was the voice of Desmond: more and more now, in fact, Alex found himself infected by these Desmond-like epithets. *Evolution, not revolution. Down with the dialectic. Make the genes pay.*

An FMLN organizer who was based in Copenhagen came through in the winter and gave a talk at a Guanarock night. He spoke forcefully and with an easy fluency, but had the stylish, well-fed look of someone who had long been out of the trenches, wearing his hair in a ponytail like the Latino street musicians you saw on Prince Arthur.

Afterward he picked Alex out of the crowd and made him his special friend.

"*Gringo!* So how do you like our Salvadoran rock?"

He plied Alex with beers at the bar, talking the movement up. Fernando, he went by. No surname, as if to make clear he was undercover.

"You know, it's not just about some bit of land you give to people to shut them up. People say negotiation, but what does it mean? You have to change the way people think. We go into towns, the first thing we do is education."

It made Alex uncomfortable to be singled out like that. He asked about Copenhagen, trying to steer the conversation to more neutral ground, but Fernando wasn't interested.

"You know where most of our money comes from? From Americans. Millions of dollars they send us, just people like you, and then their government talks about Russia. The Russians give us nothing. Sometimes

I have to carry it in a big suitcase like that, five, ten million at once. It's a joke, isn't it? The right hand doesn't know about the left one. Then we can't even say anything, or Reagan will stop it. Anyhow it's better for us—the Americans are the enemy. No enemy, no war."

At the end of the night Fernando took a group of them to an Italian restaurant nearby, a big barn of a place decked out with fake grapevines and old wine presses. An accordion player went around doing old standards like "Santa Lucia" at people's tables, though when he came to theirs, Fernando, busy holding court, waved him off. There wasn't a single woman in the group. Alex was glad that Miguel had stuck with him, shadowing him like a bodyguard the whole time he'd been with Fernando.

"So I leave them at the airport in West Berlin and send them off to Managua," Fernando was saying, telling how he'd got a group of European journalists into one of the guerilla camps, "but who's there to meet them in Managua when they get to their hotel? I am. After that I make the arrangements to go into El Salvador and I put them on the plane. *Adiós*, it's too dangerous for me, I say, I'm staying behind. Then they get to the camp, and who's the first person to see them? It's me. You should have seen their faces, like it was magic. Bombs falling everywhere, borders closed, soldiers stopping every fucking peasant, and I move around like it's nothing. We wanted them to see that, you know, that we could go where we wanted. That we were in control."

There was an appreciative silence.

"So how did you do it?" Alex said, not sure if he was needling him or just playing the straight man. "How did you get into the country?"

Fernando took a sip of his wine.

"That, my friend," he said predictably, with a satisfied grin, "I cannot tell you." And he got his laugh.

Fernando picked up the check, peeling a wad of bills from his wallet. There had been several courses, half a dozen bottles of wine—it all must have run to a good three or four hundred dollars, probably more than the night's fund-raiser had taken in.

"*Muchas gracias*," some of the men mumbled.

It was only when they were on the sidewalk that Fernando finally asked Miguel who he was, as if he were merely some servant who'd been attending to them.

His face darkened at Miguel's response.

"*El hermano de María?*"

Miguel didn't flinch.

"*Sí,*" he said. "*Es mi hermana.*"

All Fernando's expansiveness seemed to leave him. At the curb, climbing into the cab he'd hailed, he said to Alex, his voice low, "That boy is your friend?"

"Yes," Alex said, though it might have been the first time he had ever admitted this.

"Be careful, *gringo.* You don't understand our politics. Things are not black and white the way you think."

All this had been months ago, but that parting shot still rankled with Alex. *Asshole* was what he'd thought at the time, puffed-up power monger, using the war to stroke his own ego, and yet he hadn't been able to put the exchange from his mind. For one thing, it had seemed to justify all his unease over Miguel, whom even María had abandoned by then to move in with a fellow Salvadoreña. What kept coming back to him, though, was how Miguel had looked the man straight in the eye as if he saw right through him. *She is my sister,* he'd said simply. There had been something so undiluted in that, something that stood outside all the politicking.

He and María were waiting for the elevator. María was a little ahead of him and he had to stop himself from staring down at her nether parts.

"So you kept seeing her?" he said.

"Of course."

"She never mentioned it."

"You know all her friends?"

"Pretty much, yes," he said tersely. "Or so I thought."

The elevator doors finally opened in front of them.

"Now you see she has secrets," María said. "Like everyone."

They were packed into the elevator like sardines by the time they got to the lobby. María, inevitably, had drifted away from him and he had got trapped behind an old geezer trailing his IV on a stand, a flash of pasty inner thigh showing through the slit in his hospital gown. Probably off to have a cigarette, Alex thought.

He glanced at his watch: only ten minutes before his session.

"We must be quick," María said. "I haven't so much time."

They grabbed a coffee at the dingy snack shop still operating down the hall. When they were seated María said, without preliminaries, "In three days I will return to El Salvador."

Alex was floored. Miguel had said nothing of this. She was landed here now, her claim had gone through; she had her café job, her work at the sweatshop.

"Is that wise? Is it safe?"

She shrugged.

"Safe, no. But that is my country. Now they talk peace, the Americans make them talk, so there's a chance."

"You trust the Americans?"

"It's not a question to trust. They do what's the best for them. Maybe peace is the best."

They were still fishing bodies out of the garbage dumps in San Salvador, women who'd been impaled on broomsticks, men who'd been eviscerated or cut in half. He didn't know what María had done, she had never talked of it except in the vaguest terms, but he knew how little it took.

"Look, it's none of my business," he started. "I don't know, it seems stupid to me. It seems pigheaded."

Already he had lost his cool. She hadn't the right to saddle him with the thought of a broomstick up her, of her tossed out like nothing. It seemed to make a mockery of him, of his little life. It made a mockery of everything. People went along, they went to work, they did their groceries, they watched TV, and in a flash it was all beside the point.

"Maybe so," María said. "Maybe stupid. But there's no choice for me, to stay here."

She had a look on her that he'd never seen, that might have been fear.

"What was it you did? At least tell me that."

"It's not what you do. It's what they think."

It was all just evasion, this sort of sermonizing, though it had taken him a while to see that. Instead of pushing her, he waited.

"There was a boy who was killed," she said finally. "How do you say it. My fiancé. He was working with them in the city, with the guerillas, getting the guns. There were many like that. Secret people. They did the normal things in the day and then at night they helped the guerillas."

It had cost her an effort to get it out. In a minute she'd said more to him that was real than in all the months they'd spent together.

"So the army found out," he said carefully. "The death squads."

"Yes, I suppose."

"And you thought they'd come after you."

She played with her cup.

"There was a letter," she said. "It told me to go or to die. So I'm here."

That was it, then. It wasn't some vague threat, the whole union business she'd tried to put him off with. She was a target.

"Then how can you go back? It's just crazy."

"Things have changed now. It's not so dangerous."

"How can you be sure?"

"There are ways to be sure."

Her moment of candor had passed.

"There are things you don't know," she said finally. "It's not so simple, our politics."

The same old line.

"I'm not an idiot."

But the subject was closed. María stared down at the table.

"You will look after my brother, I think."

He had the sense, from the shift in her tone, that this was where she'd been headed all along, was what she had traded for. *Great,* he thought. Now he'd be truly saddled with Miguel. *Es mi hermano.*

"He's a big boy. He can look after himself."

María ignored this.

"He's like you," she said.

He wasn't sure if this was another of her Delphic pronouncements.

"You mean he likes me."

"Yes. Also that."

Fuck it, he thought. All along he had imagined that Miguel was the one who had been wooing him for María's sake when it had been the other way around. He felt past caring. If he had never met María, none of this would ever have touched him. All those bodies piling up down there, how much difference would another one make?

María glanced at her watch.

"Alex," she said, "you will tell Esther? You'll give her the rosary?"

"Of course I will."

Her voice had gone uncharacteristically tentative.

"You mustn't think," she began. "You mustn't blame her. I was the one to make the secret about us. To ask her not to say."

It was what he'd suspected. To avoid him. To keep clear of his stinky gringo flesh.

"Thanks for saying so, at least."

"It wasn't for you. Not because of our problem. It was only to be with her. I can't say so well in English what I mean. To be with someone like this. Someone with God, maybe to say, but you don't believe it."

He couldn't quite bring himself to admit to her that he understood. He didn't know what she'd taken from Esther, what wisdom or solace, but he could see at once that he would only have been an impediment.

"You will give her the rosary?" she said again.

It was her way of letting Esther know she was off the hook, he saw now, by giving him this commission.

"Yes, of course."

She had stood. He imagined her as if she were just some new refugee girl walking into his class at St. Bart's for the first time, dark-skinned and smallish, after all, with callused fingers and a bit of down on her upper lip. He had the sense he had seen her only in bits and pieces until then, never whole, as somehow more and less than she was.

"What will you do there, in El Salvador?"

"I am a teacher. I will teach."

He couldn't muster the courage to hug her and only kissed her cheeks, which felt hopelessly inadequate.

"I think you are a good man, Mr. Alex," she said. "You don't believe it, but it's so."

The benediction took away some of the sting of the many months he had felt like such a non-entity in her eyes. It was what he would have to settle for. *Good. Nice.* It was maybe what he wanted.

He was late for his session now, but had been holding his pee ever since the emergency room and felt ready to burst. He slipped into the bathroom off the lobby, but before he could get a stream going a grizzled lug with liver-colored tattoos running all along his arms stepped up to the urinal next to him. *Fuck.* It was hopeless now; he couldn't pee in company. One of the workers from the lobby, it looked like, draining off the coffee they spent the day drinking instead of working, the piss kept cascading out of him like Montmorency Falls.

Alex flushed to cover his failure. It was pathetic, this little problem of his. He couldn't help seeing it as some sort of manhood issue, like impotence or premature ejaculation. Back in the animal days of staking territory he would have been doomed, he and his kids would have starved, because he couldn't get up the piddle to claim his patch.

He washed his hands to complete the charade. On the nameplate on the hand dryer, someone had gone to great trouble to scratch out "Canada" on the company address. Probably Mr. Tattoo. By now Alex's mood had soured completely: his bladder ached; his head had started to throb from his having missed lunch. In the lobby two workers were wheeling a cart laden with construction waste toward the service elevator, moving along at a snail's pace, blocking everyone's path, and Alex thought, *Fucking Quebecois*, though they could just as easily have been Poles or Slavs or Russian Jews, who knew in this bloody waste-bin country. *Just stay home*, he thought.

As he passed the cart it suddenly veered in front of him and a jutting two-by-four jabbed his shoulder.

"*Pardon, monsieur*," one of workers mumbled, deadpan.

Alex had an urge to grab the two-by-four and bean the two of them with it.

"Next time watch where you're going."

"Eh, buddy," the other one said. "Fuck you."

– 4 –

Up in the psych ward he headed straight for the bathroom, which was mercifully empty. The pee burned as it came out from being held in so long. At the mirrors he pulled his shirt down over his shoulder and saw the patch of blue that had started to spread under his collarbone. *Assholes.* The image played in his mind again of him busting the guys' heads with a two-by-four. A couple of good wallops was all he wanted, the satisfying thunk of wood against bone.

It was in this state of bloodlust that he arrived at Dr. Klein's door. Recently the doctor's pod-person neutrality at his late arrivals had started to give way to little throat clearings and grimaces that looked suspiciously like impatience. But today he actually stood, gangly and stooped, and held the door for Alex like a young loan officer hopeful of landing a client.

He'd had a haircut, it looked like, and got a new suit, not his usual sheeny gabardine but a well-cut Sunday suit in dark wool.

"Sorry I'm late. One of the workers in the lobby bashed into me with a two-by-four."

He had gotten increasingly better over time at stretching the truth. He had been sobered, briefly, by what Amanda's therapist had said about lying, but then slowly had begun to take it as a kind of license. Everyone lied in therapy, it turned out.

"You're all right?" the doctor said, with such naked concern that Alex felt ashamed.

"It's fine. Just my shoulder."

Alex took off his shoes and lay down on the couch, which, as always, had the effect of instantly calming him. He felt the admonition go through him, also as always, that he should talk about something real for once. They had gotten a good couple of weeks out of Amanda's suicide, once he'd finally admitted to it, though even that had begun to seem merely fodder after a while. Maybe what he ought to talk about was his urinary complex, there was something real. Or those two dickheads in the lobby, and the fantasies of psychotic violence he spun with surprising frequency in the course of any given day.

"I think we were talking about your recurring dream," the doctor said. "About going back to high school."

Fucking dream work. Evasion, evasion. He started churning things out, the connections, the predictable insights—if dreams were so smart, he wondered, then why were they so obvious?—but the whole time his thoughts were elsewhere. His head was still jangling from his talk with María, which had left him with a sense of burgeoning untidiness. He could feel the clutter stretching out around him, growing more and more unruly. These sessions were merely part of the problem now, spewing psychic debris that was just left to molder in their wake. In any event, he'd be ending them soon. Once the loose ends were tied, his apartment, his grants, the okay from Jiri—he didn't let himself think of Esther, though she was the crux of it—he'd be gone. He relished the thought of making the announcement to Dr. Klein. *I have a son, you see.* Trump that.

So on the one side, there's your K. novel, if I can even call it a novel, but that's another story, and I don't mind admitting I was ready to slit my wrists when I finished reading the thing. Not exactly big on hope. But then look at your life. It's just one damned thing after another—the Galápagos, Liz, Amanda, then this amazing woman who's a novel in herself but who's dying in front of your eyes and this whole other woman who suddenly picks up and heads home though she's got a death warrant on her. And yet at the end of it: hope. This little child. This gift. It's a bit ironic, isn't it?

(Sheepish) Well, Peter, I guess just because I don't believe in hope doesn't mean it doesn't exist.

He had fallen silent.

"You haven't mentioned Liz," Dr. Klein said. "I think you met her in high school."

Liz. He had started with her and seemed set to end with her. Try as he might to get past their relationship, it kept coming back to torment him.

Klein had stuck to it with the obstinacy of a not-very-bright dog to his bone, until Alex had actually called her to arrange a meeting, as he had long promised himself to do, in the hope of clearing her from his mind.

Liz had immediately assumed her most bitter, take-no-prisoners tone, though he couldn't tell if this was her official stance with him now or just an opening gambit.

"What is it you want, exactly?"

"I dunno. Just to talk."

He had known what he'd wanted, of course: exoneration, unconditional pardon, the record expunged, though he would settle for a grudging truce. Anything to escape this sense of an accuser out there on the loose, holding intact this demon version of him.

When they met, though, at a café on Duluth, she looked merely uncertain and on edge. She was waiting for him at a little table by the window, a bottle of Perrier in front of her. The same awkwardness seemed to go through them both as he came up.

Neither of them made any move toward actual physical contact.

"So," Liz said.

He had a little speech he'd put together that consisted mainly of various levels of apology. He was sorry for the abortion; he was sorry he hadn't supported her more when they'd moved here; he was sorry for how things had ended. There were certain words he planned to avoid, certain specifics, but if it came to it he was ready to be sorry for other things as well. The speech was structured like a kind of plot diagram: rising action, conflict, awful climax. The denouement, he hoped, would be them sitting here saddened but reconciled in this café on Duluth, as in the last scene of a Woody Allen film. This was when he would tell her about Ingrid. He would tell her about his son.

It took a matter of seconds for the whole scheme to crumble.

"Look, this is stupid," Liz said. "We can't go around pretending to hate each other for the rest of our lives."

He latched onto the word like a drowning man: pretending.

"No," he said, lowering his gaze as if he were the one who was mainly at fault in this.

"We were both pretty messed up. I can hardly even bring myself to think about it. I don't know—the two of us. Maybe we're just too much alike. Maybe we know each other too well."

All of this was so far from what he'd expected that he felt he could only follow her lead until he'd figured out where exactly they were headed.

"I always thought that," he said carefully.

"It's not as if either of us is especially well adjusted. I suppose that was what I liked about you."

It stunned him that she could still talk about that, about liking him.

"I guess I made a lot of mistakes."

"Yeah, well. We both did."

She was being so reasonable, so measured. It was almost as if they were talking about some other breakup, a normal one. Maybe it *had* been normal.

"So. That was all I wanted to say." The initiative had gone over to her entirely by now. "I just didn't want to have to go around feeling all the time like there was this *thing* between us."

That was it, then. No specifics, no who-did-what, no Jesuitical haggling over the fine points of blame. She was actually letting him off the hook, more or less as he'd hoped. What he couldn't figure was why he felt so strangely bereft, as if he'd been robbed somehow of his fair portion.

"Look, Liz," he started, not even sure what he was about to say, which almost certainly meant he was about to put his foot in it. He was saved by the waitress, who chose this moment to grace them with her presence.

Alex, in his bad French, ordered a cappuccino, the first thing he could think of. The waitress gave him a withering smile.

"*Et pour madame?*"

"I'm fine, thanks."

By then, whatever urge it was that had risen up in him, the need to make a concession, the need *to know,* had passed. He couldn't bring himself to go back there now, into that swamp.

"I should tell you I'm moving back to Toronto," Liz said, looking away as if she had said something awkward.

"Oh." It was what he had always figured, that she would go. He might have felt relieved at this except for the shadow that had seemed to cross her, that had seemed to put their conversation in a different light. What he had understood was this: she was the one who didn't want to know. "I guess it never worked out for you here."

"I don't like it here, to tell you the truth. I feel like a foreigner or something."

It was true: even sitting in this café she looked out of place. Something, some quality in her, didn't fit.

He couldn't bring himself to ask about Moses.

"If you need any help," he said.

"It's fine. I'll manage."

He'd been left to drink his cappuccino alone, everything that he'd been planning to say, to get rid of, still sitting in him like a bad meal. That had been the crux of it: he had wanted to hand everything over to her, like a suitcase stuffed with a body he had cut up. *Here, take this.* It astounded him that he had even remotely considered dragging his son into the discussion, though in his mind he'd envisioned bringing pictures out and Liz growing maternal and good-humored, gently chiding him for not having mentioned the boy sooner. *Bollocks.* It was his baby, not hers; hers was in the suitcase. It would have seemed a mockery to her, that he'd been handed this grown child in perfect working order like a manufacturer's replacement for the one that hadn't panned out.

He couldn't forget that shadow. She had made up a story to spare them both, this version of what had happened they could live with.

"The thing with Liz," he said to Dr. Klein now, "was that nothing was ever clear. We were both these smart people, but it seemed like we never had the least idea why we did things. Why we were even together."

Even as he said this, Alex understood that this was exactly why they had been together, because things were unclear, because there was safety in that.

"You've never really said whether you loved her."

He was taken off guard. Clearly the doctor was not on his game today, throwing the L-word out as if it were actually some sort of acceptable clinical term.

"I guess it never came up," he said, and couldn't think what to add.

He fell silent again. Everything, somehow, seemed to go back to the child. In his mind there were two children now, his child and his shadow-child, the one who lived in Sheol or whatever they called it, the unpleasant underworld place where people ate dirt and lived on forever. The first one, at least, was no longer a shadow; Alex had laid eyes on him by then. In the week after Christmas, he had boarded a plane and gone over. Afterward, in his memory of it, the visit had quickly become a wash of different shades of ambivalence and doubt, and yet it had changed things, fundamentally. The boy was no longer abstract, a mere possibility. He had fingers and toes, all the usual parts; two arms, two legs. The whole time Alex had been with Liz in that café, the image of the boy had hovered before him—not, as he tried to pretend, as a scourge to beat himself with, but more as a kind of standard to judge by. The first thought he'd had when he sat down with Liz, if he was honest about it, was, *We could never have done that.* That was what had thrown him off, really, what had left the ball in her court, the niggling sense that he didn't feel remorseful at all, not about the abortion, maybe not about any of it. What he felt was relief—at his narrow escape, at his having come through it all with only his little guilt suit to wear, his prophylactic.

Out of the blue he felt tears welling up in him and he turned his head to one side to keep them from Klein. He didn't know what he was crying about—that he was a heartless ass, he supposed, that Liz had deserved better than him, though it was hard to make out if he was just feeling a twisted sort of self-pity or if some alter ego in him was truly coming to terms with his emotional bankruptcy. He kept coming back to that fucking abortion, kept seeing himself in that spooky waiting room while Liz went under the knife. She would have had the abortion in any event; it was what had made sense. But then it hadn't been his own body that the thing had been ripped from. It had to be like tearing out your own circuits to do that, like cutting off one of your arms. It had nothing to do with ethics: sure, it was yours, cut it off if you wanted, but it wasn't going to be pretty.

He heard the doctor's chair squeak.

"You seem distracted."

He should just come out with it, the whole story of his son. Of *Per.* The name still felt like a foreign element, some molecule of a different species he was being taken over by, like Jeff Goldblum in *The Fly.*

"I guess it just came to me," he said. "About Liz. That I don't really feel that guilty about her. About the whole relationship."

Dr. Klein's chair squeaked again, though whether in irritation or with the restrained chirp of professional glee Alex couldn't have said.

"Why don't you tell me about that."

He had gone over to Sweden on a cheap Aeroflot charter, running up the bill on his new Visa card against the hope of more grant money in the fall. The trip, a twenty-two-hour slog, had included a flight path over

Chernobyl, obscured at the time by what might have been a permanent nuclear fog, as well as an eight-hour layover sequestered in an over-heated waiting room at the Moscow airport, where Intourist hostesses served stale liverwurst sandwiches and prevented any attempts at espionage or escape. By the time he had made his way across the sound to Landskrona from the Copenhagen airport he felt like a Gulag returnee.

Ingrid was waiting for him at the terminal with Per. He was a spidery bundle of limbs, as stupefyingly alien-looking and blond as his siblings had been years before. Somehow the photos hadn't quite made clear that he was this Teuton, this pagan wood sprite of the North.

His coat sleeves were too short, his hair was too long and unkempt.

"Hello, Father," he said, in his small Swedish voice, holding a tiny hand out to Alex's big brutish one with such innocent fortitude that Alex's heart sank.

He had made a mistake. He wasn't up to this.

"It's very nice to meet you," he said desperately, and shook the boy's hand.

Everything felt strange this time around, doubled over, itself but also a kind of replica of itself, like one of those tourist villages that re-created historical eras. Here was the stucco house at the edge of town, here the white furnishings, here the kitchen table that looked out to the garden. Lars and Eva were with their father, but there were pictures of them strewn around the house that looked to Alex like the updated computer renderings of children who had gone missing years before, Lars rigorously clean-cut and blue-eyed and tall, Eva already with the housewifely look of someone soon to be married and pregnant.

"I hope you don't mind to stay in the cabin again," Ingrid said. "It's Lars's room now."

This time he felt none of the old sexual chemistry between them. Maybe it was just that, like God, he couldn't imagine sleeping with the mother of his child, though what he didn't like to admit was how old Ingrid looked, not older but *old*. Out in his cabin he felt relieved to be alone, though the place was layered now with the spoor of adolescent boy, every inch of wall filled with Lars's posters and trophies, every corner jammed with sports gear and teen accoutrements. At least the old cot was gone, replaced by a proper bed. It would have been too much, to think of Lars in the bed where he and his mother had made love.

Per was watching some show of his on the TV when Alex went in as if he were just a completely ordinary child, as if he met his birth father every day.

"It's been difficult," Ingrid said, "but I should never trade it. Not for anything."

He was drawn into a long series of getting-to-know-you activities that seemed as ritualized and laden with meaning and precise as a Japanese tea ceremony. Per showed him his bed, in Lars's old place next to Eva; he showed him his coloring books; he showed him his stamp collection, turning, at Ingrid's urging, to the Canada pages, from where little profiles of the Queen looked off into space next to commemorative stamps from Expo 67. All of it had the blare of excess information, of things that were not quite apprehendable or in a clearly decipherable code.

Under his bed Per kept a collection of bugs, just a heap of crumbling thoraxes and tangled limbs at the bottom of a Mason jar.

"It is insects," he said gravely. "Of course they are dead."

"I used to collect bugs," Alex said. This was not strictly true. "I grew up on a farm."

"Yes."

Any minute now, Alex kept thinking, he'd blow his cover. He didn't know how long he could keep this up—not days, surely, not months and years. Already his face ached from holding its fatherly look, his skin itched, he wanted to scream. He wasn't sure what he'd expected—that he and Per would fall into each other's arms, maybe, that they would unleash in a rush all the genetic blood-love that had been stymied in them. Not this, at any rate, not this polite sussing out as if they were shopping for clothes, as if they had some kind of choice. It wasn't as if they could simply break up if things didn't work out. Nothing they said, nothing they did, would ever change that Per was Alex's son.

"He says you have a funny smell," Ingrid said. "Perhaps from the smoking."

He had been taking such pains to hide this from the boy, huddling behind the cabin to smoke and scrubbing his face afterward and running water through his hair the way he had done to hide his smoking from Liz.

"It's not so good to smoke," Per said, in his textbook English.

Alex hadn't quite been prepared for this fluency of his. It was disconcerting, as if the boy had mastered particle physics or beaten Alex at chess.

Already Alex had forever lost the authority a true non-smoker would have had with the boy. He ought not to have come was what it was, not yet, not until he was ready. He'd been counting on Ingrid, he supposed, had been expecting her to manage matters from the wings the way she had always done with Lars and Eva. But something was different with Per, in a way he wouldn't have expected. Per put him and Ingrid at odds, somehow. Ingrid stood watching from the kitchen window while he made a snowman with the boy in the back garden and there seemed a part of her that would have preferred if she had never written him, if he had never come.

At some point Ingrid stepped away from the window.

"Where is my mother?" Per said at once, as if Alex were a child molester, a total stranger.

"It's fine. She's probably in the living room."

"We must go inside now, I think."

Per needed to learn to trust him, Ingrid said, but what could that mean, when he would be gone in a matter of days? It seemed a question of physical presence as much as anything, of getting the measure of each other's gravity, but Alex had been merely this phantom all of Per's life, as insubstantial as the Easter Bunny. Here the boy was, his own flesh and blood—and Alex had caught a glimpse of him, something in his expression or the angle of his face, that had suddenly seemed so much the mirror of himself that he had had to look away for the intimacy of it—and he had not yet even properly held the boy.

Their first day felt like an accumulation of little failures: maybe he was too deeply flawed, Alex thought, or the boy himself was. He was Alex's son, after all. There seemed a stubborn resistance in him that wasn't quite normal, that was like a test that couldn't be passed. If he needed a drink fetched, it was in a particular cup, not the one that Alex had chosen; if he needed a pencil, it was the one that Alex had taken for himself. There seemed nothing so simple as mere attention-seeking in any of this, but more as if there was some absolute arrangement of things which must be adhered to at all costs but whose shape revealed itself only moment by moment.

Each time Ingrid quietly stepped in to restore order Alex thought, *Wrong, wrong,* feeling erased, feeling she had already ruined the child with her indulgence of him. But then wasn't this what he'd wanted, that she should corral him, that she should keep him from error? There had been no arguments, no open battle of wills, yet by suppertime Alex could feel a kind of static building up among them all as toxic as nuclear fallout.

"You should tell me about your studies," Ingrid said. "Perhaps I haven't understood so well."

"It's just a lot of technical stuff, mainly. Theories and so on." He added, not really wanting to, "I could finish them anywhere, really."

Per sat swishing the food around on his plate, not pleased at sharing his mother's attention.

"Per, you must eat," Ingrid said.

He bent to his bowl like a wounded hunchback.

"How long will Alex stay with us?" he said, throwing the *Alex* out like a challenge.

A long second passed.

"We'll see." Alex had been waiting for a reprimand. "Some days still."

Alex could see by then that the situation was hopeless. They were a cabal already, a closed shop; they didn't need him.

He got up from the table, seething with things he couldn't name.

"I'm going out to the cabin."

He skulked out. *Why did he want me here?* he thought, but then what could it have meant in Per's five-year-old brain, how could he have understood that having a father meant a hairy lout like Alex showing up out of nowhere? Alex felt like the gift that hadn't worked out, the exotic pet brought home for Christmas that had proved less amusing than had been hoped.

Ingrid was at his door. He wanted to blame her for letting matters come to this, for leaving him out.

"You mustn't run away like a child." Her own anger took him by surprise. "At least Per can say he's only five."

Alex felt close to tears.

"He doesn't even like me."

"It's not that way with children," Ingrid said, but more gently.

"How is it, then?"

"Mostly they're afraid. Only that."

He was the one who was afraid, of being stranded here, of being turned away, of discovering he was some kind of child-hating sociopath, of waking up to find he had somehow stumbled into the rest of his life. No way out.

"We'll try an excursion tomorrow," Ingrid said. "Perhaps it will be better."

They spent the next day at the Farm. Alex had never laid eyes on the place before, yet it had touched on his life so curiously that it had taken on for him an almost mythical air. It turned out, though, to be exactly what it was billed as, a working farm, with a cattle shed and a chicken run and a thatch-roofed barn that looked like it went back to the Vikings. They wandered around in there in the narrow alleys that ran alongside the stalls and storage bays catching glimpses of barn cats and of dust motes that hung in the slats of sunlight like fairy dust.

Per was on his best behavior.

"You must show Alex your special place," Ingrid said.

Alex didn't like to think what blandishments or threats his mother had held over him. Maybe only the threat of her disapproval.

"You must close your eyes," Per said. "I will say."

Alex closed his eyes. There were low beams everywhere, projecting hooks and nails, the occasional animal splatter on the floor.

A little hand came up to take his own.

"I will bring you. You mustn't look."

He was surprised how terrified he was, how much faith it took to go forward in the dark with only that little hand to guide him. He could feel each separate finger of it, tugging him on, could feel the muscles leading up, and the bones, the pumping blood, all the way to the hollow cave where his heart was.

"You must look now."

They were in some sort of hay mow, low-ceilinged and dark. A rusting tractor was parked in the corner of it, ancient, with spiky metal wheels and a chassis that looked like the skeletal remains of a prehistoric animal.

Per still had Alex's hand.

"I think it must come from under the sea," he said strangely, as if sharing a secret. "Like a shipwreck."

The old farmer had appeared in his overalls and wellingtons, nodding and beaming at them.

"*Ja, ja!*" he said. "*Du kan driva det!*"

He went around to the front of the tractor and pulled at an old crank with a violent jerk. The engine sputtered and coughed, then miraculously rumbled to life.

The farmer pulled at the throttle until the roar filled the mow. Per stood with his eyes wide with wonder, one hand still clutching Alex's.

"Vi ser? Du kan driva det!"

Before Alex knew it, the week was over. Afterward, it seemed just a long string of missed opportunities and bad decisions. How many times had he actually dared to hold the boy? How many times had he just looked at him squarely and drunk him in, the perfection of his little body, his heart-stopping Nordic delicacy—Ingrid's genes, all Ingrid's, though maybe a few of his lurking in there, in those sudden ghostly intimations he saw of himself—as if he were a godling come down from Valhalla? To the very end he had seemed always at a remove, not quite Alex's in any visceral way. Alex had imagined their meeting differently, that there would be nothing that separated them, that they would seem to share the same skin. Instead he had found this whole other life, this bolus, this egg. From him, but not him. That seemed the nub of the problem, this having and not, this urge to possess a thing that in the very urge turned somehow alien.

In the last days, Ingrid's friend Anna had come by. Ingrid had mentioned her in her letters but not that she was alone: her husband, Erik, the burly Good Samaritan who had given Alex his coat, had left her for another woman. He had wanted children, it seemed, and Anna could have none. Instead she had become for Per what Alex had failed to be, his second parent. It seemed a Freudian fantasy made real, to be surrounded by beautiful, nurturing women who tended to your every need. What use could Per have for an Alex next to the likes of Anna? Alex had looked on as Per folded himself into Anna's arms in a way he never had into Alex's and had felt torn between pain and relief, wanting this closeness for Per but also for himself.

"Do you have a work in Canada?" Per had asked.

"Sort of. I'm a teacher. Like your mother."

This hadn't carried quite the weight Alex had hoped it would.

"But not on a farm?"

"No, no." Every day since their farm visit Per had drawn pictures of his tractor, over and over, as if trying to snare the spirit of it. "But my parents have a farm. And my sister."

Per had considered this.

"So we can visit, then."

"Yes, of course." Alex had felt gratitude flow through him. "Of course we can visit."

Silence. Dr. Klein cleared his throat. Alex peeked at his watch: still twenty minutes to go. Time enough to start in on this saga, if he had a mind to, but then there was no point, really. He had made his decision. He would go over again at the first opportunity, for a month, for three; forever, if that was what happened. There was the issue of Ingrid, of course, but that was something apart. "It's for the two of you to manage," she'd said. There hadn't been any talk this time of the man she'd been expecting delivery of from God's courier. For that matter there hadn't been any Bible readings, any speaking in tongues. There hadn't been any church.

From the tractor incident Alex suspected that Per, at least, was a free-thinker. *I think it must have come from under the sea.*

"It was hard with the church," Ingrid admitted, when he asked. "Perhaps not as you think, that they would chase me away or say this or that is a sin, but because of something in me. It's difficult to explain it. Something stubborn, perhaps, as you said once. Always wanting to have my own way."

It amazed him that these bits of him stayed with her, that she took him that seriously. It amazed him that she, like him, was afraid. Of what he might want, of what he would take. Of how he would judge her.

"Perhaps it's better now," she'd said. "We do as we wish. We worship in our own way."

In our own way. He could hardly object to that. Wasn't it what he did himself? A day didn't go by, really, when the matter didn't come up, when he didn't have a chat of one sort or another with the God he no longer believed in.

Well, Peter, I always suspected the two of you had a lot in common. It's not such a big step up from being a father figure, when you think of it.

(Blushing) I suppose this is where I ought to be saying something like, "Pay no attention to the man behind the curtain!" Though I won't claim it hasn't crossed my mind. I've always pictured him as a three-pack-a-day-er like myself, to tell you the truth, with maybe a big fat Montecristo and a highball on the weekends.

Alex heard the doctor's lips smack.

"Maybe it's time we started to move on from Liz." As if Alex had been the one to keep harping on her all these months. "You seem a bit clearer now. You seem to have worked through some of the guilt."

My ass I have, Alex thought. That wasn't his point at all; his point was that he'd never felt any, not really. But then wasn't that a good thing, in Freudian terms? Wasn't the whole goal of analysis to get beyond guilt? Yet somewhere, Alex was sure, Freud had said the opposite, that guilt was all that kept the world from merest savagery. The thin, gossamer thread that held the whole rotten fabric of civilization intact.

"I do feel that a bit. That I'm clearer."

Throw the dog a bone.

By now Alex was resigned to the fact that though poor Dr. Klein wasn't much to write home about, at least he was his own. All the mind games that Alex played with him, all the duplicity and outright lies, the crises he brought in like oblations, the little chess match of transference confirmed and denied: Dr. Klein deserved better than that, really, was just a young professional trying to make his way. Alex wasn't certain at what point these protective impulses toward the doctor had arisen in him, this dangerous undercurrent of empathy or remorse or whatever it was, but surely the little matter of having got a glimpse at his medical school files had had something to do with it. So the man was human after all, he'd had to admit then. Or maybe his softening was just another form of one-upmanship. *Take that, Mr. Poker Face,* he was saying, *Mr. Bug-Up-Your-Bum, Mr. For-All-I-Know-Makes-Jokes-About-Me-Behind-My-Back-At-Cocktail-Parties-To-Impress-Women.* At least Alex had a sympathetic nervous system. At least he had a heart.

He wouldn't get far, of course, with this line of argument.

The files had come to him through a sordid little romance he had got involved in during the dying days of his tenants' association with a perky Franglo from Laval named Marie, his María substitute, though with maybe half María's statistics and much less than that of her ethics. This was when the association had begun to function mainly as a dating service, all the fight gone out of it and people continuing to hang around the way they did at the end of parties, to see who was left. Marie had invited him over once on some pretense and had complained of her boyfriend, a come-on if ever there was one, and after that they had lain on her bed a few times in various states of dress and undress, touching each other's private and semi-private parts while Marie, a real chatterbox, kept up a running monologue of coy indecision, should I or shouldn't I. After a couple of weeks she had shuffled Alex offstage to go back to her boyfriend—either because Alex had fulfilled by then her need to feel newly desired, or because he hadn't—without having once surrendered her honor, and they had gone on greeting each other politely in the elevator afterward like the near-strangers they actually were until Marie, too, as almost everyone else in the association had done, reached a settlement and moved out.

Before all that, however, Marie had run a mission for him. It turned out she was an archivist for the College of Physicians, which happened to have its offices around the corner.

"We've got files on every doctor in the province," she said, probably while he was sucking on one of her little breasts or easing a hand into her crotch. "You'd be surprised at some of the stuff."

"Maybe you could run a check on my psychoanalyst."

Alex had said this as much to shock her as anything, but she didn't bat an eye.

"Why, what's his name?"

The next day she showed up at his apartment on her lunch break with copies of whatever she'd been able to get her hands on, transcripts, assessments, even a scaled-down copy of his medical diploma. Alex was horrified, then elated, then torn. It had to be a violation of the highest order—legal, moral, therapeutic—to burgle confidential files on your analyst. That didn't stop him from looking, though. In the end, the stuff didn't add up to much—there was nothing about Klein's psychoanalytic training, for instance, since the psychoanalysts apparently kept their own, probably more heavily guarded archives. And yet a portrait emerged, a sort of Frankenklein that Alex was able to cobble together out of the bits and scraps he had at his disposal. For one thing, he finally learned the doctor's Christian name, or his Jewish one: Daniel. Such a plain, four-square name, entirely serviceable and beyond reproach, not at all the sort of geeky one—Faivish, say, or Herschel—that Alex would have imagined for him. He learned the grade point average that had got Daniel into med school at McGill, 3.6; he learned the courses he had taken there year by year, and that he had made the dean's list three years running. It wasn't until he had to leave the books and start his rotations among actual humans that things got spottier. There was a "conscientious and thorough" from a supervisor at the Royal Vic and a "well-prepared" from one at the Jewish General, but then also a "does not take well to criticism" and, more damningly, a "seems to have problems with authority."

Very interesting, Alex thought.

"I can't let you keep copies," Marie said, with what seemed the same coquettishness with which she doled out her sexual favors. "It would be too dangerous for me."

Out of this patchwork of half-remembered statistics and descriptive adjectives Alex had somehow fashioned for Dr. Klein an entire life. A childhood in Ville St. Laurent—Klein's undergraduate transcripts gave a home address there—with a doting mother and a father who was maybe in the less profitable end of the shmatte trade; afternoons spent in the basement rec room with his stamp collection or science kit to avoid the murderous childhood politics of the street. His faultless name probably hadn't done much to save him, in the end: "Duddy," the kids took to calling him at school, which he hated, though he couldn't escape the A's he got in all his subjects, or that he belonged to the chess club, or that he dressed badly and had bad hair. By university, however, none of this mattered. "My son the doctor," his mother, a total stereotype, meaty and given to cooking at the slightest provocation, went around saying to anyone who'd listen. Meanwhile Daniel and his father, the brooder, didn't talk. "It's not enough to be a doctor. He has to be fucking Freud."

All of this seemed so familiar to Alex that he felt as if he had lived it. In fact, he had. Duddy Klein was himself: problems with authority, averse to criticism, but sufficiently skilled at hiding his deficiencies to pass as conscientious, thorough, well prepared. Where he and Duddy differed was that Duddy had taken the high road, had harnessed all his childhood sense of injured dignity and made himself into a mensch. A doctor. A success. The Jewish girls who hadn't given him the time of day back at parochial school sidled up to him now at the Hadassah Bazaar. "A good haircut and a new suit," they thought. "That's all he needs."

Which, today, for some reason, he had.

Tick, tock.

You might not believe it, but I get a bit of that myself sometimes. That sort of Jungian mumbo-jumbo about my shadow side or whatever, just because some journalist happened to run into me at a cocktail party and I didn't treat him like he was the best thing since sliced bread.

I guess that's what I mean, Peter. People used to just call it a personality. Now they've got labels for everything, so instead of just being eccentric, say, you're manic-depressive. Not that I'd call you manic-depressive.

Well, we won't get into that!

Alex had to wonder if there was any difference, really, between his little chats with Peter and these sessions with Dr. Klein. In both cases he just seemed to be making things up as he went along, whatever sounded good, whatever he could twist into a version of himself he could live with. None of it mattered then, none of it implicated him. Or maybe one version was just as bogus as any other. Maybe the postmoderns were right, and there was *nothing there:* it was all just a blaze of synapses, one of whose little jobs was to make up this thing, this person-ness. He was starting to think that consciousness wasn't some lighthouse of self-knowing but merely a little cave where you made up stories about your-self, whatever it took to hide the shit and the slime, the utter mollusk you were in your deepest nature. He wondered what was down there, under the shit, what kind of bedrock he might strike.

Take Amanda.

"I guess in some ways, with Liz, it was as if we were still back in high school. As if we were still trying to work out the problems we had then. Hating anyone who was like us. Or hating anyone who *liked* us."

The truth was, Amanda had done the world a favor: if he'd had to have one more conversation with her about third-wave feminism or the *mise en abyme,* he would have done the job himself. Meanwhile, he had succeeded where she had fucked up. He had survived. He was *alive.*

There but for the grace of God.

"I guess what I never saw was that Liz probably felt the same. That there was always a part of her that wouldn't ever accept me."

Rake back the shit, Alex thought. All his agonizing over Desmond, all these years of carrying him around like his albatross: more shit. Desmond had been a blight, a scum-sucker, a bottom feeder. Alex had wanted him dead, he had wished it, and he had got his wish. A happy ending. All the rest was whitewash, his wily ego's way of letting him have his cake and choke on it, too.

Why stop at Desmond? There was still what went to the core: Per, his little contribution to the gene pool. If Alex had any real hope about the matter, it was that he would continue getting off scot-free, making his token dad gestures and then doing exactly as he pleased. Progeny without price, every man's dream. In any event the kid would surely find a way to bash Alex's head in with a hammer if he got half a chance.

Alex was beginning to feel sick.

I suppose in a Darwinian view it makes sense, doesn't it? That the whole Freudian thing is just a sop. It turns out we wouldn't just kill our fathers if we could, we'd probably eat them for breakfast.

I'm starting to think that, Peter, to be honest. That Freud was really just Darwin stepping back from the void.

The sound from the doctor's chair was less a squeak this time than a groan.

"I'm afraid our time's up."

Alex rose heavily from the couch. Dr. Klein's suit was a bit rumpled now and his hair was already falling back to its usual boyish disorder. Alex wondered why he had made such an enemy of him, why he hadn't thought of him as on his side.

Once, after a session, Alex had found himself trailing Dr. Klein as he left the hospital, and there had been such a sad cast to him seen from behind like that—the too tight blazer, short at the sleeves, the sag of cloth at his too flat ass—that Alex had felt as if he had seen his life in a glance, the little boy walking home alone from school, the books laid out on the kitchen table while his mother cooked and his dad, taking comfort from the thought that the world was going to Sheol in a handbasket, watched the evening news. All of this had been months before Marie and Duddy Frankenklein.

I'll try harder, Alex thought, giving a last tug to his shoelace.

Dr. Klein cleared his throat.

"About our sessions."

He was standing in front of the door as if to bar Alex's exit. For a minute, they were actually face to face.

"I should tell you," he said. "I'll be leaving soon."

Alex wasn't sure he had heard right.

"On vacation?"

"No, permanently." His head moved in a strange bob, of restrained triumph, maybe, or simple awkwardness. "I've taken another position. In Toronto."

"Oh." Alex still couldn't believe he had understood. "You mean, we'll be ending?"

"I'll let you know exactly when, of course. I can direct you to another therapist if you'd like to continue. That's something we can talk about."

Alex's blood was pounding. *You'll need to make a commitment,* the doctor had said at the outset.

"I don't think I'll be continuing."

"Well. As I say. We can discuss it."

Dr. Klein had stood aside. For more than a year Alex had been coming to him, an hour a day, five days a week. Forty-three dollars a session. He didn't like to do the math. He could have sponsored a refugee. He could have fed several families in Bangladesh.

Some question was on his lips, he wasn't quite sure what it was, but before he could give it a shape the door had closed behind him.

He passed through Emergency on his way out, hoping to catch another glimpse of Stephen and Ariel, but they had gone. All afternoon he had been carrying the image in his head of Ariel clutched to Stephen's chest like a frightened chimp, though no doubt Ariel had been fully reassumed into the mother-son covenant by now.

He could still feel the whoosh of Dr. Klein's door closing behind him. Fucking careerist. *Go on and take your plum Toronto job,* he thought. *Take your filthy lucre.* Yet beneath his spite he already felt a spreading relief, a thrill of the sort he got at the end of bad relationships. He had escaped. He was free.

The sun had mellowed to a late-afternoon shimmer. Along Pine, the exhaust-embattled trees had all sprung into leaf. In a matter of days the world had been made over—all up the slope of the mountain the green stretched, impossible, but there. What little chromosome in the mind made it sing at that, what made it hope? He could feel the memory urging itself on him of the permanent spring smell of the air in Sweden, of the blue of the Öresund. They would go there together, to the coast. Per had told him of his visit to the Tycho Brahe museum on Ven—*Tikuh Brawh,* he pronounced it. He liked planets and stars; he liked dinosaurs; he liked machines. Reassuringly ordinary things, as if there was still a chance for him, as if he was a boy like any other. Alex saw, suddenly, that there was probably no special puzzle in the boy, only the usual ones. It felt as if some screen between them had dropped. The screen of Dr. Klein, perhaps. He need never mention Per to him now, had managed to save him for himself.

I suppose, Peter, it was a bit like Calvin with God. Not wanting the priests in between all the time.

You don't have to tell me about it, sir, I've got kids of my own. And while you're at it, you might as well get Mother Mary off to a nunnery.

He veered off onto McGregor from Pine rather than continuing toward Trudeau's house. After months of skulking past the place under the watchful eye of the Cubans he had finally caught sight of the man, when he had practically knocked Alex over bounding up the steps that rose from Redpath.

"Pardon, monsieur!" he had said with a grin.

It wasn't until this apparition had headed up the walk of the former prime minister's house as if he owned the place that Alex realized it was The Man Himself. He was so odd-looking and small, wizened and gnomish like a character from the Brothers Grimm. This was the man who had faced down the bottle throwers at City Hall, who had made the nation's women weak at the knees, who had brought the Constitution home. Yet here he was gamboling along the streets like a schoolboy hurrying home for lunch. The encounter left Alex with the queerest sensation, as if he had had a brush with a supernatural being but had somehow failed to make proper use of it, to take away some special power or insight.

All that had been before Alex had made the mistake of getting into a discussion about Mr. Trudeau with one of Félix's friends that had left a particularly bad taste in his mouth, all the more lingering and sharp because he had actually defended the man. Now he had to pass his house, day after day, and each time be reminded of failures he couldn't quite name, as if he had somehow fallen short of the mark in a contest he hadn't even known he'd signed up for.

From the curve that opened out to *Parc Merde de Chien* from McGregor he noticed that the bust of Simón Bolívar had disappeared from its pedestal. Anti-Fidelistas, no doubt, or maybe anti-Trudeauites. At least the placards weren't here, not in this bastion of Anglo-Scots privilege. In Félix's neighborhood, one hung from nearly every balcony and porch: NE TOUCHEZ PAS À LA LOI 101. The infamous language law. In the beginning the slogan hadn't seemed much of a rallying cry for rebellion, but then a protest at City Hall had brought people out by the tens of thousands and everything that had felt dead, consigned to the wastes by the pragmatists and the technocrats, had come alive again, all the old Péquistes crawling out of their post-referendum cocoons to spray-paint English signs and smash things in the streets. Outside his building one morning Alex had passed a car with Ontario plates on whose dusty hood someone had inscribed, apparently without irony, "Anglo go home."

None of these things made Alex feel especially broad-minded. Rather they made him feel like a redneck, a bigot, the sort of person who looked at a couple of workers whose bum cracks were showing and who stank of cigarettes and thought, *Fucking Quebecois.* At bottom he had Citizen Trudeau to thank for the whole farrago, with his precious Constitution. Alex himself didn't much care whether the city's signs were in English or French or Swahili—they were just fucking signs, after all, not Proust. But now the Constitution had come into play and principles were at stake, guillotines being sharpened in the wings while the language police tracked down each misplaced apostrophe. Big-Endians and Little-Endians. Alex wondered which side Fidel, if he were in charge, would have rounded up for the jails.

"I'm of two minds," Félix had said, in his usual Gaulish pose of fair-mindedness. "Of course, if we were separate we would protect our minorities like any state, but this way it's different. This way *we're* the minority."

There was no placard at Félix's place, at least, that wasn't his style, but nonetheless Alex had felt a sort of suasion beginning to set in there, Félix's speech peppered now with telling catchphrases that all seemed joined in some long, unacknowledged assault against an unnamed enemy. Phrases like, *Of course,* and *It's different,* and *If we were separate.* Alex had never quite forgotten Félix's argument with Louie: there was always that part of him that kept waiting for Félix to slip up, for the true fascist to show himself beneath the cultured façade.

Félix and Louie had actually met again, in the gay ghetto, of all places, one night when Alex and Michael had run into Louie prowling the streets of the East End and had dragged him to the California. The California was strictly gay lite, the refuge of straight women who didn't want to get hit on and straight men like Alex who liked to think of themselves as enlightened. It turned out Louie knew the place.

"I'm going to sleep only with white men," he said. "And only on top."

Heads turned as soon as Louie walked in. He stood surveying the room like an African prince, drinking the attention in.

He nodded toward the bar.

"Alex, look. It's your friend."

Sure enough, Félix was there, in the trademark cashmere pullover he wore in his after-hours incarnations, chatting up a young man at the bar who looked decidedly fresh-faced and sheepish and Alex-like. Alex thought he caught Félix about to turn away and pretend he hadn't noticed them, but Louie hadn't taken his eyes from him.

"Alex!" He was coming over to them, his face lit in a smile that came so naturally it seemed real. "What a surprise! And your friend, I'm sorry, I don't remember your name."

Louie held out a big hand as if all was forgiven.

"But I remember yours, my friend, I remember yours!"

The group of them settled at a table and Louie and Félix, bizarrely, talked for half an hour or more in rapid French, while Michael worked the crowd and Alex was left to make halting conversation with Félix's young companion, a boy from Rimouski who couldn't have been more than twenty. Alex couldn't figure what game Louie and Félix were at: they were acting as if they were old comrades-in-arms remembering their days battling the regime back in Port-au-Prince. Félix's hand came out again and again to touch Louie's shoulder.

"So I guess you guys made up," Alex said, after Félix had picked up the tab and gone off with his Rimouskan.

"The man is a dead man," Louie said grimly.

"What do you mean?"

"He's got it. The virus. The bug. You can smell it."

Alex didn't have the stomach to stay on very long after that.

"Did you get that?" he asked Michael. "That he's sick?"

"It's not like people wear a star. Maybe he's just old."

At their next lesson, Félix acted as if the evening had never happened. That corner of his life, picking young men up in bars and such, seemed set apart. Something had shifted between them, though, as if there was an understanding now, a sort of convoluted agreement to know and not know. *He's a dead man.* Alex couldn't get the stone certainty of Louie's voice out of his head. Félix continued to go to work, he drank his wine, he traipsed off on his holidays, yet there was a change, perhaps, he was more wan or more thin, more tired. Or perhaps the same.

Alex made an effort to stop smoking around him.

"But you must," Félix insisted. "It's the one vice I don't have. I can enjoy it from you."

And afterward Félix always had a pack of cigarettes around, Alex's brand, which he'd lay out on a side table before their lesson.

Their relationship had begun to seem a kind of theater by then. Surely their lessons were beside the point—Félix already spoke better English than Alex did, and in any event he wasn't going to have much use for it if he was dying. Alex didn't know what the average life expectancy was these days, but he knew that gay men were dropping like flies: one month they looked healthy, the next they were skin and bone. Félix ought to be getting his affairs in order, not swanning around the gay bars or wasting his time with the likes of Alex.

The invitations for drinks had stopped by then, after Alex had begged off a few times, but now Félix invited him to dinner.

"It's just a few close friends, nothing very formal," he said. "No one to be afraid of."

Alex hadn't dared refuse, wondering at Félix's intentions but telling himself that he had probably merely needed a fourth, or a sixth, or an eighth, and Alex would do. In the liquor store he agonized over what wine would be up to Félix's standards and settled finally on a thirty-dollar Barolo, then regretted the excess of it as soon as it was paid for. When he arrived at Félix's door he realized he hadn't even so much as wrapped the bottle and was ready to turn around and head back home.

"Alex! So you've come! Come in, come in, I'm just finishing up in the kitchen."

The house was filled with cooking smells. The dining room, a cavernous place with oak paneling and exposed beams that sat closed off and dark during Alex's visits, was completely changed now, decked out with tableware and flowers and billowing napkins folded into the shape of some kind of bird. From the living room came a loud hum of conversation, but Alex followed Félix into the kitchen, clutching his little offering.

The stovetop was covered in pots and pans, the counter a heap of onion skins and wrappers and greens. Alex had never seen the place in such disarray.

"So." Félix took Alex's bottle and looked it over appreciatively. "Very good, very good. You know your wines."

Someone had come soundlessly into the kitchen through a side doorway, a slightly hunchbacked man whose head was ringed with a perfect circle of baldness like a tonsure, mesmerizing in its symmetry. Below that mysterious clearing a luxuriant crop of hair that looked as if it had been under cultivation since the sixties fell away in shimmering waves down the man's shoulders.

He looked over the wine Félix was holding, then over Alex.

"*Alors, mon ami*. I didn't know your tastes ran to the Italians now." Félix let the comment pass.

"Alex, my good friend André. From my radical days."

"So you're the famous instructor. Félix has talked about you."

He set about fussing around Félix while he cooked, tidying things as if reclaiming territory.

"What part of Italy, then?"

"From the south. I mean, my family is. From Molise."

"Molise, I know it." This was so uncommon that Alex's first thought was that he was lying. "Campobasso, isn't that the town there? The Low Field. A curious name for a place in the mountains. And then of course all the Samnite ruins."

"André is a journalist," Félix said. "You must excuse him."

"Don't insult me, I'm not a journalist. I'm a terrorist."

The living room, which Alex had been dreading, was starting to look less formidable than the kitchen. He had the feeling of being stuck at the wrong end of a long evening.

A rattling pot distracted Félix while he was chopping parsley and he cut his finger.

"*Merde!*"

At the sight of the blood Alex instinctively started. It puddled on the cutting board before Félix managed to stanch it with a dish towel.

André had caught Alex's reaction.

"*C'est rien*," he said at once to Félix. "*Attends, je prends un Band-Aid.*"

He took his time dressing the wound. Félix, an eye on his pots, was getting impatient.

"*Vite, là, ça brûle!*"

André, as soon as Félix's back was turned, gave Alex a brutal look.

"*À table, messieurs et mesdames!*" he called out. "*C'est prêt!*"

Félix's notion of informal, Alex saw, stretched to name cards at every setting and an array of cutlery that looked like the armaments of a medieval battalion. A great deal of talk was given over to the cutlery as people took their places.

"*Oui, oui, de France,*" Félix said. "*Du dix-huitième siècle.*"

Matters careened toward disaster for Alex right from the start. Félix, busy with serving, left André with the job of introducing him.

"*C'est notre jeune professeur d'anglais,*" he said, as if he were a character in a Molière play.

"*Mais il parle français?*"

"*Oui, il parle fritalien, français à l'italien. C'est très drôle, apparemment.*"

With a few deft strokes André had managed to sabotage any hope Alex might have had of finding his stride. It was true—how had André known this?—that his French was peppered with Italianisms. He ought to have made light of the matter but was put off by the thought of everyone waiting to hear his funny accent. A few polite questions were put to him but he fumbled his French so badly that the overtures soon dwindled away.

"*Voilà.*" Félix had been busy in the kitchen. "*La soupe.*"

By the main course, Alex had long ago lost the thread of the conversation. The woman next to him, a stiff-backed professor from UQAM, had taken pity on him at one point and spoken to him in English, but the two of them had seemed such an island then amidst the *bons mots* flying across the table that their conversation had quickly grown stilted and forced. He was reduced now to staring into his food, all his appetite gone, or to smiling grimly as he pretended to follow what was being said, the room having taken on the menacing warp of a Dali painting. Félix had more or less abandoned him, caught up in his serving like an old queen, though all Alex could see was that Band-Aid on his finger.

"*Messieurs et mesdames, le plat principal. Filet de porc normande avec des pruneaux et des tomates farcies.*"

André had been holding court the whole meal. He had got the table onto dirty jokes, apparently a specialty of his, telling a string of them in a broad *joual* that had people guffawing and shrieking with feigned offense.

"*Qu'est-ce qu'il y a de la part de notre jeune anglophone?*" André said, at last turning to Alex again, the moment Alex had been dreading. "What do they say, over there in Westmount? *Pas beaucoup d'affiches là, je parie.* If you don't like 101, take the 401."

It was an old line, but it still got a few titters.

"*Laisse-lui, André, voyons donc,*" Félix said.

"No, I'm curious. *Voilà un anglophone* in flesh and blood, *c'est une occasion*. Maybe you can explain to us, Alex, what's the anglophones' view on 101?"

A few more titters.

"*André—*"

"*Non, non, laisse-lui répondre.*"

The room seemed poised now, waiting for the punchline that could send it safely back into laughter.

"I haven't really asked them," Alex said warily.

"*Parfait,*" Félix said. "*Exactement.*"

But André had him on his hook now, and wouldn't release him.

"What about you, then? What's your view?"

He should just have shrugged the question off as he'd done the previous one. But for the first time that evening, he had people's attention.

"I think we should follow the Constitution," he said, though his heart was pounding.

"Which Constitution is that, exactly? Mr. Trudeau's?"

André had dropped any pretense that this was just some friendly airing of views. Alex felt the sort of panic he used to get after he'd thrown the first punch in a fight.

"He has a point," Félix said to André. This came so unexpectedly that Alex felt a deep sense of gratitude go through him. "It's a perfectly normal Constitution, even if we didn't sign it."

He got a few laughs at that, and the tension seemed to ease a bit. But André wouldn't let the matter go.

"He's such a saint to you anglophones, your Mr. Trudeau. But in Quebec we didn't need Mr. Trudeau to come along to tell us who we were. You should ask him where he was in the war, with his human rights, marching down St. Laurent with a swastika on his arm like the rest."

There was a silence.

"*Ça suffit, André,*" Félix said.

A gravity had come over the room, as if André had betrayed a family secret.

"*Bon,*" Félix said. "*Ça c'est la fin pour la politique. Alors on passe à la religion.*"

If anything the exchange tipped sympathies in Alex's favor. Félix brought out his Barolo, to many appreciative murmurs, and the woman beside Alex made another attempt with him, until they finally managed to find some common ground on the subject of migrant farm workers. But he was marked now, he could feel it, like a foreign element that had to be contained.

"I really should go," he said to Félix, as soon as propriety allowed. "I have a lecture tomorrow."

"Yes, of course." He stared down at his hands. Alex saw that he had changed his bandage. "You mustn't mind André. That's just his way."

"No, no. It was interesting."

Félix saw him to the door.

"I'm away next week," he said. "For our lesson, that is."

"Oh. I'm away the one after, for Easter."

They were drifting into a zone of indecipherable courtesies.

"So we'll talk when you're back, then."

That had been nearly a month ago and they had yet to talk. Alex didn't know if he was the one who ought to call, though with each day that passed it felt more and more unlikely that he would. Two fucking solitudes. He wished he had never got near that bastard André. Their argument kept playing over and over in his head, along with the acid responses he ought to have made. *We didn't need Mr. Trudeau to tell us who we were.* Who was that, exactly? The priest-loving, wood-hewing anti-Semites that Quebeckers had been before the likes of Trudeau had come along to drag them into the twentieth century? But André's swastika comment had had the ring of truth. Trudeau had been raised by the Jesuits, after all, he'd attended lectures by Lionel-Adolphe Groulx himself. Maybe his whole career after that had just been an elaborate denial of the messed-up *Maria Chapdelaine* notion of his roots that the priests had pounded into him. It would make sense: he had had to kill off Quebec to rise above it. Classic Oedipal stuff. Alex had seen the footage, how he had promised Quebeckers the world and then delivered up only his piddling Constitution, cutting Lévesque out of the deal at the final moment and sending him home like a beaten dog.

So how did that hit you, exactly? I mean, here's this role model, this man you've looked up to all your life, this champion of human rights, and you find out he was some kind of Jew-hater.

Well, I wouldn't want to go too far with this, Peter, it's really just hearsay at this point. And if it comes to it, my own grandfather was a fascist. They were different times.

It was all beside the point, of course. None of this was what really rankled; none of it was what had kept him, all these weeks, from picking up the phone. What really bothered him, what had left the bitterest taste, was how he had recoiled like the worst sort of homophobe when Félix had cut himself. That André had caught him doing it.

Months from now, maybe, he would run into Félix on the street wasted to skin and bone and would have to face up to the fact that he'd learned nothing, that people were dying off all around him and his only reaction was, *Better them.* Or maybe he would find out that Félix was fine, that he wasn't sick at all, that he'd merely been on a diet, that the whole drama he'd been playing out in his head had just been his own bigotry. All the more reason, then, that he should call him: it would be pointless to go on shouldering the guilt of having abandoned him if Félix was actually going to carry on in his cushy life to a ripe old age.

Alex had come out to the bottom of Simpson. The gaping ruins of the Unitarian Church still sat there, monstrous and charred, virtually untouched since the fire that had consumed it a few weeks before. Another blight, now, along his path. Such a waste. It was that jerry-built woman that Alex had caught a glimpse of one day from the church doors playing the organ who had set it, out of some gripe. A transsexual, it turned out. *Brilliant! Stunning!* Alex had actually come here for a service once, not long after Amanda's suicide, and had not felt entirely out of place: this was religion, he had surmised, for people who didn't really believe in it but couldn't quite bring themselves to do without.

Whatever chance he might have had was lost now, reduced to this burnt-out shell. He had seen the smoke from his balcony and had been aghast, when he went out to it, to see that it was his own little Unitarian jewel going up in flames. It had been a fearsome sight, the great stained glass windows of the façade lit like a scene from the end times and flames reaching out above the last of the roof in building-high licks. A crowd had gathered behind a line of police tape, people stared at the fire with a kind of horrified fascination, amazed that this huge stone thing, this monument, was being consumed, and there was nothing to do but watch it burn.

Nothing much remained of the church except the rectory and the spooky outlines of the rest, jagged stretches of wall, the stumpy remnants of the façade. Its demise had left the prospect along this part of Sherbrooke hopelessly impoverished, shattering the symmetry the church had formed with St. Andrew and St. Paul up the street and the Eskine and American United further on. No trinity for the Unitarians. The fire was part of an assault against Sherbrooke that had been going on for some time, year by year its glory fading, the few old mansions that remained changing over one by one into brand-name outlets, and even the tonier shops interspersed now with empty windows showing FOR LEASE signs and middlebrow galleries selling cheap watercolors or mass-market Inuit soapstone.

The Golden Square Mile. All the good Calvinist Scots' nose-to-the-grindstone pecuniousness and hard work that had made this place was coming to naught. They were the enemy now, those old city builders; somehow they had got lumped in with the English, though the Scots had hated the English as much as the French ever had. If it came to a question of blood the English shared more with the French than they did with the Scots, by way of the Normans. Trudeau had been right about that, at least: there was no building a nation on bloodlines, that was just nuts. Like Alex's claim to the Samnites—all bunk, he'd discovered. He had actually looked them up, with an eye to somehow working them into his dissertation, and had found out the Romans had done to them what they'd always done to their troublesome vassals: they had scattered them to the winds, replacing them with Albanians, Macedonians, Turks, whatever slave race they could lay their hands on. It turned out Alex was a mongrel through and through. The purest line in him probably descended from none other than those same Normans, who had come through raping and pillaging and spreading their seed somewhere back in the eleventh century. To this day, he had cousins on his mother's side who were as blue-eyed and blond as any Swede.

He ought to call Félix. It would be a national disgrace not to make the effort. Years from now he'd be teaching in Nanaimo or Moncton or Red Deer, God forbid, and he'd be singing the same tune as every backwoods Anglo. *Oh, I lived there a few years, but I couldn't take the French thing after a while.* He hadn't been able to put the awkwardness from his mind that he'd felt between Félix and him at Félix's door that night, the rawness of it. There had been something between them, at least, some connection. Maybe his Norman blood finding its place at last across the centuries.

It was all in Darwin, the silliness of trying to separate bloodlines, of thinking of beings as discrete. It had come as a surprise to Alex—though the title of his book ought to have been a clue—how much of Darwin turned on this question, namely the niggling one of species. Everything had followed from a simple insight that all life was connected, that no difference was absolute. Alex had never seen this suggested in so many words, but he thought it was those barnacles of Darwin's that had really clinched things for him, more than the finches, those eight years he had spent on the most intimate terms with them in his little study. What he had found was this: that barnacles, by nature hermaphrodites, often carried within them little penis-like consorts, tiny fledgling males that served as a sort of insurance if their own parts gave out. They were a missing link, how creatures moved by slow degrees from vulvic all-in-ones to barnacle boy and barnacle girl. All forms were fluid, each contained part of the last and the next. Maybe the Unitarian organist could have taken heart from that: not a freak, but a link.

As blond as any Swede. He had been blond himself as a child, well into his teens. It came to him, out of the murk of high school history, that before the Normans had been Normans they'd been Norsemen: Vikings. Wearing their horns and drinking their mead and sending their longboats out across the seas. He could smell the Swedish air again, could see the pellucid sky. As blond as his son. It was the merest whim, perhaps, but still his blood went quick. It was a link.

He checked his watch as he
neared the Liberal Arts Building: past five. "Stop by my office," Jiri had
said, as if he merely had some new Baudrillard to show him, as if this
wasn't Alex's life on the line. The word was another misconduct charge
had come up against him, spurious, from the looks of it, but still. This
wasn't the old days. The more Jiri's life skidded off the rails, however, the
more inscrutably dangerous and calm he became.

Some hundred pages, Alex had given him, already formatted to
MLA rules as if to make the proposal seem more a fait accompli. The
whole framework was there, all his methodology, what he had struggled with for two years but then had miraculously taken shape over a
matter of weeks. It had been like an out-of-body experience, as if he had
become a mere conduit for some higher doctoral power. The real breakthrough, though, had come when he had finally braved an excursion
into the natural sciences and stumbled upon the sociobiologists: here
was a whole netherworld of unabashed trend-buckers, people who put
the words *science* and *art* in the same sentence without fearing they
would rend the very fabric of the cosmos. It was all total anathema to
the literary purists, insofar as they even deigned to notice anything so
reactionary—it was just biological determinism writ large, they said,
the worst sort of regression, a heartbeat away from social Darwinism
and eugenics—but that didn't mean it wasn't true.

By now he had thumbed through his own copy of the pages so often
he could quote the first paragraphs of it almost verbatim. He opened with
the Derrida quote about the road in the forest, his sop to the theorists—
talk about logo-fucking-centrism, the way Derrida went on, and yet there

was something there, a real insight—and then went right to the heart of the matter:

In the Galápagos Islands, the masked booby performs an elaborate mating ritual. The male approaches the female and after a series of gestures aimed at attracting her attention— one of which, skypointing, involves a graceful arabesque of spread wings and stretched neck, the beak pointing skyward as if in plaintive lament—he pushes before her an assortment of offerings. A stick, perhaps. A blade of dried grass. A stone. These items, there is no other way to see them, are metaphors: of food, of home, of fecundity. With them, the booby is telling his prospective mate a story. "Come with me," he is saying, "and we will have children and live in abundance." This strange collocation of all the essential elements of narrative at the most basic level of nature suggests that this oldest of stories, the happily-ever-after of fairy tales, may be older even than we have ever imagined.

A road in the forest is also a form of writing. That seems the tenor of Derrida's ruminations on the *via rupta* in *Of Grammatology*, tossed off in a parenthetical aside, in typical Derridean fashion, and yet going to the heart, really, of his radical revisioning of the idea of writing. We might even go further and say that the road is a narrative: it has a beginning, a middle, and an end; it tells another of the classic stories, the story of the journey, a journey we ourselves think to make in taking the road, though in fact we only re-create, as in a story, the journey already set out for us. Thus the road, too, is merely a metaphor, a trope, a trace of the journey already taken. Human roads, as it happens, often follow animal ones, like the ancient transhumance paths of Europe by which early shepherds, following the yearly migrations they saw in the wild, learned to move their domestic flocks between mountain and plain. Again, the narrative predates us. Like Derridean writing, it can be thought of not as belated, as an afterthought, but as originary, before speech, before language itself.

If narrative predates us, as its traces everywhere in nature suggest, if it is not the product of our self-knowing but perhaps only a means to it, then we must perforce begin to sever the sacred link we have always made between narrative and that seat of all our self-knowing, human consciousness. A booby woos his mate with a story of abundance; a bee dances out a story of food. Whatever line we draw between instinct and awareness does not change that the story is there from the outset, long before there are poets to recite it or scribes to record it. So it is that what we still think of as our unique heritage, the thing that sets us apart, what the gods have given us, the magic moment of "Let there be light," is perhaps only a passage on a much longer journey, one that is primal beyond reckoning and that goes back to the very beginnings of life itself.

Alex still felt a thrill rolling the phrases off in his mind. *Primal beyond reckoning.* He liked that. He'd been especially pleased at working in the transhumance; that should have Jiri scrambling to his dictionary. The word had the arcane ring of something cutting edge but was actually right out of his own family history: *la transumanza,* the yearly moving of the sheep between *alto* and *basso* Molise. He owed this bit of lore, again, to his cousin, who had taken him to the very paths, remnants of which still stretched across the countryside for miles, part of a network that had crisscrossed the entire region. Wild animals—bison or deer or mastodons or whatever—had cut the first swaths of them back in the mists of time, and then *Homo aeserniensis,* Isernian Man, the local protohuman, had further beaten them down in the hunt. When the shepherds came they turned them into institutions, which they had remained until his own parents had left Italy thirty-odd years before. One of them passed behind his aunt Clotilda's house, a good twenty yards across, just a stretch of grassy earth now, but with stone markers here and there along the edges that went back to Roman times. His aunt had told him about the flocks that had passed there when she was a young bride, for days on end, with bonfires every night and bagpipes playing and the constant bleating of sheep like the crying of souls at the end of the world.

After his opening he had toned down the lyricism to lay out his overall scheme, which was a kind of Frygian anatomy by way of Maslow's hierarchy of needs. Stories of Food. Stories of Home. Stories of Love. Stories of Death. Stories of Rebirth. Out of the sociobiologists he had gathered up all sorts of suitably rarefied cross-references to the natural sciences and the animal world; humans didn't really come into things until the Great Depression, as Alex thought of it, that awful moment somewhere in prehistory when somebody wondered what was the point. The rest had been easy—he'd pulled in the Greeks, the Babylonians, he'd pulled in Jesus, Osiris, even Beowulf. For his primary texts, the next hurdle, he'd given the nod to the *Odyssey* and *Ulysses*, though the former he hadn't read in ten years and the latter he had never quite finished. No matter; they would do. Joyce, in particular, was a real darling of the postmodernists, who loved all that sophomoric punning, though it was mostly Leopold Bloom whom Alex was interested in. What held the whole caboodle together, of course, was Mr. Darwin: narrative, like everything else, was a strategy. Get it right, and, like Scheherazade, you survived.

Who was it that said about Darwin—what was it?—I think it was something like, "How stupid of me not to have thought of that."

(Self-deprecatingly) I think it was Thomas Huxley, actually, Peter. Not that I'd want to put myself at that level.

It had not been easy with Jiri. It wasn't the work, so much, though Alex had made the mistake of handing in another draft before he'd really hammered things out that Jiri had summarily ripped to shreds. The problem was Jiri, his life. Ever since Jiri had stayed with him, Alex had never really got free of him. It was like being the child of an alcoholic, shoring up his lout of a dad each time he came home drunk just so the man would be around the next day to give him a proper beating.

After Alex had evicted him Jiri had gone straight back to living in his office. The dean had issued an ultimatum, which Jiri had ignored, until it seemed that after surviving every form of discipline the university had been able to mete out he would be done in by the Board of Health. Alex, out of self-interest as much as anything, terrified that he'd be shunted off to some new advisor who would make him start his thesis over from scratch, intervened. Against his better instincts, he landed Jiri a sublet in his building with a guy named Dan, a gay Quebecois temporarily decamping to Sherbrooke to look after his dying mother. Dan had been fighting his increases for years and was paying a ridiculously low rent. The arrangement was for Jiri to make his payments to him directly, to avoid having the landlords try to block an official sublet, but only a week after Jiri had moved in Alex got an angry phone call.

"His fucking check bounced. Didn't you say he was a professor?"

That was just the beginning of a long series of abuses. There was another bounced check; there were cigarette burns on Dan's furniture; there were complaints about noise and about garbage not put down the chute. Far from taking the clandestine nature of his rental as a reason for caution, Jiri seemed to take it as a license for abandon. Meanwhile the phone calls from Dan were coming almost weekly.

"They sent me a notice, for Christ's sake. I don't need this right now."

"I'll talk to him. He's going through a bit of a rough time."

"Him and me too."

Alex didn't mention that Jiri's rough time included a skinhead son up on charges of beating a gay man to within an inch of his life. This was not something that Jiri ever brought up either—dark rumors made the rounds of the department, about steel pipes and broken bones, about lawyers' bills, but Jiri himself went about with a kind of manic good cheer as if he'd just won the lottery. Alex feared for Jiri's sanity, waiting for the moment when he stepped in front of a bus or took a rifle to the top of the Hall Building and started picking people off on the street below.

Jiri's apartment—Dan's apartment—had become a safe house for every questionable associate Jiri had, young female undergrads he'd lured there despite his probation, frowzy older women who seemed ready to spill from their clothes at any instant, a host of unsavory males straight out of central casting, thin, grizzled types in smelly overcoats, or overbearing ones who silenced every opposition and held court until the wee hours. One of these—John, he went by, though really Jana, pot-bellied and with a thinning mane of silver-white that he tended like an aging rock star—came by almost nightly, claiming the best chair and draining Jiri's Scotch three fingers at a go. He was a blowhard, by any measure, full of pronouncements and easy cynicism, but Jiri sucked up to him as if he were Dubček himself.

"They're innocents, in their little world there, signing their petitions and waiting for glasnost. Glasnost is a joke. Then they still churn out their manifestos as if they've got some kind of new socialist paradise ready for us, but they'll be the first ones selling McDonald's the day the capitalists roll in. And they'll be lucky for it."

It was all the simplest sort of reactionism, straight out of Reagan 101. Alex couldn't believe that Jiri sat still for it, yet he'd be right in there encouraging him.

"That's the paradox, isn't it? That's the brilliance of capitalism—you can't deconstruct it, because it deconstructs itself. It caters to the beast, but at least it admits it."

Alex would gladly have forgone these sessions if not for the obligation he felt to keep Jiri under watch. He didn't like to flatter himself, but his presence had a stabilizing effect—inevitably, when he made the mistake of bowing out early and leaving Jiri alone with John, there'd be a complaint the next day about John Cage playing at top volume until four in the morning or two drunk men in the hall singing "La Marseillaise."

"This guy was there through the whole thing," Jiri said, as if he owed him some sort of national debt. "The Russians, the tanks, the crackdown, the whole catastrophe. Then three years in prison—all that Amnesty crowd, the ones you see in the papers these days, he knew them all at the start."

Alex was skeptical.

"So how did he get out?"

"That was the worst of it. They gave him a choice: get on a plane or let your children carry the stigma. They're very clever that way. If you stay, your children end up in the salt mines; if you go, they think you're a traitor and they turn into good socialists. Four of them, he left behind. He never laid eyes on them again—straight from his jail cell to the airport. The wife could never get them out, of course, not like mine. They watched her like hawks."

Alex understood all this, this sense of debt, that John had paid his dues when Jiri had not, yet still something stank. Maybe it was jealousy on his part: he was Jiri's protégé, his acolyte, he had dreams where Jiri led him through narrow blue-lit passages toward some brilliant truth. Yet Jiri never missed a chance to make him small, as if every obeisance, his looking up to him, his putting himself on the line to help him out, needed to be properly punished. That Jiri should turn around and shine his light on this strutting peacock was somehow doubly demeaning.

"You Canadians," John was fond of saying. "All this wringing your hands all the time, who are we, what am I? The only answer you have? We're not Americans. It makes me laugh. What did *Pravda* say once, and I don't quote them lightly: the difference between Coca-Cola and Pepsi-Cola."

By *you Canadians*, Alex knew, he meant Alex.

"At least we don't go around propping up dictators."

"With what? Your seven tanks? You're so grateful the Americans are bad, so you don't have to be. It's a nice arrangement."

Alex could always count on Jiri to pound in the last few nails.

"You have to excuse Alex. I actually found some copies of the *New Internationalist* in his place when I was staying there."

Alex almost regretted he had thrown Jiri out back then. It would have been easier to keep an eye on him in his own place rather than subjecting himself several times a week to John's bombast. There were the girls, at least. Occasionally Alex was able to hive one off from the herd and make some progress, though he had to watch his flanks.

"Alex, why don't you tell us about your little theory? It's rather clever, really, a sort of worm's-eye view of literature."

Fucking prick, Alex would think, but then trailing behind his fury like a dead weight would be the image of Jiri's skinhead son, and his anger would stall. Not a word of his son ever crossed Jiri's lips, yet still he managed, and this was the genius of him, to somehow use him to justify every rudeness, every excess. After Amanda had died, and Alex was sitting in Jiri's office one day still feeling like he'd stepped on a land mine, Jiri had said, without a trace of emotion, "I'm just glad I wasn't the one who slept with her."

Alex couldn't say where Jiri had finagled that bit of inside information. From Stephen, maybe. In any event, using it was well beyond cruel—it was practically metaphysical, it was like Satan taking him to the mountaintop and saying, "Jump." Alex had sat there dumbfounded while Jiri, not missing a beat, had gone on to talk about Heidegger or Althusser or whatever. This was back when Jiri was still using his office as his pied-à-terre, so that a sleep smell hung in the air, and Jiri's effects, all the things that had made the passage, one by one, to Alex's apartment and then back again, were neatly arrayed around him, his boxes and his books, the suits that hung in his doorless closet. Even in that moment all Alex could see was Jiri's son, all he could hear was the thunk of a pipe against flesh. There had been a group of them, from the reports: they had broken the man's arm, his leg, seven ribs; they had ruptured his spleen. How did you do that, how did you let yourself into those soft places? It was too much to think of, that your own son, your flesh, could commit such an act. You had to feel responsible. One way or the other, nature or nurture, take your pick, you *were.*

These were the thoughts that came to him, why again and again he gave Jiri a pass. Maybe not so much out of empathy as relief, that it was Jiri living with the weight of it, not him.

One night when Jiri had his new theory class up to his place, Alex managed to strike up his own little tangent of conversation with a dark-eyed urban type whom he had some fun with at Jiri's expense, ranking Jiri's course list according to degrees of impenetrability. At some point he grew aware that the rest of the class had coalesced around Jiri, riding the wave of an epic anecdote.

"This is after weeks of this, you understand, the plaster everywhere, the broken walls, broken pipes, and these two surly Russian Jews coming by every day who'd been nuclear physicists or something back in the Soviet Union."

For a moment, when he recognized the story as his own, Alex was foolish enough to feel a thrill.

"So there I am, marking my mid-terms on the sofa, when he comes in. He's huffing and puffing, carting these bags of gourmet food, nothing like the discount stuff he usually buys—clams, shrimp, fresh oysters, you name it. You should have seen his face when he saw me still sitting there in his living room. Like Mephistopheles had come for his soul. You have to understand what Alex is like—very quiet, very polite, the WASPiest Italian you'll ever meet. But suddenly he's like a man transformed—what was I doing there, and didn't he have the right to have a life, and more of the same. I couldn't figure out what had got into him. Then it comes to me: *cherchez la femme.* The poor man had a date. It all made sense. I should have figured it out when he'd changed the sheets."

The young woman Alex had been talking up was laughing along with the rest. Jiri had hit his mark.

"Alex, how did that date go, anyway?"

Alex tried to keep his tone light.

"A bit of a washout, really."

He had cut off his visits after that. He'd see Jiri in the lobby and Jiri would ask where he'd been keeping himself, but Alex would mumble his excuses and move on, determined to put things between them back on a more professional footing. He didn't need Jiri's abuse, only his approval, preferably in writing; once he had that, he could bury himself in his books and not emerge again until his thesis was done.

He kept away from the English office as well, and the sordid tales still swirling there of Jiri's trials. Word had reached him, by and by, of the new misconduct charge—*idiot*, Alex had thought, a man with a death wish—but he didn't want to know, didn't want to start making excuses for him again or chipping away at the wall he'd set up to keep himself strong. *That which does not kill me.* Let that hold for them both. In the meantime, sticking strictly to the official channels, he had finished off another draft of the first part of his thesis and dropped it off in Jiri's slot at Liberal Arts.

To celebrate he had gone out to an antiquarian bookstore he knew of in Old Montreal thinking to replace Desmond's battered copy of *The Voyage of the Beagle,* which he had been carting around all these years like a penance. The bookstore, it turned out, had closed down, but afterward he wandered through Old Montreal, past City Hall and the Bonsecours Market, along the Old Port to Place d'Youville and back up to Notre Dame. He'd been in the city nearly three years but hadn't walked these streets more than half a dozen times. It was a different century here, in all this old stone, a different country. New France. Near Bonsecours there was a plaque where Dickens had stayed in the 1840s, though the city was already old by then—the Indians had come and gone, and the French intendants, and all the *ancien régime,* to leave the British viceroys to lord it over the peasant conquered much as the French had done over the Indians and the Normans had done over the Angles and Jutes.

Near the Place d'Armes, where a monument still honored de Maisonneuve's massacre of the Iroquois back in 1644, Alex passed a gift shop where he thought he spied a familiar jowly face behind the counter: Jiri's friend John. He couldn't believe it. "Unreconstructed capitalism," John had said dismissively when Alex asked him once what he did. "Pure entrepreneur. When in Rome, as they say." Alex had imagined him in stocks or real estate speculation, yet here he was behind the counter of the kitschiest sort of tourist shop, with maple syrup and plastic moose in the window and T-shirts that read KISS ME, I'M FRENCH.

"John? Is that you?"

He turned, his features twisting into the gruesome automatic smile of a salesman. Then he recognized Alex.

"So, it's you."

It was as it seemed: this was John's livelihood, peddling tourist junk to Ontarians bridging the solitudes and Americans amazed how five-year-olds in the street spoke perfect French.

"I make my few shekels," he said peevishly. "It's easy work. In the meantime, I think, I read, I do what I want."

But there were no books behind the counter, only a little TV set tuned to some afternoon movie.

Alex wasn't sure why he had come in. To shame the man, probably, to puff himself up, though now that he was here, seeing John amidst the Canadian flags and the glass animal figures and the desk-set replicas of Notre Dame, all he felt was a mutual debasement.

The place was deserted. Alex was hesitant to leave, out of a perverse sense of obligation to keep John company.

"Here. Sit. I'll get you a coffee."

John poured some thickish liquid from a thermos into a plastic cup, topping it with a shot from a mickey he pulled from beneath the counter.

"To keep out the cold. Saves on the heating bill."

Some of the tension between them had eased. John's peevishness had lost its personal edge and shifted into a reflex Slavic melancholy.

"How's our friend?" he said, as if Jiri were some passing acquaintance.

"I haven't seen him, actually."

"That makes two of us."

He let that hang in a way that suggested he wanted Alex to pursue the matter.

"You haven't been around?"

"We had an argument, to tell you the truth. A stupid thing, it'll pass. He's a little messed up right now, the poor fucker."

John poured himself a long shot from the mickey, not bothering to dilute it with coffee.

"You know about him, don't you? About his troubles?"

"I know about his wife leaving him," Alex said cautiously, then added, "and about his son."

"Not that stuff, that's only the tip of it. I mean the past, things always go back there. Always historicize."

Alex didn't like the confidential air John had taken on. The last thing he wanted was a tête-à-tête about Jiri's skeletons.

"He doesn't talk about it much. Only that he left before the invasion."

"You're not going back far enough. Before that. During the show trials. Not Stalin's, our own. Jiri's father testified. Eleven men got the bullet thanks to people like him. All innocent, of course, but his father did it for Jiri. For his son. How do you think Jiri got his education?"

Alex felt as if he had been splattered in shit. Why was John telling him this?

John, he knew, had been barred from university. His family had been on the blacklist.

"It has to do something to you, that sort of thing." He finished downing his drink. "It fucks you up."

Alex wanted out of there. It was suffocating, this place, with its crammed narrow aisles, the curved mirrors that reflected them back distorted from every corner.

"Not a word to Jiri about this, you understand. Just between us."

Fucking jerk.

All of this couldn't help but change Alex's view of Jiri. It didn't make him pity him, exactly—pity, in any event, was something Jiri would have detested—but it dirtied things in some hopeless way. The matter of his son seemed almost small in comparison: that was part of the common run of human tribulations, the delinquency of children, the push and pull of father and son, even if it was at the extremest edge of them. This was different; it was foreign territory. Alex was out of his element, beyond the point where the murky gray of the lower depths gave way to black.

Stop by. This in one of their chance awkward meetings in their lobby, though now Alex had to deal not only with the specter of Jiri's son behind him but also of his father. Some spectacled mid-level cadre, no doubt; idealistic once, now disillusioned. *Sign.* There had probably seemed so little to fight for by that point. Only his family; only his son.

He tried the door of the Liberal Arts Building: still open. Inside, though, the place had the desolate end-of-term feeling that Alex used to like but that these days sent a throb of panic through him. Another year gone by. End of term was for real students, not for the likes of the doctoral damned such as himself. The secretary had gone, but past the warren of cubicles and work stations that lined the ground floor Alex could see that Jiri's door was ajar.

He was sitting at his desk with a blank look, his fingers tented beneath his chin.

"Ah, Alex. Come in, come in. I was hoping you'd stop by."

No jibes, no mock surprise, no pretending he hadn't invited him. All this made Alex very uneasy.

The only things on Jiri's desk were a folded newspaper and, as if he had been expecting Alex at that very moment, Alex's submission.

"I haven't seen you much. Have you been all right?"

"Just busy." He was still trying to read Jiri's muted tone. "Getting a start on the next section."

"Good. Good."

He leaned in to leaf through Alex's thesis. There were marks everywhere, Alex saw, lengthy notations in a tight script, unusual for Jiri, who tended to go in for a more global approach that consisted mainly of final withering comments at the very bottom of the last page that undid months of work with a stroke.

Alex waited for it, what little bomb he would lob.

"It's a bit schematic, of course, but that's not the real problem. The real problem is that it goes against everyone. The Marxists, the feminists, the deconstructionists, everything that's happened in the past twenty years. Don't think you're going to throw people off the scent just by tossing in a couple of quotes from Derrida."

Alex's heart fell. He couldn't do it again, he couldn't start from scratch. He saw his future stretched out before him, all the dead-end jobs teaching past participles and direct and reported speech with those damning letters branded to him, Ph.D. (ABD). *All But Dissertation.*

Jiri was still talking.

"There's Baudrillard, that's the new wave now, there's Deleuze and Guattari's *Anti-Oedipus*, that's where the whole discussion of bodies is happening. But you're not going anywhere near that stuff, not really. It comes out in the language—you have to be *in the truth*, isn't that how Foucault put it? All these guys, one way or another, they still follow the discourse."

It always came to this, even with Jiri, he saw now: toe the line. Maybe he was right. Who did Alex think he was, exactly, making up his own little scheme of things? There was a whole industry out there, pro-fessors at Yale, at Cambridge, at the Sorbonne, each of them building in tiny increments on what came before, while he was building on air.

"I can rework it," he said, his mind scrambling to think where he could shift things to bring them more in line with the prevailing order. "It's just a draft. I was planning to bump the language up a bit in the next revision."

"You're not listening to me, Alex." Here it came, the undoing. It was never a question of tinkering with Jiri—you had the goods or you didn't. "The language is the crux of it. You've stepped out into the wilderness. It's always lonely out there, but you'll have to stick to your guns if you want anyone to listen to you. It's the simplicity of the thing that's the strength of it, really, the beauty of it. Like something so obvious it's staring you in the face. What was it that Huxley said? 'I should have thought of it myself.'"

He started going through the submission page by page, noting weak-nesses, clarifying his notes, acting in every regard as if the thesis were viable. Alex sat mute, not daring to interrupt, not even daring to believe he had actually understood. An impossible crossroads seemed to shim-mer ahead of him, the place where what he had aspired to and what he had done intersected.

He didn't know what question to ask afterward, afraid to ask the wrong one, to ruin the moment.

All the bitterness he'd ever felt toward Jiri seemed washed away.

"I wasn't sure about the texts," he said. "I mean, if they'll work."

"No, no, they're exactly right. It's like a survey of three thousand years of Western civilization. I'd stick to Bloom with the Joyce, though, the rest is mainly just playing around."

Suddenly, every possibility was open to Alex—he could go, if he wanted, there was nothing to hold him back. At some point he would have to speak to Jiri about the matter, about Sweden, though at the moment the terrain seemed a bit too treacherous, trip-wired as it was with the question of fathers and sons.

Alex noticed, for the first time, how unusually tidy Jiri's office was, even for Jiri. There were no piles of books, no end-of-term clutter of essays and exams, no half-typed page on Jiri's Selectric to give Alex the sense he was merely an interruption of some more crucial task. He kept waiting for the peremptory tone that always signaled the end of their meetings, but Jiri was still eyeing him.

"There's something behind this," he said. "Something personal. I can feel it in the writing."

"We talked about it. About the Galápagos."

"Yes. You and Darwin. Some sort of epiphany, I suppose."

Alex hoped he would just drop the subject, as he had done before.

"I guess."

"So? What was it? What was your finch?"

There was something plaintive in Jiri's tone that tugged at him.

"If you want to know the truth," he said, before he could stop himself, "someone died there. Someone I was with."

It was the first time he had ever spoken of Desmond.

"A friend?" Jiri said, with uncommon delicacy.

"No. Not a friend. Just someone I'd met. A researcher."

Jiri's attention was still on him.

"What was it, an accident?"

"There was a storm. He fell off our boat. It was all a bit complicated. He was a jerk, really, it was stupid. It's not even worth talking about."

It had been a colossal miscalculation to bring this up with Jiri. Battened away in his mind Desmond's death had had a kind of integrity, a kind of amplitude, but to speak about it seemed to make it instantly amorphous and vulgar.

"So you felt responsible, was that it? Because you didn't like him?"

Jiri had said this charitably enough and yet the easiness of this casual interrogation made Alex's blood rise.

"Something like that. To tell you the truth, I was ready to push him myself."

"But you didn't."

"Didn't what?"

"You didn't actually push him."

He was treating Alex like a child.

"No, I didn't fucking push him."

"And afterward. When he fell. You didn't look for him. You didn't try to save him."

"Look, I get it, I didn't actually kill him, if that's your point." He was practically shouting. "Don't make fun of this. Just don't. I could hear when he fell, for Christ's sake. I heard it, and I didn't do anything."

He felt so angry. *Choke on that,* he thought. *You're not the only one with a fucking past.*

It was always a mistake to give Jiri an entry, Alex knew that. He always made you shovel your shit to hide his own.

"Have you ever told anyone about this?"

"What's the difference?"

"Seriously. How long have you been carrying this around?"

As if he ought to feel unburdened now. As if Jiri had done him a favor. He didn't feel unburdened. All he felt was grief, a hole, as if he had given up something important.

"It's not such a big deal. I realize that. Let's just drop it."

Jiri stared down at his desk.

"Look, Alex, I'm not trying to minimize what happened to you. You got a look at a part of yourself most people never have to see. It changes you. But don't make a monument out of it. People hoard their guilt in these rich countries like it's some kind of commodity. Don't fall into that trap. Save your agonizing for the important things, not some asshole who just happened to die while you were having bad thoughts about him. I'm sure I did worse things than that in the last week that I've already forgotten about."

He said all of this with such directness it was like being sprayed with a water cannon. Alex felt such a mixture of things he couldn't form a proper reaction, not sure if Jiri was belittling him or actually, for once, treating him like an equal.

"Here." Jiri shoved over the newspaper on his desk. It was another *Toronto Star.* "Page three. You'll hear about it soon enough. In case you're wondering what it's actually like to kill someone."

The article looked so minor and inconspicuous, tucked to one side next to an ad for women's leatherwear. "Man Dies from Injuries Following Brutal Attack." Alex couldn't bring himself to do more than scan it, glossing over the details and names. Kidney failure. Apparently one of the kidneys had been damaged in addition to the spleen.

From injuries sustained. It took Alex a moment to realize the legal import of that.

"You know, I went to see him after the attack," Jiri said. "I don't know why. To apologize, I suppose. A stupid thing. He was out cold, of course, he must have been pumped full of morphine—it was like a joke, the way he was trussed up, like one of those cartoons where someone's been hit by a bus. This hunched-up immigrant man was sitting next to the bed, the father, I figured. He hadn't even taken his coat off. He might have been sitting for hours like that, half out of the chair as if he was going to leave any minute. A big sour-faced old bastard with those worker's hands, you know, that skin like cracked plaster. Kazlauskas. Lithuanian. I didn't know what to say to the guy. I told him I was an old high school teacher of his son's, that he'd been a good student, and he just nodded as if he couldn't care less. Who knows what he was thinking, maybe that his son had just got what he deserved. But it was the same, you know, it only made everything worse. The only thing that kept me from putting a gun to my head was thinking, that's it, it can't get any worse than this. The rest'll be easy."

They had reached a funny plateau, one that gave a good view of things but was rather barren and windswept. *That which does not kill me.* Alex had to guard against showing anything like sympathy—he'd be made to pay for that.

"What about your son?" he said. "What'll happen to him?"

"That's the irony. This'll probably help him in the end, now that they've got a good charge against the ringleaders. I know it's funny to say it, but he's not a bad kid. He was probably terrified at the time. He'll testify against the leaders and if he's lucky he'll be home by Christmas. Then there's just the rest of his life to worry about."

He would testify to save his skin. *History repeats itself.* That had to be going through Jiri's mind.

"Have you seen John?" Alex said cautiously.

"You mean Jana?" Jiri laughed. "What, you want to make sure I've got someone to look after me, is that it? That's very kind of you, but you needn't worry about me. I won't be all right, but no worse than usual. As for Jana, he's gone back to Czechoslovakia."

John had never mentioned anything of the sort.

"Can he just do that? Won't he be arrested or something?"

Jiri shrugged.

"He'd had enough, it seems. We had a big argument, in fact, but I couldn't talk him out of it."

"What about his shop?"

"Oh, so you knew about that. That should tell you everything. He just locked the door and got on a plane. There were a few debts, I guess, but it wasn't really that. It was the children. He wanted to see them. His wife turned them against him when he left, he never really got over that. Who knows, maybe glasnost will save him or maybe the party will use him as a poster boy. It's a coup for them, in a way, to get him back. Fleeing the capitalists."

Jiri set Alex's dissertation in front of him.

"I should tell you that I'll be moving to Toronto, of course, with the trial and everything. I've taken a job at one of the colleges there, composition, mainly, though they promised to throw me a bit of literature now and then."

"But you'll still be coming up here? I mean, you'll still be on the faculty?"

"I handed in my resignation about an hour ago," Jiri said cheerily. "A clean break."

Alex twigged: he was heading off being sacked. He could have commuted otherwise, taken a leave, whatever, instead of languishing in the backwaters of community college composition.

"What about my dissertation?" Alex blurted.

"You'll be fine with it. You're well on your way. I suspect you'll be getting tenure somewhere long before I ever do."

That was it, then. Alex couldn't quite figure out what had just happened between them—it seemed they had revealed their darkest selves, then carried on as if it were nothing. Maybe this was what passed for friendship with Jiri, these perilous thrusts and feints, the constant raising of stakes until disentanglement became impossible.

"I liked your use of the transhumance, by the way," Jiri said. "I assume that came out of some sort of family history."

Out on the street Alex felt a peculiar lightness, though not quite the cathartic one he might have wanted. It was more like being reduced: he had one less thing to set him apart, one less excuse. He didn't like to give up his bogeymen any more than anyone else did.

So let me get this straight. Here's this bastard you've been trying to get rid of like a bad penny for what, six or seven years, and then you actually miss him? I know you're not big on Freud these days, but come on. Oedipus Redux or what?

(Chuckling) I don't know if you're exactly in a position to be criticizing my father figures, Peter.

Touché. Or your bastards, for that matter. But you have to admit it's a little, pardon my French, fucked up.

I don't want to sound too mystical about it, but I guess I sort of became him, in a way. I took his place.

The air had cooled. A lingering smell of winter wafted over from the shadows of the Hall Building: *I'll be back,* it said. Things had a way of doing that, of coming back, especially the bad ones. The eternal return. Look at Jiri. He was running from himself, you could have said, he was running from the monster in the maze. But that didn't really sound like Jiri. Maybe he ran as a dog did, because it could. There was a field and open space, no leash, and only the pounding of your blood. *Run.* Over the hill to who knew what, with just the wind against you and the roar in your head of being alive.

O utside the light was fading. Already the thrill of Jiri's approval seemed a distant memory.

A line of clouds was setting in over the river, maybe bringing with it a last rogue snowfall. Alex knew he ought to pick up some food, but he hadn't the will. Each time he went home now the same fatigue came over him: he seemed surrounded by so much *stuff*, all of which he would have to pack up again and store or cart home or toss out so that one day he could start the whole cycle all over again.

He felt the familiar roil in his blood as he hit de Maisonneuve and his building loomed up before him. His renewal notice had come a few weeks before, proposing another insane increase, as if the previous year had never happened, and Alex, as was his right, had accepted the lease but rejected the increase. By now it was all tactics, though the object of them grew more and more obscure as the day of reckoning receded further and further into the distance.

He entered the foyer and checked his mailbox. The weekly Steinberg's flyer, with a coupon for Folgers; an entire booklet of coupons from the already struggling Faubourg. Nothing more. Alex's mood dipped. No letter from Per in over two weeks.

Across from the mailboxes, a thin young man with the washed-out look of a heroin addict was struggling to make sense of the new telephone entry system. The system was about the only real innovation in the building after all the months of work, a completely useless device that seemed to require an understanding of some of the finer points of integral calculus, so that every time Alex entered the place these days he was faced with the same dilemma, whether to quickly pull the door closed behind him like an asshole or let through whatever petty thief or serial killer was puzzling over the keyboard.

Alex turned his key and held open the door.

"Thanks, man," the addict said, disappearing into one of the elevators without even bothering to hold it for him.

Alex dumped his junk mail into an empty planter. A rough hand-lettered sign had been posted between the elevators for several days: LEASE RENEWALS, 2ND FLOOR. This time around the landlords were getting smart, calling in the refuseniks early on in an effort to nip any group solidarity in the bud. Alex himself had got a call, but had politely declined to meet. As was his right. *I prefer to let the Régie decide.* He had somehow been thinking of this as part of his plan—he'd have them over a barrel, with two years' increases still in abeyance—but the truth was that the closer he got to departure, the less leverage he had. All his claims were still tied up at the Régie, and he might be forced simply to drop them all when he left. The lease renewal had just been a stratagem, a ruse, but it could easily turn against him. He was responsible for the place now for another year, and might have to spend weeks finding a subletter, or might be refused one and then be stuck paying his rent until the landlords chose to replace him. He could just abscond, of course, but that would be burning his bridges, and giving the bastards not just the legal victory but the moral one.

The tenants' association had long ago imploded, the victim of its own internecine bloodbaths and of the Byzantine vagaries of the Régie du logement. The association hadn't stood a chance, really—since it had no official standing and no right to the details of individual files it was no match for the owners, who knew every claim and every hearing and had only to hive people off one at a time and cajole them into submission. It had all begun to seem positively Orwellian. People living a few inches of drywall from each other were stuck in their little boxes of paranoia and fear, while the owners, with their direct line to the Régie, knew every time anyone farted or flushed a toilet or turned on a light.

Alex's own claims had slowly wended their way through a nightmare of bizarre twists and turns. A series of letters arrived announcing hearings and then deferring them, combining some of his claims into single ones according to criteria that were never made clear, then separating them again. Finally, in January, his first hearing came up, on the actual increase. He trudged through the ice and slush to the Régie offices, carting letters from the landlords, association minutes, photographs, timelines, double-registered reply cards, and sat in a windowless waiting room on the sixth floor of a downtown office tower while one by one people were called in before the *régisseur*. After two and a half hours the bailiff called out a mangled version of his name and led him to an open area set out with a few rows of auditorium chairs and a dais up front where the commissioner sat at a flimsy table like someone doing a product pitch at a convention. There were so many people milling about, assistants carrying files, young men with coffee cups, a worker who was changing a fluorescent light, that they might as well have been in the middle of a train station.

He was seated at his own little table. A few lonely faces stared out from the back rows of seats, but none that Alex recognized. The *régisseur*, a pleasant-looking Quebecois in a stylish suit who spoke impeccable English, had the air of someone who had accidentally wandered into the midst of an argument and had gamely agreed to help settle it.

"For Le 1444 Mackay Enregistré?" he called out.

But no one came forward.

The bastards had stood him up. Alex was livid—after all the letters, the lists, the postage, the months of waiting, they hadn't even bothered showing up.

"So what does that mean, exactly?" he asked.

"I suppose it means you've won," the *régisseur* said, with a whimsical smile. "You should get your notice in a couple of weeks."

So they had just lain down like that without a fight. Alex didn't get it. Maybe it wasn't worth their time, paying a lawyer or whatever to sit twiddling his thumbs waiting for a hearing; or maybe they knew they didn't have a hope. The whole affair left Alex oddly deflated—he had wanted his day in court, had wanted to spin out the whole saga, the strong-arming, the threats, the outages, the insidious injustice of it. Instead he was walking away, like everyone else, with only his few bucks of saved rent to show for it all, and maybe not even that, since it still fell to the Régie to settle on what it deemed a reasonable increase.

At least it was over, he thought. But a few days later someone slipped a sheet of paper under his door in the familiar pink foolscap of the Régie: a notice of appeal. The owners hadn't even bothered to send it double-registered, as if daring him to claim he hadn't received it, to stoop to their level. Under "Reason for the Appeal," someone had written, in the worst sort of scrawl, "Unable to attend original hearing." That was reason enough, it seemed, to start the whole process all over—more counter-forms to file, more months of waiting, more trudging down to offices, another smiling *régisseur*. Then, beyond that, surely another appeal or maybe even a judgment against him, because of heating costs gone up or necessary repairs done or costs for bylaw compliance, who knew? It was maddening; it was hopeless; it was criminal. Bucketloads of taxpayers' cash had been spent to set up this vast instrument to guard tenants' rights, laws had been drafted, offices built, civil servants hired, thousands of forms printed up, and it was all just another tendon in the long arm of The Man.

Alex knew then that he had already lost. He had neither the stamina nor the will to follow the matter through, not to mention that he was already thinking by then of being gone by the summer. In the worst-case scenario nothing would be settled by then and not only would all his damage claims be dismissed but the outrageous increase would simply be rubber-stamped, so that he'd actually have to send a check over from Sweden for back rent or risk having his credit rating ruined forever, never able to rent an apartment again in the country or get a mortgage or buy a car. This was how, from the smallest of things, whole lives were unraveled and spirits were crushed. He might as well live in China or the Soviet Union.

He ought to have settled and put the matter from his mind, but instead he kept tilting at it, pushing his forms and mailing them out, filing his lease renewal by the required date. His hearing for damage claims came and went exactly as the other, with the landlords' side of the bench conspicuously empty. In a matter of days, wonder of wonders, a judgment came back to him, heartbreaking in its reduction of weeks and months of political struggle to the most finicky of sums: for the loss of water in the months of July and August 1986, thirty dollars; for electrical outages, two dollars per outage; for the loss of the pool, five dollars per month. And so it went. In total, the settlements, which covered the six or seven months when living conditions in the building had spiraled down to Third World levels, came to ninety-six dollars. Then two days after the judgment had reached him came the familiar pink form again, slipped under his door like the last one, the iniquitous notice of appeal.

In the elevator now he went to press the button for his floor but at the last instant hit the one for the second floor instead. Before he could change his mind the elevator doors opened and there before him, sitting hunched at his little desk in his office-cum-storage room, was Mr. Shapiro, looking a bit paunchier and a bit balder than the previous summer but not that much worse for wear. Alex felt a queasiness come over him at gazing like that on the baby-cheeked face of the enemy. The banality of evil.

He ought to just turn around and go home.

"Alan, isn't it?" Too late. "Come on in, I'm just getting organized."

The air on this floor still reeked of chlorine, though it had been many months now since the pool had been open. Another half-eaten sub sat in front of Shapiro, maybe the same one as the summer before, a cunning prop. To one side on the desk was an open banker's box that looked stuffed with rumpled renewal forms, the building's address scribbled across the side of it as if this were merely one enterprise among many.

"Sorry, refresh my memory about your last name. It's a bit hard to keep track."

Alex had to admit he was impressed that the man remembered him at all.

"Fratarcangeli. Alex Fratarcangeli."

"Right. Alex. Sorry. Italian, isn't it?"

He had turned from the banker's box to what Alex hadn't noticed resting on a low side table behind it: a gleaming state-of-the-art Compaq Deskpro, complete with a big CRT screen and a long row of fancy function buttons.

"You have one of these yet? I can keep that whole box of stuff on one disk."

For a moment then, his eyes fixed on the screen, he was pure geek. He was running some kind of fancy data program, dBASE, it looked like. After a few glitches a screen came up with Alex's name at the head of it. It gave Alex an eerie feeling to see all that data about him pixelating against the blue.

"Right. Right." Shapiro's brow furrowed as he scrolled through the file. "There's still last year outstanding, I guess."

He said this as if Alex were some shuffling deadbeat who'd come begging to him.

"So," Shapiro said heavily. "How are we going to solve this?"

Alex saw his brother Gus in Shapiro's place again, and his father, battling the welfare moms, the drifters, all the low-lifes who turned their hair gray and sucked away their tiny margin of profit.

It didn't matter, he thought. He just wanted out.

"I'm not sure I'll be staying, it turns out. I might need to leave in the middle of the summer."

There, he had blown all his advantage. Now he was the one asking a favor.

Shapiro leaned back in his chair.

"I think we could work something out. I think we could manage that."

It was all very dispiriting. Alex ended up agreeing to a five percent increase, backdated three months so it would have been in effect long enough to use as a basis for a new rent when he left, though Shapiro agreed to kick back the difference. The only other concessions he got were the right to break his lease on thirty days' notice, and the ninety-six dollars the Régie had deemed he was due.

"Here, I'll make the check out right now," Shapiro said. "I'll include the extra you're paying on the rest of your lease, so you can just make out your rent for the full amount."

There were half a dozen forms to sign. A new lease renewal, with the thirty-day clause, barely legible, scratched in in pen; then the agreement to backdate the rent, several retraction forms for the Régie. Alex felt like someone who had agreed, for the merest baubles, to sign a false confession.

Shapiro had taken on an unabashedly pleased, helpful air.

"Concordia student, right? What was it, history?"

"English, actually."

"I always loved English. Shakespeare, Dickens, all those guys. I wish I still had the time, you know?"

In the elevator Shapiro's check, for a hundred and thirty-six dollars, his damages plus his paltry kickback, felt like a scorpion in his pocket. He had given himself over to the zeitgeist, to profit and loss, just like everyone else. Social Darwinism was alive and well.

You can see it in the language people use these days, Peter, the metaphors, this whole mental shift. It's all economics now. It's not values anymore, it's value.

Well, to coin a phrase, I guess that's the price we pay. What is it they say about Thatcher? A shopkeeper's daughter.

Exactly. Meanwhile, no one thinks of the social costs.

That's the bottom line, isn't it? But it doesn't look like anyone's taking stock.

María would never have taken the check. She would have stuck the thing out.

He ought to have clipped that coupon for Folgers. It was a cut above Maxwell House, if not quite Van Houtte's. It occurred to him that he likely had Darwin to thank for Van Houtte's: it was Darwin and his ilk who had displaced peasants around the world, so that great latifundia could be pieced together in places like El Salvador to grow things on more scientific principles than dumb peasants would ever manage. Liberals, they were called then. That had been Darwin's camp. The conservatives, meanwhile, the bloody paternalists, had thought the rich should look after the poor, not realizing that that merely encouraged them.

He still remembered that awful coffee he'd had at Miguel's apartment. It was all in the roasting, he'd heard. The thought of Miguel set off a little alarm at the back of his head. *Shit.* Their lesson. He had completely forgotten. He glanced at his watch: a half-hour late. If he was lucky, Miguel had waited. Or not lucky, exactly, but he was in charge of him now, María had put him in Alex's trust. The least Alex could do was not make a botch of it.

– 8 –

Miguel was sitting up against Alex's door thumbing through another of the glossy magazines he went through like candy. Cheesy men's stuff, mainly, of the sort that Michael sometimes bought for the bods, but also fashion magazines, *National Geographic, Chatelaine,* anything he could lay his hands on. He never read them, from what Alex could tell, only leafed through them looking at the pictures, pausing over these with the childlike curiosity of an extraterrestial marveling at Earth culture. Alex felt a jumble of emotions seeing him squatting there so innocent-seeming and absorbed. Relief that he hadn't missed him and a grudging protectiveness, but also the inevitable irritation that Miguel had managed to worm his way into the building as if he was no better than all the other riff-raff that waltzed in off the street, that he was poring through his trashy magazines rather than doing the worksheets Alex had given him, which he surely wouldn't have finished, that he was simply there, still in Alex's life, practically his ward now, so that they would probably end up bound together in unholy alliance until the end of days.

"Hey, man. Is not normal for you, so late."

Normal for Miguel was to waltz in forty-five minutes after the appointed time as if it were nothing. Now this one occasion that he actually seemed to have been punctual he had the gall to lord it over him.

Alex went straight for the door, leaving Miguel to scramble clear of him.

"Been waiting long?" he said tersely.

"No man, I'm jus' coming now."

In the elevator Alex had started gearing himself up for a possible man-to-man on the subject of María's departure, but already he felt the minginess that always came on him around Miguel, the unwillingness to let him imagine he took him seriously.

"I saw your sister."

"Yeah, man, she's going home. Is jus' crazy."

"So you know?"

"She's my sister, man, you think I don' know?"

Man this and *man* that. You'd think the place was crawling with men. Meanwhile the real men, apparently, were off fighting the war.

"If she's your sister," Alex said, aiming below the belt, "then why don't you stop her?"

"She's my sister, man, not my kid," Miguel said gloomily. "You know what she's like. Even back home she's always been breaking my balls."

Though Alex didn't feel he had given him any encouragement, Miguel had never wavered from his first attachment to him. After things had soured between Alex and María, Miguel had commiserated with him as if Alex was the one he'd been watching out for.

"Is better for you, my friend. She's my sister, you know, but very hard. Very tough. Not like you."

Since then Miguel had kept up the connection between them as if it had never been in question, calling at all hours, showing up unannounced at Alex's door to drag him to some friend's place or function. The simple fact was that he actually seemed fond of Alex, had grown attached to him as if Alex were a young naïf in a bad neighborhood whom he had taken under his protection. Alex, post-María, post-Amanda, didn't have the will to fight him off. It was a relief, really, to let Miguel take charge, to fall into the rhythm he had of coming and going without plan as if he were still roaming the streets of San Salvador trying to keep his finger on the pulse.

"What did you do back there, exactly?" Alex had asked him, not entirely sure he wanted to know.

"This and that. First my father's factory, then when it closed down jus' little jobs for money. To carry things and so on. Like a messenger."

An innocent. Except that in El Salvador there were no innocents, only sides. The army there organized youth groups to stand on street corners and watch everyone who came and went, a sort of demonic Boy Scouts that formed the recruiting grounds for the death squads and paramilitary.

Miguel still had his network of mole-like associates, short, slick-haired young men who would come together in little nodes at the

Salvadoran events and stand laconic and dark-eyed and watchful like boys at a high school dance, then melt into the crowd again. Alex was lucky if he ever heard a complete sentence pass among these boys—it was all Miguel's *unibersal language* with them, a nod, a grunt, a wave of the hand. Not like the politicos, with their heated talk. Alex couldn't have said if they were simply scoping the place for women or arranging names on a hit list. More likely they were doing the sort of "little jobs" they had done back home, since none of them ever seemed to lack for cash. Miguel sometimes would open a wallet packed with wrinkled twenties and hand over a few bills to this one or that one like a mafia overlord, a separate economy unfolding within his little cell that seemed to have nothing to do with the normal Keynesian flow of the refugee world, the welfare payments or the low-end service jobs or the remission of funds to family and freedom-fighters back home. Never once had Alex seen Miguel express what could pass for an unambiguous political position—he stood above all that, or beneath or beside it, wherever, it seemed, he'd be clear of the line of fire.

"The rebels, you know, they have guns like the army. You shoot, someone will die. The bullet doesn't care if it's left or right."

It was Alex who had suggested the tutoring, in that way he had of bringing upon himself the things he most dreaded. He thus managed to institutionalize a relationship that might otherwise never have survived its flimsy foundations. He had hoped to keep some sort of connection to María, he supposed, though he never actually asked about her. It was only by chance that he learned she had moved out on her own—he dropped by their old apartment once when he couldn't reach Miguel on the phone to find María's room had been taken over by one of Miguel's ferret-eyed young cohorts.

"Sorry, man, she take the phone with her," Miguel said. "A couple of days, I get another one."

She had moved up to Jean Talon to be closer to her work, Miguel said. Her departure looked suspicious to Alex, but Miguel took it in stride, over the next few months taking in an alarming number of new roommates, as if he were running a sex trade operation or underground railroad. Each one seemed as transient and shifty as the one before, but they all had a story, had smuggled up from the States or been evicted because their welfare had been cut off or were the cousin of an in-law on Miguel's mother's side.

Then out of the blue one day Miguel told Alex he had moved, like his sister, to Jean Talon.

"I thought you said there were too many Salvadorans there."

"No, man, you don' even see them. Is all Italians. Good people, like us. Latin people."

Alex wasn't sure whom exactly Miguel meant to include in that "us." His apartment, when Alex saw it, looked like a carbon copy of the last, except that instead of clotheslines strung with laundry out back there were the elaborately trellised and furrowed back plots of the local Italians. Alex had never spent much time around Jean Talon but now suddenly he was there every weekend—Miguel would call and wheedle and cajole, say Alex's brain would rot if he was always working, until Alex would lose the will to resist.

"You become a machine, man, is no good. You become a fucking Canadian."

Somehow Miguel had already so understood the instinctive self-abnegation that formed the bedrock of the national character. It was true that there was hardly an outpost of Alex's emotional landscape these days that didn't feel colonized by an almost Presbyterian sense of chastisement—most recently Katherine had dropped out of school and taken a shit job as a receptionist and his parents had canceled a trip to the Holy Land because of some funny bleeding from his mother's nether parts. Miguel took him to bars up in Little Italy that were worlds away from all of this, full of overdressed Italian girls on the lam from their nineteenth-century parents and gold-chained Ginos who drove up in muscle cars. It was everything he had fled from back home, but it felt like a kind of anaesthesia now, familiar and without pain. Miguel had abandoned his own kind the instant he had moved in amongst them and cleaved himself to the Italians, which suited Alex fine—he didn't know how many more cumbia nights he could have borne, how much more of seeing María across a room and feeling like a eunuch. In the bars he got mildly or totally drunk and even managed to fraternize with the womenfolk, because Miguel, who looked at home here with his black pants and lamé shirts, had wasted no time on that front. They might end up dancing until two in the morning, something the normal Alex simply didn't do. But then it wasn't the normal Alex who went out to these bars, but some other sleazy, devil-may-care one, the sort of person that back in high school he had despised and desperately longed to be.

He never made the mistake of trying to take any of these Italian girls home. Even if that had been remotely possible it would surely have led to unmitigated disaster—within a week he would either have found himself bound up in a web of soul-strangling obligations he would never have got clear of or paralyzed with ethnic shame. But Miguel never left with anyone either. Alex suspected he had never had sex with a woman, for all his talk, and indeed he always looked relieved at the end of a night to have Alex to rescue him.

If the trains had stopped Alex crashed at Miguel's, stumbling home with him through streets that looked surreal in the nighttime desertion. The houses were mainly poky two-story townhouses built right up against the street, but half of them were done up with the rococo flourishes of ducal palaces, fancy brickwork or pillared doors or Juliet balconies in swirling metal that seemed straight out of the grand apartment houses of Milan. Once Miguel tried the door of the big Romanesque church off Dante Street, and found it open.

"Let's check it out, man! Come on!"

He was already inside. Alex imagined alarms going off and the pastor appearing from the rectory half-dressed and furious, but there was only the cavernous silence. He made his way through the dark, ghostly shapes looming up from every direction.

Miguel had found a light switch.

"Over here, man."

A couple of sconces came on in the chancel to send grainy light up into the dome above the altar. It was adorned in a massive fresco crowded with iconography, a Madonna ringed by the angelic host and below these the saints, perhaps, and lower still the mere mortals, every creature in its place. The bottom tier was a veritable mob, fat-cheeked clerics and dewy-eyed altar boys and a man in a suit who looked like he'd wandered in off the street by mistake.

Miguel pointed to a figure in the bottom corner. "Is your hero."

Alex had to strain in the light to make sure he'd seen correctly: it was Mussolini, in full military regalia, a bit more hirsute and robust than in life, perhaps, but clearly him, sitting astride a charger flanked by a host of cardinals and by the pope himself on his throne.

"He wasn't a hero," Alex said. "He was a dictator."

"You are wrong, my friend. He was for the poor. Schools, hospitals, all of this."

Alex felt irritated that Miguel knew these things.

"That doesn't make him a hero."

"Is depend what was before. For some people, I think, he is a hero."

"Is that how people think back in El Salvador? That it's better to have a dictator?"

Alex was surprised at how wounded Miguel looked.

"No. I don' talk about El Salvador. Is different."

Anyone other than Alex would surely have softened to Miguel long before. He was just a child, really, nearly ten years Alex's junior, just someone trying to make a life. Yet each time Alex saw him he felt the same little node of resistance form in him.

Miguel had taken his place at the dining table and was leafing through the notebook Alex had given him for his exercises. Sure enough, he'd done barely half of what Alex had assigned him.

"You know, you got to move from this place, man," he said. "Is not good people here."

"I like them well enough."

"Is too many English, man. Too many racists."

This wasn't quite what Alex had expected.

"I wouldn't think they're any worse than the French."

"No, you're wrong, one hundred percent. The French, maybe they say it in words, but the English say it in their eyes. Is the worst. The French know that. They know what it is, when someone looks at you. Like that book. White niggers."

Alex was astounded.

"You read that?"

"No, man, I seen it on your shelf the first time I came here. *White Niggers*. Is all I need to see. Is something you feel in your bones. The Quebecois, they feel it. They're like us."

The ambiguous "us" again. This time, Alex was pretty sure it didn't include him.

"You know, I come to your door downstairs," Miguel said, "with that fucking security you got, it doesn't work, and is like a dog coming from the street how people look at me. I'm just saying to you, man."

Whatever will Alex had had to start tackling the past perfect tense had gone from him. Instead he pulled a couple of beers from the fridge, left over, for all he knew, from his end-of-term party a year ago, and handed one to Miguel.

Miguel brightened.

"My friend. I thank you."

They set chairs out on the balcony and sat drinking and smoking like mestizos in the village square. The office towers downtown reflected the sun as it sank behind Alex's building. Out over the St. Lawrence the cars were crossing the bridges into Longueil, where Félix had lived in his fifties bungalow and Pierre Vallières in his tarpaper shack. Miguel had a photo tacked to his kitchen cupboard that showed a white stucco ranch house in San Salvador that looked much more like Félix's bungalow than Pierre's shack, though a sort of militarized version of it, the doors and windows barred, the garage battened down, the garden ringed with twelve-foot walls topped with barbed wire and broken glass.

"Do you think it's safe for your sister to go back?" Alex said.

Miguel picked at the label on his beer.

"What's safe? How can you say *safe* in a war?"

Alex felt all the questions he had never dared to ask hovering between them. He knew too much by now, was the problem, enough to piece things together. *Little jobs*, Miguel had said. *Like a messenger*. Maybe watching people come and go. Once they grew out of the youth groups, young men like Miguel normally graduated to the Organización Democrática Nacionalista. ORDEN. Order. This, depending on whom you asked, was either a fabrication of leftist propaganda, or a loose association of civic-minded peasants interested in controlling crime, or a CIA-trained counter-insurgent paramilitary organization that was the main recruiting ground for the death squads for government informants.

"She said there was a boy there she'd been involved with," Alex said. "That she'd got a letter. A threat."

"She said so?"

Already Alex felt he had overstepped.

"She seemed to think she was safe now. She wouldn't say why."

Miguel kept picking at his bottle.

"Is only for her to tell. Before, I was there, I could see things, but now who can say?"

See what, Alex thought.

"Did you know this boy? The one who was killed?"

"Did she say so?"

"She didn't mention you." Alex had never seen him like this, so wound up. "Only that he was killed."

"Is better you don' ask too many questions, my friend. Is not Canada, my country. You don' know the things there."

He had hit the usual impasse. It was as if a crust covered the real truth of the place, as if there was what could be seen and known but beneath that a kind of sinkhole where everything was darkness.

Any next question he could ask seemed like stepping too far.

"You know, in El Salvador," Miguel said, "every day you wake up, you have to decide, am I going to live or die. That's it. You just have to decide."

The comment settled between them a moment like a stone sinking down.

"This boy. Yes, I know him. Not from María. From the street. She never brings him to the house, but I know him. Is my business to know. One day someone can knock on the door, and if you don' know, they can kill you. They can kill your family."

They were at the heart of it now, the awful thing, unfolding just as Alex had feared.

It wasn't too late to stop.

"Is that what happened?"

"Why do you want to know this, man? It doesn't matter now."

"But she's going back there. It doesn't sound safe."

"What did María say? The letter. Who was the one that sends it to her?"

Alex wasn't following.

"She didn't say. The military. The death squads. Whoever sends those things."

"Was not the right, my friend, was the left. When the boy was killed."

Twilight had set in. Miguel was growing dark beside him. The goodwill Alex had felt between them when they'd come out here was gone. Miguel had been right. They should never have talked of these things. In his mind Alex saw the bungalow in white stucco with its barred windows and bunkered doors, the men who came knocking. A name was whispered, an address, and an hour later the army stormed some hovel in the barrio. It happened every day.

It came to him that María must know all of this.

Miguel had risen.

"I'm going, man. You call me or something."

Alex didn't know what to put his hand to afterward. He picked up *White Niggers of America* from the shelf in the living room, no doubt right where Miguel had seen it a year before. Vallières was living out in the country now. He had done time for a bombing but then had renounced violence and The Revolution and gone back to the land. Even the kidnappers who had got free passage to Havana had gone straight—they had grown so despondent and bored in the hotel life Castro had provided for them that they'd preferred to come home and do jail time. That had been his own country's brief flirtation with the violent overthrow of the established order, completely unglamorous and incidental and banal. It was something to be grateful for.

The twilight hour. Alex rummaged around in his fridge, found nothing, then stretched out on his couch while the light died.

9

H‌unger finally drove him into the streets. He headed toward the Casa Italia. The restaurant's sign had been removed at some point and Alex almost walked past the place, so anonymous had it suddenly become, with the half-illicit look of a speakeasy or a gray-market eatery in Eastern Europe.

The restaurant was packed. Domenic, his round mountain face beaming, his mongrel face, it turned out, the face of slaves, was holding court from behind the cash.

"Alex, what's the matter with you, you look like your dog died!"

His mother's face. He must remember to call her.

It's my mother, actually. The Big C.

"I'll just take whatever the special is."

In the three months now since his mother's diagnosis he had barely let himself think she might actually die. He felt too young for the death of a parent. He hadn't worked through his issues yet. He hadn't got around to mentioning who he really was.

Oh, by the way, Mom, before you die—I'm not sure I told you about my son.

Domenic's attention had already shifted to the man in a suit and tie who had come in behind him.

"I've been h'eating in every place in the city, and yours h'it's still the best."

"Then you should write in your newspaper and tell them to give me back my sign."

"Yes, it's just crazy, I know."

She had had her operation a few days before Easter, a convenience for Alex, since he'd been able to make two family events for the price of one. They had all sat in the hospital waiting room, the six siblings, her whole crop, while the doctors had cut out the thing that had given them life. It had done yeoman's service, it had ensured her genetic line, then had tried to kill her. Alex pictured it lumpy and flaccid like an old valise, a battered immigrant's handbag.

"I guess we're both on intimate terms with my mother's uterus now," Gus said to the surgeon afterward, a good line, though Alex always thought of Gus as a humorless neo-con. He had Alex over that evening to his new house on the lake and his girls gave Alex such a hug he thought they'd mistaken him for someone else.

"Wow. What did I do to deserve that?"

"All you have to do is show up," Gus said. "That's all it takes."

The surgery, apparently, had gone well. By Easter his mother was already home and going about her chores in her usual tortoise-like shuffle, as if she'd merely had her tonsils out.

"How're you feeling, Mom?" In the hospital Alex had caught a glimpse of the blood-encrusted stitches across her belly, just around the spot where his father had had half his stomach removed for an ulcer.

"Oh, *'n'g'e male*. Not too bad."

It had all happened with the quickness of catastrophe—the bleeding, then the tests, and then in a matter of weeks the surgery. To make matters worse, Mimi, the family's backbone, the only one who was any good in a crisis, had fallen into a slump that had taken a sharp turn for the worse not long before their mother was diagnosed. It had started, really, with her new house, the place she had planned out and longed for all of her life and then had ended up hating. After that everything seemed to sour for her, her marriage, her children. Then an NFB film crew had come through to interview her on the pioneering work she'd done on her greenhouse farm in areas like pest control and bumblebee pollination, but when the film came out she discovered she'd been duped.

"They twisted everything," she'd said on the phone, beyond distraught, ready to leave her husband, her kids, to move out of town, to change her name. "They made me look like an idiot. It's like I've wasted my life."

It turned out the film hadn't been a profile of the town's burgeoning greenhouse industry but an exposé on the treatment of Mexican migrant workers.

"The woman was so nice," Mimi said, practically in tears. "Just this little Chinese woman. She spoke English so well."

Alex prayed Mimi hadn't actually said that to her.

"It's probably not as bad as you think."

But then Alex had caught the documentary when it aired on TV, and it had been bad. The main figure, interviewed with a J-Cloth tied bandito-like around his face to protect his identity, was actually a disgruntled migrant who worked for a big fifty-person operation whose owner was never named and never chose to appear. Meanwhile perfectly upstanding people like Mimi had been lured by flattery and indirection into saying things they ought not to have said.

"Oh, yeah, we have to kick 'em in line once in a while," one of Alex's uncles was seen to say, clearly relishing his moment in the spotlight. "But, you know, they're the workers and we're the boss. That's how it goes."

The death blow for Mimi was a particularly cruel one, strategically placed toward the end of the film like a coda.

"It's true they go into town sometimes and get drunk," she said, in answer to some question that wasn't heard, "and then their owners have to go and pick them up."

Their owners. The filmmakers must have been rubbing their hands in glee at that one. Where had Mimi been the last forty years, when everyone else was learning never to say such things? But the whole matter apparently turned on an unfortunate semantic shift: the local greenhouse owners, who had been known as "growers," had found themselves competing for the term with a new class of professional managers-for-hire and had decided that henceforth they would be known as "owners."

"It was just in my head," Mimi said. "It was stupid. It was stupid. But then you say it, and you can't take it back."

The whole affair was more depressing to Alex than he would have expected. Of course these farmers were racists, who wasn't in these little towns? The Germans looked down on the Italians, the Italians on the Lebanese, the Lebanese on the Portuguese, and the Anglo-Saxon gentry on everyone. This was a town where there had been a law on the books well into the fifties banning blacks from spending the night. And yet the film was a travesty, through and through, the sort of thing that gave social action a bad name. It had divided the church, after one of the new priests had started a union drive; it had divided the migrants themselves, most of whom were just anxious not to kill the goose that laid the egg. What the film seemed to miss was that there was a whole ecosystem at work in these places, full of the minutest subtleties of interrelation, that you couldn't really understand a piece without understanding the whole.

In Montreal, Alex had seen a Chernobyl film at the Cinémathèque that was part of a new glasnost series coming out of the Soviet Union—it was all propaganda, of course, a shining tribute to the workers who had risked their lives for the nation, but at least it was honest propaganda, at least it showed enough of the poor sods scraping through the radiated earth in their shirtsleeves to let you piece out the truth. There were shots of the emptied town, the meals left behind uneaten, the desolate apartment blocks, as chilling and still as the final scenes of *On the Beach*.

Jana had seen the film and had dismissed it at once.

"It's still the same story. They're all dead by now, those heroes of the revolution. Even the filmmaker's dead."

But Alex had found it oddly moving. Part way through, it had shown the interrogation of a technician who had fled the site after the initial blast, hangdog and shamefaced now like the worst sort of shirker, good only for the Gulag. Alex had squirmed then much as he had when he had watched Mimi: the guy was just another poor filmic scapegoat. He couldn't help thinking—maybe this was the point, what was there to be read between the lines—that he would have done the same, he would have run, just as he probably would have been caught out by that film crew like his fellow townsfolk. People couldn't bear this sort of close scrutiny, it was asking too much. That was surely what had bothered him so much about Mimi's film, his survivor guilt.

By the time of the surgery, however, Mimi had pulled herself together.

"I don't even want to think about all that anymore. All that matters is that Mom gets through this."

Alex was relieved. It had reached the point where she'd actually been turning to him for advice, a clear measure of how desperate things had got.

Easter Monday, he had shown up at her place. She was out in the greenhouses winding tomato plants up their support strings along with the Mexicans, who were still putting in their ten-hour shift despite the holiday. Recently they had come to Mimi afraid that because of the film, they would be forced from now on to take holidays off.

Alex stood watching Mimi at her work, feeling instinctively guilty at being at leisure and clean. The air was rank with the steamy earth smell of his childhood, the pungent odor of the vines. The steam pipes clanked as the heat fed into them, with a sound like bullets whizzing through them.

"I don't know how to say this, exactly," he started.

Mimi kept her eyes on her work, winding her plants with unthinking expertness, her hands moving like dancers.

"This better not be something bad. If it's something bad I don't want to hear it."

He was afraid to go on, watching her hands move. One little slip in this sort of work, and the plant snapped. That was the Great Sin of their youths, to break a plant.

"I guess that depends on how you look at it."

"It sounds bad already."

The first few sets of flowers had opened on the plants. All up and down the rows they hung with their brazen yellow anthers heavy with pollen, utterly promiscuous and unabashed.

"The thing is . . . I have a son."

Mimi kept at her work with a dangerous calm.

"You're joking, right? Tell me you're joking."

It seemed briefly possible that he was.

"Not really. I mean, I could lie if you want."

Her hands rose up and up another plant, then the smallest miscalculation, and the head snapped off.

"Fuck! Fuck!" For a moment they both seemed to relive all the old childhood terror. "It's all right. There's a sucker. It'll come back."

They went up to the house. Alex knew better than to ever comment on any aspect of the house by now, or to use the upstairs bathroom, which had been a particular disappointment.

"So. I guess you better tell me everything."

This was one instance where talking about something actually seemed to bring a measure of relief. Not that Mimi was easy on him: she was completely scandalized, in the most Old World sort of way. Once she'd realized that this wasn't simply some nascent indiscretion that could still be hidden away, she began to circle the wagons.

"You can never tell Mom and Dad about this, do you understand? Never!"

"What do you mean, never? I have to tell them eventually. He's not just going to go away."

"You don't understand, Alex. This isn't something Italians do. Not around here."

"You were going to leave your husband."

"That was different. I didn't really mean that."

"I didn't really mean this either."

They left it that he wouldn't say a word to anyone until their mother was in the clear. After that, Mimi would feel things out for him. Their mother, at least, was a possibility—nobody ever knew what she really thought about things, but that, in a way, was an advantage.

They didn't even mention their father.

"At least he's in Sweden, thank God. At least he's not going to show up at the door."

He ought to have been angry at her, as anyone normal would have been. This was an actual child they were talking about, this was the twentieth century, the modern world, not the village back home, where people used to abandon their bastards at the local convent in the dead of night or leave them to die in the cold. But afterward Mimi began to call him almost daily in Montreal, never mind the long distance, asking questions that all had the same grudging tone of interrogation but that seemed to have less and less to do with the issue of avoiding scandal. What did he look like, she wanted to know, did he speak English, did his mother own a house? He was part of the family, after all; provision would have to be made for him.

"What does this mean legally, have you thought about that? Maybe you should talk to Gus. I mean, wouldn't he inherit everything if you died?"

Alex didn't relish the thought of a man-to-man with Gus on the subject of his bastard son.

"There's not really a lot to inherit at the moment."

Their mother, meanwhile, still awaiting a follow-up from her operation, had carried on with her duties as if the specter of death had been a piece of lint she had brushed off. Already she was hard at work in the little greenhouse his parents had built at the back of their new house, starting seedlings for the few acres of land they planted in the spring to stock the roadside fruit stand she watched over every summer like a hawk.

"How are you doing, Ma?" he would ask her on the phone.

"*Eh,'m'beh.* Not too bad."

Alex had wandered through the Jean Talon market a few times watching the Italian women at their shopping, silent old ones in black whose lined faces read like history books, or thick-legged *molisane* from Campobasso or Agnone doing their shopping for Sunday dinner. *Lasagn' a tacchun'*, his mother used to make on Sundays, her local specialty, homemade lasagna noodles cut into squares and sopped with tomato sauce. Alex had never really liked them much. He'd preferred the real lasagna, in the oven, with meat. Most of his childhood, in fact, had been a matter of not liking things much, what he was, where he'd come from. He hadn't liked his mother, for instance: he couldn't remember what had triggered it, but suddenly, at eight or nine, everything she did had become loathsome to him. He couldn't stand being touched by her, the least sign of affection—false, false, it all seemed, as if it were some kind of play for him. He had forgotten that. He was always thinking that she was the one, a cold fish, but she had tried and he had repulsed her, in the heartless way of a child.

His meal had come up. Tony, the second son, the sensitive one, maybe, slimmer and more morose than Carmen, brought it over. No doubt he wanted to be a poet or hockey star instead of languishing here in his father's restaurant.

"Dad wanted to know if you wanted a cappuccino after. We just got the machine in. On the house."

So they had sold out like the rest.

"Sure. Thanks. Why not?"

He felt comforted by the familiar hodgepodge of the place, the hockey sticks, the Paris street scenes, the maps of Italy, the family photos near the cash. There were grandchildren, it seemed, two beefy Domenic-like boys of three or four, identical twins, from the look of them. A photo showed them with their mother, beefy and Domenic-like in her turn, the whole lot of them hopelessly ungainly and unattractive, with their round balloon faces and sausagey limbs, yet somehow necessary.

Alex ate his special. Spaghetti and meatballs, Disney cuisine, but his secret favorite. As he was finishing, Domenic himself came waltzing over with his cappuccino, done in the Italian style, with just a whisper of scummy foam across the top.

He rested a wide butt cheek on the corner of an empty table.

"What is it, Alex? Woman problems, I'll bet. That's what it looks like."

"Something like that."

"My sons, you know, they used to bring girls home all the time, a different one every week. Finally I said, enough. Just bring the one you're going to marry. Otherwise it's a waste of time."

The old story. They all got together, it seemed, these immigrant oldsters, and thought up ways to screw over their children.

Domenic's eye was already scoping the room for someone more important to talk to.

"And your family? They're okay?"

"Everyone's fine, I think."

Domenic dropped his voice down to his preaching tone.

"Don't ever forget your family. They're all you've got in the end, don't forget that."

He was off again, glad-handing. Not like Alex's mother at all, really. Someone like Domenic you could read with your eyes closed; not his mother. If she died, she would take all the stolid mysteries of herself to the grave, all the things he had never asked her about.

Some years earlier two of her brothers had been killed in a car crash in Italy. This was at the point in Alex's undergraduate years when he'd been going through his first round of therapy and had thought it important to talk about your emotions.

"How are you feeling about your brothers?" he had finally ventured, in his halting dialect.

There was a long pause. Maybe the question merely baffled her.

"You can't say what it is when something happens like that," she said at length. "There aren't words for it. I can't tell you."

She was like him, maybe, only more so, more distilled. She was someone not much for this world.

He got up to settle the bill. Domenic took his cash, all the while talking around him in a florid, execrable French to the man in the suit and tie, who was working on his gnocchi at one of the counter seats. Alex noticed Domenic had charged him for the cappuccino but said nothing, paid his money, and headed out to the street.

10

He couldn't bear returning to his apartment and kept walking east on St. Catherine, past Ogilvy, now liberated of its apostrophe, past le Pub Peel, past le magasin Eaton. Before he knew it he'd gone beyond Place des Arts and St. Lawrence, and the chain stores and designer shops had given way to the gay bars, the hookers in alleys, the discount shops and empty lots. It was like shedding history, like slinking out to its seedy outskirts.

He passed the California. He hadn't seen Louie since their night there. There had been something angry in him then, something reckless. The situation in his homeland had gone bad again just as he had predicted, but he hadn't wanted to speak about it, as if he was a free element now, as if the place had ceased to exist for him.

He cut north at St. Denis. The landscape grew briefly civilized again—UQAM was here, with its reclaimed church front, the Bibliothèque Nationale, a few jazz bars, a string of student eateries. He and Liz had come out here one of their first nights in the city, when the place had still seemed exotic, then never again. There was an empty stretch up the hill between Ontario and Sherbrooke that was flanked by a ruined church, another fire victim, a huge barn of a place sitting gaping and charred like a casualty of war.

He crossed Sherbrooke, just anonymous high-rises here, and walked up to St. Louis Square. The place sat quiet and still in its mellow lamplight as if it had never left the nineteenth century, the trees and shrubs that bordered the walkways offering out their little gifts of trembling leaves. Around the square sat the houses of the old bourgeoisie, with their mansards and scallops and turrets, most of them newly regentrified after dereliction, so that even the down-and-outs who mainly peopled the square had the dignified look of young clerics or bank clerks out for their promenade. In one of those ironies that gave Alex black-hearted pleasure, the square's French name, Carré St. Louis, was a misnomer: the correct word in French for this sort of square, as it happened, was *square*.

He doubled back toward downtown along Prince Arthur, where the first straggling sidewalk merchants and performers of the season had set up shop, and crossed again. Without quite realizing it, he had instinctively kept to his own little shoal of city, the few dozen blocks he had hardly strayed from his entire time here. Over on Milton was the ominously named Last Word bookshop, whose dusty, narrow aisles he had spent many hours among; then St. Urbain, former heart of the old Jewish ghetto, and the monstrous apartment-cum-shopping complex at Parc, for which whole city blocks had been razed. Up Aylmer was the Yellow Door, a basement hole-in-the-wall: Margaret Atwood had read there, and Leonard Cohen had played.

He had reached McGill. Around the residences great heaps of belongings had been piled up along the curbs, beanbag chairs, stereos, green garbage bags full of clothes, while squealy girls in tennis gear or sloppy sweats hugged each other and cried and made fusses and their fathers stared off into the middle distance or loaded things into their cars. Another year gone. Alex cut across the quadrangle, already ghostly with abandonment, and hiked up McTavish to Pine. From there the mountain stared at him, and from its peak, with its grid of Christmas lights, the Saint-Jean-Baptiste cross. All his time here that damned cross had loomed over him from every angle and he had never been up to it, had yet to piss on one of its girders or give one a kick to say he had come and seen.

He started up the mountain. It was a lot darker here than on the streets, positively spooky, the greening trees whispering in the half-wind with the high-pitched trill of winging bats. He had no proper sense of the mountain's network of paths, and as soon as he had started up, his objective, the cross, was cut off from view. He would just keep going upward, he figured, until he reached the top. At least the weather was holding: the stars were out despite the earlier clouds, clearly visible here away from the haze of light from the streets, and the temperature actually seemed to have risen since the dip of the afternoon, hanging in the pleasant zone between muggy and cold that marked the city's few good days of spring.

The gay romping grounds were around here somewhere, but Alex had never been able to pin down exactly where. In his mind they were like some ancient Greek woodland or the forest of *A Midsummer Night's Dream*, sylvan and unpredictable, bacchanalian, though the reality was probably a bit more sordid. Maybe the Honorable Mr. Trudeau was frolicking out there at that very moment, in his secret life; maybe Lévesque was there as well, and Fidel with his riding crop, and they were sorting out the question of bottoms and tops. "You fucked me," Lévesque had apparently said at the constitutional talks. Maybe he had meant it literally.

Now, isn't all that stuff just rumor? I mean, he practically made his name because of his way with the ladies.

Yes, but just look at the ladies, Peter. Look at his wife—what was she, all of sixteen when he met her? Meanwhile he was pushing fifty. There's got to be something funny there.

Well, I don't mind the occasional sixteen-year-old myself, when I can get one.

(Laughing) I think you're going to see some mail on that one, Peter.

All kidding aside, yuk yuk, sure, I can see the whole manly thing, the canoeing and the spearfishing in Cayo Largo and all that. I'm thinking of that scene in D. H. Lawrence where the two guys wrestle naked in front of the fire. But when it comes down to the crunch—

Making babies, I guess you mean. Ensuring the line.

That wasn't exactly what I had in mind, but I see your point.

Alex continued upward. He passed a jogger, then no one. It was amazing how quickly the city disappeared here—a few zigs, a few zags, and it all fell away, the noise, the traffic, the lights. He was in the middle of bush. He could smell the damp of the earth, the metallic after-smell of old cold, the rot resurfacing from the fall; he could hear every rustle of leaf and crack of twig. Everything was shadows. It was only once he had gained the wide path that led up to the lake that the small fear in him began to abate—there were cyclists here, other walkers. He had forgotten what a beast the dark could be, how the fear of it was coded in his cells. Maybe that was the main job of civilization, to ensure adequate lighting.

He came to the curve that overlooked the lake, which was just a crater of inky black now. Just below was the spot where Jimmy had smashed Ariel's head with a rock that morning. So long ago. He ought to leave a little marker of what had happened, a pictograph or something. Then a million years from now, when the fossil record had grown patchy and the achievements and failings of this particular phase of human development indistinct, archeologists would puzzle over it and form a theory of a lost subculture of protohumans, a warlike tribe of limited brain and primitive culture that had flourished briefly, then vanished from the earth.

At the Chalet he paused for a smoke. He had never figured out the use of this place: it was the size of a banquet hall, with buttressed rafters and Group-of-Sevenish paintings ringing the walls like the stations of the cross, but no concessions, no place to sit, nothing but empty space, as if it was still awaiting its august purpose. Beyond it, at the lookout, little clusters of hooligans and lovers stared out at the lights of the city, which were nothing but the incandescence of tungsten yet seemed to promise a million mysterious things, on and on beyond the snaking river until they gave way to the night.

Signs had started appearing for the cross, but they led into the deserted frontier that was the far side of the mountain. He rounded a curve and it was as if he had gone over to the dark side of the moon—to the west was the floodlit dome of St. Joe's, the city's great tit, and beside it the lights of U of M, but then beyond that was black. It took him a moment to make sense of this blighted dark: it was the cemetery. It seemed to stretch as vast as the park itself, rising to a second peak that was like the first one's doppelgänger. Alex felt a little chill: all along, this second mountain had shadowed the first. He had the dim sense he ought to be able to wrest some sort of meaning out of that, maybe that things came in twos: the male and the female; the quick and dead; the yin and the yang; the light and the dark. The French and the English.

He was alone out here now, walking the line between the opposites. Some thug could come out of the bush, some wild animal, some fearsome monster of the soul. *I shall tell you all.* Or maybe Satan himself, come to take him to the pinnacle.

Lucky you brought old Peter along with you, at least. You couldn't spare one of those smokes, could you?

His shoes crunched in the dark with the gut-rattling distinctness of a soundtrack. He couldn't have mapped his route but had the sense he'd been spiraling around and around up the mountain, as in those pictures you saw of Mount Purgatory in the *Divine Comedy*. Then at last the cemetery ended and the city began to reappear again in occluded swatches through the bush, though at angles Alex had never seen it from before, that made it appear completely unfamiliar. Views north into the streets of Outremont; views east, the lights stretching flat as a prairie, flat as the sea. It was more or less alien territory in that direction—*pure laine* Quebecois who went back to the Conquest; Azorean fishermen who had come from a world as lost as Atlantis and sold Tide and Mae Wests now in corner grocery stores; Chinese who had been here for decades but whom no one knew anything about. Then the Italians, the Guatemalans, the Hasidic Jews, and more Quebecois, as cultured as courtiers or the worst sorts of louts, Gitanes-smoking, Pepsi-drinking cursers of the tabernacle, but who might as well have lived beyond a wall like East Berliners for all Alex had had to do with them.

He still couldn't see the cross. With each step he grew leerier, hearing bogeymen in every movement. It was colder up here—he had come out in only a workshirt, growing clammy now with the sweat from his climb. He had begun to think that maybe he had taken a wrong turn or that the pathways were some kind of trick; or that the cross itself didn't exist, was some sort of illusion, a mass hallucination that had long held the city under its spell.

Then he rounded a corner and the cross appeared in front of him, just a collection of metal and forty-watt bulbs, not perched atop some towering promontory or windswept crag but sitting placidly in the middle of a little knoll that rose up like somebody's bald spot.

Its construction was rather more workmanlike than he'd expected, an assemblage of rusting angle irons and metal struts with an Eiffel Tower–style support arching up from the bottom. A spiked metal fence of a gauge sufficient to deter terrorists and Huns ran around its perimeter, though Alex knew of no assault that had ever been mounted against it. The story went—this was the sort of trivia he'd picked up through CanLit—that it was the sieur de Maisonneuve himself who had put the first cross here, presumably after he'd finished slaughtering the Iroquois. It might not have been such a walk in the park in those days getting up here, bush and bears and poison ivy and maybe more Iroquois hiding in wait. If it had been Alex, he would have turned tail and headed right back to La Rochelle—the sight of untamed wilderness gave him a sensation somewhat akin to having an icicle poked through his heart. But de Maisonneuve had probably looked out and seen God's country, a virgin paradise.

The New World. Not especially new, really. The chances were the Iroquois had been coming to this spot for a million moons already by then, for picnics or lacrosse or maybe to send messages the way the Samnites had done with their high points, by building fires from peak to peak. To them the place wasn't virgin but old, they had almost finished with it. Hochelaga had come and gone by then: a thriving town according to Cartier, complete with palisade and fields, but vanished without a trace by the time of de Maisonneuve. One theory put the place just about where McGill was, which seemed right—Alex could picture it, the longhouses lined up just where the buildings were now, with the quadrangle in between. As if the ghost of the old had risen up in the new. They might be living their shadow lives there at the moment, those Hochelagans, wandering the residences and lecture halls in some simulacrum of what might have been.

Not virgin, but old. He stared out and for a moment he saw it, that alien view, the vision of a world passing.

In its truly virgin days the mountain had been a volcano and everything around it barren waste. That was a bit harder to get his mind around, that this landscape had once been Galápagan in its newness. Against that scale of things all this elaboration around him, the lights stretching out like a bridal train, the suburbs beyond and the farms and the vacation homes, the network of highways leading to concession roads leading to dirt tracks and forest trails and footprints through the snow, was an afterthought, a minor blemish, just as fleeting as what had come before. They were insects burrowing away; time would close over them like sand over an anthill. Unfortunately there was no prize for knowing this, except maybe getting off the occasional good one on the nature of time and human endeavor among the doctoral set.

So he had made it here, to the top. He felt a tenderness in his bladder and pulled his zipper down, alone here in the open air, to lay his trace at the foot of the cross.

It was past eleven by the time he got home. She'd be asleep now, but not in bed: the news would be on and she would be stretched out in her La-Z-Boy.

There was a phone right there on the side table next to her.

"Mom? It's me. It's Alex."

Today was the day that she got the results of her follow-up.

"Eh? *Chi è?*" Slowly rousing herself. "Oh. *Ahlix. Sci tu.*"

She had never quite managed his name, really, that clipped final syllable.

"*Scti vuon'?*" she said. Are you well?

Given how rarely he used it now, their dialect had begun to feel like so much Arabic in his mouth.

"What did the doctor say, Ma? Your test?"

"Oh, you know. It's okay."

He knew this was about all he was going to get. It would do. He felt a tension he hadn't even known he was carrying give way like a clog inside him.

"So it's okay, then. It didn't come back."

"*Sci. Sci.* It's okay."

Another rush of feeling, this one seeming as much for his own sake as for hers, that he had actually called, that he hadn't fucked up. He wanted to give her something, some sign he would change, make things up to her, be her son.

"Ma, I might be going away," he said in English. "I might be going to Sweden."

"Eh? What are you saying?"

She had kept on in dialect. It was like playing a game of telephone on the telephone.

"I might be going to Sweden." He felt his heart rate spike. "I have a son there."

A pause at the other end of the line. What had he been thinking? This was no gift. The woman had just come through a near-death experience, and he was throwing her back in the pit.

"What are you saying? I don't understand."

He couldn't stop now.

"I have a son. In Sweden. *Tinghe nu figl'.*"

"What are you trying to say? Let me get your father, I don't understand."

Alex's blood froze.

"Never mind, Ma. Never mind. It's nothing. Just forget about it. I'll call again tomorrow."

"Are you in some kind of trouble?"

"No, no trouble. We'll sort it out tomorrow, Ma, it's nothing."

He grew utterly paranoid the moment he had set down the phone. He had botched his filial moment. *I have a son.* It had sounded like gibberish, random sound. *Aihevusuhn.*

He took his Per letters out of his new Per drawer, as if to assure himself not so much that the boy was real but that *he* was, that this notion of Alex-as-father wasn't the figment it sounded like. There was quite a stack of these letters now, sometimes in Per's own beginner's hand but mostly in Ingrid's teacherly transcriptions, notebook perfect but always true to the five-year-old mind. Alex read them as if they were riddles, palimpsests, ancient scrolls, as if there was some deeper message to be got to beneath the obvious one, though each one seemed as staid and formulaic as the one before, as beside the point. He'd done this, he'd done that, he had got a new toy. Alex had to remind himself Per was five, that this was what passed for being open for a five-year-old, for telling all. Later, he suspected, he would only get less.

There were many pictures. These Alex kept in a separate stack: one day he would mount them, pin them with magnets to his fridge for all to see or paste them to the walls, laminate them, make a book, blow them up poster-size or paint them on the ceiling. *I have a son.* For now, though, the matter still felt too private. For now, it was his own.

He always went back to the first one, the tractor with spiky back wheels and lopsided front ones. Per's tractor, it turned out, the one from under the sea. Then beneath it, Per's careful scrawl in the corner. Alex could hardly bear to look at it or bear to hold off, each time saving it and avoiding it as if it were obscene, too good to be true.

For Father. Only that. A little bombshell.

epilogue

And in short, I was afraid.

T. S. ELIOT
"The Love Song of J. Alfred Prufrock"

Alex was in Esther's hospital room. Blip, blip, went the monitor—ninety-eight point four, ninety-eight point three, ninety-eight point four. It was late now, way past visiting hours. He kept waiting for the shadow to appear in the door that would send him away, but though the lights had been dimmed in the ward and a hush had fallen over it, broken only by occasional muted laughter from the nurse's station, no one had come. The sense had begun to build in him that he had been left here by tacit agreement. The only light in the room was the grainy one filtering in from the hall and the glow of Esther's monitor, which together cast a bluish aura over her like the haunted light of horror films.

He was feeling oddly light-headed, occasionally straying into the strange back alleys that separated waking from dream. Ninety-eight point five. From the monitor his eye drifted to *Les Misérables* still on Esther's bedside table, many weeks untouched, and he thought, *Fahrenheit 451.* The temperature at which books burned. Why had he thought that? There was a film, by Truffaut, he'd seen it, but who had written the book?

Savonarola. The bonfire of the vanities.

It must have been a bit of a blow, I'd think. All that work and then just to have the thing gathering dust in a university library. But what's that quote from the Royal Society about Darwin? How it was too bad nothing big had happened that year?

(Chuckling) I think it was the Linneans, actually, Peter, though I'm not sure we're dealing with quite the same situation. I'll be honest with you, half the time I didn't even know what I was talking about.

Well, join the club, then, sir, join the club. I'll let you in on a little secret myself—I sit here every day making everyone feel like I know them better than their mothers do when mostly I'm just thinking about my next cigarette.

Ever since his meeting with Jiri, Alex had been blocked. At first he had blamed his and Jiri's fucked-up dynamic, but he was beginning to think the matter had as much to do with Esther as with Jiri. She'd been his muse, he figured, because she'd believed in him without warrant and without restraint; because of those hours he'd spent reading to her, when something had seemed to shimmer before him like a grail, radioactive with meaning. All that mystical sense of impending revelation was gone now, replaced with a kind of positivist funk. The logical end of things, in his scheme, was a hopeless determinism: that was where you ended up once you took consciousness out of the picture, once you made it just one more adaptation like the rest, no more important than the third eye of a lizard or the illusory owl eyes on the wings of a moth. Even the randomness of the process was no escape—theoretically, it, too, could be plotted out, if you had all the data. All it would take was a mind big enough to hold the whole of creation, every breath, every birdsong, every flutter of a bird's wing. The mind of God, perhaps. If you could do that, if you could trace every link, every cause and effect, every mistaken notation in a ledger that lowered a balance and lessened a return and ruined a business and collapsed whole economies and so shifted the entire course of human history, you could show that it wasn't possible to so much as sip your tea on your terrace without the cup, the way you held it, the brand of tea, having already been chosen for you way back in the first instant of the Big Bang, for all the illusion you had that you did things as you pleased. Alex couldn't believe this, of course, that he was just an automaton, an insect, an ant, otherwise how could he go on? But that didn't mean it wasn't true.

Ninety-eight point two. He wondered why they had left him here, what they weren't telling him. Some new bug had taken hold of Esther, he'd learned that much, pneumonia-like but not pneumonia, a *Pneumonia sapiens*, maybe, or *Pneumonia habilis*. Earlier, she had had her oxygen hooked up, but then one of the nurses had come to remove it. Why? Maybe they pumped the whole building full of oxygen at night, hence his weird light-headedness. Or maybe they simply couldn't be bothered to keep checking if she'd knocked her mask off or strangled herself with the strap.

Esther's mother used to bring houseplants into the room, begonias and African violets and wandering Jews, but they'd been banned now: at night, apparently, he hadn't known this—how could he not have known this?— they actually started sucking the oxygen up and giving off CO_2. Plant poo.

Her family had been by, the entire contingent. Mother, father, siblings, even Molly, alias Wamalie, coming and going in overlapping sets like a Venn diagram. Lenny had arrived with his new girlfriend, a nice Jewish girl who exuded warmth like a hearth and treated Alex as if she had known him from the womb and who clearly had a will of iron. Lenny deferred to her with such gentlemanly courtesy and attentiveness it was obvious at once that he must marry her. It was heartbreaking, really, this Victorian decorum between them. It made all of Alex's past relationships look like schoolyard brawls.

In a lull after the girlfriend had gone and it was just Alex and Lenny, a woman had come in whom Alex had never seen before. Slightly older-looking and a bit chunky and suburban and ill at ease, with too much makeup on and a polyester dress that clung to her in the wrong places.

"I guess you haven't met," Lenny said. "This is Sarah."

It was the fugitive sister. Not what Alex had expected at all. No combat fatigues, no windburnt leanness, no narrow-eyed look from gazing out to the far horizon for incoming mortar fire.

"So you've come back from Israel," he managed, then at once regretted the "back."

He asked fumbling questions about her life over there on the kibbutz, which she answered in the same slow speech as her father, still thick with the twang of Côte St. Luc. She lived in a house with her husband and son— "We get a two-bedroom," was all she said in the way of description—and worked at the kibbutz's credit union, doing accounts. Alex asked about sharing the farmwork and all that, but she acted as if she was hearing the idea for the first time.

"Oh, we don't really do that sort of thing. I just work in the garden sometimes."

He didn't dare ask about the communal child rearing.

"It's not like before," Lenny put in. "People just live their lives. Like here."

She might have been living out Esther's shadow life, though not the exotic version Alex had imagined for her, but the banal one with a Jewish husband and a kid and a job, even if she had had to decamp to a war zone on the other side of the world to do it. He could see her there in her different house in her different country as if in one of those long takes in a foreign film, while her husband snacked in the kitchen and her son watched TV. Something seemed about to happen, then nothing did.

Not ten minutes had passed before she started making motions to leave. She went up to Esther's bed with a look that seemed to require some next action, her hand coming up to touch Esther's cheek or brush a strand of hair away, but the action never came.

"How much is a cab home?" she said, making a show of rifling through her purse. "I've got ten, is that enough?"

"Don't be silly, I'll drive you," Lenny said at once.

Alex was on his own after that. The image of Sarah lingered with him. She must have moved to Israel out of some homeland instinct, that dangerous meeting point of the radical and the reactionary. He knew the family had lost people in the camps—it was all a bit gray to him, though Esther had mentioned a great-aunt on her mother's side who was a survivor, living somewhere in Europe now.

"She came over once, but she and my grandmother didn't get along. I guess because of the war and everything."

All that history. It was too much to hold in your head. Sarah came at the end of it, on her kibbutz, and Esther lying here in her bed with her hospital bracelet, her different tattoo.

He thought of the trains shunting back and forth in the night behind Esther's house, how Lenny had hated them. But not Esther.

"It looked so romantic, all those lights in the windows at night. That's all I thought about then. All the places I'd go."

She hadn't opened her eyes the whole evening. He didn't know these days if she was asleep or unconscious, or even what the difference might be between the two. No one bothered anymore with keeping their voices down around her when she was asleep. She had become a sort of thing, lying there—it wasn't pleasant to think in those terms but they had all fallen into the habit of it, of carrying on as if she weren't there. Maybe she wasn't. Over the course of a day she might surface to consciousness any number of times, but it was hard to say anymore what she registered, how much her battered optic nerves could take in, or her lesioned brain. It had been weeks since she had shown any definite sign of volition, anything more than a turn of her head or the shift of a limb that could as easily have been a spasm; months since she had uttered a word. Somehow her body had continued to persist, hadn't simply wasted away to nothing, but there was a quality to it, with its cut tendons and IV-sodden flesh, that made it seem to be melting there into her bed, to be losing integrity, whatever it was that made you discrete and whole, an entity, and not simply random particles slowly drifting toward perfect dispersion.

Entropy. The second law of thermodynamics.

How had he known that?

So there you have it, I guess, that's where we're headed, perfect disorder, not the other way around. I don't know how that squares with your Mr. Darwin, but it makes you think. Of course, that's assuming the universe is actually a closed system.

I'm not sure I follow you, Peter.

Well, it's sort of obvious, isn't it? The white light. The Prime Mover. The God spark. That would throw a monkey wrench into things, wouldn't it?

(With mock surprise) Peter, I didn't know you were allowed to talk about these sorts of things on the air. To even think about them.

Well, I have to think about something, don't I? I hope you don't believe I give a good goddamn about some quilting competition in Regina!

In one of the science journals, Alex had come across a study of people who had lost their sense of meaningfulness after they had had experimental brain surgeries of one sort or another. "God, a tree, a cup of coffee, it doesn't matter," they said. "It's all the same." That was what the world looked like beyond meaningfulness: no one thing mattered more than any other. Mental entropy. The theory was that a sense of meaning was itself just another adaptation, what allowed otherwise perfectly rational people like Alex to deny the obvious, that there wasn't any.

He had purchased his ticket. It had seemed pointless to wait, macabre, almost, as if he were willing Esther to die, as if she were malingering. But then once he had booked a flight Esther had taken a turn for the worse, as if she knew. It was not a good sign that The Sister had come. A few weeks, she had said she was staying, as if that was all she was giving her.

In Sweden it had been one glorious long summer's day after another, by Ingrid's account. Ingrid was biting her tongue, Alex knew; soon her patience, her goodwill, would wear thin. "Per is always asking if you will come," she had written lately, and the "if" had made his heart stop. Already most of the summer was gone, and all the outings he had planned in his head, the kite-flying, the days by the sea, would have to be crammed into the last hurried weeks before school.

Esther's monitor had dipped into the ninety-sevens. He had seen it go as low as the ninety-threes and no one had batted an eye, though technically you were supposed to be dead by then. There was a call button whose cord was bandaged to one of Esther's wrists, but Esther had grown so famous among the nurses for its overuse in her early weeks that Alex was always reluctant to consider pressing it without hard evidence of crisis. The trouble was that he wasn't getting enough data—what he had always thought of as the plethora of machines surrounding Esther actually came down to a few minor ones, her temperature monitor, her oxygen feed, her IV, none of them the kind that could pinpoint the moment of crossing over like the ones on TV. She could slip into death without anyone noticing, she could be slipping this very moment.

Ninety-seven point one. He watched her until he'd seen her head shift, until he could make out the heave of her chest beneath the sheets.

He had brought his Joyce but hadn't been able to bring himself to crack it open. He had made it through the *Odyssey*, at least; it hadn't been nearly the slog he had feared. Sex and violence: the old story. He was using the Butler translation, because Darwin and Butler had had a history, one of those mentorships gone sour, the sort of thing Alex might be able to work up into a clever meta-commentary about fathers and sons. *If you are truly your father's son*, everyone kept saying to poor Telemachus. Alex could see the possibilities. Joyce was going to be a harder row—he made the *Odyssey* look like a potboiler. Alex had dug up a throwaway reference to Darwin in the Ithaca chapter, but that sort of thing was worse than useless—what he needed was what showed up in the text in spite of itself, what was coded in its DNA. So far the only thing he was absolutely sure of was Bloom's gorgonzola sandwich at Davy Byrne's.

I notice how you're trying to slip in the Italian content. It's not the first thing we think of with Joyce, is it?

Well, he did spend all those years in Trieste.

He could lead off with something more accessible—"The Dead," say, the feast scene, to tie into Homer. Such a perfect little story. Maybe Joyce should have quit while he was ahead. *The time had come for him to set out on his journey westward.* What was it in that that cut him to the quick? The music of it? The sense of a journey? Of going west?

There was nothing in his theory that accounted for any of this.

He scanned Esther for signs of movement again. There, a little twitch, though this was followed by such a sudden thrashing about that he thought she had gone into a seizure. His hand went for the call button, but then the movement ceased as abruptly as it had started. He waited again for the heave of her chest. There. And again. It had crossed his mind that it could happen this way, those last throes. *Not gently.*

He made a mental list of what he needed to do before leaving. Pay his credit card, get kronor, go through his things. Sort out what to toss into the fire—his matchbook collection? his Amnesty files? his high school memorabilia?—and what to save from it. Rent a van. Bring things home. Tell his father about his son.

The shock had been his mother's reaction: he had made a special trip home and sat with her in the kitchen while Mimi spoon-fed the details to her in little increments.

"What are you saying? *Sandr'*, tell me what she's saying. What does she mean, you have a son?"

Alex stared at the floor.

"His name is Per," he said, as if that would help.

He waited for her to break into wails.

"Oh! A son!" Her face had lit up as if she had solved a great riddle. "A son! That's what you were saying on the phone! *Ah-san, ah-san!* I couldn't understand what you meant, this *ah-san!*"

He had never seen her so animated.

"*Ah-san! Ah-san!* But how long did you know? Why didn't you tell me? Did you think we would chase you away?"

Her reaction was so far from what he had expected that he could barely gather his wits.

"I don't know. I didn't know what to do."

She reached out impulsively and pulled him to her in a gesture that was half mock-aggression and half embrace. She had never done such a thing.

"You idiot! What did you think I would do? I'm your mother!"

For a moment he and Mimi sat speechless. Mimi, if anything, looked disappointed at how well she had taken the matter.

"Ma, we have to work this out," she said. "It's not some little thing."

"What is there to work out? It's done. He's not a boy anymore, I can't tell him what to do. If he has a son, he has to go to him."

It made the tears well up in Alex to hear such a bald statement of faith.

"But what about Dad?" Mimi persisted. "What's he going to say?"

"What can he say? He'll have to accept it."

Nonetheless, they had all agreed to put off telling him. Now Alex would have to bring the matter up—and he had to be the one, that much was clear to him—when he was already backing out the door, when there wasn't time for the usual pattern to play itself out of psychotic anger followed by oppressive silence leading to weeks of depression which gave way to resignation and grudging acceptance. Which could be seen as a good argument in support of the delay.

Or maybe, who knew, he would sit across from his father at the kitchen table, that awful place where everything had always happened, the fights, the recriminations, the shame, the whole family history across three generations, and he would speak to him for the first time as a sort of equal. He would tell him the truth. His father would have to respect that. He would have to see that the matter joined them as much as it set them apart.

Eventually, at any rate.

Blip. Ninety-six point nine.

Why did the readout keep going down? Alex wasn't even sure what it showed, exactly, her body heat or the heat of the pad underneath her, and so couldn't say if the machine was fighting to cool her from a raging fever or she was in some sort of thermal failure and it couldn't keep up. Why didn't he know this? He eyed the call button dangling from her wrist again—it was entirely useless to her there by this point, her fingers having long ago severed any sort of formal communication link with her brain—but instead of going for it he leaned in to put a hand to her forehead. Not burning: cool. He felt his own head, then hers again. Normal, maybe, or close to normal. Her skin still had the same soft feel he remembered, for all the months of hospital air. The feel of something alive. That needed touching.

Her head shifted away from him.

"What is it?" he whispered, but she was still deep in her sleep.

He looked at his watch: past midnight. He felt that he had crossed the point where leaving her would have been normal, correct, that he ought to be thinking now about settling in for the night. He wondered if there was some sort of twenty-four-hour depanneur in the place where he could get cigarettes. Not bloody likely. Three days now he had gone without, or most of three days. He had to be ready for when he left.

The stuff's going to kill me, I know it, but still I won't stop. You have to wonder what that's about. If I don't actually want it somehow. It'd be such a bloody relief, if you want the truth. No more of this fucking blather, day in and day out.

(Sotto voce) Uh, I think your mike's still on, Peter.

Well, fuck the mike. There, I've said it. Just fuck it.

He could feel sleep coming on now in earnest, though he was usually at his most lucid at this hour. Not enough stimulants: he had had to cut out coffee along with the cigarettes, they were like symbionts in him. Though also maybe the linchpins of his own private ecosystem: by midday now the whole organism had started to fail, his head would be throbbing, his eyelids drooping, he'd find it impossible to hold a thought or remember the simplest things, appointments, where the margarine was, his own name. If this was his life after cigarettes, he might as well swallow the hemlock. Then there was that anguish in him, the sense of looming dark, as if he were losing the one friend who'd been true. It was just his addiction speaking, he knew that, but what if the demon had so threaded its way into his parts, like those viruses that took over their hosts from the inside, that turned them into their own private motor homes, that he couldn't cut it away without destroying his very self?

A sad man he was, very sad, if sucking on a cigarette was the sole pleasure he'd managed to wrest from life. He might as well have been a slug, a barnacle, a stone.

At least the barnacles had been of use.

Blip. Ninety-six point six.

Old Charlie Darwin, slicing away at his barnacles in the quiet of his study, finding the little penis-ones nestled in the folds of their brides. The Ideal Husband. Was he happy there, did it please him to putter alone among his specimens? He had rigged that mirror outside his window to keep watch for visitors, so he could take a powder. Not much of one for human intercourse. Better the barnacles.

The spat with Butler: he had to give it a closer look. There was something truly rotten there, he could smell it. The matter had cast a pall over Darwin's last years: he had sought advice from every intimate, drafted a dozen letters he had never sent, pondered every course of action, then in the end had done nothing. It was beneath him, his counselors said; Butler was a nut. And yet there'd been cause enough, from what Alex could tell. He couldn't remember all the details—a dispute about dates was what it was, over a piece a German acolyte had written on Darwin's grandfather Erasmus but then revised when it appeared in English in the light of Butler's own new book on Erasmus. The problems arose when Darwin wrote a preface for the piece that implied it was being reprinted unchanged, though he himself had sent Butler's book to the German. It would have been easy to dismiss all these convolutions as just the usual sort of academic hairsplitting, except that the effect of the German's revisions, for anyone who didn't know they'd been done after Butler's book, was to make Butler look at best a little foolish and at worst a plagiarist, since the revisions had carefully pilloried Butler's arguments without however once making actual reference to him. Even this might not have looked so bad on Darwin if Butler's book hadn't been a sort of coming out against his old mentor, pushing Erasmus's theories over Darwin's.

Such had been the moral contests of the putative founder of the post-theistic world. Darwin had written Butler claiming he'd known nothing of the revisions, though in the absence of any sort of public amends Butler grew increasingly rabid and embittered, firing off letter after furious letter to the *Athenaeum*, so that Darwin went to the grave with the shadow of the dispute still hanging over him. What was it in Alex that took comfort from this sort of pettiness and intrigue, from the thought that behind even the greatest of minds lay a wounded ego? In one of his letters Butler had made cutting reference to the "happy simplicity" at which Darwin had been declared a master by the newspapers of the day: all his life he had played the handwringer, the invalid, the innocent, and had got what he'd wanted. The rich wife, a good breeder to boot; the country retreat; the respect of his peers. In every regard, the English gentleman. In Downe he had been appointed the local magistrate, doing his dining room over in Queen Anne, more stately than the Victorian clutter of the rest of the house, and holding court there from his throne, pronouncing yea or nay on stolen chickens and disturbing the peace. Then, at his death, whisked off to Westminster. A little plot in the village churchyard was all he'd asked for, though within hours of his death the movement was already afoot for a proper state funeral.

Alfred Russel Wallace—could this be right?—had been one of the pall-bearers. That "Russel" had always stuck with Alex, limping along there with its missing *l* like a little cripple. If Darwin's was the sort of fate Alex aspired to, Wallace's seemed the one to which he was doomed: the poor cousin. Whenever he came across references to Wallace in the literature he always wanted to avert his eyes, though in this way, of course, through the back doors, Wallace had taken up an increasingly stubborn tenancy in Alex's brain. Alex didn't like to go there much, to the Alfred Russel Wallace room, but there it was, with all its pathetic little collections and memorabilia and drafts of letters seeking preferments that never came.

They had had two versions of the same life, Wallace and Darwin, good homes, professional fathers, decent pedigrees, though it seemed there had been air enough in the world for only one of them. Darwin's father had prospered where Wallace's had failed; and so the die had been cast. At thirteen, Wallace was pulled out of school and apprenticed as a draftsman; Darwin, meanwhile, flunked out of medical school but then spent several years swanning around Cambridge, gambling and riding horses and collecting bugs and meeting the old boys who ran the Establishment. Darwin's father paid his way aboard the *Beagle*, the trip that made his career: he returned home with cratefuls of specimens, mainly secured by his hired shooter but paving the way for his entry into the upper echelons of the scientific world. It was only in hindsight, once the specimens had been properly classified by real professionals, that the first glint of a bright idea began to flicker in Darwin's head. He owed a debt in this to his very same shooter, who had carefully labeled a collection of finches from the Galápagos that Darwin himself hadn't thought worth the bother.

Wallace, too, had set out for South America. Self-taught and self-financed, he hoped to bankroll his own research on the species question by selling specimens to armchair naturalists back in England. He carried with him a copy of the same *Principles of Geology* by Charles Lyell that had made almost daily reading for Darwin aboard the *Beagle*, and whose observations on the shift of continents and the anomalies of the fossil record had first led Darwin to question the accepted notion that the world had been created in its entirety somewhere around 4004 BC. Wallace, however, had a run of bad luck. First he grew ill while traveling up the Amazon and had to cut his trip short. Then when he returned to Pará he learned that his brother, who had been working there, had died of yellow fever. Meanwhile the specimens Wallace had been sending to the coast for two years to be shipped over to England had unaccountably been held up at the docks, so that he had to arrange to bring the whole lot back with him on his own passage. A few weeks out to sea, his ship caught fire and sank, and all his specimens were lost. He survived in a leaky lifeboat until he was picked up by a passing cargo ship, which almost sank in its turn before finally creaking into port some two months later.

It was like something out of Buster Keaton, this strange shadow dance between the two men, Darwin ambling obliviously past the open manhole, the tottering ladder, the sheet of plate glass, while Wallace, shouting warnings from behind, suffered every pratfall. In England Darwin settled into his comfortable marriage and home to work out his theory at his ease while Wallace was forced almost at once back into the field, this time the Malay Archipelago. It was there that Darwin finally entered the annals of his life, as one of his clients. Wallace sent him the skins of local domestic fowl and such, and Darwin grumbled, half in jest, about the carriage costs. Meanwhile Wallace published a paper on the origin of species that was ignored by virtually everyone except Darwin, who wrote him a cheery letter on the subject and mentioned in passing his own many years of work in the field. "It is really *impossible* to explain my views in the compass of a letter," he said coyly, in the way of warning Wallace off his turf. Wallace, after all, was merely a lowly chore boy, while Darwin, by then, was the Great Man of Barnacles.

It was while recovering from a bout of malaria, what apparently passed as leisure for him, that Wallace happened to make a connection between the origin of species and the theories of Thomas Malthus. This was where matters grew positively uncanny: it was that same conjunction of forces, the far archipelago, the Malthusian spark. Wallace sent his paper on the subject not, as anyone more secure in his reputation would have done, to a scientific journal—how differently matters might have turned out for him—but to none other than Darwin himself. It beggared the mind, this unlikely intersection of forces. Darwin by then had toiled over his theory for half his life, refining and delaying, afraid of upsetting all those old boys who had given him a hand up. "It is like confessing a murder" was how he had put the matter to a friend, when he had dared to confide to him the theory's barest outlines. Yet here was Wallace coming to him like a whelp, an innocent, seeking the Great Man's approval, having whipped off the same scheme between rounds of fever. It was almost as if none of the getting there had really mattered, only that this moment should come when the two men were suddenly faced with the specter of their other selves.

Blip. Ninety-six point four. Would an alarm go off, would he know? He needed a cigarette, badly. This time he took her hand: still warmish. Still a pulse.

"Esther," he whispered. "Esther."

But she didn't turn.

It had begun to irk Alex how Darwin's apologists always made so much of how sportingly he had handled things with Wallace. Twenty years, Darwin had slaved. A life's work. Then along comes this upstart. Wringing his hands, Darwin had put the matter to the objective judgment of some of the top scientific minds of his day, who also happened to be his best friends. At their urging he drafted a quick summary of the views he had claimed were impossible to summarize and presented it, along with Wallace's paper, to the Linneans, to their general bafflement. Wallace, meanwhile, was still off in the islands awaiting a yea or nay from his *père manqué*. He had not been informed.

The rest, as they said, was history. After all the years of skulking and shirking, Darwin managed to rush *The Origin of Species* into print in a matter of months, so that by the time Wallace had straggled home from the East, Darwin was already safely ensconced as the father of evolution. He'd handled things expertly: he had covered his ass and got the prize. By then he had managed to surround himself with faithful supporters to mop up the shit when it hit the fan, men he had cultivated one by one to replace all the former supporters he had betrayed. Smiling and shuffling, pleading his stomach troubles, he retreated to his garden and his study. Wallace, for his part, put out a flurry of publications, none anywhere near as successful as *The Origin*; fell into penury again; veered off into spiritualism and socialism. He earned his living grading government exams and doing editing work for people like Darwin, never quite able to land a proper job. And yet still he had been there, an honor, after all, bearing the Great Man's remains into the Abbey.

Ninety-six point three. Blip. What was left of them now, those remains? Food for worms. Such a piece of work, the human body, to come to that. Everything so finely tuned, seeking its balance; of the billion things that could go wrong, so few of them did. A masterwork: the work of an artist.

The portrait of an artist.

All right, he admitted it, he hadn't really liked that one. A bit pompous. Self-indulgent. While he was at it, what of that turgid bit in "Scylla and Charybdis," was that really necessary? An extra appendage. An appendix. Should have cut it out.

See, he could do it too, all that childish punning.

It sounds like you've got a bit of a love-hate with Mr. Joyce. I know you'd like to move on from Freud, but it looks to me like the old anxiety of influence. And didn't he also teach at Berlitz, if I'm not mistaken?

(Wryly) So I guess these are what pass for the tough questions with you. Though I'm not sure everything comes down to that same old dynamic, Peter. Look at you and me.

Well, here's my question to you, then, sir: Who's really in control here? Because all I hear in my headphones is my producer screaming at me to get that blanking a-hole out of the studio!

The appendix hanging there, a little blob of flesh. A little penis. A pen. Upon. What did it do, exactly, upon a time? For eating leaves or something. It could kill you, but there it was, refusing to go. Vermiform. Vermin. Worm. Darwin had liked worms. He'd had a little worm stone in the back garden that sank as the worms worked away underneath it. You could still see it there—had Alex actually done this? had it been the original?—by the beech tree at the back of the lawn.

Not a masterwork, really: a hodgepodge, a mishmash, a mess. Things wore down; they turned against themselves; they sat crammed in their flimsy body bag like so much underwear and socks packed in a hurry. There was no artist, really, that was the problem. *No plan.* This happened, then that; something worked, then it didn't. The way his father had run things on the farm: whatever was handy. Try this coupling. Try this bolt. Look at Esther there, with her T cells pinging away at her myelin sheath like mice gnawing the covering off a wire. You've got mice. You've got MS. Myelin sheath. It was all connected. So little went wrong, but then it took so little: one microbe amiss, one link, and the whole system ran amok. It was like those petri dishes in science class: a bit of this, a bit of that, see what survived. A bit of mold, maybe, and presto: penicillin. Penis. Pen. All connected. Esther was a petri dish in there, her own little habitat, a human test tube, to see what survived: something, maybe, but maybe not something human. What was alive out there at Chernobyl? Massive carrots the color of Mars; little glow-worms that fed on strontium 90.

Blip. Panic went through him: the readout had dropped to the ninety-fives. This time he pressed the button. What if this was it, what if she was fading away? Her parents ought to be here, not him; he didn't deserve it.

There is nothing worse than to watch the death of your child. Where had he heard that? Esther's mother could have said it, the tone was right. But what she had actually said was, "What can we do? It's God's will."

It seemed no one had broken the news to her yet of his demise.

Fear was all it was, he figured, what had kept Darwin silent all those years, simple animal fear. *Like confessing a murder.* He had killed off the biggest father of all. People lost jobs for that sort of thing, they became villains, they were raked over the coals by every institution. Darwin had done the math of who his allies were: Hooker could be counted on, maybe Lyell as well; but not Henslow, the old codger, Henslow who had taken him under his wing at Cambridge, who had given him his start. Henslow would have to be sacrificed. The romantics who claimed Darwin had kept his peace those many years for the sake of his Emma, to spare her Christian sensibilities, were on drugs, as far as Alex was concerned. He had acted at every turn for his own preservation, had marshaled his forces and then, when the moment had come to move forward, had done so with brutal resolve. All his wringing of hands over Wallace had been to wipe the blood off them: he'd needed Wallace was what it was, had needed his symbiont, his other half, to show he wasn't merely some crackpot, some flake. That he was-n't alone. He had needed him to fertilize the thing, to bring it to light, to make it whole, and then to crawl back into his cranny like the little penis mates of those barnacle mothers.

That was a way of looking at the matter. It made sense. Even Emma had

had to forgive him then, when it came to a matter of legacy; even the church. The smiling public man, the happy simpleton, red in tooth and claw.

I dreamed I went to heaven, and everyone liked me.

No one had come yet. He was about to go out in search of someone when the monitor blipped, then again, and was suddenly back up into the mid-ninety-sixes. That wouldn't make sense if you were on the way out. The reading probably changed if she so much as shifted a leg, if the air current from a closing door wafted in, if Alex leaned an elbow on the underpad.

Which he was doing. Shit.

A nurse appeared in the door. Not one of the regulars: she was small and dark and decidedly Wamalie-like, a Filipina, surely. His first thought, which immediately fell under the scrutiny of his mind's subcommittee on racism, was, *Good for her. She has a proper job.*

She made a kind of friendly wince at finding him there.

"I don't think you're supposed to be here now," she whispered.

"I know. It's just—her monitor. It keeps going up and down."

She came over and gave it a look.

"It's nothing. It's normal. We have it there at the station, also. The numbers."

"Oh. I didn't know."

She had come for Esther's turning. With an effortlessness that seemed remarkable for her size, she got Esther onto her side, rearranging her limbs and her bedsheets until she actually looked like herself.

Alex was waiting for her to send him away.

"It's okay." She put a finger to her lips. "You stay. It's good."

When she'd gone he felt like he'd just got word that some seemingly inevitable punishment had been waived. He wasn't going to be kicked out; Esther wasn't going to die. He took Esther's hand again, wanting to reach her somehow.

"Esther," he whispered. "Esther. I have a son."

Nothing. Nothing there.

There was room enough in his scheme for God, according to Darwin. It wasn't his place to pronounce yea or nay. And yet in his heart, in that rat's nest, that bag of blood. It was his Annie, some said, who had taken his God, not his theory—he had doted on her, she was simple and pure, she brought him snuff when he'd passed his quota. It was simpleminded to think that it hadn't occurred to him people died, even innocents, that he would rest the matter of faith on such a trifle, and yet Alex could see it. It wasn't a question of theology. It was that sense of being abandoned, of being alone. Nothing there.

Where's the guy when you really need him? Correct me if I'm wrong, but I think you've had a few dark nights of the soul yourself.

I'm not sure if that's something I feel comfortable talking about here, Peter. What? Do you think anyone's listening? Do you think anyone cares?

He squeezed Esther's hand.

"Esther," he said again. He felt her hand in his, the crooked fingers, the little bones, the feeble thump, thump of her heart. "I have a son."

He was growing maudlin again. He would keep admitting his son's existence until it was real.

Darwin had kept a box all his life, Annie's box, filled with her goose quills and pen nibs and sealing wax.

Esther had turned.

"Esther!" He squeezed harder. She was looking at him in her unfocused way, with her pools for eyes. "Esther, it's me. It's Alex."

Orbs, her eyes had become, little satellites. Lost in space. Who knew what they saw?

"Esther, I'm leaving, I'm going to my son. His name is Per. He lives in Sweden. I have to go to him."

He felt the imperative of this as he said it, of going: it was not a choice.

"He's my son, I have to go."

Esther's eyes took him in for the briefest instant with what might have been actual focus, actual recognition, then closed. He had killed her, he thought. He had used up her last ounce. But then he felt her tiny pulse again, saw her chest lift and fall, like the waft of a feather.

She had heard him, that much seemed certain. Maybe not so coherently as to make sense of him, but to hear, at least, to feel the vibrations of air, to feel spoken to. No one did that now; no one spoke to her. He ought to keep talking, say anything, the way they said you should. He could entrust his secrets to her. He could give words to things he had never dared to speak of. *I shall tell you all.*

He picked up *Les Misérables* and began to read softly from where he'd left off.

Such a strange thing, these little scratches on a page, what a million years before or a million hence might seem without remotest pattern or intent but conjured a world up now, so that the room slipped away, and the stink of illness, and the infernal machine, and they were in the streets of Paris. The barricades were ahead of them, and the sewers, and Javert in the Seine; and then Jean Valjean alone on his deathbed, forsaken by Cosette for her lover. It seemed to stretch out before them for weeks still, for decades.

How did it turn out, in the end? He couldn't remember.

She had never been to Paris. All that he took for granted, she had never had, the little towns in the Netherlands, the German autobahn, walking through the wheatfields to the Puttgarden ferry and then collapsing on the beach on the other side, where the sun rose over the water at three in the morning.

He didn't know—who did?—how the mind worked at the end. If things flashed by with some sort of meaning or pattern or just sputtered out like ruined computer files. Decaying sense: what the Enlightenment thought imagination was. Entropy. Not Paris, just Spain, and not Spain, really, only her version of it. Then there were the car trips she had told him about with Lenny: he would drive her to Tobermory for treatment in the divers' tanks. Some doctors said it helped. Hyperbaric oxygen. Sensory deprivation. Like death, she had said. Then had added, "But not in a bad way."

What did they talk about on those drives? Did they take solace from one another, did they broach the important questions? Did they fight over where to stop, when to eat? All the promising names of things, Alexandria, Cornwall, Belleville, and then the same straggling outskirts of fast food and strip malls and the same endless stone and wind-bitten trees.

The worst rides for him were the long ones home from the train station with his father, the rote mumbled questions, the rote gruff replies. Who knew what it was: something beyond dislike, not more than it, but different, a sort of rawness, of injury. Once, where the road curved at Staples, they had seen a line of cars on the road ahead inching along as if it were a funeral cortege, half a dozen or more moving perfectly spaced like a single entity, though the road stretched deserted before them.

"Damn cops," his father said, with a grunt that would have been a laugh if he had been with someone else.

Alex saw it then, the cruiser at the head of the file. It turned off at one of the concession roads, and one by one the other cars sped away.

The incident had put his father in a good mood.

"That's how people are," he said. "They're good until nobody's looking."

He could hardly remember another time when his father had done that, when he had shared anything like a worldview with him outside the context of a bitter argument. Afterward that line of cars had become a sort of koan for him of the strange ambivalence that surrounded anything associated with his father. What had he meant, exactly? Had this been just another of his knee-jerk attacks against the welfare state or some protective truth he was passing on like a talisman? If a truth, didn't it fly against every supper-table argument Alex had made that the human animal was perfectible, that it deserved things like unemployment insurance and special rental units that were set aside for welfare moms? The real battle, of course, was the one within: his own private suspicion, amounting sometimes to a dastardly hope, that his father was right, that humans were rotten to the core, that the only thing keeping the farmers on those concession roads from slitting their neighbors' throats and stealing their combines, keeping the mucky-mucks in town from raping the farmers' wives and then stringing them up till their legs twitched, was the fear of being punished for it.

Of course, it was possible that his father had only been making a joke.

Note to oneself: Molly Bloom's orgasm as the Big Bang. He had never actually got that far in the book, but he'd heard of the scene so often he felt like he'd fucked her himself.

He was drifting. It had been some time since he had actually been attending to what he was reading: they were with Little Gavroche, haunting the wineshops and eating dandelions in the street, though when Alex pictured him he saw Per. It was that Norman blood. There would still be time, he thought, they could still fly their kites on the coast as he had years before with Lars and Eva. It kept coming back to him, that day, the smell of the air, the not-quite-describable *thingness* of things, the gray cliffs, not gray, the not-green grass, the unbearable un-blue of the sea. What was the point of these longings, these hearkenings back? They seemed to want to be the very thing they recalled, and show that they couldn't be, and be the thing in between. To make you long, and long for longing. To say there was a chance, and a chance, and a chance, yet all was lost.

Such a *funny* thing, Ingrid had said. The whole of it, she'd meant, every beat of a wing, every breath.

Out in the sound you could make out the island of Ven. Tycho Brahe had sat there, jotting his numbers down, but though they had stared at him, speaking their truth, they had not shaken his faith. Earth at the center; sun to the side. Little circles and circles within circles to explain the anomalies. That had been the Ptolemaic World, all this figuring and working out just to buttress people's pigheaded assumptions, as if knowledge was always merely the handmaiden to belief. Who knew what circles they were drawing now, to explain away what they had misunderstood. It was all darkness and ignorance, Alex figured, more profound than the human mind could fathom. If God was the thing that passed understanding then there was still God enough in the world, for surely every truth, every fact, every faith, that was now held sacrosanct would one day prove the merest superstition.

Note: The end point of evolution, if there was one, would be the perfect creature: contradictory impulses resolved, no thoughts, no needs, no rage; able to see through rocks; to survive without eating; to change things by force of will. To live forever. It would be exactly what it had displaced. It would be God.

Ninety-six point seven: going up. Menswear. Lingerie. Home furnishings.

It was not much more than a year, he thought, since he'd met her. Walking then, on her cane; chatting about Chernobyl. *Isn't it awful?*

In *The Gazette* that day there had been an article, small and buried in the back pages but there, about the worldwide ban on CFCs. From the most unlikely places came hope. María had backed the right horse. Now that she was home, he expected to hear any day that she'd ended the war.

This was what would happen: he would go off to Sweden like Wallace to the Rio Negro, it would be cold, he and Ingrid would argue, Per would dislike him in some covert, lingering way. He would teach English as a second language, part-time, for peanuts; he would work for the university marking exams. He would never finish his dissertation. Or he would finish it and it would be ignored, or scooped, or, worse, turn out to have been unconsciously plagiarized and have to be shredded. Meanwhile he would be stuck with his no-name degree from his no-name university. He would give up and come home. He would teach English as a second language, part-time, for peanuts.

This was the likely scenario. And yet, and yet. There it was in his breast, he could feel it battering away at his ribcage like a trapped bird, hope.

He had stopped reading. It was miracle enough, maybe, the thing-ness of things, their funniness. That there were clouds, that there was air, that stones formed from the sand and then turned to sand again, on and on. What were these things, where had they come from, what could they mean? How could they fill the mind and yet be so small? There might be gods beyond them, and gods of gods, and, beyond these, things unimaginable, that the human mind could not name or give shape to and yet it could think they were there, it could marvel at the immensity of its own ignorance. Somehow through the chance of events, the slow building of things with No Plan, the mind had become fitted for such thoughts, for such moments of wonderment.

A shred of memory came to him, or perhaps something he'd dreamed, beckoning there at his mind's mid-horizon. He was in a northern country, walking or cycling, it wasn't clear which, and it was raining or had rained or the sun was out, and he was traveling, he was on a journey. He had been here before. For a moment the place took on such a vividness he thought he could hold it whole, could possess it: there were farms, clapboard houses, the outskirts of a town, a view across woods to a lake. The smells of things, the clarity of them, even while they slipped from him and refused to take on their meaning. It was like living a thing and losing it in the same instant. Where were those houses, that lake? He had been here. It was like a place in the mind he returned to to find its meaning, only to find that the meaning of it was simply that it was there.

He took Esther's hand again, and knew he was about to go. If he were to tell the story of this moment, all the important things would be missing—the slightly clammy feel of Esther's skin, the pilled thinness of her sheets, the scuffed floor. The feeling like sadness in him, not sadness, and then that part of him that was already elsewhere, that had finished with this.

Alex heard footsteps in the hall. Likely one of the other nurses on her way to send him packing. The footsteps had the hollowness to them of nighttime desertion. Things would end, and they would end, and they would end, they seemed to say, and still go on.

"Good-bye, Esther. Good-bye."

She hadn't turned.

Outside, he knew, the city still lay stretched, just an instant's remove from the wildness it had been once, and would return to; the planet was still hurtling through space at untenable speeds. He kissed Esther's hand, then slipped quietly through the door and into his life.

acknowledgments

For their help with my research and with this manuscript I am deeply grateful to the following: Marvin Luxenberg; Rafy Winterfeld; Benjamin Cornejo; Nubia Diaz de Cornejo; Francisco Rico Martínez; Rivka Augenfeld; Colin MacAdam; John Montesano; Oscar Rangel Manjarrés; Ana Escobar; José Escobar; Myron McShane; the Centre for Refugee Studies, York University; Marshall Beck; Lisa Kowalchuk; Tanya Basok; André Jacob; Eusebio García; Roxana Valencia; Alfonso Valles; Salvador Torres; Iliana Hernández; Nancy Giacomini; Nicola Martino; Don Melady; Alex Schultz; Lorena Leija; Stephen Henighan; Daniel Poliquin; Paul-Antoine Taillefer; and Paul Quarrington. I owe a special debt to my wife, Erika de Vasconcelos; to my agent, Anne McDermid; and to my editor, Martha Kanya-Forstner.

In the course of my research I consulted many sources, foremost among them the works of Darwin himself. Apart from those, I will mention only *Darwin: The Life of a Tormented Evolutionist*, by Adrian Desmond and James Moore; *The Moral Animal: Why We Are the Way We Are: The New Science of Evolutionary Psychology*, by Robert Wright; and *The Boy on the Back of the Turtle: Seeking God, Quince Marmalade, and the Fabled Albatross On Darwin's Islands*, by Paul Quarrington. And, of course, Wikipedia.

For their material support I am grateful to the University of Windsor Department of English; Assumption University, Windsor; the Canada Council Writer-in-Residence Program; Mitch Kowalski and the Toronto Writers' Centre; John Carroll University, Cleveland; Steven Hayward and Katherine Carlstrom; Jimmy, Eddie, and Frances; and Barbara and Dr. John Schubert and the Schubert Foundation.

NINO RICCI'S first novel, *The Book of Saints*, won the Governor General's Award for Fiction, the SmithBooks/*Books in Canada* First Novel Award, and the F. G. Bressani Prize. A longtime national best seller, it was followed by the highly acclaimed *In a Glass House* and *Where She Has Gone*, which was short-listed for the Giller Prize, and the national best seller *Testament*, which won the Trillium Book Award in 2002. He lives in Toronto.